Unacceptable Risk

Hidden Wolves Book 1

Kaje Harper

Editing by Amanda Faris

Proofreading by Ashley VanBuren and Jonathan Penn

Cover art by Jay Aheer

Formatting by Beaten Track Publishing – beatentrackpublishing.com

License Notes

Acknowledgements

I want to thank all the members of Josh Lanyon's M/M Crit group, who put their own projects aside to give this a read and weigh in on some burning questions. You guys are the best. Thank you to my editor, Amanda, who believed in the first book I sent her, and every one since then, and has made them all better.

The second edition would not have happened without all the readers who asked for it, and Ashley and Jonathan, the wonderful proofreaders who polished up my revised sentences. My formatter Deb fits me in without complaint, and Ali Ryecart made my blurb better. And isn't that Jay Aheer cover gorgeous? I can't wait to share this version with readers.

My deepest gratitude still goes to my husband, whose patience has passed remarkable and is approaching legendary.

Chapter 1

Stepping out the clinic door took Paul Hunter's breath away. The winter sky had cleared to reveal a glowing crescent moon, and the night was *cold.* The snap of frigid air froze his breath in his mouth, as the sparkle of fresh snow and the graceful curves of new drifts caught at his soul. Six inches of new white powder had landed since the parking lot was last plowed. The wind had shaped a fantasy of snowy dunes, interspersed with glistening black ice where the pavement was exposed. The boring parking lot looked like an Ansel Adams photograph.

Paul knew he should stop and appreciate the beauty. This was why he was still in Minnesota, after all. The impulse to leave his childhood home far behind had never been quite strong enough to make him actually go. He loved this state; the cold, clean whiteness made him believe in fresh starts, and a new snowfall like this could usually raise his spirits. Unfortunately, tonight he was so tired his eyes were crossing. The beauty of black ice under white powder meant an hour to drive home instead of fifteen minutes. And he was *so* damned tired.

He considered staying at his veterinary clinic, sleeping on the floor, but he'd done that last night. Another day without a shower or a shave and his clients were likely to notice. He really needed to hire more help, another veterinarian or an office manager, someone to take a little of the load. But when he tried to work the budget to make an assistant possible, the money just wasn't there.

He pulled his collar up around his chin and stepped carefully onto the glazed pavement, considering his options again. Maybe he could get someone really part time, a woman with kids who only wanted a few hours a week. He snorted as he unlocked the door to his old Explorer. While he was fantasizing, how about a beautiful woman who was brilliant with finances and happened not to be dating anyone. And who had a thing for geeky veterinarians. *Not happening.*

At least his truck started. A blast of icy air from the vents blew across his neck, and he quickly switched the controls to defrost until the heat could come on. He reached into the backseat for the brush, hauled himself out, and worked his way around the vehicle clearing snow off the windows. He didn't bother to scrape the layer of ice on the rear. That's what defrosters were for.

When he got back inside, the first wisps of tepid air from the vents had raised the temperature from cryogenic to merely cold as hell. He backed out of his space carefully, feeling for the level of traction on the pavement. *Slippery* was the answer. He eased the brakes, shifted, and crept forward. Visibility wasn't bad anymore, despite the snow blowing across the road from the fields. At least it was late enough that there were almost no other idiots on the road to contend with.

Accelerating carefully to a daring twenty miles an hour, he concentrated on staying awake and trying to stay in his half-concealed lane. Moonlight and headlights cast conflicting shadows over the rutted slush. He ignored a dark drift on the road ahead of him until the thing moved and his headlights glinted off a flash of green eyes. *Something alive! Shit!*

Paul stomped on the brakes. The anti-lock chattered, ineffectually trying to prevent a slide and spin. Paul steered into the spinout, cursing. The truck turned, turned, slipped sideways, tilted slightly, and stopped. He'd ended up facing backwards and canted off the road, but the tires had caught the rough gravel verge in time, and he wasn't in the ditch.

He swung himself out of the door and the cold hit him again, making him shudder. The wind drove fine snow from the open fields down his neck, and the swirling flakes stung his eyes. The dark shape on the road was still there, too weak or injured to run.

Paul approached cautiously. He couldn't make out what the animal was. That dark bulk was the right size for a sheep or deer, perhaps, but the wrong eye color. Too big for a coyote or a dog. Too small for a horse.

The creature raised its head and the red rear lights of the truck outlined a long heavy muzzle, pointed ears, and gleaming eyes. *Wolf!* For an instant, Paul's heart pounded. Then common sense kicked in. This dog was much bigger than any wolf, with a broader head. Anyway, while northern Minnesota had free-roaming wolves, this was the Twin Cities. There were no wolves in the Minneapolis suburbs. *Just a big dog.*

Paul murmured soothingly as he eased toward the dog. "Hey, boy. It's okay. I'm not going to hurt you. What happened, baby? Did someone hit you and drive off?" As he spoke, he pulled the scarf off his neck and twisted it into a rope. This might not be a wolf, but an injured dog could take his hand off just as easily. Easier, given that thing's size. *One try with the scarf, then I go back to the clinic for the rabies noose pole.*

When he got close, he dropped to a crouch, looking at the dog. The snow had started drifting onto the dog's hindquarters, which suggested it had been lying out in the cold for a while. The poor thing was either too badly injured or too hypothermic to move, but its dense coat looked thick enough to withstand cold. The way it lay splayed on the road screamed injury.

Murmuring, keeping his motions slow, Paul reached out with the scarf toward that broad head. The dog just looked at him, unmoving. He waited for a snarl, flattened ears, a lift of lip, or a snap that would send him back to the clinic for the pole. *Show me a sign, baby. Are we okay?* The dog's eyes followed him as he shifted position, but he read no visible threat. Slowly, slowly, he lifted the scarf rope up, and in one practiced movement, snapped a loop tight around the muzzle, then back behind the ears and fisted the crossover hard. And felt foolish, because the big dog didn't move a muscle in response.

After a pause, Paul eased his grip enough to knot the improvised muzzle into place. The dog might be tolerant now, but lifting it would no doubt be painful. He rubbed his gloved hand across the wide head and pointed ears. "Good job. You're a good pup, aren't you?" Holding the knotted muzzle in one hand, he slid his other hand firmly down the dog's neck and back, waiting for a pain response. As he brushed the snow away from the dog's flanks, he began finding pink tinges and then red, soaked with blood from multiple cuts. Either stoic or numb with cold, it neither moved nor whined, even when Paul's exploring hand found a gaping gash over the ribs.

"Jesus, baby," Paul breathed, keeping his voice calm and reassuring. The dog would respond to the tone, not the words. "You're cut to hell, aren't you? We need to get you back to the clinic now. Just hold tight, okay?"

He straightened up and took two steps toward his truck. For the first time, the big dog whimpered. When Paul glanced back it was scrabbling its front legs, trying to get up. "No, puppers," Paul said firmly. He went back and pressed over the dog's shoulders to hold it in place. "Down. Stay." Apparently someone had trained it well, because it subsided immediately and held still. It twisted around to look at him over one shoulder, that odd blue-green color reflecting from its eyes.

"I'm going to bring the truck closer," Paul soothed, as if the creature could understand him. "I can't carry you that far. You're a big, big guy. Just stay, and I'll get you. Stay. Stay."

Slowly, he walked backwards toward the truck, keeping his eyes locked on the dog, repeating the stay command. It seemed to hear him and held still obediently. Paul breathed a prayer that it would stay put when he backed up toward it. The last thing he needed was to run it over.

His truck was askew on the shoulder, but the engine was still running when he climbed in. The blessed heat from the vents blew across his chilled skin. Slowly, trying not to spin the tires, he backed up off the shoulder onto the road and toward the dog, peering intently at that dim shape in the rearview. When he was as close as he dared to get, he put on the parking brake and the flashers, jumped out, and opened the tailgate.

The dog raised its head as he approached. He noted that it was working to breathe, its neck strained and its mouth open the fraction that the scarf loop would allow. *Dammit, got to get that muzzle off soon.* Paul rubbed its ears again. "Good pup. Sweet baby. I'm going to try to pick you up, okay. Try not to bite my face off."

He slid his arms under the dog's body, scrabbling with his fingers against the ice. The dog's fur was frozen hard to the freaking pavement, and it was so big! He strained to move it. The dog began pushing too, digging in with its hind legs. There was a lurch forward as its fur came free, and the dog whimpered, short and sharp. Paul gave a quick look. *Intact boy. I hope his balls didn't freeze, poor baby.*

"It's okay, boy. I know it hurts, but you're loose now. Just a little more. Four steps. Three steps." Soothing, murmuring, slipping on the ice, unable to lift more than the front half, he dragged the dog toward the truck. Damned thing had to weigh two hundred pounds. The dog pushed with his rear feet as if to help. Harsh puffs of air escaped from his lips around the muzzle, but otherwise he was silent. Paul was sure he was hurting the poor pup, but he neither whined nor growled.

At the open tailgate, Paul wrapped his arms around the wide chest and heaved up and in. He didn't worry about where his face was in relation to those big teeth anymore. He just put everything he had into the lift. The dog's front paws reached the carpeted floor, and he scrabbled and dug his claws in. Paul shifted toward the furry stomach and hauled up and forward.

The dog's big body lurched higher and slid inside. Paul fell against the furry flank, breathing hard, his mouth full of hair.

"Good boy, good boy, brave boy." He untangled himself, and pushed and shoved the dog forward, until he got room to close the hatch, careful of the long, plumed tail. The dog's fast breaths spurred him on as he jumped back in the driver's seat, heading for the clinic as fast as was safe on the icy road.

§ § § §

Simon *hurt*, worse than he ever remembered hurting before. And that was saying something. Over the years he'd had torn muscles, lacerations, even broken bones, from fights, from punishments. He was barely tolerated in the pack, and plenty of wolves had made that plain to him, with fists or teeth. But he'd never felt pain like this.

They didn't kill me, but it feels like they came close.

The pack Second and his followers had dumped Simon on the road, laughing about his odds of freezing or getting run over, and he'd understood that stopping before they did the final deed wasn't meant to be a kindness.

He'd landed bleeding in wolf form on the icy pavement, unable to force himself to his feet, barely fighting off unconsciousness as his tormenters drove away. Even in fur, he'd felt the pavement's chill seeping into the very marrow of his bones, felt the flesh of his paws numb and begin to freeze. The cold had slowed his blood loss, but heat and life seeped out of him onto the black ice.

Shift. Heal. Better. Less pain. Shift. That promise tempted him as he lay fighting for breath. But a shift took more energy than he had left and would've left him naked in his human skin on the snow. He drifted, dreaming of shifting and healing, too weak to try. By the time he raised the energy to even push to his feet, he was frozen tight to the surface.

He'd fought then to free himself, his efforts too feeble to work. He couldn't catch his breath. A great weight seemed to press on his chest, binding his lungs and robbing him of air. He'd thought his legs were moving, but black spots filled his vision and he was no longer sure. Then as he paused to gasp for air, he heard the rumble of tires. Saw headlights approaching. He'd raised his head to look his fate in the eye. Werewolves were hard to kill, but in his condition, he'd never survive being hit by a truck. He wondered dully if death would at least stop the pain. The vehicle approached slowly, inexorably, tires crunching on the icy road.

And then it stopped.

Now he swayed in the back of the SUV, feeling the truck slide as the driver pushed the limits of safe traction. The heat was on full, blasting warmth over him. It was glorious and excruciating, as the throbbing burn of returning circulation clawed its way up his legs and down his ears. He shivered uncontrollably, feeling his cells suck in the heat. Werewolves were tough, and his body was doing its best not to die after all.

The scarf muzzle around his face was driving him crazy. He wanted to rip it off, except his legs didn't seem to work right. He strained his jaws apart as hard as he could, and the soft fabric gave a little, but the added opening didn't help him get his breath. His vision tunneled in around the sole task of pulling in the next gasp of air, and the next.

He barely noticed as the truck slowed, turned, and stopped. The driver got out, letting in an icy draft that shook Simon out of his daze. His sensitive hearing picked up a building door opening, then after a pause, an unfamiliar metallic rattle. The back door of the truck opened.

"Okay, sweetie," the man's light tenor said behind him. "I'm going to pull you out now. Don't fight me, baby. Just stay, okay. Stay." Hands gripped Simon's hips, pulling him backward. For a moment pain flared, and he hung onto consciousness by a thread, clenching his whole body on the brink of darkness. Then he was flat on his side on a cool surface, moving, vibrating and swaying. He forced his eyes open, and recognized some sort of metal trolley, barely big enough to support him. The man pulling it cursed as the wheels bumped and caught in the snow. Then he was hauled through a doorway into wonderful warmth and dryness.

"Stay. Just stay." The man pushed the cart down a hallway and into a larger room, switching on the lights. Simon looked around and choked, a half-sob half-laugh coming out like a strangled cough from his laboring throat. *It's a veterinary clinic!*

Had to be. There were posters of the internal organs of a dog and cat on the wall, and a microscope on the counter beside other medical-looking equipment. Glass-fronted cabinets displayed pill bottles and supplies. A rack held fabric muzzles.

Out of all the gin joints in all the world, I've been plucked from my icy grave by a veterinarian.

He was so fucked. Even if he lived through this, the pack would tear him apart. They'd kill this Good Samaritan with the gentle hands too.

Simon would've cared more if he could just fucking *breathe*.

The man pressed a stethoscope to Simon's chest, then switched some humming power on, one hand on Simon's furry shoulder to hold him in place. "Gonna take some quick pictures, baby. No big deal, no need to worry, you'll be fine." The vet's soft soothing tone might be intended to keep a frightened animal quiet, but the reassurance was working on Simon too. Fear and pain grew distant, beyond the dizzy lack of air. Simon lay still, gasping, feeling a man's friendly hands touching him, hearing a man's voice call him sweetie and baby. *If you only knew.* An illusion, of course, meant for a furry mutt, not him, but it felt nice.

Pain jolted through him as he was lifted onto a bigger, sturdier table. A whirr bothered his ears, followed by a clunk and beep. Then he was pushed sideways, and there was a rasp, another clunk-beep. Dully, he wondered what that was. X-ray, probably. He couldn't muster the energy to open his eyes and look. A distant part of him was scared that he didn't care. *What happened to self-preservation? Unquenchable curiosity? Get up off your ass, Simon Conley.* But he was so tired, so sore, and there wasn't enough air in the universe. Oblivion sucked him down, and he let go.

§ § § §

Paul cursed under his breath as the big dog slumped limply. He yanked his scarf from the dog's muzzle and lifted his lip. *Gum color… damn, he's getting paler.* Ducking into the surgery, he hauled the anesthesia machine to the end of its hose and started the oxygen. His biggest cone barely fit around that broad muzzle, but he got a good flow going and was relieved to see the dog's membranes pink up quickly. *Better.*

He grabbed his stethoscope. The dog's heart still sounded okay, but lung sounds were dull. And everywhere he looked there were wounds. Among numerous lacerations, he noted deep punctures and ragged tears, the marks of another dog's teeth slicing through flesh. *Some bastard's been dog-fighting this sweet giant, and let him get torn almost to shreds. And then dumped him to freeze to death.*

Paul considered himself even-tempered, but if he ever found the person responsible for this… He pushed the thought aside, running practiced hands over the dog's body. None of the wounds was bleeding worse than sluggishly now. The left front leg felt broken, and he worried about some ribs, and where the breathing problem was coming from. The X-ray would answer that, once he had time to check it. He took another listen. *Stable. Fucked up, but stable on the O2 for now. Deal with blood loss and hypothermia.*

After placing IV catheters in two unbroken legs, he microwaved the fluid bags until they were close to blood warmth, wishing once again he could afford a real fluid warmer. He started the fluids running at the shock dose and draped a heating pad over the dog. *Temp? Thermometer in the butt, sorry, dog. Ninety-five degrees. Crap.* He added warmed fluid bags packed in against the dog's belly.

I don't like that he's still unresponsive.

Nonetheless, it was an opportune moment to put the X-rays into the processor, which churned, rumbled, and spit out the films. Going back to put a hand on the dog, just in case, Paul held the X-rays up to the ceiling light. *Yup.* He didn't need a light box to spot the fractures across both bones of the left front leg, or count five broken ribs. *And a pneumothorax and collapsed lung. You've been through the wars. Stay with me, baby.*

He gathered equipment and supplies, one eye on the dog, preparing to tap his chest. *Sedation?* The dog was still unconscious, and he decided to take a chance with just the local, sliding the needle home. Each syringe of displaced air he pulled off visibly eased the dog's respirations. By the time he sucked out the last few ccs, the dog's labored breaths had slowed and deepened almost to normal. *Better. You might just make it.*

Dog bites called for a shot of antibiotics and a rabies vax, so he gave them. He hooked up more fluids, and began clipping over the worst of the wounds. As he cleaned a deep laceration, he realized that the dog was awake and watching him.

He lunged to pin the dog's head and shoulder safely to the table, and felt a little foolish when he didn't try to move. The dog's eyes just gazed into his own, oddly colored eyes, pale blue-green, like glacier water in the mountains. The iris formed a thin ring of turquoise around big dark pupils, dilated with pain and shock. *I've never seen eyes like that, even on a Husky…* Paul blinked and broke the stare.

"Okay, boy," he murmured, gradually easing his weight off the furry shoulder as the big dog continued to hold still. He stroked gently across the broad skull, rubbing at the untorn ear. "Just lie still. I know it hurts, but we're going to make you better." He reached for a sedative syringe, and the dog's lip lifted in the first hint of a threat that Paul had seen. He froze, hand extended.

The dog's gaze locked with his own, fiercely and demandingly boring into him. If Paul were a canine, he thought, he'd have been rolling on the floor exposing his throat in submission. As it was, he stood unmoving, his eyes lowered, and spoke softly.

"Good boy, brave boy. You've been so good so far. I don't want to muzzle you again, sweetie. I want to give you a pain med, so I can go on fixing these wounds." The dog blinked once. "Just a little morphine, baby, just to take the edge off." *Well, morphine and a sedative, but the tone mattered, not the words.* "I won't hurt you. You need stitches. You need to let me help you." Slowly, slowly, he reached for the syringe again. The dog looked at his hand, as if tracking the motion, but held still as he picked up the dose. Paul slid his hand carefully to the IV port on the fluid line, well away from those big jaws, and slowly pushed the plunger home. The dog's eyes returned to his face for a long moment, and then furry eyelids drooped as the medication hit home.

He used two hours under anesthesia to stabilize the broken foreleg in a splint, and clean and suture all the major wounds. And at that, he was leaving a host of smaller cuts to heal on their own. The dog's breathing had eased and his membrane color was better by the time Paul finished. The floor of the treatment room was awash in shaved tufts of beautiful gray fur.

Paul ran a hand over one of the remaining intact patches of coat on the dog. The dense silky undercoat was black, overlaid with guard hairs tipped in bands of gray and white. The color rippled from smoke to black to light gray as he stroked across the soft, unmatted fur. This was no lost stray, no backyard reject given to pit bulls to learn their bloody trade. Every line spoke of breeding and care. Either this was a fighting breed he didn't know, or a pet that had been stolen for vicious use.

He caressed the dog, feeling heavy bone and solid muscle under his hands. He would have to go online to try to match the breed— something Nordic, wolflike except for the bulk of that frame and head. He hadn't seen any tattoos, or implanted microchip on the X-ray, but if this was a stolen purebred, someone would be looking for him. *I'd be turning the neighborhood upside down if he was mine.*

Paul rubbed his eyes tiredly and reminded himself, *don't get attached.* That was his mantra. He had no dogs or cats at home. He wasn't home enough to be fair to a pet. But knowing that didn't keep him from aching to take in every abused and unwanted creature that passed through his hands. The clinic already had three cats. Sometimes when Turk and Toby were tussling across the floor, that was two too many. There was no room for a dog. *Say it with me, there's no room for a dog.*

He leaned on the table, half-hypnotized by the gentle movement of his own hands, swaying, dangerously near sleep. He needed to crash, and the dog would be safer in the kennel than on the X-ray table. After one more set of films. He took the X-rays and developed them, yawning.

Air was no longer leaking in the dog's chest, and the leg was set straight. A quick exam found the dog's body temperature up to ninety-nine degrees, gums pink, lungs clear. There was no more major bleeding, no signs of shock, and when he disconnected the oxygen, the dog continued to breathe easily. *This is what all those years of study were for.*

He arranged the stretcher as an improvised ramp and slid the dog from the table to a blanket on the floor. With effort, he pulled him back into the kennel and wrestled the huge limp body into one of the new big bottom cages. *Close the door, lock the latch.* He was operating on autopilot by now. *Hang the fluids, slow the drip rate.* He dumped a pile of clean towels on the floor outside the cage and stretched out, fighting to keep his eyes open long enough to be sure the dog's anesthetic had worn off safely before he slept. *That you, boy? Yeah, blink for me. Looking better, up, sternal, breathing, looks good.* Paul's last awareness was of eyes like jade, watching him from the other side of the bars.

§ § § §

Simon blinked hard, trying to clear the cobwebs from his brain, still fuzzy from the drugs and pain. He shook his head and had to grit his teeth. *Ouch! Dumb move!* Outside the front of his cage, the veterinarian snored lightly, curled up on a heap of fabric on the floor. Simon had watched the man fall asleep as he'd waited for the drugs to give him back control of his body.

Simon took a deep breath, and sweet, lifegiving air flowed into his lungs. Pain bit sharply along his left side, but the suffocating pressure was gone. His chest rose steadily, in and out. *Hell, yeah. Breathing can't be overrated.*

He pushed himself up higher onto his chest, experimentally, and gasped as he jarred his broken leg. The man outside woke immediately, sitting up to look into the cage.

"Are you okay, boy?" The vet reached out to check the fluid lines dripping into Simon's veins, and looked him over carefully. "Does it hurt? I can't give you more pain meds now. In an hour I'll pull up some more of the good stuff for you. Okay?"

Simon gazed back, trying to look calm and pain-free. The last thing he needed was more drugs. Just his luck, he got a Good Samaritan with the hearing of a bat and the instincts of a mother. He held his stoic pose until the veterinarian lay down, and his breathing slowed back into sleep.

I should not *be complaining about my luck.* He'd been inches from dead, then found by someone who not only knew how to save his life, but took the time and effort to do so. His leg was even set right, so the rapid healing of a werewolf wouldn't knit the ends back together out of alignment. He just needed rest, food, and time, and he'd be good as new.

The problem was, he also needed to get out of here, and soon. He could pass for a dog for a while, even up close. His wolf form was outsized, conserving the mass of his human body, but it would look canine, would X-ray canine. The genetic blood tests that would pick up his shifter differences should be way beyond what a small clinic could do. But in another day, his injuries would be healing faster than anything possible for an ordinary dog. A good veterinarian wasn't going to miss that.

Simon opened and closed his mouth, turned his head slowly, and curled and uncurled his three good paws, trying to be silent. Everything hurt, down to the hairs in his ears. He needed to plan how to get out, and which form to use for what part of his escape. He could shift back to human, but shedding his wolf form and going human was neither instant nor silent enough to avoid the notice of his keeper. Any shift would have to wait until the vet was elsewhere.

As a human, he could reach through the bars and undo the latch to get free of the cage. A shift would also speed up healing. But in human form, he'd be naked with no money and no transportation, and his arm and ribs would still be broken. *And this tight splint won't fit over my human arm.* He'd have to chew the bandages off before shifting, unless he wanted his arm to be really screwed up.

Simon sighed silently. Splint off, go human, get out of the cage and the room, and then hopefully have the energy to shift again to wolf, because a naked guy wandering around would draw a hell of a lot more attention. He'd have to find a route out of the building, and make his way home on foot and in fur. His stamina was excellent and even though he was no faster than a canine wolf, he was sure he could get there eventually, even on three legs.

Probably.

If his chest didn't start closing in on him again. Worse than the pain, he remembered the crushing panic when each breath came shallower and less satisfying than the last, like drowning in his own chest. He didn't know enough about medicine to be sure that problem wouldn't come back if he pushed himself too hard.

Okay, maybe not running out into the snow yet. Simon let his eyes drift closed. Because really, what did it matter if he waited a few more hours? At some point the vet would get up and go to the bathroom or get himself some food. That would be soon enough to make his escape. A little more healing time before then could only be a good thing.

But through the night, the vet never left Simon's side to go farther than a duck into the next room with the door open. Twice he injected medications into the fluid lines, although he didn't tell his supposedly canine patient what he was getting. On the second dose, the warm rush blanketing over Simon's pain told him it was morphine. He couldn't fight the soft darkness that sucked him down to sleep, waking hours later, groggy but healing.

His time sense told him it was almost dawn when the veterinarian finally crawled stiffly out of his pile of towels and stood up. Simon winced sympathetically, hearing the pops and creaks as the man stretched. He had spent too many nights on the floor himself. He could imagine what the man's hipbones felt like.

"Hey, boy," the vet murmured, opening the cage door to check on Simon. "You look much better this morning. You must have a strong constitution." He reached out and stroked Simon's head. Simon resisted the urge to duck. He was being a dog, and a friendly one at that. A dog would rub up against that hand, would take comfort in the long, strong fingers massaging his neck. A dog might even lick at that wrist beside his face.

Simon gave in to temptation and licked. The taste of man and sweat with a hint of antiseptic soap burst on his tongue. His wolf senses were acute; he would know the taste of this man again among a thousand others. The vet giggled at the rasp of his tongue, a surprising sound from that tired and drawn face. He cupped Simon's head in both hands and stared into his eyes.

"You're a sweet boy and I like you too," the man crooned, fingers digging gently into Simon's fur. "I was worried about you, but you're going to be just fine, aren't you?" Simon stared back. The vet was young, although fatigue had put lines in his cheeks and circles under his eyes. *Those golden eyes.* He thought he had seen them somewhere before, eyes that were hazel, almost amber, like old honey. A faint spider-web of gray overlaid the gold, darkening as the man's eyes widened in surprise at Simon's un-dog-like, steady return stare.

Simon dropped his gaze submissively, as he had taught himself to do so often with the pack. The vet rubbed the base of his ears with strong thumbs and Simon leaned in. Then the man slid a finger under Simon's lip and lifted it, pressing above Simon's fang. Simon barely aborted a reflex snarl at the presumption. *You're a dog, you're a dog.* He converted the sound to a short cough.

Immediately the vet looked concerned. "Your color's good, but I'd better check that chest," he muttered, reaching for his stethoscope. *Idiot*, Simon told himself. He held still for a careful going-over, making no move or sound even when fingers probed around the throbbing wound on his ribs. Every touch hurt, despite the obvious care the man was taking, but the less Simon responded, the less the vet would hover.

Simon was impatient to be alone, to be able to shift. The transformation would pull together torn flesh and begin to knit bones. He was tired of being so vulnerable. He wasn't fond of the pain either.

After what seemed like an eternity of prodding, the vet reached in his pocket for a thermometer. Simon tucked his tail under tightly and stared at the man hard. *The next time you stick something up my ass,* he thought as clearly as he could, *it's only going to be if we* both *want it there.* Some message obviously got through, because the vet looked back and forth from the thermometer to Simon, then put it away again. "Maybe later."

His fingers ruffled Simon's good ear. "Rest now, baby. You'll be better soon. I've got to go clean up and start working." The vet backed up, locked the cage, and left the kennel room.

Finally. Finally! Simon pulled the fluid lines out of his legs with his front teeth, ignoring the trickle of blood from each site, and the flood of saline dripping onto the floor. He bit into the edge of the leg bandage and twisted. He knew this elastic stuff; unwrapping was far easier than tearing it. The self-cling peeled off easily enough. The gauze and cotton underneath yielded to his strong jaws. His leg ached badly, the pain worse as the splint fell away, but his human arms were much burlier than his canine ones. The bandage would've become a tourniquet biting deep into his arm during the shift.

Simon curled himself up on the steel floor of the cage, in a position his human body would be able to accommodate. He controlled his breathing, stilled his muscles, and *reached* for the change. *Reached—* And fought back panic as he touched nothing.

Okay, okay, try again. He went through the exercises his mentor had taught him, back when he first learned how to touch shift energy, and reached out again. *Nothing.* No sweet current of power to pull into himself, to drive his body through its forms. His mind grasped and reached and came up empty. He knew the energy had to be out there but he couldn't touch it. Like there was a pane of glass between him and the change. Or, he realized, a wall of steel.

The fucking cage! It was stainless steel, top, bottom, sides, and grill. And the whole room was lined with banks of similar cages. All steel, dense and reflective— the one metal wolves were wary of because, unlike mythical, harmless silver, steel blocked that sweet flow. The metal absorbed and rechanneled the shift energy away from Simon. His body ached to bathe in that power and find his human form, but couldn't.

At the realization, Simon went nuts. That was the only way he could explain coming to himself to find his body slammed against the bars, his muzzle jammed painfully far under the corner of the door, his whine a high-pitched painful sound. Was that really him? He shut up abruptly. *Control. Never lose control.*

Before he could untangle himself, the vet ran in, knelt, and yanked open the barred door to free Simon's muzzle. With Simon's weight unbalanced, he fell out of the cage into the man's arms. And was caught and held.

"What?" the man murmured. "What, boy? It's okay. You're okay. Hush, baby, hush. Jesus, what did you do to your splint?"

Simon gathered himself to pull free and run. Then he froze, holding the impulse back by the skin of his teeth. *Not yet, damn it.* A young woman in animal-print scrubs had followed the vet in and shut the door firmly behind her. She reached for a noose pole standing in the corner.

"Doctor Hunter!" she said. "Are you okay? Do you need help?"

"I'm fine, Sarah. This guy just panicked or something. He fell on me. He's not trying to bite me." The vet— Dr. Hunter, apparently— was petting Simon, rubbing gently, fingers somehow missing all the sore spots and finding the perfect zone on Simon's chest.

"I don't remember that dog," the woman said doubtfully.

"I found him last night. Someone had him in a dog fight and then dumped him. He's cut to hell, but he's really sweet. I dragged him all over the place last night getting him here, with a broken leg and a bunch of bad ribs, and he never so much as lifted his lip. He's really tolerant."

"But if he's a fighting dog… He's awfully big."

"I don't think he was a fighter, I think he was bait. They steal pets, huskies, golden retrievers, even little dogs, they don't care. They dump them in with the real fighting dogs to teach them to kill. This guy is so sweet, I wonder if he tried to fight back at all."

The hell I didn't fight, Simon thought. *You try it with five to one odds and see how you do.* But as a cover story, it wasn't a bad guess.

"Bring me some Ace injectable." Hunter added, "And materials for another splint. We need to get this guy fixed up again before the clients start arriving."

Simon tensed, but he'd missed his chance. He could hear someone else beyond that door. These people were accustomed to handling dogs, and set up to prevent escapes. He could get away, no doubt, but only if he was willing to really hurt them, or if he shifted in front of them. If he broke that first commandment and let them see what he was, he would have to kill them. Pack law was inflexible on that point.

He was trapped, for now. He allowed Dr. Hunter to drug him, re-splint his leg, and replace the catheters. Only when he was waking up in the cage, and the vet brought in a bucket collar designed to keep dogs from chewing their bandages, did he balk. *Hell, nope.*

He might still be groggy from the drugs, but damned if he was wearing that thing. He locked eyes with Hunter, staring hard, watching the man's eyes darken with apprehension. This time Simon didn't look down, didn't soften his gaze.

"Come on, boy," the vet coaxed. "You can't keep chewing off your bandage. That leg needs to heal." Simon kept on staring, his best almost-alpha look. "It doesn't hurt." Hunter moved the collar closer. Simon got up unsteadily and drew back deeper into the cage, so the vet would be forced to come in close if he wanted to trap Simon in that bucket. "Damn," Hunter muttered. "Should've put it on while you were sedated."

Simon snarled his disapproval of that idea.

An instant later, he found himself wagging his fucking tail as hard as he could, and panting a canine laugh. Anything to erase the flash of fear that had crossed Hunter's face. He wasn't sure why, but he couldn't stand having this man afraid of him. *I owe him too much.* It took a minute of his best damned ingratiating dog behavior before the vet's body language relaxed.

"Guess you just don't like the collar." Hunter put it behind him. He reached into the cage very slowly, watching Simon's eyes. Simon looked down and tried to take all the alpha out of his posture. He kept a steady thump going with his tail, despite how sore his hindquarters were, and licked the man's hand. *Clean male sweat, skin, familiar taste.* Simon closed his eyes for a moment, and when he opened them again the cage door was closing.

"Be a good boy and leave that bandage alone so we don't need the collar, okay?"

Simon thumped his tail once in agreement. The vet looked at him, startled, and then smiled and left the room. Simon curled up in his crate, biding his time. *At least no one will be looking for me here. Only my Alpha could track me down and he almost certainly won't bother. And I can heal.* There was that.

Chapter 2

Paul's clinic day turned out to be pretty routine. He did a couple of cat neuters, and removed a poodle's skin mass. He saw a vomiting cat and a dog with an ear infection, the usual cases of limping and itching and diarrhea. All in a day's work. With the snow still blowing and drifting, several of the annual appointments elected to reschedule.

He took his charts into the kennel to work on whenever he had a break, to keep an eye on his recovering patients. The first time he went back there, the clinic cats followed him to perform their daily inspection of their territory. He watched in amusement as fat elderly Sally led the two males on their rounds. They surveyed the groggy cats and the poodle, waking up from surgery, with their usual disdain. Then Sally led the way to the front of the new dog's cage.

All three cats stopped dead at the sight of the big dog. The dog had been resting, but opened his jade green eyes and stared flatly at the three felines. Paul saw no threat, no movement at all from the dog, but all three cats suddenly decided to be elsewhere, immediately. Sally's shrill Siamese voice commanded Paul to jump up and let them out immediately. The trio leaped through the gap as soon as the door cracked open, and sprinted off across the treatment room.

"What was that about?" Paul asked the new dog rhetorically as he closed the door. "You didn't growl, you didn't even move, and Sally backed down. I've seen that cat put a German Shepherd in its place. What's so special about you?"

The dog looked at him, mouth opening in a canine grin, and thumped his tail once. "Yeah, you like being special, don't you?" Paul opened the crate to check the bandage and look his patient over. Whatever breed this dog was, he must've had an iron constitution, because the wounds looked damned good. One would never guess the dog had been on death's doorstep just hours ago.

Paul settled down on the floor to write, where he could reach in the cage and pet the big dog. "I bet someone's searching for a beautiful boy like you."

He opened a chart as he scratched absently with his left hand. "But if we don't find your owner, I'm keeping you. You can stay here at the clinic while I'm working, so you'll get plenty of attention. There's a fenced exercise yard you can run in when the other dogs aren't out. I don't care about being sensible." He stopped, concentrating on writing in the chart for a while. But this was a dog. This was only a dog. Sarah was on her lunch break, and Elise wouldn't leave the desk, so he could say these words, here where no one else would hear him.

"I'm so fucking lonely… I haven't had a dog in so long." He laughed at himself. "Or a date, or a life, but there's not much you can do about that. But you're lost, and maybe you need someone too." The dog crept closer to him and nudged him with his big head. Paul smiled and rubbed the proffered ear. "I'm going to call you Wolf." The dog snorted, as if amused. Inching further forward, Wolf settled down beside him, his big head on the edge of the cage against Paul's hip as he wrote. Paul combed his free hand through Wolf's smoke-gray fur.

Something eased in him as he petted his dog. All those single-minded years of working toward his goals had been necessary, of course. He'd managed the narrow determination to get top grades, get the acceptances and scholarships that'd made becoming a vet possible. He'd put in many long hours making himself indispensable to the previous owner of the clinic, then even longer hours when he had the chance to buy the place. But the goal he'd envisioned for himself, one where he was successful and content with his life, always seemed to move out of reach.

He was tired of chasing a mirage of happiness, where every step looked like it would get him there, and then the target slid a little farther down the road. He'd cut everything extraneous out of his life in the quest to finish school, to make this clinic his own, to pay his staff, to never miss a loan payment, to give his clients and patients the care they deserved. And he couldn't regret it, not really. His goal was still there, shining ahead of him, if he could just get on top of the workload. But if he had no time in his life for making human friends, maybe he could allow himself the unquestioning companionship of a dog.

He rubbed across Wolf's broad skull. The lacerated ear was clean and dry, well scabbed over. It might not even heal notched. The dog watched him with that unique concentration in his pale eyes. Paul, of all people, knew better than to anthropomorphize but he could talk to the dog and pretend Wolf understood him, as long as he knew he was pretending.

"Hey, Wolfers. Maybe I'll even go back to running regularly, if I have you needing exercise. Maybe I'll finally meet my neighbors when they see me out with you. No one talks to a lone guy, but I'll bet you're a chick magnet of the first order."

Wolf snorted softly and rubbed his cheek against Paul's ribs, knocking him sideways. He hugged the dog's neck gently.

"Of course, with your size, feeding you will probably have to be a budget line item. It's a good thing I'll get your meds and supplies at a discount. And you'll need a good foam bed, especially until those injuries heal. And a license…" He paused, running through the dog's needs in his mind. It *would* cost a mint to keep a dog this size. *Totally worth every penny.*

"I haven't had a dog of my own since I was a little kid. Not since…" His throat closed. Even to a dog, he couldn't talk about that time. He set his charts on the floor and buried his face in the dog's mane. Wolf's fur smelled of alcohol and antiseptics, but underneath that was a clean scent of dog and pine woods and outdoors.

"Am I being unfair to keep you, when I don't have a big space for you to run in?" That wild outdoors scent suggested this dog spent a lot of time running free, as did the lush thickness of his coat. The clinic exercise yard was small and relatively bare. "Maybe I should find you a good home with a big property." His chest ached at the thought of giving Wolf to someone else. *So much for not getting attached.* But he should do what was best for the dog.

Wolf twisted under his cheek and a big wet tongue stroked across Paul's neck, as if the dog had caught his tone. Paul sighed. "Not yet. I can't do that yet. We'll see how it goes. There are off-leash parks and places you can run. I swear I'll find the time."

The dog made a rumbling sound deep in his chest. Not a growl, judging by the steady thump of his tail. Almost a purr, but what kind of dog purred? Paul sat up and picked up his pen. "You're a good listener, Wolf." The heavy furred head nudged against his hip and the dog's eyes closed sleepily. Paul bent over the charts in his lap again. For once, he was reluctant when it came time to put his writing down, shut the cage, and go back to seeing clients.

The cancelled appointments meant that, for a change, Paul had finished most of his paperwork before the clinic closed. He took his dog out for a last walk in the fenced yard, Wolf's leg splint carefully protected with a plastic bag. The dog paced beside him on three legs through the hallways, head swinging back and forth as if checking out the place. Outside, Wolf led him along the fence, looking up.

"Don't even think about it," he told the dog, amused at his own fancy. "That's seven feet; you can't jump it, especially on three legs."

The dog gave him a look that seemed to say, *want to bet?* But he made no move to try. Paul was glad, since walking this dog was a matter of mutual consent. Wolf outweighed him by thirty pounds, and with the leash looped back around one of the dog's shoulders to keep pressure off the wounds on his neck, Paul had very little leverage. Fortunately, he'd invested in good double doors and fences. A friend of his had gone through the nightmare of having a patient escape and get hit by a car. He'd made sure that was *never* happening to him.

Back in the kennel he ran into a snag. The dog refused to get back into his crate. Wolf didn't bite, or even growl, or threaten him at all, just put on the brakes and lay down like a lump. The crate was barely big enough to begin with. Without Wolf's cooperation, Paul could wrestle one part of the dog inside, only to find that the other end was back out on the floor. After ten minutes he stopped, breathing hard.

He could hear Sarah and Elise still up front, closing up. He could ask them to come help, but he wasn't sure even three people could make this dog do anything he didn't want to do.

"What's the problem?" he asked the dog. *As if he's going to answer me.*

Wolf looked at the crate, then paced to the other end of the room to sniff at the row of old concrete runs Paul hadn't had time to replace yet. They were much bigger and roomier, of course, but the gates were old and rusty, and the curved shape left a nasty gap open at the bottom corners. A boxer had got its head stuck in that triangular space a year ago and almost choked to death. He hadn't put a dog in one since. The stainless-steel crates were much safer.

"Come on, baby," Paul said. "My house isn't dog-proofed. I can't leave until you're safely locked up for the night, and I am so freaking tired. Kennel up." He pointed to the crate, hoping the dog would obey the command.

"Kennel up. Go to bed. In your crate." *What other commands might an owner have used?*

Wolf just stared at him, pale eyes unblinking. Then the dog walked over to the first concrete run, stepped in, and lay down neatly, well back from the gate. Paul couldn't imagine a much clearer response. He sighed. The effort to move two hundred pounds of dog seemed unachievable, and after all, the previous owner of the clinic had used those runs for twenty years without problems. And this dog's huge head was never going to fit in that risky space.

"Okay," he told his stubborn pet. "You can stay in there. But if I come in tomorrow morning and you've strangled yourself on the gate I'm going to be seriously pissed." The dog gave him that open-mouthed smile he usually saw on golden retrievers. He would've sworn the jade eyes were amused. Paul bent to pet Wolf once more. Not that he had to bend far. He had no business taking on a dog, especially a big one that would need a lot of exercise. But somehow, he couldn't resist. Dropping to one knee he hugged the dog, rubbing his face in the soft fur over Wolf's shoulder.

"I'm really glad I found you." He stood up straight, latched the gate securely, and put a stern look on his face. "Now no chewing off the splint or pulling the wrap off those catheters. Or you'll be back to the bucket head."

The dog gave him a tiny wuff, as if in agreement, and he laughed. "Yeah, like you understand a word I'm saying. Good night, Wolf. See you in the morning."

He whistled as he left, despite the fatigue, looking forward to an actual dinner and a full night's sleep for a change. Even the slippery, snowy drive home couldn't dampen his mood. His pillow was soft, his bed luxurious, and he smiled as he fell asleep.

But his mood didn't survive being woken by a call from the police about a break-in.

Paul pulled his SUV up in front of his clinic and jumped out. Flashing blue and red lights from the police car at the curb lit the front door. The sound of his on-site alarm reverberated in the still, cold air. Any hope this was a false alarm vanished at the sight of a gaping hole in the plate-glass front window.

The police officer got out and came toward Paul as he hurried for the door, holding out a hand for Paul's keys. "Why don't you let me go in first and look around? In case there's someone still in there."

"Absolutely. Thank you." Paul stood shivering on the step while the cop disappeared inside. After a few minutes, the officer returned. "No sign of anyone. Why don't you check the money and drugs, and tell me what's missing?"

Paul followed him inside. He punched his code into the alarm box, and the cessation of the noise was a relief. As the cop watched, he hurriedly checked the cash box and the drug lock-box. Both were intact and untouched. Even the drugs on the shelves were in their places.

"Maybe it was just vandalism," the cop suggested. "Someone breaking the window for fun. I thought from the size of the hole someone must've gone through it."

"Shit!"

"What?" The cop hurried after Paul as he ran toward the back. Paul lunged into the kennel room and stopped. His fast breaths echoed in the empty room. The first concrete run contained only a drift of gray fur, a few pieces of Vet-rap bandage, and a mound of torn cotton batting. Wolf was gone.

Dammit, no! "There was a dog here. A valuable dog, and I think he was being used for dog fighting. Someone broke in and took him."

"Maybe he got out. Why would anyone bother to steal a dog? And then not take money or drugs or computers?"

Paul wanted to protest, but he was stopped by the look of the bandages lying on concrete. The last time Wolf chewed his leg free, the debris looked exactly like that. *Fool me twice. Shit.*

He followed silently as the cop led the way back to the broken window. "Yep. Look. The fragments are all on the outside. Something broke the window out, not in. I'm betting that dog went AWOL all by himself. I just hope he didn't get hurt on the glass."

"Damned dog." Paul gritted his teeth. "Well, thanks for your time, and for calling me. I'll check around some more, clean up the glass. I should cover the window with something."

"Want help?"

"No, I've got it." Paul shook himself out of his scattered thoughts and held out his hand. "Thanks again."

"Just doing my job." The officer hovered for a moment. "Are you going to be in big trouble for losing the dog? I can tell the guys on patrol to keep an eye out."

"Um, sure, that would be great," Paul said, although without enthusiasm. Somehow, he didn't think anyone would catch Wolf if he didn't want to be caught. But he showed the cop a photo, taken on his phone, and described his dog. *Well, not my dog, not anymore.*

After the cop left, Paul found a cardboard box and improvised a patch for the broken window to keep out the cold. He tried to look on the bright side. At least the escapee wasn't the pet of a client who would sue his ass. At least it wasn't a small hairless breed that would freeze to death out there. At least it was a dog smart enough to stay off the roads. Hopefully.

He went out looking, flashlight in hand. The cleared sidewalk outside the window showed no traces, but in the snow at the edge of the parking lot he finally found the huge paw-prints of a dog traveling on three legs, heading northeast. He followed as far as he could on foot, calling the dog's name. *A name which he's heard about twice in his life, and is never going to respond to.* When he lost sight of the trail in the blowing snow, he went back to his truck and cruised, aimlessly, searching the roadside for sight of a big smoke-gray body. Every mound of gray slush and drift in the ditch made his heart beat faster, until he proved it wasn't Wolf. *He's too smart to get hit by a car,* Paul told himself. *Damned dog probably went home.* But he didn't give up his search until the gray light of dawn forced him to head back to work.

§ § § §

Simon stared at a full color picture of himself in wolf form. The photo was on a flier stapled to a pole. "*Have you seen this dog*?"

"God damn it!" He'd hoped that he would walk away from his vet hospital stay with only the healing scars on his body to deal with. The almost-breach of security should've been over, just another case of an injured stray that disappeared. Dealing with his attack and his position in the pack was complicated enough without bringing a human into his mess. But he might've known that vet was too damned stubborn to let a patient go missing.

Simon pried the flier off the wood and eyed the photo. *When did Hunter take the freaking picture?* From the groggy look on his wolf face, he'd been doped up pretty thoroughly at the time, but it was a clear likeness. If his few friends in the pack spotted a flier, they would razz him about being called a dog, and about the bright turquoise wrap that adorned his injured leg in the picture. If anyone who *didn't* like him saw this, the question of concealment would be raised. Then if he couldn't prove the pack secrets had stayed safe, both he and Hunter would pay the deadly price.

The description of his wolf form as "very big but sweet-natured and gentle" made him snort. Sadly, the irony of a gentle werewolf couldn't hide the fact that he was so in trouble. Simon roamed the streets, locating and removing fliers as he spotted them. He was going to miss one, he just knew it, and that would be the one Karl would see. It was pure luck that he'd even found the first one.

He hadn't thought his damage control through well enough. He'd called in sick to work, because his arm wouldn't let him do the job right. Rebandaging it himself had been a bitch, and his makeshift splint wasn't solid enough to safely use his hand. The broken ribs still made walking painful. So he'd set out to entertain himself by driving aimlessly, steering with one hand and knee and fudging the turn signals. He'd been trying to make himself harder for Karl to find, and yeah, he had cruised past the North End Veterinary Clinic, just out of curiosity, just to look at the place with human eyes. But he hadn't thought about how the vet would handle his escape. He'd never expected the wanted posters.

He found seventeen more fliers scattered through the neighborhood in his first two hours of searching. Knowing human nature, there were probably an even twenty. He absolutely had to locate the other two. Unless there were twenty-five. He realized he'd better talk to Hunter. Soon. Otherwise even if he found all of these, it was a good bet he'd see a new set posted tomorrow. Simon decided to take a break indoors, drink something hot, and plan his approach.

The coffee shop he located was warm inside, the air redolent with the scent of freshly-baked cookies. Simon licked his lips. Werewolves didn't have super-strength or scary mind powers, like in so many stories, but his senses were acute. Smell and hearing were enhanced in his human form, vision was clearer than canine-normal as a wolf. Sometimes the sensitivity was a curse, like when something was rotting in the garbage. Sometimes his excellent nose was useful. Right now, it was telling him that this bakery used real butter and lots of cinnamon and chocolate. His stomach growled.

He ordered cinnamon cocoa and a giant cookie, and gazed around as he waited for his drink to be made. His eye was caught by the community bulletin board beside the front door. *Bingo, flier number nineteen!* He was folding the page up into his pocket when a voice behind him said, "Dr. Hunter just posted those this morning." He turned sharply. The girl from behind the counter held out his cup, looking questioningly at him.

"Yeah," Simon said quickly, "But that's my dog, and I know where he is. He came back home last night."

"Well, you'd better tell the doc. He seemed pretty worried."

"Right. I'm on my way over there as soon as I've warmed up a little."

"Oh, good." She smiled and handed him the drink. "Enjoy."

The girl headed back to her station, and Simon found a table in the back. The cocoa was rich and hot, the cookie crumbled just right, but Simon sighed. Usually he was good at enjoying the moment, regardless of what freight train was bearing down on him next. That skill kept his life tolerable. But this situation had the potential to be a real mess. He ate and sipped slowly, and gave his options some thought.

Eventually he made his way back to his truck, and drove to the clinic. Despite the approaching lunch hour, the clinic parking lot was full of cars. Simon wrapped his scarf around his neck and pulled his hood up, making sure the healing cuts on his neck and ear were hidden. He eyed himself in the rearview mirror. Other than a bruise on one cheek, none of the damage showed. He took off his sling, got out, and tucked his left hand into his jacket pocket to support the broken arm. *Shit, that hurt.* But he couldn't let the vet see matching injuries in his human form, even if the chance of him making the connection was basically zero.

Simon made his way to the door, wincing when he spotted the piece of cardboard taped over the broken front window. *Oops, my bad.*

Inside, a middle-aged receptionist was dealing with a woman juggling a cat, handbag and checkbook. Simon got a brief glance and a nod. He waited his turn, eyeing the room with that odd deja-vu sensation that came from experiencing a place in one form that he had only known in the other. The waiting room seemed bigger, brighter and less full of smells than his wolf-self remembered.

Finally, the client was done. She tucked her amazingly compliant feline under her arm for the trip out to the parking lot. Simon held the door for her, then stepped up to the desk.

"Can I help you?" the receptionist said brightly.

"Is Dr. Hunter available?"

"I'm afraid he's pretty busy this morning. Can I tell him what it's about?"

Simon pulled one of the fliers out of his pocket. "He was looking for this dog, and I've found him."

"Oh, yes," she said eagerly. "He'll be so glad. Just wait a few minutes and I'll tell him as soon as he comes out of the exam room." She disappeared back into the clinic. Simon roamed the waiting area, noting the shelves of shampoos and toothpaste, the dog food and rawhide bones. He spotted a bulletin board adorned with pictures of pets for sale, pets for free, lost pets. There, front and center, was flier number twenty. Simon quickly pulled the page down and added it to the collection in his pocket.

"You were looking for me?" Hunter's voice asked from behind him.

Simon turned. His first thought was, *wolf senses are not always more acute.* The man in front of him was familiar, voice and size, movement and scent. That mix of clean skin and light sweat, with something herbal and minty, faintly overlaid with disinfectant and alcohol, shouldn't have been so appealing. But the scent went right to the wolf side of his brain as *comfort* and *friend.* The amber eyes, looking at him warily, were right too. But his wolf hadn't realized that this man was gorgeous.

The sight of Hunter hit Simon like being dropped in scalding water, every nerve alight. *I want that man.* Streaked brown-blond hair fell in tousled, untrimmed strands above those gray-flecked gold eyes. High cheekbones stood out starkly in a face pared down to the thin side of healthy. A curved upper lip met a full lower, barely a shade darker than the pale, pale skin, and there was a faint bruised look of fatigue around the eyes. The man was all fine muscle over clean lines of bone, like a racing greyhound that had been worked too long and too hard. Simon wasn't sure if he wanted to fuck him or feed him. Both probably. He settled for holding out his hand.

"Dr. Hunter?" he asked in a calm, friendly voice. "I'm Simon Conley."

"My receptionist said you came about the dog." Hunter's hand was smooth and cool, the grip firm but brief. "The one in the posters?"

"Yes. He's my dog. Well, half mine."

Hunter's eyes brightened with hope. "Do you know where he is?"

"Sure. The dumb mutt came home on his own, late last night. Wolf is at my house. But I appreciate the effort you put into looking for him. Posting twenty fliers…?" He let his voice rise in a question.

Hunter smiled in relief. "It was no problem. That's great! I was really worried about him. And hey, I called him Wolf too." The joy in his expression put color in his cheeks and eased the bruised fatigue around his eyes. With that smile, he looked about eighteen.

Simon bit his cheek to keep from grinning in response. "The name fits, I guess. He looked a little beat up when he got home, but not too bad. He ate fine."

"When can you bring him in?" Hunter asked. "I'm booked pretty full today, but I'll squeeze him in whenever you can get here."

"Um, bring him in for what?"

"He needs to be checked over. For one thing, his front leg is broken and he chewed off the splint. He needs a new one. I should re-X-ray his chest too. He had a collapsed lung, and God only knows what he did to all his lacerations, going through plate glass and then running the whole way home. Unless you took him to a different clinic?"

"He looked pretty good to me. I mean considering his injuries. My friend, who co-owns the dog, knows a lot about animals. He wrapped the leg, and said the rest of the dog looked okay."

"That dog needs professional care," Hunter said firmly. "He almost died."

Too true, Simon thought. Unfortunately, there was no way he and the dog could appear in the clinic at the same time. In any case, he was healing too fast for an exam to be safe. The lacerations were closing, and an X-ray would show the broken bones well on their way to being mended. He trotted out his planned story.

"The problem is, I have to get back to work right now, and my friend who owns Wolf with me is moving to New Jersey tonight. He's picking up the dog and heading out. He bought a house out there, with lots more room for Wolf to run. I'm sure he'll take Wolf to a vet near his new place as soon as he gets there. In fact, if you give me the dog's records, I'll make sure my friend brings them along with him."

"No."

Simon blinked. "No, what?"

"No, I am not giving you this dog's records so you can disappear with them."

"What are you suggesting?"

"I saw the injuries to that dog," Hunter said coldly. "That was no simple dog fight. Maybe if he was a little poodle, I could believe he just happened to run into a couple of roaming pit bulls. But Wolf is two hundred pounds, and no matter how sweet he is I don't think he'd hold still to be attacked. That was severe aggression, by several dogs. The kind of thing that dog fighters do to train their dogs. And to cap it off, he was dumped. I found him on a road. He was bleeding out into the snow, but there was no trail. He didn't crawl there on his own. Someone shoved him out of a car and left him to die."

"Who would do that?" Simon asked, sounding artificial in his own ears.

"I don't know. But you tell me that the dog is fine, except you can't bring him in, and he hasn't been to any other vet, and by the way he's going to be taken out of state tonight, after which he won't be seen again." Hunter glared at Simon, fury and challenge lighting his eyes. "Is he even still alive?"

"Of course he is! If he was deliberately abused, it happened after I lost him."

"Then prove it," Hunter insisted. "Let me see him. He needs antibiotics, and his leg really needs to be re-set. If he's going to another vet, I'll be happy to copy his records for them, but I'm not giving you anything until I see the dog."

Simon sighed. "Wow, you are demanding." He couldn't help grinning. "That's okay. I like that in a man." He watched Hunter closely, but the only reaction he got was a slow blink and a tensing of muscles. Message noticed, but no clue about how it was received. That wasn't amusement, or interest, but it also wasn't disgust or running screaming. *Let it go, idiot. Starting anything with a human man right now is crazy.*

"How about this," he suggested. "You can go by my house. Wolf is there now. He has the run of the house and yard while I'm out. I have to get back to work, but if you stand by the fence and call him, I'm sure he'll come over and you can check him out."

"He should be confined inside, with those injuries. Not running loose in the snow."

"No, he shouldn't," Simon argued. "If I try to confine that dog I'd come home to a destroyed house and he might hurt himself doing it. He's best with some space. That's why he's going to New Jersey. My yard is too small and the fence is too low for him."

"Okay," Hunter replied. "Give me your address. In fact, let my receptionist make up a complete file for Wolf. I'll need his previous vet's name, and his shot record. I gave him a rabies shot when he was here." Simon winced. *So that's the odd feeling in my butt, the one that's sore but not a bruise.* "I held off on everything else. But you'll need him updated with a health certificate for travel across state lines."

"Sure," Simon agreed, biting back his frustration. *Like I have a fucking shot record.* The man's thoroughness was moving beyond inconvenient. "And I can pay the bill now and get his record closed out."

"After I've seen him," Hunter said coldly. "I'm not taking your money until I'm sure you're not responsible for his condition." He glanced over at his receptionist, who was gesturing at the waiting room full of patients. "I'll go by your place at lunch time. You can stop in for his records after three. We're open till seven."

Simon watched the man head back to his work with a mix of admiration and irritation. So much for thinking a simple little visit would get things cleared up. But at least the fliers were down off the walls.

He gave the receptionist enough information to start a file, mixing truth and invention with I-don't-knows about previous vet visits. He blamed his imaginary friend for the uncertainty. Once the file, uncomfortably combining "Wolf" and "Conley" on the tabs, was shelved, Simon headed out to prepare for his home vet visit.

Simon owned a tiny house on a small suburban lot. The yard had a low white fence, which he could easily hurdle in wolf form. Even returning last night on three legs, he'd made it over the fence and through the dog door in the back before collapsing on his own floor. He'd crashed there for hours of sleep and eaten a big venison roast, raw and bloody between his teeth, before he felt restored enough to safely make the shift back to human form.

In his battered condition, the two shifts he'd needed to get out of the clinic had almost been too much. On the second one, from man back to wolf to run home, he'd almost trapped himself between forms, with too little energy to go forward or back. He wondered if Gordon, his Alpha, would have sensed it and come to tip him over the edge. Or would he just have died there, naked and deformed on the clinic floor?

Today he was much better off. He hurried in his front door, gathered supplies, and then stripped and wolfed. The energy flowed, sweet and abundant all around him in his wood-frame home. His body obediently found its other form, sliding through the genetic code, shifting the shape and density of bone and muscle.

Shifting hurt, though. It was always somewhat painful, an ache and burn like the day after hard exercise. But today, with his broken bones, there was a sharp edge to the pain. He kept silent by habit, holding the agony inside himself as the broken ends of bone in his arm ground, changed, and sought each other to knit a little more together. When the shift was over, he lay panting for a while, letting the pain endorphins ebb and waiting for his heart to slow back down.

Then came a half-hour struggle to wrap his broken foreleg in a splint that looked like a bandage applied by human hands. The job would have been easy before shifting, except any wrap on his human arm would have fallen right off his canine leg. *Fuck!* He finally had something workable, but the pain of banging his half-healed front leg around was causing spots in front of his eyes. He collapsed on the floor, breathing hard.

Karl would be laughing so hard right now. Karl and his toadies had meant his injuries in the cold to kill him, Simon was certain of it. But failing that, they would just love to see him fail his concealment. Forcing his Alpha to kill him for breach of secrecy would work even better for them than murder. He'd be damned if he'd let that happen, and not just because he liked living.

Don't worry about it now. As wolf, he had a practical attitude, so he put his nose on his paws and took a nap. *Get sleep when you can.* He woke to the sound of a car pulling up outside. *Showtime.*

The vet's voice called, "Wolf? Here, boy! Treats!" Simon waited just long enough for a show of independence, then sauntered out the dog door into the snowy yard. Hunter was standing by the fence, holding out his hand. The scent of something delectable, bacon and liver and toasted grain, wafted from that hand. *Trust a vet to know the best treats.* In truth, the man's own scent was almost as appealing. His wolf-self wanted to go over and get rubbed on that perfect spot on his chest, and eat the whatever-it-was in the bargain. His human-self locked the impulse down. He didn't dare get too close. His coat was already re-growing in the shaved spots, and the stitches were all gone. The threads that hadn't been rejected in the change he had snipped out, cursing at the way they pulled the healing injuries out of shape on his human body. But Hunter would surely notice if he got a good look.

Simon sauntered toward the man, walking on three legs with his bandaged foreleg held clear of the snow. *See Mommy, I'm keeping it clean and dry.* He stopped fifteen feet away and barked softly, wagging his tail. Actually, he didn't have to do that deliberately. His wolf was glad to see this man. He remembered the first time he'd felt himself wagging at some pleasure as a wolf. It was an odd reflex, like smiling but more physical, like an erection at the sight of a pretty man, his body taking over without conscious intention.

He paused to assess how he felt. He had never faced a man he'd been attracted to as a human while in wolf form. He was a little relieved that his wolf wasn't turned on. He wanted to get close, and touch, but for comfort and friendship, not desire. His wolf wanted to treat this man as pack, protect him, feed him. He snorted, as the image of hauling a deer carcass over to dump in front of Hunter came to mind.

"What's up, boy?" Hunter was saying in that soft coaxing voice. "Do you remember me? Come on, sweetie, I've got goodies for you. Come here and let me look at you."

Simon wagged harder, deliberately, and let his jaw drop in a canine smile, but moved no closer. *How to reassure this man, so he'll leave?* He ignored the little voice that didn't want Hunter to leave. He needed to look healthy, healing, but not impossibly so. He walked around, shoved his nose in the snow and tossed clumps in the air. He did a little play-pouncing, like killing a mouse, but carefully and keeping on three legs.

Hunter watched him, talking softly. After a while he threw the treat into the snow, halfway between himself and Simon. Simon eyed it, and then let himself smile again. He took off around the yard, running hard enough to kick up the powder. On his pass by Hunter, he suddenly swerved, snatched the jerky strip in his teeth in a concealing shower of snow, and was away again.

Hunter laughed. "Yeah, you're not stupid, are you?" He put a hand and foot on the fence. "What if I climbed over?" Simon chomped down on the treat, chewing rapidly. *There, eating fine.* As Hunter pulled himself up on the fence, Simon backed away a couple of steps slowly, eyeing him. Hunter reached an arm over. Simon backed up two more steps. Hunter pulled his arm back, and Simon moved forward two. Reach; two backward: stop; two forward. Hunter sighed and dropped back to the ground on his side.

"Okay, dog. I'm not stupid either. I'm never going to touch you if you don't want me to." Simon wagged happily. The vet sighed again. "You look better than you did last time I saw you. I wish there was a way to know if that guy is really good to you."

Simon goofed around for a while, watching the vet out of the corner of his eye. The man smiled at his antics, but didn't seem ready to leave. Simon racked his brains for a clincher. He made his way back into the house through the dog door and glanced around for something that could look like a dog toy. *There.* Eric had won him the purple stuffed bear on a trip to the State Fair five years ago. He'd bet Simon that if he walked around the Fair carrying it, he'd get hit on within fifteen minutes. Then they had argued over whether getting hit on by women counted. A good memory, but Eric was in California now and it would serve another purpose.

He rose on his hind legs, snagged the fuzzy toy off the shelf and hauled it outside. In front of Hunter, he gave the best performance he could come up with of silly-dog-with-a-teddy-bear. He tossed and chased and leaped over the thing, until Hunter was laughing.

"Okay. Okay, stop. You're going to hurt your leg. Stop, Wolf, settle. I believe you. You're fine."

Simon paused, mouth full of bear, and looked at him. Hunter headed over to his car and pulled out a white plastic bag.

"I'm going to put your stuff on the front door-handle for your master," he said. "He'll have the antibiotics and directions there, and a photo of the X-rays, the best I can do. I'm still keeping the originals." He paused a moment longer. "And I'm talking to a dog again. But you're an unusual dog, Wolf. You take care, don't reinjure that leg, and enjoy New Jersey. And if that guy isn't good to you, you do a Lassie-come-home and work your way back here and I'll take him on for you." He sighed. "As if. I hope I'm doing the right thing." Simon wagged and tossed his head to wave the purple bear. Hunter gave him one last long look, then carried the bag around the house to the front. After a moment he returned and climbed in his truck without looking at Simon. And although Simon watched until the truck was out of sight, Hunter never looked back.

Simon made his way back into the house and spat the bear out on the floor. *Purple fuzz in the mouth, blech.* He shook himself, yanked the slipping wrap off his leg, and shifted back to human. It was slow, and even more painful. The lengthening and stretching of his bones lanced through him in sharp needles of sensation. For a moment he almost lost himself in the currents of pain, sliding sideways away from the shift, looking for refuge. *Safe, warm, golden space where I can rest.* He caught himself up and controlled the impulse, focusing will and concentration on the changes he was making. His body stabilized, panting and nude on his kitchen floor.

Shit, maybe he wasn't as healed as he'd thought. It wasn't safe to be so vulnerable, and his body desperately wanted food. After scrounging up some sweats to wear, and rigging a towel in a sling for his arm, he set about decimating the contents of his refrigerator.

Food was good, lots of food. He made a sandwich that Dagwood could've been proud of, dumped a bag of chips on the plate, added cookies, and carried his meal one-handed to the couch. His left arm ached abominably, but the pain was worth tolerating to get rid of the vet. Hunter was too inquisitive and nosy. And he'd cared far too freaking much for a dog he'd had less than twenty-four hours. He'd been all worked up on Wolf's behalf, ready to take on Simon's human form. Simon's muscle and bulk hadn't intimidated the man at all.

He had to smile at the memory of Hunter getting in his face. Of course, Simon been working to soothe the man, not intimidate him. But he had a feeling intimidation would have been difficult even if he'd tried. Hunter cared, really cared, about doing the right thing. There weren't enough people like that in the world.

Simon took a big bite of his sandwich and cursed as bits of tomato dropped onto his sweatshirt. What he really should do now was finish eating, then have a hot shower and a nap. Then if he had the energy, he should shift again, twice if he could manage it, until his arm bones quit separating. And then eat more, and sleep, and gather strength to heal.

There had to be a reason he'd been attacked far worse than normal by Karl and his flunkies, but he couldn't figure it out. Even less clear was why they hadn't come back to finish the job, or hauled him out for a formal Challenge while he was injured. A sneak attack like the one he'd faced was against every rule the pack had, and the pack lived by its rules, fiercely enforced and unbreakable.

Unfortunately, it was his word against five of them as to who started the fight. He couldn't bring them to the Alpha for judgement with no evidence. But they had to be at least slightly nervous. Why would they break every rule, put themselves at risk, and yet not finish him off?

Simon's head ached almost as much as his chest. Karl played games and loved to manipulate. As pack Second, his long-range goal was control of the pack. No one could doubt that, not even the Alpha. Gordon stayed on top of Karl by the skin of his teeth these days. But how Simon fit into this game Karl was running wasn't clear.

No one had come back to kill him. Yet. But no one had spoken up to support him either. Not that he was expecting much. The wolves he got along with were mostly too low in the rankings to risk coming to Karl's attention. Hell, Simon was an object lesson in how dangerous that could be. His pain over the pack bonds had no doubt told them how close he'd come to dying. A few had called his phone, leaving tentative messages about how they were glad he was still alive. *Gee, thanks.*

Simon finished his sandwich and stuffed two snickerdoodle cookies in his mouth. The taste of cinnamon reminded him that he'd had one visitor. He'd woken that morning stiff and sore to notice an odd scent of sugar and spice. The fragrance was seeping through the window he'd left cracked open to give his ears and nose an early warning of anyone approaching. He'd barely made it out of bed before the front doorbell rang. Simon had grabbed for a big, loose robe, sniffing hard in an attempt to identify his visitor. All he got was the glorious smell of fresh baking. He didn't sense a packmate though.

Passing the bathroom on his way to the stairs, he'd grabbed a towel. By pulling the robe low over his bad arm, and slinging the towel thickly around his neck, he could cover most of the evidence of his injuries. He made an effort to move silently and easily. No way he wanted to sound vulnerable, coming down those stairs.

When he pulled open the door, the woman on the steps brushed past him casually. "Let me in, Simon. This coffee cake's going to be frozen again if I stand out here much longer."

Simon stepped aside to let Megan, his pack Seventh's bondmate, into his kitchen. Megan was a lean, active woman as tall as Simon, and although he probably outweighed her by fifty pounds, when Megan had a head of steam up, you stepped out of her way and said, "Yes, ma'am."

He followed her to the kitchen. The hot pastry she set on the counter made his mouth water but he ignored it, despite his inner wolf clamoring for food. "Does Mark know you're here?"

Megan turned and leaned on the counter, still bundled in her parka, her hazel eyes serious. "Of course. He's watching Karl. We have half an hour before Mark has to go on duty. So talk fast. How bad are you hurt?"

Simon shrugged carefully with one shoulder. "Arm's broken. I'll heal."

"Mark was on duty when it happened." Megan's husband was a police officer with the Minneapolis department. "He couldn't get away. By the time he was off work, he said you seemed better. And we thought we wouldn't rock the boat. But then you didn't answer your phone."

True enough. His phone had been left home with his clothes. When he was home and human again, and awake enough to care, he'd found the few missed calls, including one from his Alpha. He'd called Gordon back and left a message that he was fine. The others he'd let wait. They would know over the pack bonds that he hadn't died. His exhausted stupor had tunneled his attention down to food and sleep. And since then, no one had bothered to try again.

"I was getting to that." Eventually.

"Mark and I, well, we wanted to be sure you weren't hurt worse than it felt."

"I appreciate that." Her arrival, even without the baked goods, was more than anyone else had done. "Karl won't be happy with Mark if he starts taking my side, or with you for showing up here. It's dangerous."

"Karl should eat shit and die." Megan sighed. "I hate this. I hate the way we're all walking on eggshells, waiting for something to snap. I hate the fact that Mark, my Mark who's willing to go into a dark building after a man with a gun, is so overwhelmed by Karl that the most we can do for you is bring coffee cake."

"Hey, I love your coffee cake," Simon told her. "The second you're out the door, there will be nothing left but crumbs."

She smiled faintly. "It's not homemade. The cookies are. But… Simon, Mark said to tell you, well, he would stand by you if he thought his backing would do any good. But he advises you not to make a formal complaint to Gordon. Right now, the Alpha can ignore this, but if he has to confront Karl…"

"Yeah." That was the problem. None of them were really sure Gordon could take on Karl anymore. In fact, maybe that was the goal in attacking him. Force a confrontation…

"And Mark's worried about me and our boy. Karl has never played by the rules." Pack wives and kids should've been absolutely off limits, but Simon wouldn't have trusted Karl to keep those boundaries either.

"I'm fine, Meg. Go tell Mark I understand. I'll see him around."

Megan had hesitated, but then made her way to the door. In the entry she'd turned and touched Simon's arm. "Be careful, Simon. Eat and rest, okay. You look like shit. We really would hate to lose you, even if Mark doesn't dare get his own scent on your doorstep. Even if the best we can do is have me show up as the busybody wife."

He'd managed a smile. "I know. It's fine."

He'd watched her hurry back to her car and pull away.

Not one wolf had taken the risk of approaching Simon's house that morning. Not even his best friend Andy had come. They knew he was alive and healing, of course. Pack bonds meant that everyone knew when a packmate was in real danger, and whether they lived or died. Their absence was a measure of how scared they all were of Karl. But he had to admit a little pang in his chest, when the phone and doorbell stayed silent. Even though their caution was logical, even though he'd have warned them away if they asked, it did hurt that no one tried.

Inadvertently, his thoughts fastened on the glowing gold of Hunter's eyes, demanding to know if Wolf was okay. Up in his face for the sake of a dog. There was a guy to have on your side. Not a fighter, of course, but he'd never give you up just because it was the safe thing to do. Pity he was human. Although if he'd been a wolf, he'd be facing the threat of pack violence too, and Simon had enough to do taking care of himself without a more submissive wolf to protect.

Of course, the fact that Paul was human laid open a far more appealing possibility. *Mmm.* Simon leaned back on the couch, sprawling, licking the last of the cinnamon from his fingers luxuriously.

That man was everything that pushed Simon's buttons. The streaked hair, lean body, high cheekbones, gold eyes, might have come straight from one of his fantasies. Although when he thought about it, he'd usually chased after guys with more muscle and more height, not the starving runner types. And yet, there was nothing about Hunter that he would change. Not one thing.

Shit. Simon forced himself to sit up straight. When did he get so stupid? Chasing Hunter was a fool's idea. The vet was linked to Simon's wolf, which made it a bad, bad idea to get mixed up with him in human form too. What if they were out somewhere and met one of the pack? Imagine that conversation. *"How did you and Simon meet?" "Oh, I treated his dog when it was attacked."* And wouldn't that lead to a come-to-Jesus meeting with the Alpha. Even if they couldn't prove a breach of security, the risk would be considered unacceptably high.

So stay away from the man. How difficult could that be? Hunter had left Wolf's medical records and antibiotics for him. He'd gone away satisfied. There was still the matter of payment, but Simon could phone the receptionist with his card, or mail in a check. He had no reason to meet with Hunter again. None.

Although it might be wise to check back with a fake update on Wolf's condition. Before Hunter took it into his head to come around asking more questions. And, shit, there was that window he'd broken escaping. That had to cost something. He owed Hunter for the damages; at some point he'd have to offer payment…

Simon shook his head. He was rationalizing, but he knew himself too well. He wasn't going to stay away from Hunter. Playing it safe had never been his style. Surely there was room for a little contact, a little friendship with an attractive human. Not even Karl could be suspicious of every person Simon met.

He could do this. Just see the man casually, get to know him. Because something about Hunter made him realize how empty his life was of friends right now. The pack that had once been family, however dysfunctional, had become a time bomb. And he had no one else. Simon remembered how his whole body seemed to react when Hunter was around, relaxed, focused, more centered than he'd been in weeks. He was fascinated by those amber eyes, that quick mind, skilled hands…

He hauled himself stiffly up off the couch, wincing at the pull on his ribs, and carried the empty plate to the kitchen. Time for a shower. The water would sting in his cuts but he wanted that safe, clean pain. Maybe it would clear his head. Maybe after a warm shower he would be able to sleep. *Maybe in the wet enclosed space, I'll find an extra reason to be glad it isn't my right hand that's injured.*

Chapter 3

Paul hadn't thought he would see Wolf's owner again. Despite how good the dog had looked in the yard, some part of him continued to be suspicious of the New Jersey story. But when he stuck his head into the waiting room before closing time that evening, to see what he had left to do, Conley was sitting in one of the plastic chairs in jeans, a turtleneck, and his parka, leafing through a *Dog Fancy* magazine. He wore a knit hat in heather greens pulled low over his ears.

"Hey," Conley said, standing up at the sight of him. "I came to pay my bill and all, but your receptionist said you hadn't made one up yet. I told her I'd wait for you." He smiled cheerfully.

Paul wondered if Conley knew how appealing that grin was. *Of course he does. He probably charms birds out of trees and girls out of clubs with it.* Or maybe boys, if Paul had caught that off-hand quip right that morning. *Not that it matters to me which way he swings.*

"Sure," he said. "I've been busy. Give me a few minutes and I'll put something together." He glanced over at the front desk, where Elise had paused in the process of packing up her things to raise an eyebrow in silent enquiry. "You go on home," he told her. "I'll take care of his payment when I'm done. See you tomorrow."

"Thanks, Doc." She shrugged on her coat. "Angie has choir tonight, so I need to run."

Paul held the door for her, then flipped the sign and locked the deadbolt, so clients would know they were closed. His feet ached. "Sit tight. I'll have that for you in a moment," he said, turning back to Conley.

"Here." Conley held out a paper bag. "Brought you something to eat while you work."

Paul eyed him, perplexed.

"It's from Subway. A meatball sandwich." As Paul hesitated to take the proffered bag, the young man's face fell. "You're not vegetarian, are you?"

"No." Paul reached slowly for the food. "But why are you bringing me this?"

"I know your type. Married to your work, never slow down, don't take the time to eat right." When Paul still hesitated, Conley pushed the bag into his hand. "Go on. It's just a sandwich. A thank you for taking care of my dog. Take it."

Somehow, Paul found himself heading back to his office, food in hand, with Conley trailing behind him.

"Sit there," Paul directed, pointing out a chair. He settled in front of his computer and started an invoice. It was hard to decide what to charge for. Technically, Conley hadn't given consent for any treatment in advance. He had the right to refuse to pay anything. Clearly, he wasn't going to do that, but Paul didn't want to push his limits— a guy his age was unlikely to have a lot of spare cash— although the clinic could use every penny it could get.

"Don't hold back," Conley said, as if sensing his thoughts. "I'm not rich, but I can afford a few hundred. Saving Wolf's life is worth a whole lot to me. You should charge for what you did."

Paul made some entries. The numbers added up fast, especially when he put in the emergency exam and monitoring. He took it back out again.

He hadn't noticed when Conley got up, but the man was suddenly looking over his shoulder. "Stick that back in. It's more than fair. And I don't see any charge for oxygen on there." When Paul looked up in surprise, Conley shrugged. "You said he had a chest wound. I'm assuming you gave oxygen."

Paul included an hour's worth, wincing at the total, but Conley pulled out his wallet and peeled off bills. Paul noticed that the roll was much thinner when he was done, but Conley laid down the money without hesitation.

"Thank you," he said. "I'll get your receipt printed."

"I should be thanking you. Not a lot of people would take on a big injured dog like that, and put this kind of money and effort into him without knowing if they'd ever get paid, just because it's the right thing to do."

"It's my job."

"You did more than that. I'm grateful."

Paul printed the receipt and went up front to fetch the page off the printer. Conley hadn't followed him, and when he brought the receipt back to the office, Conley was back sitting in the spare chair, long jean-clad legs stretched out in front of him. He looked relaxed, and despite still wearing his hat and parka, not like a man about to take his paperwork and leave. Paul wondered if there was a polite way to hurry this along so he could get back to work.

"Um, have the vet in New Jersey contact me," he said, holding out the paper. "I'd love to know how Wolf does."

"Sure." Conley folded the sheet into his jacket pocket without standing up. He nodded at the paper bag. "You should eat your dinner before it gets cold."

"I have some work to do…" Paul began.

"Which can wait while you eat a hot meal. Come on. Unless you can tell me you had a big lunch?"

Paul felt the heat rising along his cheeks. So he'd skipped lunch to make the trek to look at Wolf. What made his eating habits any of this young man's concern?

Conley smiled at him, with enough warmth to melt ice caps. "Yeah, I figured. Sit down and eat, Doc." He pulled the bag back toward himself and opened it, pulling items out. "Sandwich for you, bottled water because the last thing you probably need is more caffeine, chips, chocolate chip cookie for you, chocolate chip cookie for me." He pushed Paul's food to his side of the desk and bit into his own cookie with enjoyment. "Now these aren't bad," he continued conversationally around a big mouthful. "For mass market. They've got the texture just right. Dig in and don't get the meatball sauce on your keyboard, Doc."

Paul sat down helplessly and began unwrapping his sandwich. He wanted to protest, but what he heard himself saying was, "My name's Paul, not Doc."

"Paul." Conley's eyes met his, intense gray-green with an odd hint of jade. "I'm Simon."

"Yeah," Paul muttered. "Okay." He bit into the sub. Maybe a few calories would help get his brain back on track.

As he ate, he eyed Simon surreptitiously. The man acted unaware of his scrutiny, although a small smile playing around his lips suggested otherwise.

He wasn't tall, maybe an inch above Paul's own five-nine, but despite his youth, he could've made two of Paul in width. He was built solidly, with biceps that filled the sleeves of his parka, and wide thighs in those jeans, enough muscle that Paul revised his age estimate up a couple of years. *Twenty-two? Twenty-three?*

Simon's skin was copper-gold with a deeper undertone that suggested ethnicity rather than a tan. The hint of an old bruise showed on one cheek. Those odd gray-green eyes sparkled at Paul from behind the longest lashes he had ever seen on a man. His hair was black and wavy, a few ends escaping from under the knit cap, and his face was wide, with a determined jaw, straight nose, and a hint of epicanthic folds around the eyes. Paul wondered if he had some Hawaiian or Native American ancestry.

Paul realized he was staring. He looked away, feeling his face heating. But instead of commenting, Simon said mildly, "Tell me what you think happened to my dog."

Paul described Wolf's injuries, and his treatments. This was his expertise and the words came easily. Simon was interested and knowledgeable, asking relevant questions. After a few minutes, Paul dug out the digital photos he'd made of Wolf's X-rays for the next vet's benefit, and put them up on the computer screen to show Simon.

"Here, and here," he said, pointing out the air in the dog's chest around the collapsed lung. "And this one's after I tapped the chest. You can see how much better it looks." He clicked forward. "This is the leg, pretty obvious. This is after I splinted it the first time. And this is after the second time, when that dog of yours chewed his bandage off." He peered at the screen, clicking on the magnification button. It made things bigger, but fuzzier. "It's weird," he told Simon, looking at the screen. The image blurred and he blinked to clear it. "These are less than a day apart, but if I didn't know better, I'd think there was already a healing callus starting to form on the second one. It's too early of course." He looked at the radiograph again. "I'm worried that Wolf did some damage to the ends of the bone when he got the wrap off. Maybe that's fine splintering instead of callus." He looked over his shoulder at Simon, who'd come around the desk to see the pictures. "You should tell your friend to get this X-rayed again soon, and that splint had better stay on at least six weeks."

He tried more magnification, but the image splintered into unintelligible pixels. *I want digital x-rays. As soon as the clinic can afford them.* He took the image back down. His vision blurred again, his head spinning, and for a moment he wondered if Simon had somehow spiked his food. A jaw-cracking yawn gave a more mundane explanation. Three days and two nights with almost no sleep were catching up with him. He shut the computer system down with a sigh. There were still charts to write, and purchase orders to plan.

"I hate to chase you out," he told Simon, "But I still have work to do, and I don't know how many conscious hours I have left to do it in. You can get out the front. Except you can't," he realized, dragging himself to his feet. "The door's locked. I'll come along and let you out."

A warm hand closed on his elbow. "And then what?" Simon asked, sounding almost angry. "Come back here and work some more?"

"I have charts and things. I won't stay late."

"You're going to fall asleep at your desk. And wake up with a horrible crick in your neck. You need a bed and a good night's sleep. Work in the morning."

"Who elected you my mother? Well, not really my mother, because she wouldn't…" Paul shut his mouth firmly. Jesus, he was more tired than he thought if he almost started talking about his mother.

"You need to take care of yourself."

"I'm fine. I mean thanks for the food, but I need to work now. Anyway—" A little irritation broke through. "—it was your damned dog I looked all over creation for last night."

"Sorry. I am sorry. He's a brat. Look." Simon took Paul's jacket off the hook on the wall and held it out. "That doesn't change the fact that any chart you write in tonight is going to be impossible to read in the morning."

Paul began to retort and stopped. Simon was pushy, but he wasn't wrong. No point in being stupid, just to be contrary. "Okay." He accepted the parka. "Yeah, you're right." He blinked at the wide smile Simon gave him. Good thing someone was happy. He kicked off his shoes and pulled on his snow boots. Wallet, keys… he was forgetting something, but his brain felt like each thought was wading through molasses. Wallet, keys… mail. He needed to take the mail past the box. He picked up the pile and stuffed the envelopes into one oversized pocket. Leaving was good. The cold air would wake him up.

Outside, Simon hovered at his shoulder while he set the alarm and locked the door. Or tried to. After the second time he dropped the keys, he felt compelled to comment, "I'm not usually this clumsy, you know. I do surgery and stuff. I just… I guess my fingers are cold."

"I guess." Simon's voice was a bass rumble as he held out the snow-dusted bunch of keys he'd retrieved.

"Thanks." Paul concentrated, locked the door, and pocketed the keys. "There." Except no, he needed the keys for his truck.

He fished them out again, then looked up in surprise as Simon took the bunch from him and dropped them back into his pocket. "You're not driving."

"What? Hey, all I had to drink was water."

"Tell me you're not so tired you might drift out of your lane and hit someone," Simon challenged, his hand in Paul's pocket holding the keys in place.

Paul glared at him, then sighed. "Fuck. I need a cab."

"No, you don't. My truck's over this way. I'll give you a lift. After all," Simon added when Paul hesitated, "it was my dog you were chasing all over last night."

That seemed fair. Surely that was fair? Paul nodded and followed him to the big black pickup.

"Bad-ass boys drive bad-ass toys," Simon quipped, opening the door.

"You don't have a bad ass," Paul tried to joke. That didn't come out right.

Simon grinned. "I would cherish that, if I thought you knew what you were saying. Come on, Rip-van-Winkle. Let's get you home."

§ § § §

Paul glanced around the clinic the next afternoon and decided he loved Saturdays. His new favorite day of the week. Half a day's work with clients and their pets, on top of hours of real sleep, and then the whole afternoon to get caught up.

He'd caught a cab, come in early that morning, and finished his Friday charts. Appointments had gone smoothly and all the clients were out the door on time. The purchases were ready for Monday. He just had today's records left to do, and month-end taxes. And maybe he should review the budget again. Still, he might even have time to read some journals.

He was deep in his finances when a knock on his office window surprised him. He looked out to see Simon, standing outside in the snow where the flowerbed would be in summer. Simon grinned and waved a checkbook at him. When Paul glared at him, he waved the book again and pointed toward the front door. Paul sighed. Clearly the man was not going away.

He unlocked and opened the door, standing firmly in the gap. "Simon. What part of 'Your account is paid up' did you not understand?"

"The part where I remembered that my dog broke your window," Simon replied cheerfully.

"Insurance will cover it. We're square."

"Hey, you don't want to make an insurance claim for that. Your rates will go up more than the window's worth, especially if you tell them the culprit was a loose patient. I'll just cover it. How much could it be?"

Paul took a malicious pleasure in telling him.

"Youch," Simon commented. "Big fucking window. But okay, can I come in to write this check before my fingers freeze?"

"No. I mean, yeah, come in." He stepped out of the doorway. "But you don't have to pay for the window. That's what insurance is for."

"No, it's not." Simon brushed past him and opened his checkbook on the reception counter. "Insurance is for fires and tornados and other disasters. For the little stuff, you're better with a big deductible and pay for it yourself."

"I can't take more of your money," Paul protested. "You already had the biggest bill of the week, and without a signed consent form first."

"Hey, you saved my life. I'm not complaining."

"I what?"

An odd look crossed Simon's face. "I mean, Rick would've killed me if anything happened to Wolf. He's pretty attached to him. That's worth more to me than this money." He tore off the check and passed it over.

Paul looked at the total, then glanced up at Simon, whose expression was subdued. "It must be hard for you," he offered, "losing your dog and your… friend, at the same time. New Jersey's a long way off."

Simon shrugged. "Yeah, but it's not like you're thinking. Rick's just a friend, and Wolf hasn't been with me very long. That's why I don't know about his shots and stuff. Rick was living in Washington state, near Bellingham. He dropped Wolf off with me when he headed east, to keep him safe while Rick was house-hunting. So I'll miss the big moose, but he's only been with me a couple of months."

"It wouldn't take long to get pretty attached. He's something special. Do you know what breed he is?"

"Nope. Humane Society special."

"He might be half wolf," Paul speculated, "But you don't want to register him that way because then he becomes wildlife instead of a pet and treating him at a regular clinic becomes illegal. I put Malamute mix on his chart."

"Close enough," Simon agreed.

"Have you heard how he's doing? Did your friend find a good vet? I haven't gotten a call for follow-up. Or are they still on the road?" The dog might've had an amazing constitution, but a long trip and all that stress… Paul would feel better once he'd talked to Wolf's new vet.

"He's good," Simon said. "They're still driving out. Rick's probably going crazy trying to keep him quiet in the truck."

"Well, if you get the new clinic's name let me know. I'll give them a call. Pity we'll never know who was responsible for him getting attacked." Paul put a little edge in his voice. Simon's dismissive attitude about his dog's injuries still struck a false note. But when Simon just nodded, Paul mentally told himself to let it go. He liked Simon, and he'd made the decision to trust him about Wolf. He'd go crazy second guessing himself.

Which left him standing there, looking at Simon, his mind a blank. *I must still be more tired than I thought.* The silence between them stretched.

Simon glanced toward the door. "Well, I just wanted to pay for that window."

Suddenly Paul was reluctant to see him go. "Can you afford this?" he asked, waving the check. "I mean, really?"

"Yeah." Simon sighed. "I've got some savings, for a project I'm planning. This isn't really that big of a chunk."

"Still…"

“Tell you what.” Simon’s eyes were suddenly brighter. “You take this check, and in return you can come out with me and see my project. Tell me if you think I’m as insane as some other folks do.”

“I don’t need to see any project to know you’re insane,” Paul teased, heartened by the change of tone. “And I was the one who didn’t want to take the check, so how come I have to do you another favor?”

“Oh, come on. You’re just feeling guilty about taking my money. Do me a favor, and then you can cash that with a clear conscience.”

“Somehow I’m not following the logic. But I’ll give you the benefit of the doubt. I’m still working, though.”

“You’re always working. Tell me when I can walk through that door and not find you working.” When Paul hesitated Simon said, “Hah, you see? Get your coat and let’s go.”

Without meaning to, Paul found himself sitting high up on the passenger seat of the big pickup, watching the Minnesota roadside go by. He tried to remember how long it’d been since he’d taken a drive out in the daylight in winter, and couldn’t. The roads were melting down to bare pavement, although every crossroad and curve held a layer of brown slush. Away from the road, the snow was still fresh and bright. Pristine fields were marked only by the occasional trail of deer or, being Minnesota, of snowmobiles. Fence posts and barns held caps of white, beginning to sag into crooked garlands as the sun’s warmth loosened their hold on the wood. A fresh snowfall in the night had dusted branches and trees. The smallest twigs were beginning to shed their loads as they stirred in the light breeze. Paul sighed.

“Sometimes I forget how beautiful this is,” he said quietly.

“You like the winters here?” Simon steered competently one-handed through a patch of ice.

“Yeah. That’s part of why I stayed.”

“Why you stayed when…”

Paul shrugged. “When I could’ve left.” That stuff was not for sharing. “How about you? Skiing or swimming?”

“Snow-shoeing,” Simon said happily. “And hiking and skating. I like cold a lot better than heat. Although I don’t object to a nice warm drink after the cold, or a nice warm bed.”

Paul wasn't going to touch that line. He looked out the window. "How far is this project of yours, anyway?"

"Another fifteen minutes. Can you think of anything better to do than drive through the countryside with good company and gorgeous scenery?"

Paul thought about tax forms and the budget and an article on skin grafting in cats. "Nope. I can't."

Eventually Simon left the paved roads for ice-covered gravel, and then rutted dirt. After a final five minutes working out the truck's suspension, he pulled into a lane, up a small hill, and around a bend to a dead end. He put the truck in park and killed the engine at the end of the road. "Here it is."

A battered old farmhouse loomed up in the untouched snow, its windows dark and a few of them boarded over. The square, gabled shape stood two stories high, fronted by Minnesota round fieldstone. Its peaked roof looked like a mix of slate and asphalt, as if patched several times in different eras. Paul was about to make a crack about picturesque ruins, but the quality of Simon's stillness as he looked at the house made him hesitate. There was a quiet dignity about the old place.

"It has nice lines," he said tentatively.

Simon's face lit up with pleasure. "Yeah, it does." He jumped down out of the truck. "Come on. Let me give you the tour. Although I warn you, this place could make a fixer-upper look like the Taj Mahal."

Paul followed as Simon forged a path through the new snow to the front door and hauled it open.

"Don't you lock the door?"

Simon snorted. "Nothing to steal. I'd rather they didn't break in if they're coming in anyway." He stepped inside, and Paul followed. The front hall opened onto two big rooms, one on either side. At the back on the left were the remains of a kitchen. On the right, remnants of a dividing wall suggested a parlor and possibly a pantry. Central stairs curved up to the second floor, a heavy oak banister guarding the stairwell. The floors were wide hardwood boards, and the steps mirrored them. The middle of each stair dipped slightly, in silent tribute to generations of feet.

Simon shut the door and laid a hand like a caress on bottom post of the railing. "I won't show you upstairs. The staircase is fine, but the upper floors are a little iffy. The last thing you need is to fall through."

Paul walked slowly into the left side room. Sun slanted through the cracks of the boards over the window, laying golden stripes across dusty oak flooring and the faded, flowered wallpaper. Heavy beams in the ceiling echoed the wood tones of the floor. Despite the cold, the house felt welcoming. He put out a hand and swept a layer of dust off the edge of the wall molding. The wood was silky under his fingertips.

"Someone built this with care, to last," he said. "How long has it been empty?"

"I don't know." Simon looked around, eyes unfocused, as if he saw more than was there. "I ran across it one night, when I was out wandering. The old farmer who owns the property said the house hadn't been used in decades. It was his grandparents' house once, but they built a new place closer to the main road."

"A shame to see a home like this falling apart. If the roof's leaking and water got in, it'll all rot eventually."

"I fixed the roof. At least, I covered the bad parts with shingles, and I stay on top of the leaks. Sealed up the windows that were broken."

"How long have you owned it?" Paul asked.

"I started fixing it even before I put money down, on the sly. Now I have a written agreement with the old guy. I pay him some each month, like a private mortgage, and when he's ready to leave the farm and move to town, I get the deed for this place and fifty acres that it sits on. We've marked the boundaries. He'll sell the working farm to someone else, and I'll keep making him payments on this."

"And until then?"

"I'm doing a little at a time. The roof and the windows first, and I've sanded the main floor but I won't refinish it yet. I'm working on replacing the upstairs floorboards now. The beams are solid, and the walls were built to last. Time and money are the problem. And there's no electricity for power tools, so I have to run a generator and that eats gas."

Paul nodded. He wandered back into the house, toward a sunlit spot of floor. The kitchen had a long wooden counter, with an old tin sink set in it. The walls showed where cabinets once hung. Out the small window above the sink, the snow stretched over open ground for fifty feet. Then the woods closed in, tall trees and a tangle of undergrowth. Sun streamed in the small window, giving the illusion of warmth. There was a stillness about the place that was soothing.

"Will you live here eventually?"

"I hope so." Simon shrugged. "It's a big job. Sometimes I think I won't live long enough to bring this place back to what it should be. But if I make a start, maybe someone else will finish it."

Surprised, Paul punched the man's arm lightly. "That pessimism sounds more like me than you. Where's the raving lunatic that I know and…" He stopped.

Simon raised an eyebrow at him, and his grin came back full wattage. "You want to finish that sentence?"

"Nope." Paul stepped back. "Your ego is already inflated."

"Nice. I show the man my favorite place and he starts insulting me." His smile faded. "You don't think I'm crazy to take this on?"

"You may be crazy, but not for this. Sure, it'd be a lot easier if you had a ton of money and a degree in engineering." He paused, realizing that for all his comfort hanging out with this man, he knew very little about him. "You don't have a degree in engineering, do you?"

"No. But I work in construction."

"So there. You're even in the field. No, I can see how you might take one look at this place and feel that you had to save it. It's a little quixotic of you, but not crazy."

"Don Quixote went around fighting windmills," Simon pointed out. "That's not the best example of sanity."

"You can't win if you don't try. I like this place."

Simon smiled at him, slow and sweet and miles removed from his usual quicksilver grin. "I'm glad," he said simply.

Paul stared back, caught by that expression. Something hung in the silence between them, but then Simon broke the moment with a laugh. "I'm not going to make you hang out here in the cold. I just thought you might be interested in the place. And now that we've explored my obsession, what do you want to do with the rest of the afternoon?"

"Um, I probably should get back to work," Paul suggested.

"No, you shouldn't."

"Excuse me? Since when did you become my social director?"

"Since you failed to have a social life to direct," Simon quipped, heading toward the door. "Tell me truly, how long since you took an afternoon off just to play?"

"I take every Sunday off."

"And do what?"

Cleaning, shopping, laundry, bills. "I have fun when I want to."

"Okay," Simon said, pulling the front door shut behind them. "Quick, name one thing you've done for entertainment in the last month."

"I like to read," Paul told him. "And I run in the park sometimes and..." He couldn't remember. "I do lots of stuff."

"Well today, you're going bowling." Simon swung up into the cab and started the truck.

"Bowling?" Paul stared at him. "I think the wood glue fumes have gone to your head. I don't remember saying anything about bowling."

"You do know *how* to bowl, don't you?"

"Of course I do." Paul fastened his seatbelt as they headed down the bumpy lane. Bowling was a solitary activity, and cheap, and therapeutic. You took this heavy ball, threw it as hard as you could, and made things go smash. If you liked, you could imagine anyone's face on the pins. A strike could bring a lot of satisfaction. "I haven't bowled in years, though." He was about to disclaim any desire to change that, but paused. He used to be pretty good at bowling. In fact, he used to be damned good. "I probably can't even keep the ball out of the gutter anymore."

He must've laid it on too thick, because Simon eyed him sideways. "Why do I get the feeling I'm being hustled?"

"Not likely. Anyway, I don't bet."

"I do. Dollar a pin?"

Paul calculated. The sum was unlikely to break either one of them. "You're on."

Two hours later, Simon was in the hole for fifty-seven dollars, and they were on their third game. Paul lifted his ball out of the return track, hefted it thoughtfully, and made his approach. Back, bend and throw. The ball sped down the lane, tucked neatly in between the head pin and the third, and blew the rack apart.

"Strike," he told Simon, unnecessarily since the alley had automatic scoring. On the overhead screen, little animated bowling pins fell over in heaps, just to rub it in. He dropped into his seat.

"Ouch," Simon protested. "I knew you were hustling me. Whose idea was this stupid bet anyway?"

"Yours, smart man. Now get up there and give me some competition." Although Simon apparently had fallen on the ice a few days before and hurt himself, so his injuries took some of the fun out of the hustle.

Simon was bending stiffly for his ball when a voice from behind Paul drawled, "Hey, Simon Conley, who's your friend?"

Paul barely had time to turn before Simon was there between him and the newcomer. Paul stood up and found himself looking over the bulk of Simon's shoulder.

"None of your business." Paul couldn't see Simon's expression, but his voice was cold in a way Paul had never heard before. "What do you want, Tommy?"

The young man, probably still in his late teens, was taller than Simon and looked athletic, but couldn't match Simon's muscle. Something about the way he and Simon faced each other made Paul think that mattered. Tommy glanced at his companions, a couple of teens standing behind him, and seemed to gain support.

"I have a message for you." The teenager waited, as if expecting Simon to comment. After a moment of silence, he added meaningfully, "From Karl."

"Running Karl's errands for him, are you? What a good boy."

The boy's face colored. "Everyone does what Karl says." After another long moment he sneered. "Well, maybe except you."

"Are you going to give me the message?"

"It's from Gordon too. Karl says Gordon wants to be sure you'll be at the meeting tonight. Karl thought you might need a reminder."

"How kind of him," Simon said sarcastically, without moving a muscle.

"Well," the boy said impatiently. "What should I tell him?"

"Tell him you passed on the message. You've done your job. Now run along and play, boy." Simon's voice snapped hard on the last words.

The young man took two quick steps back, as if shoved, and then looked angry. His gaze darted around, and lit on Paul's face. "Shall I tell Karl you have a new chew toy?"

Paul didn't think Simon moved, but the hard muscle in front of him became stone. "Do you really want to go there?" Simon's voice was pitched barely over a whisper.

One of the boy's companions grabbed him by the arm, speaking urgently in his ear. The boy shook the grip off, but his expression turned wary and he backed away from Simon step by step, as if afraid to turn his back. Simon remained planted, implacable, until the three youngsters had faded into the crowd. Then he sighed and turned back to the lane. Walking over to the rack, he bent and picked up his ball, not looking at Paul. His throw sailed six feet forward before meeting the polished lane with a painful crack. Pins flew on impact, but the five pin was left standing untouched. Simon swore softly.

"You want to tell me what that was about?" Paul asked quietly.

Simon eyed him sideways. "No." After a moment he added. "That kid was my cousin, of sorts. Distant family anyway. I have a lot of extended family around, and we all share in a family construction business. My uncle Gordon runs it. There's a meeting tonight I can't miss."

"So I gathered. Who's Karl?"

"Another uncle." Simon frowned. "It's complicated. Family politics. My family loves to play politics." He looked at the single pin waiting for him at the end of the lane, and then back at Paul. "Would you mind if we called it a day here? You're up another twenty-six points on me. I'll pay off on eighty-three bucks."

"I don't want your money," Paul said quickly. "I was hustling you. I used to average two-oh-eight, when I played regularly. And anyway, you're injured."

Simon had been moving more and more gingerly and deeply favoring his left arm. He'd ended up lifting his ball entirely one-handed. Simon argued that bowling only took one arm anyway, but his awkward approach looked uncomfortable. "I'll give you another chance sometime," Paul offered. "This was just for fun."

Simon frowned, as if to protest, then gave Paul a grin that seemed tired. "Thanks. My house's upstairs floors thank you too. Although I'll never complain about being hustled by you."

Paul kicked his ankle. "Give me a ride back to my truck and we'll call it even." He hung a little closer to Simon, letting their shoulders bump as they returned the balls and passed ugly two-tone shoes back behind the counter. "I had fun. You were right. It's been way too long since I've done that."

Simon nodded but without looking at him. He seemed preoccupied with his own thoughts.

They headed back to the clinic in a silence that slowly became heavy. "So," Paul added eventually, "will I see you around?"

"Oh, undoubtedly. If I survive this meeting."

Paul squinted at him across the truck cab. The tone was light and facetious, and yet somehow it… wasn't. "Will you call me?"

"At the clinic?" Simon wasn't looking at him.

"You can usually find me there." Paul pulled out an old receipt from his parka pocket and located a pen, scribbled for a moment. "Otherwise, here's my cell." He held the paper out as he opened his door. "Call and tell me how it went."

Simon looked at him for a moment, as if memorizing his face, before he reached out and took the paper. "I had fun too." His expression lightened, although the effort showed. "Now I get to watch the uncles being pretentious and the cousins being obnoxious. It will be the highlight of my week. I'll talk to you soon." He waited for Paul to climb down and get clear, and then peeled out of the lot, deliberately spinning the tires and fishtailing on the snow. Paul watched him go, with a formless anxiety inside him. Despite Simon's playacting, he heard "if I survive" echoing in his head. But how bad could a family business meeting get?

Chapter 4

Simon was wondering the same thing. Of course, when the family business was a werewolf pack, bad took on a whole new meaning. He stopped at home to shower and change. The routine was familiar. Disinfectant soap first, stinging his nostrils, burning across the deepest of the healing cuts. He put pressure over the one on his ribs to stanch a new trickle of blood. *Damn it.* Then he used a sandalwood herb gel scented enough to gag a horse, and then rinse after rinse with the unscented stuff until all trace of other people— *of Paul*— was gone from his skin.

He'd always erased his bed-partners from his body before meets. He didn't hide who he was from the pack anymore— that was an exercise in futility. But he saw no reason to print the scent of his lovers on unfriendly noses. And even though Paul was just a friend, and they had barely touched, unfriendly covered a whole lot more territory right now. Better safe than sorry. Especially when they'd had the bad luck to be seen by a youngster dumb enough to misinterpret things and unfriendly enough to talk about it.

Bowling had been stupid. He'd wanted to spend time with Paul and said the first thing that came to mind. But not only had it put them out in public, the bending and swinging had his arm and ribs aching like fire, which would be a handicap if this meeting went bad. He chewed a couple of aspirin, put a new stretch-wrap support around his arm, and tried to shrug his idiocy off. Nothing he could do about it now.

He dressed in loose black sweats, fast to remove, elastic enough to shift without undressing in an emergency. The healing gash on his neck showed without the turtleneck to cover it, but the rest of the pack knew he'd been injured. They'd certainly all felt his attack, by the end. Getting that close to death would've pinged everyone's radar. No point in trying to cover it up.

Grabbing his keys and driver's license, he headed out. As he drove, he thought about how often he had taken this route, from his first time as a thirteen-year-old beside his mentor, to last month's uneasy get-together, with everyone on edge and walking wide circles around each other. Sometimes he'd been eager to see his packmates. More often he'd dreaded it.

Until a year ago the pack had been a kind of home. A somewhat dysfunctional and violent home, perhaps. Werewolves seemed to be programmed to react badly to homosexual males among them. But he had his Alpha's provisional support and protection, as long as he didn't step too far out of line. He'd made a place for himself in the middle ranks. He never backed down from a wolf he thought he could easily beat, but didn't Challenge unless he absolutely had to. And he'd been tolerated, for the most part. He was usually treated like part of the pack. Arthur, Gordon's massive, cool-headed Second, had kept bickering to a minimum. The man's calm presence had ensured that the only beatings Simon got were clothed in legitimate Challenge and stopped before permanent harm was done.

But then Arthur died in that stupid private plane crash, and since then the pack had been spiraling down. Karl, who'd been competent and edgy as Third and enforcer, was downright scary as Second. Without Arthur's leash on him, the rules bent around him like bamboo in a strong wind. Karl did as Karl pleased, and his pleasure had always included other people's pain. And Gordon watched, letting infractions slide as he never would have before.

The pack held its collective breath, snapping and growling at each other when the principals were absent, lowering their eyes and walking softly around Karl and his cronies. They were all waiting, Simon thought. Waiting for Karl to do something bad enough to force Gordon to take him down. Except they'd all begun to wonder if Gordon did nothing because he wasn't sure anymore that he could take Karl. Better some pretense of oversight than a pack that truly ran with Karl as Alpha. Without Gordon reining Karl in, Simon would be dead.

Of course, Simon was surprised to be alive and breathing today. Karl knew he hadn't died on the road that night. They all had enough pack sense for that. Simon could touch the bright flare in his mind that was Gordon, and the swirl of amorphous energy around it that was the pack. He couldn't sense each member, as an Alpha was said to do, but he knew enough to tell if one of them was badly hurt. If someone died, he knew when and who. The pack would've known when he was near death, and they would have all known he survived.

Scattered memories came back to him, clearer than before. That attack had come as a surprise. The first warning he'd had was a swish of many other feet through snow, as he ran for the joy of it on four legs through the trees.

The sound could've been packmates joining him in his run for fun, but he knew it was not. He'd swerved and ducked in time to meet a lunge of teeth with his shoulder and not his leg. Pain flared at the slice of fangs along his skin, and he had whirled to meet his attackers.

They'd ranged around him. Karl, massive and pale gray in the moonlight; Frank, his closest follower, tawny, heavy and stupid, but very dangerous in a fight; Cory, young and hotheaded; Zach, his lithe dark form quivering in eagerness for a rumble; and behind them Marcus, grizzled and wary. Simon knew his chances were bad before the violence began. Pack rules said only one-on-one fights, except to bring down a law-breaker. Pack rules said for any offense short of the worst, submission and a bared throat ended things. Simon had broken no laws, but he looked at them and knew that baring his throat would mean having it ripped out.

Karl let the youngsters begin his dirty work, and Simon caught them by surprise. No holding back this time. As they came at him from opposite directions, he feinted toward Zach and then caught Cory's front leg as he leapt in and crunched. Bone gave way and the young wolf struggled back, screaming. Simon let him go and went for Zach, who'd expected to be the one forcing the next attack. Zach scrambled backwards in a flurry of snapping, and Simon dove under in a very unwolflike move. He slashed across Zach's hamstring as the younger wolf tried to hurdle off him. Zach went down hard in the snow and came up dragging his leg. Simon allowed himself a second's satisfaction. His mentor had taught him well, especially once they'd both realized Simon would desperately need the skills. Simon had been careful since then to let himself be underestimated.

But a second of grim pleasure was all he allowed, because now he faced Frank and Karl, and that was a different story. They moved together with the smoothness of old teamwork, not getting in each other's way as the inexperienced youngsters had done. Simon met their lunges, but when he faced one, the other came in from behind. He was soon bleeding from a dozen lacerations. Frank's ear was torn and Karl had blood dripping from his shoulder, but Simon knew he wouldn't last as long as they would. Once, he almost broke free and ran, knowing escape was his only chance, but Marcus caught him. Not a bite, just a slam from the old wolf's heavy body, but the force took him down. When he rolled to his feet, Frank was in front of him and there was no escape.

He fought on, because it wasn't in him to lie down and quit. Eventually, as he twisted his body away from Karl to leave neck fur instead of jugular vein in Karl's teeth, Frank's heavy jaw crunched down on the curve of his ribs from the other side. Simon felt the sharp pain of bones breaking. His next leaps left him breathless and panting, and when Karl moved in low, Simon's evasion was slow and short. His front leg gave under crushing teeth just as Cory's had. When he broke free, he stood on three paws, snarling his defiance. He kept snarling, and fighting, until he was flat in the snow and there was no air in his chest for anything but breath. Darkness had closed in and he'd waited for the death blow.

He'd heard the sound of an engine approaching and stopping, and then sensed the wolves around him shifting back to human. He took bitter satisfaction in the pained whines of the younger two.

"Shit!" Cory grunted. "Shit, shit, shit! Motherfucker broke my arm. I'm gonna kill the bastard."

"No, you're not," Karl said, low and cold. "You're going to do as you're told."

"But it fucking hurts!"

"Quit whining." Zach's voice was contemptuous. "He fucked up my leg and you don't hear me crying about it. Shift again a couple of times. It'll heal."

"I can't," Cory complained. "Not for hours now."

"Then go to the emergency room," Marcus told him. "Get it set straight, before it heals like that. Tell them it was a stray dog. Of course, they'll make you get rabies shots." There was a dry satisfaction in his voice.

Cory's footsteps passed Simon's rump, heading for the vehicle. "Faggot," he cursed softly, giving Simon's body a kick he hardly felt through the other pains. "Gonna be a dead faggot. Bastard."

Then hands rolled Simon over, dragging him. He snapped at them blindly, smelling Frank's human skin, and missed. He was shoved into the vehicle, and a bumpy ride began. He tried to open his eyes, tried to smell who the driver was, as if it mattered anymore to tally his enemies. Pain and motion and the crowding of bodies around him defeated him. Then he was shoved out onto the icy road. His head hit with a crack that almost took him under.

He heard Cory whining, "I don't see why we don't just finish him" and Karl snarling "I want each of you to look Gordon in the eyes and say you didn't kill him. Now shut up. We don't have to kill him. The next truck along this road will do the job."

"What if he gets away?" Marcus's voice was low. "He's stronger than we thought."

"I can make that work too," Karl said, "but okay." Booted footsteps sounded in the snow, and then Simon's side exploded with a kick right over the bad bite. He heard more ribs go. A second kick glanced off his skull, leaving him in whirling darkness. Far away, he heard a voice say, "There. He's not going anywhere." And then they left him.

Of course, that's why they didn't finish me there. Deniability.

He'd lived the past two days expecting Karl to come back and finish the job the road hadn't done after all. He was braced for an attack from behind, or even a shot. Wolves settled most pack matters with teeth and will, but Karl might actually turn to modern weapons if they suited his purpose. Karl didn't follow rules. But the blow had never fallen.

Deniability must still matter, he decided. Maybe Karl was as uncertain as Simon about what their Alpha could still do. Maybe he wasn't ready for an open Challenge to Gordon yet. Or maybe by not having any one of them deliver the fatal blow, he had hoped to make them all equally guilty. Everyone had helped deliver him up to death under some vehicle's wheels, and in the aftermath, Karl would have owned a hold on all of them. Karl would've liked that.

Simon parked his truck on the gravel, next to a Hummer he recognized as Aaron's. Aaron was as close to neutral territory as he was likely to find. As he headed for the door of the pack's big lodge, a red pickup peeled into the lot behind him, spilling young men out of its cab. The driver jumped down and joined them.

"Hey, Simon," Tommy's voice called, bold among the company of his friends. "How's the new boyfriend?"

Simon turned and sighed wearily. "He's just a friend, little boy. Jesus, only a virgin would confuse bowling with sex."

Tommy's cronies hooted and shoved him, their laughter sharp and on edge. Simon headed inside before Tommy could come up with a retort.

The lodge was divided into two big rooms downstairs. On one side, a warm lounge area held couches and chairs, faced with small tables and dominated by a large fireplace. A wall held a giant-screen TV. In times past, they had gathered there for holidays or football games. Even tonight, there was coffee and cocoa, pop and water set out, along with pans of cake and sweet breads. Werewolf appetites were notorious, but this spread seemed lavish for a regular meet.

From behind a laden table, Mark's wife met Simon's eyes and gave him a small, strained smile. She busily straightened the piles of food, her hands unsteady. Simon wondered if the wives were trying to feed the men into a better mood. The women here were the bonded wives who could tell how on edge the pack was. *Must be hard for them— attached to the pack but locked out of the decisions, nothing for them to do except try to feed us mellow.*

Simon took a Coke, found a wall to put his back to, and stood, sipping slowly. Wolves filtered in from the cold, alone or in small groups. The young wolves were boisterous and unsettled. The older wolves were quiet and wary. Many of them looked at him, a quick assessing scan of his body. Few of them met his eyes. Even Andy, the closest he had to a friend in the pack, approached sidelong via the food table and a couple of stops for conversation.

"Hey, Sim," he said when he finally landed nearby. He kept his voice low, glancing around to be sure nearby conversations were screening them.

"Hey." Simon waited to see how Andy would start the conversation.

"You look good. I mean, considering."

"Arm still hurts. But I heal fast."

"Look, man," Andy said quietly. "I'm sorry. I mean, I wasn't nearby. It would've all been over, one way or another, before I got there."

Simon nodded. He almost didn't ask, but he decided he wanted to know. "Did you even start to come after me?"

Andy's face colored and he looked down, which was answer enough. "It was Karl, Simon. The way you felt over the bonds, those injuries, I knew you had to be fighting Karl. You know me. I'm as close to the bottom as makes no difference. I can't take any of them on, even if I wanted to, least of all him."

"It's okay," Simon told him, although they both tasted the lie. "It's Gordon's job anyway. If he's not going to do it, there's no way you can."

"Sim, what do you think's going to happen?"

"Karl is going to Challenge," Simon said. "That's obvious. The only question is when. All the shit he's doing, scaring people, dividing us up, it's all preparation for that. I don't think he's quite ready yet, but I could be wrong. This thing with me was meant to give him an edge, somehow."

"Jesus, I miss Arthur," Andy breathed.

"Oh, yeah, me too. Now get out of here, buddy. Hanging with me right now is not going to be good for your health."

"I'm sorry," Andy said again. "Be careful." But he went.

The only other wolf to approach Simon was Aaron. He came inside alone, stomping snow off his shoes as if he had been walking for a while, and scanned the room. His olive skin held a flush from the cold air, and his damp black hair was burnished to a shine under the lights. A quick look at Simon, and he crossed the room to him directly.

"Are you all right?"

Simon raised an eyebrow. "I'll heal."

"Good. Good. I was down in Bemidji when I felt it happen. Damn near went off the road on the ice trying to get back here. By the time I was close you felt okay, so I decided to wait, let it ride. He didn't come after you again?"

"No," Simon said, glancing around. The other wolves had stayed far away from him, as if his problem was contagious, so no one was standing near them. But Aaron was still being awfully direct for a room full of sharp-eared wolves.

"Okay then. We'll see what happens next. Watch your back." Aaron strode off, his movements smooth and controlled, but tension in the lines of his back.

Simon stared after him. He hadn't expected that. Aaron was in the pack, but not really part of it. He'd joined by petition a few years ago, after leaving his home out west somewhere and wandering for a while. He was one of the few wolves whose true dominance in the pack was unclear. In meet, when they gathered by strict rank, he took the sixth slot. He'd fought only once, the first time he had been Challenged for position. The fight had lasted eight seconds and ended with the pack Seventh challenger down on the ground, his throat pinned in Aaron's black jaws. After that, no one below him objected, and Simon thought the wolves above Aaron were relieved that he was willing to hold place. For the most part, they walked wide around him to avoid provocation. Even Karl didn't push Aaron.

Aaron was as silent and controlled in human form as he was lethal as a wolf. Simon couldn't recall a conversation with him that went past hello and pass the chips. The man kept his mouth shut and reacted to nothing. His rare comments in meet were astute and to the point, but if he was contradicted, he didn't argue further. If he had been asked, Simon would have said that Aaron disliked him, but today it hadn't felt that way. He breathed out heavily. Having Aaron on his side might make survival possible. If it didn't get Aaron killed.

Gordon's entrance was like bringing a magnet into a room of iron filings. Every head turned, every conversation stopped. Gordon moved casually, as if unaware of the scrutiny. He handed his coat to his wife and sent her with a gentle push toward the other women behind the tables. He sauntered toward the food, tasting one cake and then another. Behind him, a few conversations resumed since it seemed the Alpha wanted it that way. Simon bet that no one was paying attention though, and two dozen pairs of eyes followed Gordon across the room.

The Alpha was still a big man. His presence loomed like a thunderstorm, heavy in their minds. His wolves were still his, reacting to him as they always had. But Simon thought the Alpha moved a little more stiffly than before and his hair was grayer. Simon was sure he wasn't the only one measuring, assessing.

"So, my brothers," Gordon said, turning. "You seem more in a mood for business than pleasure, so perhaps we should meet." He scanned the room. "Is Karl here?"

"I'm here," Karl said from the door. He came in with Frank, moving swiftly and powerfully across the room. Simon thought he was doing it on purpose, as contrast, but Gordon just smiled warmly at Karl. "There you are, Second," he said. "Shall we begin?"

The meeting room was a big empty space, halfway down a bare hallway. Concrete floors and walls, and a sturdy sound-proofed ceiling kept it secure.

A hose coiled on the wall and a drain in the center of the floor were there for a reason. There was a cupboard, and a desk in one corner where writing could be done, but for the most part the paperwork details of pack business were taken care of elsewhere. Meetings were for discussion, for arguments and policy, for punishment and Challenges, and for bonding the pack into one whole with a common will and goals. Gordon had been good at that.

Simon realized he was beginning to think of his Alpha in the past tense.

They filed in and sat on the floor, a host of athletic, graceful men. In concentric arcs in front of Gordon, from Second through the youngest pups, they found their places. Simon sat in his usual, below Mitchell, above Connor. He noticed that they both slid away from him more than in the past, so the ring of empty space around him was twice its usual size. Not that either had ever been touchy-feely with him, but now they knew he was trouble. Whatever was coming, they didn't want to get caught in the fallout.

When they were all in place, Gordon cleared his throat and began.

"We are met as a pack," he said, in ritual opening.

"We are met." The response came rolling back to him. Simon could feel the echo of the words in his mind, as his sense of the pack around him grew deeper and clearer. That was Gordon, tuning them all in. That connection was the Alpha's power.

"We have several items of business today," Gordon said mildly, in contrast to the vibrating tension of his wolves. "The tithe may need to be altered slightly, as our expenses have changed. Our north run will have to be rescheduled, because a big winter snowmobile group has signed up at the local motels. We will gain a life in the pack, as Christopher's wife has completed her sixth month of pregnancy, and we will lose one, as Anderson has decided to Pass."

There was a collective intake of breath, although the news was not unexpected. Werewolves did not age gracefully. The healing and shifting helped to extend life, but not forever. Most elders, if spared the rare diseases they were susceptible to, elected to end their lives when they felt themselves slipping. Some committed suicide by usual human means. But most chose to go out as they had most intensely lived, as wolves.

Gordon added, "Joshua, Anderson has asked you for the honor."

It was a challenge and a responsibility, to fight a man whose mind wanted to die but whose wolf body might not agree. It was hard to do it right, to cut no flesh, cause no pain, until the opening came for one swift humane strike. Arthur had been the master at it. Simon had seen him end half a dozen lives that way over the years, quick and clean. Since Arthur's own death, only one wolf had Passed. He had requested the honor from his own son. The old wolf had the nerve and will to hold still for the blow, and the young man had not faltered until after he had shifted and his father's wolf body lay still in his arms.

Joshua, a spare quiet man who held Third, nodded his acceptance. "I will."

Simon took a quick glance at Karl, but if the Second was insulted at being passed over, he showed no sign. No one who wanted a humane end would take a chance on Karl, but Simon thought Karl still might make Joshua suffer for the slight, later and in private.

"Before we discuss the tithe," Gordon said, "is there other business that should come before us?"

Simon stayed silent, waiting to see if anyone would bring up the topic of his attack. Most of the wolves were carefully not looking at him. Cory stared angrily, but held still. Karl's slow gaze swung to Simon. Simon raised an eyebrow at the Second, but said nothing. He wished he knew if Karl wanted their fight discussed or not. Given the risk of playing into Karl's hands, Simon wasn't about to raise the topic. Better to pretend nothing happened and not rock the boat.

"What about Simon?" Aaron asked in a clear voice. Simon winced. So much for having it blow over.

"Yes. Simon," Gordon said slowly, as if he too was reluctant. "Come stand before us, Simon."

Simon rose and paced out to the front of the group, taking a position where he could face Gordon and still see Karl out of the corner of his eye. He forced himself to bend his head. "Alpha."

"You were Challenged two days ago, Simon," Gordon said. "Would you care to comment?"

That was no Challenge and you know it. "A completed Challenge is old history," Simon said.

"Who Challenged him and why?" Aaron asked. "Because that did not feel like a fight within the bounds of law."

For a long moment there was silence. Wolves tensed uneasily, but no one spoke. Then Karl stood, languidly, and spoke directly to Aaron. "Cory came to me because he wanted to Challenge Simon, but felt unable to do so. The insult he said had been committed was… unpleasant. I offered to help Cory with the form of the Challenge, but it turned into a fight before terms could be properly set." Karl turned and gave Simon a cold look. "Fortunately, no permanent injury was done."

"Cory." Gordon's voice held a whiplash of displeasure. "What was the substance of your Challenge?"

Cory stood in the back ranks, his arm still supported in a sling. "Simon insulted me," he said hoarsely. "He tried… he touched me, put his hands on me, *that* way."

Simon felt the other wolves' distaste like a film on his tongue. "Oh, spare me," he drawled. "Or at least give me some credit. If I was going to make a pass at another wolf, which I'm not, I'd choose one who was a lot smarter and better looking." Cory's narrow face flushed.

"You deny it?" Gordon asked Simon.

"I do," Simon said earnestly. His Alpha had supported him in the past, when pack opinion would have made it easier not to. He wanted Gordon to know that he had not broken the conditions of his acceptance. "I have done nothing that would justify a Challenge." He met Gordon's eyes and opened his mind. His Alpha could tell truth from lie, coming from one of his wolves.

Gordon nodded slowly. "Truth."

"And yet Karl felt he should support Cory," Aaron pointed out. Simon wasn't sure if he was taking a dig at Karl or just stirring the pot to see what fell out, but the ramped-up tension felt dangerous.

"I expect he believed Cory's story," Simon said cautiously.

"Is that how it happened, Second?" Gordon asked. "Did you take action, based on a mistaken belief?"

Fear and anger and restlessness vibrated down the pack sense. Wolves looked at their neighbors, wondering who would jump where, if Karl took this opportunity to defy Gordon.

But Karl looked back calmly at his Alpha. “Perhaps I was so disgusted at the image of Simon bringing his perversions among our young wolves,” Karl said, “that I didn’t investigate far enough. But after all, when it’s a case of one wolf’s word against the other, a Challenge is appropriate.”

“We could do it again here,” Simon offered, unable to resist. “Get the Challenge right. If Cory would like, I can prove my truth on his body now. Or vice versa, of course.”

Gordon sighed, but he turned to Cory and raised an eyebrow. Cory choked. “I think we’ve done enough. I mean, we’re both injured.”

“I would never take unfair advantage,” Simon said easily. “Perhaps some other time, if you still want to hold to your story.”

Gordon frowned and sent Simon back to his place with a wave of his hand, emphasized with a push against the pack bond in his head. “I think we’ve wasted enough time on this,” he said. “Let’s move on to something near and dear to all our hearts, the money.”

Simon sat and listened as the pack members argued over the need to raise the tithe for unmarried men, to support the growing size of the pack. Voices were high and quick with relief. Karl wasn’t challenging Gordon, at least not tonight. Perhaps he’d hoped Gordon would come down more strongly in Simon’s favor, alienating the traditionalists in the pack and driving them to Karl’s support. Or perhaps Gordon still seemed too strong. Simon frowned. They all must know that the reprieve was temporary.

Agreement on the tithe was reached after a shorter-than-expected discussion, as if no one wanted to provoke the others tonight. Anderson’s death date was set, and pack duties assigned. Eventually, Gordon called the end of the meet. The assembled wolves rose and filed out. Simon judged his exit from the meet carefully. Not too soon, so he could avoid Cory and the other youngsters hurrying to their cars and better entertainment elsewhere. Not too late, where the wrong man might catch him alone. His choice was thrown off when Brian, the pack Fourth, fell into step beside him.

“You really didn’t touch Cory,” Brian said quietly. It was not quite a question.

"Shit." Simon turned off into a quiet corner of the great room, hearing Brian keeping pace behind him. He wasn't afraid of the big man, although Brian stood just below Joshua in rank. Brian at least had a sense of humor. Once or twice, when Simon was being punished for some ill-timed snark, he'd caught a glimmer of amusement in the other man's eyes. But he didn't want to have any *discussions* right now. He wanted to go home and think.

Not an option. Brian still outranked him.

Simon turned to face him. "Cory's an ugly, stupid kid with a cruel streak and a bad temper," he said flatly. "I wouldn't go near him with a ten-foot pole." He couldn't resist adding, "And I'm big, but not that big."

Brian blinked, but what he said was, "Cory's not ugly."

"He has a face like a weasel. God. If I'd known what they were going to say, I could have brought my last boyfriend along. Stood Jos and Cory up side by side in the great room and let the pack judge for themselves whether I'm that desperate."

"You wouldn't." Brian actually seemed alarmed.

"Bring a strange human here who wasn't my mate? Flaunt my sex choices in front of the pack?" Simon snorted. "You *do* think I'm crazy."

"You are crazy. But you keep your word. Even if you are…"

"Queer," Simon supplied.

"Yeah. That. Tell me about the Challenge."

"There was no Challenge."

Brian nodded. "Tell me about the fight, then."

Simon hesitated, considering. Brian was old, perhaps a decade younger than Gordon. No physical match for Karl, but power of will still rolled off Brian and kept him in his rank. "They came at me out of the trees as I ran. No warning and no Challenge."

"Who?"

Simon told him. Brian's mouth twisted, as if he tasted something bitter. "Cory just straight out attacked you? I noticed his arm, and Zach is limping."

"I could handle Cory and Zach. I couldn't handle Karl and Frank." There was no shame in that. Possibly only Gordon in his prime, or Arthur, could've taken on the second and fifth wolves in the pack together and won.

"You don't look hurt that bad now."

"I heal fast." Not even Brian could safely know the details of his injuries or how he survived them. "But I was meant to die."

"If Karl meant to kill you, he would have."

"For some reason he wanted their hands clean. They dumped me unconscious on a road. It was only luck that I came to and got free before I was run over." *Luck and Paul.*

"Damn," Brian said. "He's always maneuvering for an advantage. I almost wish the waiting was over, except we all know who'd end up Alpha."

"You don't think Gordon can still take him?"

"I think it would be close. But Karl won't risk a Challenge until he's certain he can win. He'll keep trying to swing the pack behind him first. He's ruining half the youngsters as it is. They follow him like puppies. He gives them excitement, thrills, and they won't listen to us boring old-timers."

"Well, they sure as hell won't listen to me."

"No!" Brian said sharply. "You keep away from the pups like you've promised. Breaking your word now, when Gordon forced the agreement on half the pack, would be worse. That's probably what Karl thought. If you were dead, the wolves who don't like you would've believed Cory. It would have shown Gordon was wrong to trust you, and thrown his judgement into doubt. Even worse if he continued to defend you afterward. Getting rid of someone who's a thorn in Karl's side was just the bonus."

"Not much of a thorn. I keep well clear of him."

"You do more than you realize. Every time you mouth off at some absurdity of his discipline and get beaten for it, some of the wolves are on your side. Karl wants absolute obedience from everyone below him. He knows he's never getting that from you, and other wolves know it too."

"I follow rank," Simon protested. Sometimes he bent himself into a pretzel to submit to the right people in acceptable ways.

"When you agree with it. Otherwise you have the form, but not the content." Brian shook his head at the alarm in Simon's eyes. "Don't worry. Gordon knows our hearts and he accepts us. But Karl won't."

"Us?"

"Oh, yes. Did you think you're the only rebel in the pack? If you were straight, you could be me fifty years ago. I've learned to put in my two cents where I might be listened to now, and not get slammed for speaking up in hopeless causes. You'll learn too, if you survive."

"That's becoming a big if," Simon said soberly.

"You should seriously think about running, if Karl Challenges. Find another pack, like Aaron did."

"Perhaps." He'd thought about leaving. A lot. But the chance of finding another Alpha who would accept a new gay wolf into his pack was almost nil. Running would mean either living alone, his head empty of packmates, no job, no history, and the color of his skin a strike against him among humans. Or petitioning a new pack and going back deep into the closet. So he was still here, waiting to be forced to go.

Of course, he was a realist. If Karl ever did Challenge, Simon had his escape plans ready. He wasn't going to share them with anyone, though, not even Brian.

The older wolf eyed him for a moment and then slapped his shoulder. Simon wondered if it was coincidence that the hard hand landed on one of his healing wounds. He hid the wince. "Walk softly," Brian said, "and keep your ears open."

"Always have," Simon told him. "Always do."

He watched Brian cross the room and head out into the cold. If Gordon fell, Brian would be an Alpha Simon could live under. But unless Karl was so weakened by a fight with Gordon that he couldn't hold on, Brian would never beat him. He was probably too smart to try.

The snow in the parking lot whipped Simon's exposed skin with stinging pellets. He ducked his head, but kept his eyes open and ears alert as he made his way to his truck. He even paused to sniff around the vehicle for signs of tampering. But at least to his duller human nose, no one had touched his ride.

He thought about calling Paul, but he hadn't brought his phone. By the time he got home, he was thinking about not calling Paul. He liked Paul already, probably too much, but he wanted even more to keep him free of this mess. Anyone who might be leverage against him wouldn't be safe. Already Tommy was linking Paul with Simon out loud. Usually, human friends and contacts were strictly outside of pack business, untouched by the upheavals inside the circle. But Simon didn't trust Karl to give up any kind of advantage.

What he and Paul had couldn't be called more than a shallow friendship at this point. They'd had what? A few conversations? Three games of bowling? Surely, after a few days of being blown off, not calling and not getting together, Paul would move on and be safe. *Ignore him. Let him find someone else.* No matter how bitter that tasted, he knew it was for the best.

Simon was lounging in front of the TV in his sweatpants, not really watching the end of an old movie, when his doorbell rang. *What the hell? At midnight?* A quick check of his pack sense found no one hurt, no one dead. He opened the door cautiously.

Paul looked up at him from the front step, a bag redolent of sugar and chocolate in his hand, and smiled tentatively. "Hi. Care for some donuts?"

For a moment, Simon thought about closing the door in his face. Because his heart had leaped in his chest at the sight of Paul's face, and he knew he was in trouble. He'd made the decision to walk away once tonight, and it had been harder than he'd expected. If he let Paul in, he wasn't sure he could make it again later. But he saw Paul's expression become more and more uncertain, the fear of rejection growing. Simon sighed and threw the door open wide.

"I never turn away a gorgeous man bearing gifts," he said. "Come on in."

Chapter 5

Paul had spent the evening working. After an afternoon of play with Simon, he'd come back to the clinic with new energy. In fact, he'd reworked the budget and decided maybe he could afford to pay a professional to do taxes and payroll for him. The thought of letting someone else carry the responsibility of dotting i's and crossing t's for the IRS was wonderful. Simon had been right. Time away from the job made him work better, not worse.

Which brought him back to thinking about Simon. He would've imagined that nothing worried that man. A big vet bill, floors that were collapsing, a sore arm, losing at bowling, all were greeted with acceptance and a glint of humor. But whatever the business meeting had been tonight, Simon had been… concerned. In fact, from the moment that kid Tommy had spoken up, Simon had seemed like a different person. Bigger, harder somehow, and much less lighthearted.

The way he'd stood between Paul and the teenagers suggested physical protection, although Paul couldn't see why Simon would think he needed protecting from a bunch of teenaged bowlers. This was Ham Lake, not the mean streets of downtown. Still, he waited impatiently for Simon to phone him back, to tell him all was well. And Simon didn't call.

Paul let the clock go around. Perhaps it was a long meeting. Perhaps they went out for drinks afterward. Perhaps Simon had lost his number. Both his numbers. By the time eleven-thirty came and went, Paul knew he was being stupid, but his imagination had taken over big time. Perhaps Simon's Uncle Gordon was Mafia, and they'd drowned Simon in a lake. Perhaps they were cheating on their taxes and they'd shot Simon for not going along with it. Perhaps…

He got Simon's address and phone number from the files. Wolf's chart, with the photo attached, made him smile. He'd have to see if Simon had heard from his friend yet. A pity Simon didn't still have Wolf to take with him to that meeting. Paul would've worried a lot less.

He could have called, but… he wanted to see Simon's face. He picked up donuts and cocoa on the way as an excuse, or a peace offering. He wasn't sure Simon would want to see him at that hour but treats would help. *Right?* As he rang the doorbell, it occurred to him that perhaps Simon had brought someone home after the meeting. He might be interrupting. The door opened before he could panic.

"I never turn away a gorgeous man bearing gifts," Simon said, with a hint of his usual humor. "Come on in."

Paul stepped past him into the main room. The house seemed bigger on the inside than it had from the yard. The living room was filled with old, battered, comfortable-looking chairs, and a long, black leather couch. A modest TV was playing an old black-and-white movie at barely audible volume. There was no other light on. The subdued glow flickered over walls papered in a faint stripe, and heavy blue drapes. And over Simon's bare chest. The man had *muscles*, cut and clean, covered with a light fur of dark curls. No extra fat there. It was hard to tell in the faint light, but there were a couple of crusted lines on his skin across his ribs below one nipple, like scabs of blood. Like maybe he had been hurt. Any bruising was hidden by the dark hair on that strong body. Paul realized where he was looking and felt his face heat.

He held out the bag. "Here. Donuts and hot chocolate for you, coffee for me."

Simon took the food, smiling. He laid the contents out on the coffee table in front of the couch, then grabbed a dark sweatshirt off a chair and pulled it on. Paul breathed a little easier. Not that he cared what Simon wore, but just… it was winter. No good reason for the guy to be walking around half-naked. He sat on the end of the couch where Simon had put down the coffee. Carefully, he picked up the Styrofoam cup and hid his face in it, inhaling his first sip.

Now that he was with Simon, all his fears seemed ridiculous. Simon had moved easily. Even his sore arm didn't seem to bother him much as he put on the sweatshirt. Simon had a business meeting with relatives he didn't like. No reason for Paul to get worried. Which made his coming over look like… something else.

He scrambled for something to say. "I see you survived the meeting. I was working late and stopped for a snack on the way home, and I thought, well, that I'd bring you some and make sure you were still employed. If money is tight, I haven't cashed that check for the window yet."

"That's nice of you." Simon took a big bite out of a donut. "But not necessary. The money's fine. The meeting went as well as could be expected."

"I guess I should be going. I have stuff to do tomorrow." Paul took a big mouthful of coffee and coughed, choking, spilling a few drops on the floor as his hand shook and he couldn't catch his breath.

A strong fist thumped him between his shoulder blades, and then Simon took the cup out of his hand. "Raise your arms straight up. That's my mother's cure for choking, and it actually works."

Coughing, feeling stupid, Paul tentatively raised his hands.

"All the way." Simon's warm fingers ringed his wrists and hauled his arms upward. "It opens the chest."

To Paul's surprise, it helped. A couple of wheezing breaths and he was fine. Simon released him and he lowered his hands. "Now that was smooth of me," Paul said ruefully. He bent to mop at the spill with a tissue.

"No problem." Simon sat back on the couch and sipped his cocoa. "A man who brings me food can be forgiven anything."

"Anything?" Paul looked up and caught a laughing glance in return.

"Almost anything. Of course, it depends on the food. For donuts, you get a pretty big pass. Not so much for lutefisk."

"Ick." Lutefisk was Norwegian pickled jellied white fish. Actually eating it was said to be the sign of a true Minnesotan. If that was the case, Paul was remaining an outsider forever. "You eat that stuff?"

"Not without a gun to my head."

Paul felt able to ask. "Was the meeting as bad as you thought?"

"Could've been worse." Paul thought that was the end of the topic, but Simon added, "My Uncle Gordon runs the business. He's getting older but he has no intention of giving it up. My Uncle Karl wants it bad, and he doesn't want to wait. The rest of us are choosing up sides and holding our breath. It could get messy."

"Do you have to work there? I mean, I don't even know what you do, exactly, but the economy's not so bad that there aren't other jobs out there somewhere."

"It's hard to walk away from family."

"I did." Paul would have taken that back an instant later.

He waited for the inevitable questions about why, but Simon cocked his head to one side. "And how did that work out for you?"

"Better than staying. Better lately." That much was true, for sure.

"Good." Simon took another bite. "Now we address the question of why a guy like you is here talking to me on a Saturday night, instead of out on a date with a hot woman."

Paul laughed. "Hot women don't date skinny geeks in glasses."

"You don't wear glasses."

"I used to. All through school. Lasik surgery was one of the first things I bought myself when I graduated, but in my head I'm still the nerd with Coke-bottle lenses. Anyway, dating has never been my thing. I'm busy, and I don't do small talk well, and the girls I might be interested in would never be interested in me."

"Jesus, set yourself up to fail, why don't you? Go to the right bar, and the girls would be all over you."

"Where's that? A bar where anyone who's not months behind on the rent is a good catch?"

Simon stared at him. "You really don't think you're good looking?"

Paul stared back. "What planet are you living on?"

"Okay." Simon stood up and grabbed Paul by the wrist. "Come on. We're going out."

"What?" Paul let himself be pulled to his feet. "It's midnight. What have you been smoking?"

Simon stepped into boots with his bare feet. "You have this warped image of yourself. And I'm tired of it." He caught Paul's chin in his hand. "You are one gorgeous guy." He gave Paul a small shake and let go. "But you won't take my word for it. So I'm going to prove it to you. How open-minded are you?"

"Um, open, I guess. You taking me to see if I can pick up blind girls?"

"Nope." Simon threw on a parka and pulled Paul out the door, locking up behind them. "Your truck's still warm. You drive."

Bemused, Paul climbed in the driver's seat and started the engine. He backed out carefully into the dark street. "Where are we going?"

"Turn left here, and get on Central going south." After Paul followed through, Simon added, "I don't know which straight bar your kind of girls would hang out at, although I guarantee you it's out there. But all I said was

I'm going to prove to you how good looking you are. I'm taking you to a gay bar, and if you don't get five guys hitting on you in the first fifteen minutes, I'll… replace all the cabinets in your clinic for free."

Paul stared at him, then forced his attention back to the road. "I'm not going into a gay bar."

"Chicken? You said you were open-minded."

"I am, but…" Paul tried to wrap his mind around this. "I don't want guys to pick me up."

"Of course not. I told you they'll try. I'll be right there and you don't have to say yes. Look, men and women may have somewhat different standards, but gorgeous is gorgeous. This is just a test, okay, to prove a point."

Paul opened his mouth, closed it, tried again, and finally said, "All the cabinets?"

"Every one," Simon grinned.

"Okay. It's a bet." He could use new cabinets, and somehow, secretly, he wondered if maybe Simon was seeing something he didn't when he looked in the mirror. A familiar voice in his head sneered, *you're nothing, stupid, geek, skinny, ugly; no one will ever want to touch you.* But he wasn't stupid, he'd proved that. And maybe the rest of it was wrong too. "Where are we going?"

"A place downtown. Keep driving."

An hour and a half later Paul's head pounded with the music, his mouth tasted like too much beer, and he was surrounded by men. Most of them were paying no attention to him as they drank and talked and cruised. But several had. Simon, at his shoulder, chatted, ordered drinks, and guided him through the crowd. Simon drew his own share of attention even in old sweats and scuffed up boots. But Paul couldn't deny that other men had been looking, and sending out tentative feelers, in his own direction. Whether five in fifteen minutes he couldn't say. But he was prepared to concede the bet. For some reason, he was getting hit on, and not by the ugliest men in the bar either. The attention felt weird, but not as unsettling as he'd expected.

A hand grabbed his ass, and he whirled, not open-minded enough to let that go. A big man stood behind him, but the hand that had touched him was now imprisoned in Simon's fist.

"No touching without asking," Simon growled.

The other man twisted loose and held his hands up. “Sorry, man. I didn’t know he was yours.”

“He’s not. But you still need to learn manners.” Simon watched coldly as the man worked his way back into the crowd, then bent close enough to Paul’s ear to talk without yelling. “You ready to give me the win?”

“Yeah,” Paul agreed. “You ready to leave, or are you looking for a date while we’re here?”

“I’m a gentleman. I always leave with the man I came with.”

The air outside the bar was clean and cold. Paul dug in the pocket of his jacket and found his keys. He tossed them to Simon. “You drive. I’m not sure I could pass a Breathalyzer.”

Simon caught the keys. “Sure. I’ll take you home.”

“I’ll be sober by the time we get to your place.” Paul felt pleasantly sleepy as the hum of the engine warmed the cab. “I can drive myself home from there.”

He dozed as Simon drove smoothly and competently. The swaying of the truck lulled Paul, and he leaned his head against the window, feeling the cold glass kiss his forehead. “Guess I’m not that ugly,” he admitted after a while. “She was wrong about other stuff. I don’t know why that one stuck so hard.” He was drunker than he had realized.

“Who’s she? Old girlfriend?”

“M’ mother,” Paul admitted. “Told me I’d never amount to anything, ugly, stupid. But I’m showing her, aren’t I?”

“Your mother said that?”

“Oh, yeah. Dear old Mom.” Paul laughed. Everything felt good, the warmth, the motion, the beer, and the quiet man beside him. “I was all she had and I was never enough. Never good enough. Never anything enough. But now I’m here and I don’t have to be enough. And she can rot on her own, like I was, alone like I was.” He laughed again. “’Cause she’s not here and I am. I’m here and I’m free and I’m happy.”

“You sure are. And pretty drunk too. I’ll listen to anything you want to tell me, sugar, but I don’t want you to say anything you’ll regret.”

“No regrets. I left and never went back. No regrets. And now I have my own business, and employees and clients. I even have a friend. You are my friend, aren’t you, Simon?” He was suddenly anxious about that, through the haze.

"Yeah, I'm your friend. You don't drink much, do you?"

"Don't drink at all. But I may start. I think I like beer. I like this."

Simon laughed softly. "At least you'll be a cheap drunk if four beers can put you under. Did you eat dinner?"

Paul peered at him, trying to remember. Simon's hair was mussed, and his cheeks were shadowed with half a night's stubble. He would bet the man had to shave twice a day to stay clean. Although unshaven wasn't a bad look on him. He smelled of beer and whiskey from the bar, but under that Simon's scent was cool and clean, something outdoorsy. If it was aftershave, Paul would have to find out which one. As the streetlights swept past, lighting the cab in flashes, Simon's gray eyes had an odd green glow to them. Maybe that was why his gaze felt so intense when it landed on Paul's face.

"Well?"

Paul blinked. "Um, what was the question?"

"Did you eat dinner?"

Paul thought about it. "I don't remember. What day is it?"

"Okay." Simon pulled into his driveway and turned off the engine. "You are so not driving home right now. Come on." He appeared at Paul's door, opening it and hauling Paul out.

"I can make it home."

"Bullshit." Simon unlocked his front door and led Paul inside. He snapped on a lamp and pushed Paul down into the couch. "You sit there and I'm going to find you something to eat."

Paul smiled up at him and picked up a donut. "I can eat these. Lots of good sugar, and, and stuff. Sugar is food, right? And then I can go home." He took a bite, and lemon filling squirted. He licked at his lips. "Tha's okay. I like the lemon ones."

Simon sat beside him, eyes glowing softly. After a moment he said, "You missed some." He reached out and ran a finger under Paul's lip, coming up with a glob of lemon.

"Thanks." Paul licked it off Simon's finger before he could pull it away. "I like lemon."

"You said that." Simon stared at him, then reached out again and brushed the corner of Paul's mouth with a fingertip, brought it to his own lips, and licked it clean. Paul watched the gesture, for some reason breathing harder. He was confused. Food would help. He took another bite of donut and felt the sweet goo escape again.

"Oh, hell," Simon said softly. His big warm hand cupped Paul's cheek as he leaned in. "You're sticky again." His mouth found Paul's, his tongue tip licking Paul's lip. Paul opened his mouth a little, and the tongue slid in, just a fraction, gently touching. Then Simon pulled back.

Paul looked up at him confidingly. "You taste like lemon."

"That's you, babe." Simon leaned forward again, and this time there was no mistaking it for anything but a kiss. Except this kiss was warm and sweet, and Paul's mouth seemed to know how this should go. He leaned closer and parted his lips.

Simon groaned softly and Paul pulled back a little. "Am I doing it wrong? Am I hurting you?"

"You're killing me," Simon muttered. When Paul felt ready to panic, Simon's hands held him, firm against his face. "I'm kidding. You're doing this right. Too right." Simon kissed him again, softly. Paul sighed and relaxed into it. It had been so long since he was last touched. Simon's mouth was expert, hot and open. And his tongue found places Paul hadn't known he had. He opened his eyes when Simon pulled back.

"What?" he asked muzzily. "Are you stopping? I don' want to stop."

"You're drunk. And we're not doing this."

"I like this," Paul said plaintively.

"We're not doing this now. Maybe later. Right now, you're going to sleep, and sober up, and then we'll talk."

Paul smiled happily. The room was rocking, just like the truck, and it was almost as warm. He felt like he could sleep. "Okay," he murmured. "Later." Simon lifted his feet onto the couch and pulled him down. He giggled as he slid on the slick leather, his head slipping from the arm to the seat. Then a soft, heavy blanket draped over him. It smelled like Simon, clean and outdoorsy, pine and a hint of musk. A big hand under his cheek raised his head to slide fabric underneath. A nice pillow. A soft, squishy pillow. He curled himself into his usual tight ball, arms around his head. This was comfortable. This was good. The light switched off. He heard Simon's voice say, "Don't barf on my couch when you wake up."

"No barfing."

In the warm darkness, Simon laughed softly. "Good night, sweet prince."

"Tha's Shakespeare."

"Go to sleep." Simon's voice was firm, and Paul obeyed.

His first reaction when he woke was panic. He didn't recognize where he was, and that was bad. That was always bad. His head throbbed and the room was dark around him. He tried to sit up and get to his feet in one movement, which resulted in an ungainly slide toward the floor. Hands caught him before he hit.

"Hey," a deep voice said. "Slow down."

Deep voice. Simon. Paul relaxed, comfort flowing in. He was okay, because this was Simon's place and he must have drifted off and… *Oh, shit!* The memory of what he'd been doing before he drifted off suddenly came into focus, in full Technicolor. His mouth remembered warmth and sweetness, lips and tongue, and his brain remembered kissing Simon. His own voice in his head said, *I don't want to stop,* and then what? Nothing came to mind. Had he…? Jesus.

Paul squeezed his eyes shut and tried to make it go away. "You okay?" Simon's voice asked. "You promised no barfing, remember."

"I'm not going to throw up." Paul was pleased that his voice was steady. He was a little nauseous actually, but not that much. His head pounded painfully. "I'm sorry. I guess I looked like a fool last night."

"You looked like a smart, sweet, sexy man who gets drunk on four beers. I gathered you don't drink on a regular basis."

"Not often." *Not ever. I'm such a freaking nerd.* Paul opened his eyes. Simon's outline was barely visible against the faint hint of light behind a curtain. Simon was sitting next to him on the couch. Sitting too close. Paul straightened up and pulled away. "What time is it?"

"Six AM. It's still dark out."

"I should go. I need to get ready for work."

"It's Sunday. You don't go in to the clinic on Sundays."

"Not usually." Paul knew his voice was high and fast, but he couldn't seem to slow down. "But sometimes. Like today I should, because I took half of yesterday off. And then I need to do some laundry, or I won't have clean lab coats for next week. And grocery shopping. I need to get some groceries."

"Okay, slow down. You're freaked. I understand. You can go if you want to. You don't have to make excuses to me. But I thought maybe you'd want to talk."

"Not now." Paul could feel his face flushing red, and was glad the room was too dark to show it. He was still fully dressed, except for his boots and jacket. Did that mean nothing had really happened? How the hell did he get drunk enough to let his control slip? He remembered talking about his mother, too. That was almost worse, not remembering what he'd said. He scrambled to his feet. "I really need to go." Where were his boots? He fished around on the floor with his hands.

Simon switched on a lamp and sat blinking in the soft light. He didn't get up or move toward Paul. "Your jacket's in the hall closet. And your boots too."

"Thanks." Paul hurried over there, moving sideways because he didn't want to look at Simon, but he didn't want to turn his back on the man either. He pushed at the bifold door, which stuck for a moment and then gave way, dumping him a step forward. His face landed in the soft wool of an overcoat, and that scent of Simon's filled his nose, of outdoors and pine woods and male skin. He jerked back, and pulled his own coat from its hanger. His boots were there, ready to step into. His keys were in his pocket.

He hesitated with the front door open, because it wasn't polite to just rush out. Simon was sitting unmoving on the couch, watching him go. "Thanks for taking me out." *Shit, that sounded like they had a date.* "I mean, it was… interesting and stuff."

"Especially stuff," Simon said with a faint smile. "Will you call me? Because I still want to be your friend, even if you never so much as kiss me again. And I don't want you to run out into the dark and disappear."

Paul couldn't answer. He couldn't believe Simon had mentioned kissing, when he thought he was getting out of the house without bringing up last night. He couldn't stand there with the door open. The cold air was getting in. He shut the door carefully behind him, headed for his truck, and prayed to every god out there that it would start.

Chapter 6

Simon held his smile in place until the door shut behind Paul's back. Then he let himself slide down the slick leather to the floor, and pounded his forehead rhythmically on the couch. He'd fucked that up. Done it wrong at every level and he had known it at the time. But his good sense often fought a battle with his dick, and this time he'd finally lost.

Paul said he liked it. Well of course he'd said that. You take a young, lonely man, no friends, terrible self-image. You tell him he's beautiful and make him believe it, and then you get him drunk and kiss him. Big surprise when he goes along with it. Bigger surprise when he freaks to hell and gone in the morning.

At least Simon could give himself credit for stopping. He could have taken things further— maybe a lot further— last night. But even he had known that would be wrong. He could hope he hadn't done anything Paul wouldn't be able to forgive.

He needed to get out of the house. His whole body was stiff, after a night spent curled in an armchair, dozing lightly. He'd wanted to be nearby when Paul woke, in case… Well, in case of anything. In case he freaked out. In case he was really hung over and needed aspirin, or something. *In case he wanted to kiss me again.* He really was an idiot.

He got together building supplies, loaded the truck, and headed for the farmhouse. The current task was ripping out the old upstairs floor where it was rotting through. It would suit him perfectly. He needed to rip and destroy something. His wolf wanted to go hunting, but it was almost daylight. His wolf wanted to catch a deer and haul it back for Paul and go find him and feed him. His wolf was deluded too.

He'd always had good control. Better than good, actually. Self-control had been a life-and-death necessity at one time. Werewolves were hidebound traditionalists, with family and pack at the center of their lives. A young boy who was gay would usually out himself to the pack within the first year or two as a wolf. Teach him to shift at thirteen, put him in a situation where he was naked around friendly, athletically-muscled men on a regular basis, and sexual attraction was hard to hide. Even if you could hide the physical signs, arousal had a scent the others would notice as they passed from man to wolf and back. And your Alpha was there in your mind if he chose to be, feeling what you felt. And when the pack found out, gay meant dead, killed, disposed of, erased. No chance, no appeal.

Simon had probably been saved by his parents' sudden death when he was twelve. Their loss had been a devastating blow. He'd been dearly loved and cherished, and lost without them. Finding himself alone, cared for by an elderly great-uncle who seemed cold and distant, Simon had withdrawn. He'd locked all his feelings down deep— love, hate, grief, want, fear— he'd bottled all of it up and moved through life like an automaton. He wouldn't let anyone matter to him ever again.

Then a few months later, his great-uncle brought him into the pack, told him his true nature and taught him to shift, and his life was rocked sideways again. His wolf lived in the now, and that had a seductive way of easing his pain. In the months and years that followed, he ran as wolf as often as he could, beating his grief and loneliness back with sheer physical exhaustion. In human form, he lifted weights, swam, climbed. Being around the other men and boys only made him impatient for the moment when he could be alone again. He avoided everyone.

So in his isolation, he hit fifteen before an interest in sex really emerged in his life. By then, he knew what the pack thought of gay men, and how dangerous the first awareness of his desire was. He kept himself to himself, as he always had. Even away from the pack, he practiced locking his feelings down. He imagined the men in the pack as their wolves, imagined hate and teeth, when he might be looking at muscles and skin. Three years of iron control served him well.

His great-uncle Martin noticed, eventually. Who would expect a man of that age to be able to track down computer files and figure out what pictures he was browsing? The old man had surprised him again by helping him hide, instead of turning him in. He also began to seriously teach Simon to fight, both in wolf and human form.

By the time Simon was eighteen, he was a lot more deadly than most of the pack probably realized. He had dominated, stared, and occasionally fought his way up to the top of the youngsters, aiming for a mid-pack status that would keep him safer without making him a target. He'd also figured out that a joke, a quip, a quick deflection, could serve him well. His sense of humor began emerging, and he thought he had the world figured out. Then Uncle Martin contracted the shift-cancer, for which there was no cure. A few months later, Simon was alone again.

He'd never found out what eventually tripped him up. He had managed for several more years, keeping his rare sexual encounters hidden. He stayed distant from his packmates, but at the same time made himself useful whenever he could. He became known as a loner but an asset to the pack, helpful, dependable, if a little less respectful than most youngsters. His smart mouth wasn't always under control, but usually the pack chose to be amused. And if not, he took a beating well. Until someone, somewhere, at the wrong moment, noticed him.

Karl had waited until Simon was naked on top of another man, bodies pressed together, mouths engaged, before he came into the motel room. Simon never knew how Karl got the key, either, to open the carefully locked door. Distracted by his lover, Simon's normally acute senses had detected the beep of the lock only in time for him to raise his head before Karl was standing in the doorway, anger rolling off him like a cloud of smoke.

Simon knew he was dead. There was no reprieve, no room for misunderstandings here. But the man under him was human, and unaware. The pack shied away from killing humans if at all possible. It was seldom worth the risk.

"What the fuck?" Pretty, innocent Mick had cursed against Simon's neck, wriggling to get a better view of Karl. "Who the hell are you?"

"This is my uncle." Simon told him, rolling off and sitting on the edge of the bed. He didn't look at Karl or try to cover himself up. He gave Mick his best smile. "He apparently wants to talk to me. His timing sucks. I'm sorry."

"You want me to leave?" Mick's wide blue eyes looked confused.

"You'd better. Whatever he wants, his attitude will only be worse if you're here." Simon sighed. "Maybe I'll make it up to you another time."

"Are you sure?" Mick reached for his clothes, slowly getting dressed, but looking concerned. "I'm not sure I should leave you alone with him."

Simon gave Karl a quick glance, telling him to tone down the murderous glare, and then turned back to Mick. He reached for the younger man's shirt, helping close the buttons. He wanted Mick safely out of there, and if making Karl squirm was the last fun he was ever going to have, he was going to get the most out of it. He took Mick's shirtfront in his fists, leaned in and kissed him, long and deeply. "Don't worry, babe. He looks tough but he's a big teddy bear underneath. He might yell at me, but that's all."

"If you're sure…" Mick kicked on sneakers and headed for the door, slowly and reluctantly. "Will you call me tonight so I know you're okay? I can give you my number."

Simon thought it was just his luck, to have for once picked up a man who was more than just a pretty face. "Look, don't get involved. I have lots of family around, and things may get messy. You deserve someone less… preoccupied. Okay? But thanks."

Mick eventually went out. Karl kicked the door shut behind the human without looking. Simon and Karl stared at each other, unmoving, both listening as the man's footsteps on the concrete were followed by the slam of a car door, and then the hum of an engine, driving away. When Simon was certain Mick had safely gone, he stood, eyes still locked on Karl's. He knew what was coming, but he had to try.

Simon might've had the best fight training Martin could give him, and he was young and fit at twenty-three. But even then, Karl was Fourth and had been enforcer for a decade. He was six inches taller, fifty pounds heavier, and as fast as he was big. Despite the best Simon could do, Karl slowly and methodically beat him unconscious.

He came to, naked, on a hard cement floor. The iron grate of a familiar drain was making a print on his hip. There was no moment of disorientation. For years, he'd had nightmares that began like this. He knew exactly where he was.

"Karl." Gordon's voice cut through the buzzing in Simon's head, "I asked you to bring him here, not beat the shit out of him." Simon struggled to his knees, shaking his head to clear it.

"He didn't want to come with me," Karl said from somewhere behind him.

"You're not my type," Simon snarled thickly. A hard kick took his legs out from under him again and spilled him face down on the concrete.

"Enough." Gordon's voice was sharp. "Find your place, Fourth. Simon's not going anywhere, and this is a matter for all the pack to decide."

Simon struggled up again and opted for sitting on the floor. His left eye wouldn't open, but through his right he could see Gordon in his place as Alpha, and out of the corner of his eye the rest of the pack ranged around him in precise rank order. They were dressed in more mixed garb than usual, business suits and work clothes side by side with the more usual loose sweats. None of *them* were naked.

"Simon Conley," Gordon said formally. "Can you hear me?"

"Yes, Alpha." Simon bowed his head carefully. Defying Karl was one thing; defying Gordon was altogether different. The weight of his Alpha's anger burned in Simon's head. He'd never been so aware of that bright presence, pressing painfully against his mind.

"We are met as a pack," Gordon said.

"We are met." Simon's whisper was lost in the rolling echo.

"Simon. We have a report that you have been having sex with other men, which is against the laws and code of the pack. If this report is false, now's your chance to say so."

Simon swallowed thickly and opened his mouth. "No."

"No, what?"

"No, it's not false."

"Do you have anything you want to say?"

Simon could tell Gordon was already moving away, distancing himself from what would follow. Suddenly he was more angry than he was scared. "Yeah, I have things I want to say."

"Why do we have to listen to him?" a voice called from the circle on Simon's blind side. He thought it was Frank. "He's confessed, the remedy's clear. Why make us wade through the filth anymore?"

"Simon has been a member of this pack for ten years," Gordon said coldly. "I think we can at least give him a chance to speak."

"Speak then, boy." That was Karl. "But make it short."

"What are you all so afraid of? How does my being gay make me such a threat to the pack that after ten years I suddenly need to be killed, without any hesitation? What have I ever done that has been a risk to any of you?"

"It's not the risk," Gordon said. "It's pack law."

"But why?" Simon persisted. "You claim to cherish every pup born. We all support the families, hold our breaths for each pregnancy, rejoice for each live birth. And then you're willing to wipe out one in ten of our youngsters, just because they're attracted to men instead of women?"

"It's not one in ten." That came from behind him. "It's a rare perversion and it must be eliminated."

"Not so rare," Simon protested. "Uncle Martin told me about Christopher, and about Joey. Jesus, Christopher was just thirteen. Kid was probably still a virgin when you killed him. Isn't it time to stop? I've supported the pack, paid my tithe, run with all of you. I've never risked the pack, never come close to giving us away. How do you know Christopher couldn't have done the same? Isn't it time to stop killing your own children?"

"You are no one's child here," Karl growled.

"Not anymore. But the next one will be." Simon stared at Gordon, willing him to stop and think. Martin told him that when Christopher was killed fifteen years ago, there was the beginning of discussion about why such drastic measures were necessary. But Christopher, like Simon, had lost his father young. There was no one in the circle who had cared enough to overcome instinctive distaste. Simon hoped the world had changed enough in fifteen years for some of them to hear him. "What does homosexuality have to do with risk to the pack? Because that's what we reserve death for, isn't it? Keeping the pack safe."

"And so we are," Dan's voice hissed from off to his left. "Keeping the youngsters safe from you and your perversions. Keeping this from spreading."

"You think being gay is so wonderful that if you leave me alive, all the pups will want to follow in my footsteps?" Simon said. "Now there's a switch."

"We're keeping you from touching them."

"And is that the risk you see? That I might seduce one of the cubs?"

"Faggots are promiscuous. It's sick and disgusting. We don't have to justify what's been law and custom for a thousand years."

"We wolves drive cars, and use computers, and contact other packs on the Internet," Simon said desperately, "and none of that has been law and custom for a thousand years. The pack's had to change and adapt to survive." His head spun and the pain was making it hard to remember his planned arguments. He'd always known he would end up here someday, his life held in Gordon's hands. He had prepared. But staying conscious was hard. He put his hands flat on the floor for support. If he passed out here, he was dead. It would be easier for them to just finish him then.

"Perhaps in the past, gay wolves were a risk because they could be blackmailed, or were considered worthless because they brought no young to the pack. Maybe there were other reasons. But the world around us has changed. Our pups go to school with gay kids, they see gay athletes and entertainers, they know it's not that big a deal. What if you have to kill one of them next? Can you really make them believe that's the right thing to do? Will they still believe the pack only uses extreme measures at last resort, to keep us safe, if this is enough to make you kill one of us? Or will you drive the youngsters away, with your extreme reactions? You could risk the safety of us all by alienating wolves who should be bonding to the pack."

There was silence for a moment. Then Gordon said, "Did you practice that speech?"

"Would that make it less true?" Simon asked wearily.

"You're asking us to ignore pack law."

"Why is it law? It's not written anywhere. There was pack long before we knew how to write. It's more like a custom, carried from one generation to another. It's not infallible, not scripture. Our imperative is *protect the pack.* I'm saying that nothing I have done, or will do, is a risk to the pack."

"You soil us just by being here," someone called out.

"Yeah, filthy slime," Frank added.

"That's not what you said last month when you asked me to hunt with you. And I haven't changed."

"I didn't know you liked to bend over and get fucked," Frank hissed.

"Oh, I'm always on top."

"Enough." Gordon's voice was harsh. "Insults are not the point here. Simon has raised the question: why, after ten years with the pack, does finding out that he is queer suddenly make it necessary to kill him? And when I think with my mind, and not my gut, I have a hard time answering him."

"You're kidding!" Karl shouted. "You want to risk him spilling our secrets to one of the hundreds of faggots he's been fucking?"

"Hundreds?" Simon laughed and then coughed, as pain in his ribs speared him. "Hardly. But why should my bed partners be more risk than all the women Lucas goes out with? He's closer to hundreds than I am."

"Over it, pup," Lucas' deep voice rumbled from the left. "And not one of them the wiser, nor ever likely to be. And if a sweet girl can't worm our secrets out of me, I don't know why Simon should be different."

Simon almost choked at the first words of support he had heard. He looked up at Gordon as silence stretched again.

"What about the youngsters?" Frank asked. "You can't want this perversion spread among them."

"I can't see why you think it would," Simon said. "Why would any wolf want to be gay, if he had a choice? But if you like, I can take oath to never go near any wolf younger than me, or near any wolf for sex. I don't care. I have no interest in them. I'll swear on anything you like."

Gordon was nodding. "Perhaps…"

Suddenly Karl leaped out of his place, shoving Simon down on the floor. "You can't!" he shouted at Gordon. "You can't be thinking about leaving this piece of filth in our pack. What kind of Alpha are you?"

There was a sudden silence. Gordon seemed to get taller without moving a muscle. "Are you Challenging me on this, Fourth?"

Karl had stood before his Alpha, and every muscle in his body quivered. The whole pack knew that he wanted to make the Challenge. The whole pack also felt the weight of Gordon's commanding presence and knew that Karl would lose. Winning a Challenge depended on fighting skill, but also on strength of will, and on the support of the pack, especially when one fighter was Alpha. Gordon still had dominance in will and the pack was still behind him then. After a long moment, Karl bent his head a fraction and dropped his eyes. "No."

It was barely submission, but Gordon nodded and turned away from him in clear dismissal. "What do you think, Second?" he had asked Arthur.

The huge dark-skinned man had been silent so far. Now he looked at Simon for a long moment. Simon tried to pull himself up and return that look. He tried to keep hope and fear and pain out of his eyes, and give his Second the gaze of a wolf of the pack. After a while Arthur spoke directly to Simon. "Would you take an oath to never sleep with a man again?"

"No," Simon had to say. At the rumbling of anger from the pack he added, "That would be swearing celibacy for the next hundred years. I have no interest in women. If I don't sleep with a man, then I'm alone forever. Would any of you swear to that and expect to keep to it?"

"Perhaps not," Arthur agreed, despite the growls around him. "But you would swear to touch no packmate in a sexual way, and to avoid the company of all wolves younger than yourself, forever?"

Simon opened his mouth to agree and heard himself say, "If I live to be very old, that could get difficult." He bit his own tongue sharply.

"Those younger than twenty-one, perhaps," Arthur suggested. "I assume adult wolves can handle their own sex lives." His glance around the circle held enough scorn that any objector thought better of it.

"Yes," Simon said clearly, "that I would swear to."

Arthur looked at his Alpha. "I would accept that. Because it was my job to kill Christopher, and Simon is right. I never want to slaughter one of our pups like that again, just because he gets hard when he sees a naked man. I can't see where this custom of ours adds safety for the pack, in this day and age. It may even endanger it, if we drive some wolves to hide or leave us at a young age for fear of being discovered."

Several voices spoke up together, but a look from Gordon stilled them all. He swept his eyes over the assembled men, gauging their attitudes and where their support lay. Finally his gaze came back to Karl, still out of his place in the circle. Gordon's expression hardened.

"As Alpha, it's my job to decide what serves the pack best. Simon has been with us, wolf and man, for ten years. He has said things today which

I have thought about before, but never followed to a conclusion. I will not kill one of my pack without due cause, and I'm no longer sure this is due cause." He frowned at a rumble of discontent from the ranks. "I said I am not sure. We will take oaths from Simon, here in front of all of you, and we'll see if he can hold to them. Death is still a choice I can always make, if it seems best. But *I* will make that choice." He let his glare fall on Karl. "Is that clear? If anything fatal happens to Simon, and I find one of the pack is responsible, that wolf will answer for murder to the full extent of pack law, no matter what his rank. Do I make myself clear?"

Karl stared back, his eyes hot. Gordon raised his eyes to look at the rest of the wolves, and then back at Karl. He raised his voice for all of them, his dominant will bearing down on them. "Do I make myself clear?"

"Yes, Alpha." It was a ragged chorus, begrudged in places, but even Karl repeated it.

"Good." Gordon looked at Simon, who sat on the floor, unable to believe that he had won his reprieve. "Then let's get these oaths done, so we can move on, boy."

Simon thought it was ironic that he probably owed his life to Karl. He didn't know what Gordon would have decided, if slapping Karl back for his insolence hadn't become part of the equation. Even then, with Arthur and Derek alive above him, Karl's ambition had been clear. Gordon had held the reins though. Until just this week, Karl had roughed Simon up whenever he could manufacture a reason, but he'd never let it become lethal.

Karl hadn't been the only one unhappy with Gordon's leniency. Simon had spent the next two years fighting. He was Challenged by every wolf below him who felt that they couldn't stand being topped by a gay man. He was roughed up by every wolf above him who hated what he was. He had won when he could, and felt it was safe. He had rolled over for a beating when he had to. Hiding his skill became less vital than surviving, and ironically, he ended the two years significantly higher in the pack than he began. Only once had he completely backed down from a fight. Christopher's older cousin had Challenged him, and as they stripped for the shift, Simon had caught the man's strangled whisper of "Why should you live when he had to die?" He'd bared his throat at the first exchange. The combination of grief and rage hit him hard in the gut, and he chose to neither win nor lose that fight. He took back his place in rank later, when shifts in dominance led to the next contest.

Lately, he'd seldom had to meet another wolf out on the floor. The pack had gotten used to him. He kept his love life carefully out of sight and tried to control his tongue on other topics, with varying success. He had no really close friends, but he participated in gatherings and meets. He ran with the pack when they got together up north for a long weekend as wolves. A few people greeted him in a friendly way, shared brief conversations, and would hunt at his side in wolf form.

Andy would occasionally call and suggest a ball game or bowling. And some of the wives were friendly enough, when he wasn't avoiding them because kids were around. Most of the pack ignored him. Perhaps a few of the younger wolves would have been more sociable, but he held to his oath and left them strictly alone. He'd always been aware of Karl, watching for some excuse to bring him down.

It wasn't a bad life. He had work he enjoyed, outdoors in the summer and in the shop in the winter. He was working on a set of cabinets right now that would be beautiful when finished. Building and crafting was satisfying. He had lovers now and then, in parts of the city where his packmates seldom went. And he had the sheer joy of being wolf. Running on cold snow under the trees, with only starlight to guide him, was as close to heaven as Simon could imagine. But if Karl had his way, Simon's life was going to blow up in his face soon.

At least we got through that last meeting. Holding our breaths.

He thought about pack business as he entered his old farm house, as he examined and made plans, as he began removing boards from the floors. It was easier than thinking about Paul. Running down the pack roster was familiar, this tallying of wolves and their opinions, relative to rank and strength. He was disturbed to find he'd let his pack awareness slide in the ten years of calm since he was forced out and stopped looking over his shoulder, just keeping his distance well.

Too well. His alpha's protection had made him complacent. There were now eight wolves he knew very little about. He had their names, their shapes, their scents, clear in his mind. But how they felt about Karl's ambition was speculation. Seven of them were young and off limits to him. One was a new addition, like Aaron. Back in the day, he'd have found roundabout ways to study them, to know where they stood in relation to his enemies and allies. He was a fool to have let his vigilance slide.

As he worked, the strain in his healing ribs nagged him. He had only limited use of his injured arm, and a couple of careless moves sent flashes of pain through him. When his fingers became chilled, and his back asked for a break, Simon stripped and shifted, pleased to feel his arm sore but stable though the process. As a wolf, he stretched, feeling his spine ripple and flex. The shift had further healed his bones, and he reveled in the easing of his pain.

He gave himself an hour, for the sheer pleasure of it, chasing rabbits in the snow with no intention of catching them, and leaping, still on three careful legs, through drifts until his fur was frosted white. Life was too short to miss out on moments of joy. Shifting again in the unheated privacy of his house, he was pleased to feel his human bones stronger yet. Even the bite on his side was healed down to thick new scars, pulling but not painful as he tugged on his sweatshirt. He shivered, chilled despite his werewolf metabolism, eyed his day's work, and decided to call it quits.

The truck's engine heated the cab quickly. Simon opened his jacket as he drove and put on sunglasses against the low angle of the setting sun. Then he finally he let himself reach for his cell phone and check it.

Paul had his phone number. Simon had put that information in the "Wolf Conley" medical record himself. But there was no message. Not even a missed call. Simon whistled carelessly, but zipped his jacket up to his chin again, feeling the renewed chill as the sun went down.

Chapter 7

Paul looked around his clean, neat apartment. There was nothing left that demanded his attention. He'd spent his Sunday productively, mopped, and scrubbed, and done laundry. His refrigerator was restocked with food, half of which would probably spoil before he cooked it. He'd sorted his veterinary journals, and put the old ones in recycling. Of course, he could always catch up on his reading. There were a dozen journals still waiting to be looked at.

He sat in his desk chair and picked up an issue of *JAVMA* determinedly. Two pages later he realized he couldn't even remember what disease he was reading about. He put it back down.

His computer stood there on the desktop, waiting for him. He'd been walking around the temptation all day. Because he had scientific training, and that training said if you wanted to answer a question, you did the research. And the Internet was out there, offering to let him do just that.

Paul rubbed his palms on the thighs of his jeans. Kissing another man meant nothing about who someone was, especially if you were drunk when you did it. He'd always been attracted to women. Always. He'd never thought about men that way. He didn't intend to start now.

Except he couldn't forget how he'd felt with his face cradled in Simon's hands as his mouth was possessed. A man's kiss should've been unpleasant, or at best neutral, if he was straight. But neutral was definitely the wrong word for the way he'd reveled in Simon's touch. Drunk or not.

So, research. While sober.

He booted up his computer and turned off the room light, letting the screen illuminate the dimness. He didn't have a lot of porn bookmarked, but he was a young, single guy. He had some. After a moment's hesitation, he clicked on a favorite site with short video clips of women getting undressed. Suggestive, sexy, but not explicit. You could pay for explicit of course, but Paul had always liked subtlety better as a fuel for his fantasies.

He browsed through the stills, looking at one after another of the pretty women in their clothed pose, waiting. There; there was a young woman, maybe twenty or twenty-one, with long dark hair and pale blue eyes. He clicked on the box. The image of the girl turned to him and smiled, as her hands went to the first button on her blouse. Paul watched as the woman on the screen moved almost shyly through her routine. She was elegant and slender. Her breasts in the revealing white lace bra were small and high, rosy-tipped through the fabric. Her skin was fair, her legs long and slim. He breathed faster and slid a hand to his lap as she undressed for him and paused, naked, her body turned away, her smile a promise. Okay. He was touching evidence that this still turned him on. He pulled his fingers away. No touching, just the women. He continued to browse.

A surprising number of the offered women were busty and blond, a combination that did nothing for him. One woman looked slim in her coy over-the-shoulder opening pose. But when he clicked, she moved like a seasoned stripper, revealing big, unnaturally-solid breasts. He shook his head. *...like a whore, shaking her tits at any man who walks by. You like that, don't you, little pervert. I've seen you looking...* He bit his lip and forced his mother's voice out of his head, moving to the next still.

His body did like women though. He was proving that. Slim, dark, subtle women made him hard. Several of these girls were worth a second or a third look, and tempted him to do more.

He could've stopped there. He was straight, surely, since his reaction to these women was to reach for the lube. Positive evidence. He wanted to stop there.

But science was science. All the positive evidence in the world wasn't proof. You could claim that every animal in the world was a cat, and each cat you saw would support that theory, but the first dog you saw would destroy it. You had to check the negative.

He entered "gay men naked sex" in his search window and made himself click the button. The sheer number of hits was surprising. He clicked on one at random, and closed it fast. *TMI. Jesus, not going there.*

After careful searching, he located a site that was more... artistic. Nude photos of men, subtly lit, without explicit sexual content; these were images he could look at without having to squint sideways. He studied the first shot. The model was a muscular black man, his body illuminated by the single candle he held, light spilling off the wide arcs of his pecs. Paul thought some men went too far with the weights, and probably with the steroids. There was a point where the body-builder physique became almost a caricature of maleness. This man was not over that point, but he sure was pushing the edge of it.

The next was more subtle, a slim pale man bending in front of a thinly-curtained window, his body a silhouette except where a slash of light from between the two halves of the drapes carved a line of white down his chest and thigh. There was a beauty in the lines of his body that Paul could acknowledge, but he didn't think it turned him on. Not really. The photo was well done though, that line of white skin sliding past the dark shadow of the groin, keeping the shape there hidden. Paul wondered if the model had been aroused by posing that way. Probably not or he would've seen… He moved on quickly.

The fifth model was the most like Simon. Paul made himself pause and look closer. This man's skin was a little darker, the planes of his face narrower and craggier. The model had straight black hair spilling almost to his waist over his muscled back. This shot was a rear view, face barely turned to profile, but there was no mistaking that back and ass for female, however long the hair. No woman had that cut and play of muscle from one exposed shoulder down along the spine. No woman's ass dimpled tight and hard like that, curving above thick powerful thighs. Paul began flipping through the other pictures. Models began to repeat in the images. The muscular black man was a favorite of the artist, in photos where light was made to caress every cut and curve of that big dark body. Those still did nothing for Paul. The slim brown-haired guy was given gauzy sprays of water, filtered moonlight. Then the Native American was back, his lines broken by the dappling of sunlight through leaves. The effect was almost like camouflage; naked brown skin against brown fallen leaves, blended by the dappled lines of bright and dark. The man's head was down, his face hidden in shadow.

You could almost believe this was Simon. Although Simon was more compact than this man, less rangy. Simon's chest was more muscled, his arms shorter and more curved through bicep and forearm, and more heavily furred… *Shit.* Paul didn't have to touch himself to know. His body liked this too. Liked the play of light over male skin and muscle. Liked the tight curves and angles, and the thought of seeing them moving…

Paul flipped to his favorite of the bookmarked girls. He imagined her coming toward him, dropping to her knees in front of him. His hand fell to his lap unbidden. He imagined her full red lips opening for him. *Okay.*

He flipped back to the man. Imagined him lifting his head, looking up, smiling. Would he come to Paul, or would Paul go to him? Simon was friendly but there was a core of toughness there. He couldn't imagine Simon dropping to his knees and… or maybe he could. *Fuck!* He clicked back, missed his mark and got an older, slender red-haired girl. He'd liked her at the time but now, no. He clicked on the brunette. He liked girls, he really did. *Mother was wrong, with all her fag and sissy talk. As wrong as every other insult she threw my way—*

He found himself searching the remaining photos of the men, wondering if that Native American was in any others. No, no, no, yes. Free-climbing on a rock face, ten feet up, no clothes, his hands and toes jammed into the cracks of stone a weathered red-gray that set off his brown skin. The light was mellow gold, the setting sun sending long angled shadows of the man's body across the rocks. His muscles strained, taking his body weight upward. Paul looked at the broken lines of the shadows, and blushed even in his own home as he realized why he was studying their shape around the hips so intently.

He slammed himself out of Google with rough fingers on the keyboard and sat staring at the screen. His whole body was achy and unsettled. Now what?

He was turned on by some of the girls, so he wasn't gay, right? But he couldn't deny that at least one man had made him just as hard. But only the man who looked like Simon. The others did nothing for him. Well, not much anyway. That slim guy by the curtains, maybe. More than the blond with the pneumatic tits, at least, but less than the sweet little brunette. So was he bi? Or had he somehow imprinted on Simon, like some stupid baby chick following the first thing it sees when it hatches out of its egg, even the wrong species? He had been alone so long, and Simon walked through his walls like they weren't there. Maybe he was just so fucking desperate for attention he didn't care who it came from.

Was he so needy that he'd do anything to be touched by someone? He hated that idea. Simon was smart and good-looking and, okay, sexy, with the way he moved and the light in his eyes. Simon could have anyone. *So why's he spending time with me? Doesn't he have any fucking gaydar to tell him I'm straight?* Or maybe he did, and it was telling him Paul wasn't as straight as he'd always thought.

Paul turned off the computer and headed for the shower. He ran it cold first, as long as he could stand it, but the heat in his groin didn't disappear. The simmering need just drew back deeper in his shivering body, waiting.

He turned the water warm. Punishing himself was stupid. Not like he'd never been horny before. That's what you got for spending an hour looking at porn. He visualized the pretty brunette, coming into the bathroom and undoing those small pearl buttons. She was stepping out of the skirt, unhooking the lace bra.

Paul took himself in hand, letting his soap-slick skin slide through his fist. He imagined the girl getting in the shower, kissing his chest, kneeling down, reaching up to touch him. He pulled faster, twisting his hand up and over himself. Red mouth, dark hair. His body thrummed with need, hovering on the brink, unable to cross. Dark hair, wet with spray, gray eyes looking up at him, strong clever tongue swirling around and taking him in, strong hard hands on his ass pulling him forward into a willing mouth. As he fell into the fantasy, gasping his climax, those gray eyes smiled at him, ringed oddly in green.

Paul held the safety bar in a white-knuckled grip as his body shuddered down to stillness. He wasn't fooling himself. He knew whose eyes those were. And whose hands. *Simon kissed me first.* He held to that. He'd been drunk, but not so much that he didn't remember that. No matter how needy he had been, or what he'd done in invitation, Simon had made the first real move.

He stepped out of the shower, toweling dry, shivering again as the air hit his wet skin. The mirror was fogged, hiding the bathroom. He could imagine someone else stepping out of the shower stall, big and warm. He sighed. *We need to talk.* He could go to bed now, lay down his temporarily sated body and try to get some sleep. Or not.

§ § § §

Simon recognized that truck engine, even through a light sleep. He'd heard it before, man and wolf, and woke for the sound immediately. He'd slid out of bed and was pulling on sweatpants before the engine stopped outside. Then he was leaping downstairs, fighting the lock on his door, and hurrying out into the snow when he heard it start up again. He grabbed the driver's door handle and saw Paul jump at his sudden appearance.

After a second Paul powered the window down.

"Hey," Simon said softly. "Fancy meeting you here."

"I'm sorry. I didn't realize… I just looked at the clock and… I didn't know it was so late."

"Or so early. Depending. That's okay. Come on in."

Paul sat there for a moment, staring out the windshield as the truck engine rumbled. "I really shouldn't."

"Yes, you should," Simon interrupted, "and it's too freaking cold out here to argue with you. Come on in the house."

Paul looked at him again and did a double take. "You're crazy! You're half-dressed and it's freezing out here. Fuck, you're barefoot! Get in the house, you fool."

"Only if you're coming in," Simon insisted, not letting go of the door handle.

"Yeah." Paul sighed. "I'll be right behind you."

Simon waited until the truck was switched off before letting go and leading the way inside. He flicked on one light as he went, but kept things dim. Dim was always easier for difficult conversations. Even better would be something to keep them from having to look each other in the eye. "You want some hot chocolate? Or coffee?"

"Since when do you have coffee in the house?" Paul asked, diverted. "You told me you never drink it or buy it."

"I picked some up. Should I make it?"

"Thanks." Paul looked everywhere but at him. "You should make yourself something hot too. What possessed you to come outside like that? This is Minnesota, you know."

Simon discarded several answers before saying lightly, "The weather ain't the boss of me," as he headed to the kitchen.

"You sound about four years old." Paul followed him, gazing around.

Simon liked his kitchen. The house was just a rental, but he had done a deal with his landlady to get a break on rent in exchange for some remodeling. He'd built cabinets from a blond maple, with antique brass knobs. The counter was dark granite, and the floors were slate-gray tile. Simon set a copper kettle on the stove to heat water and got out coffee and cocoa. Mugs were on a bottom shelf. He couldn't resist giving Paul the one that said, *Homolicious*.

"Don't you want to put on a sweater or something?" Paul asked tentatively, as the kettle began to edge toward a boil.

"I'm fine. I like the cold." Werewolf metabolism made low temperatures easier to handle, although his human body could get frostbite if pushed too hard. But he was indoors now, and the cuts on his body had healed to fading scars. Wherever this was going, Simon wanted every advantage. He knew what he looked like without a shirt. After all, he made an effort to keep it that way.

The kettle whistled, and Simon filled the two mugs. The smell of chocolate and coffee rose together in a comforting blend. Simon didn't mind the smell of coffee at all. Some werewolves were more sensitive to the underlying bitterness of the brew, and Simon was one of them. As he watched Paul take a sip, he reflected that he even liked a hint of the flavor on another man's tongue.

Slow down.

He let the silence grow comfortable as they drank quietly, each leaning against a different piece of counter.

"This is good coffee," Paul said eventually.

Simon laughed. "I can pour water through a cone. It's an essential life skill." He ran a finger around the rim of his mug, picking up spilled cocoa powder, and then licked the chocolate off slowly. Paul was pretending to ignore him, but Simon's acute hearing picked up the slight speeding of Paul's breath. *Good.*

Paul seemed permanently stalled in silence, so eventually he said, "What brings you here tonight? Not that I'm complaining."

"You said we could talk."

"Talking is good."

Paul took another four sips, one of which Simon suspected was camouflage with an empty mug, before he said, "You kissed me."

"I did. I'm not going to apologize. You're extremely kissable."

"I wasn't… I didn't expect you to apologize. I just…" Paul stared down into the mug. "I was just wondering why."

"If I have to explain that to you, you're even less experienced than I thought," Simon teased.

Paul's fair skin flushed red. "No, Jesus, I meant why me?"

"Because I wanted to. Because I like you, and you're beautiful, and you didn't seem unwilling."

"There were lots of beautiful men at the bar," Paul said slowly.

Simon didn't say, *Oh, you noticed.* He could feel the tension in Paul, and knew that if he pushed too hard, even in fun, Paul would be gone. "I didn't want lots of men," he said softly. "I wanted you." After another long silence, he added, "What do *you* want?"

"I don't know," Paul said plaintively. "That's the problem. I've always been straight but…"

"But?"

"But I liked… what we did."

"And?"

"But I was drunk, which I never am, so I don't know if liking kissing you was for real, or some weird part of being drunk and having guys hitting on me and being horny and… all that."

Simon nodded gravely, hiding a small smile. "Are you drunk now?"

"No." Paul's eyes were huge and dark in his pale face.

"Okay then." Simon reached out and took Paul's empty mug from his hands and set it carefully on the counter. He put his own next to Paul's. Paul stared at the empty cups as if there were answers there. Simon stepped forward, cupped the man's elegant chin in one hand, and raised his face. He leaned forward slowly, an inch at a time, giving Paul a chance to pull away. Instead Paul tilted his head and opened his lips obediently.

Simon kissed him, slow and soft and warm. He tasted the coffee on Paul's tongue and the chocolate on his own, as he slowly explored Paul's mouth. After a moment he pulled back to gauge his reception in Paul's face. Paul's eyes were closed, waiting. Simon groaned softly and took back the kiss, deeper, harder. He clasped the nape of Paul's neck in one hand, feeling the soft brush of tawny hair over his fingers. He ran his other hand over Paul's silky, clean-shaven cheek and then down his neck, shoulder, biceps, forearm. He slid his arm around Paul's waist, pulling them together. And then he wasn't the only one doing the kissing. Paul's tongue met his, stroking, probing. Paul's hands locked in the small of Simon's back and pressed their bodies closer, tightly, like they were trying to climb inside each other.

Simon broke the kiss to nip at Paul's neck and jaw. He ran the edge of his teeth over the cords of Paul's throat, and Paul's head fell back into Simon's hand to give him access. Simon thrust his tongue into the hollow at his collarbone and Paul whimpered, a small needy sound. Then his eyes opened, and Simon leaned back a little to meet his gaze, without letting go.

"What's the verdict?" he asked roughly. "Is kissing me only fun when you're drunk?"

"Shut up." Paul tangled a hand in Simon's hair, pulling him back into the kiss. Simon moved so his thigh was between Paul's, and they pushed together, grinding. Simon hadn't felt like this in a long time, needing someone so urgently that he didn't want to stop to get naked or plan his moves out. The press of hard bodies together, and panting breath, was enough. His hands on Paul's ass, fingers digging in hard. Paul's hands on his back, locking them together. Then Paul moaned, "Simon. Oh, God, wait. Don't—"

Paul shuddered, body tight against Simon's. Simon knew the sound and scent, felt Paul go over right there, like teenagers necking in their parents' kitchen. Simon held him tightly but gentled his movements, supporting him, kissing his neck softly, as Paul shook and gasped in his arms.

"I'm sorry," Paul moaned. "God, Simon, I'm sorry. I'm so stupid. I'm…"

Simon kissed his mouth to shut him up. "You're sexy. And sweet, and hot, and horny, and now also wet and sticky." He laughed softly. "You only beat me by seconds, and if you move again too fast, I might join you."

"I've never done that." Paul's eyes were rueful. "I didn't expect to lose control. I'm sorry.'

"Stop apologizing. There's no better compliment than making a man so hot he comes just from being kissed. I haven't been that close to losing it in forever either." He relaxed his arms to allow space between them, but didn't let go completely. He smiled and stated, rather than asked, "You're okay. I'm okay."

"But you didn't…" Paul blushed.

"The morning is young. If you'll stay."

Paul looked away, and wriggled loose of Simon's grip. "I didn't plan this. I was just going to… I thought maybe…"

Simon let him flounder for a while, then said, "Life is what happens while you're making plans. Anyway, you can't go back out now. You'll freeze your dick. At least come upstairs and get cleaned up. I can loan you some clean briefs."

Paul finally looked up and met his eyes. "All right."

Simon pushed Paul ahead of him up the narrow stairs, afraid he still might bolt. At the top of the staircase, doors opened to two bedrooms and a bath. Simon guided Paul into the bathroom and flipped on the light.

"What?"

"You could use a shower." Simon turned on the water.

"I just had one."

Simon kissed him hard. "Then you could use another."

Steam rose in the bathroom as the water heated. Simon leaned against the counter between Paul and the door, arms folded across his chest. But Paul looked so bewildered that he backed off, loosening his stance and moving aside from the door.

"I don't mean to rush you," he said quietly. "I'm sorry too. You are so hot, and it's been a long time for me, and I'm taking a mile here when you've given me an inch. Well, maybe seven inches." He couldn't resist a grin. "Anyway, you can shower alone and I'll bring you a change of clothes. Or I can show you why I like a shower big enough to kneel in."

Paul opened his mouth to respond several times. When he finally spoke, it was a bare whisper. "Who gets to kneel?"

"God, I do, of course. I want to taste you, and I want to show off my hard-won skills. And I do mean *hard* won." He wiggled his eyebrows comically at Paul.

"And you like doing that?"

"Been dreaming of you that way. Literally." He leaned on the door and smiled his best boyish grin. "I love showing off to an appreciative audience."

Paul nodded slowly. "I guess I could be appreciative. If you have a little patience."

"Patience is my middle name. Well, actually it's Michael, but that's close." He moved closer and raised his hands to the buttons on Paul's shirt. "Come on," he murmured. "If you're going to shower, you have to lose the clothes."

§ § § §

Paul gave up fighting with himself. If this was only a dream, he'd let it play out all the way. If it wasn't… After his porn revelation, he'd argued with himself half the evening about whether to talk to Simon or not. He'd picked up the phone a dozen times, but "what the hell are we doing?" didn't seem like the kind of thing you could discuss over the phone. Finally, he'd just headed over. If you could say "just headed" when he took the time change and shave first.

He'd felt so stupid, arriving at the house only to realize he'd dithered until almost one in the morning. He would've turned around and left. Except Simon showed up at his truck window, barefoot in the snow. And Paul had to get the crazy man to go back inside. And then…

He'd been telling the truth when he said he'd never done that— never dry humped with a date until he lost control. He'd never even come close. Simon's mouth and hands and taste and smell went directly to some part of Paul's brain he thought had never been touched before. He wasn't a virgin. He'd had sex, and liked it. But this was different, something so essential the need bypassed thought and went straight to his body.

Now the shower ran warm behind him, slowly fogging the mirror. He stood paralyzed, as Simon's hands barely brushed his chest, opening his shirt, one button at a time. When the front separated, Simon slowly pushed the fabric off Paul's shoulders, roughened fingers running down Paul's arms as he peeled his shirt off. Then those fingers ran back up his bare skin. Paul looked down, watching, as Simon traced the line of his collarbone. Brown fingertips slid across his ribs, before dipping to mark the sharp ridge of one hip bone, jutting above his low-slung belt.

"Jesus, babe, you need feeding up. What have you been doing to yourself?" Simon sounded almost angry. "You must be a good fifteen pounds underweight."

"I'm fine." Paul twitched away from the wandering finger. "If you don't like how I look, I can go."

"No, sugar, no," Simon said quickly. "You're beautiful. But you're not taking care of yourself. Come on. If you were someone's pet, what would you tell them?"

Paul looked down at himself, noticing his ribs through his skin and the way his jeans hung from his notched-tight belt. "I guess I've been kind of busy."

"Kind of." Simon's voice softened again. "Okay. First I eat you, then I feed you. Sounds like a plan."

Paul choked at the words, then gasped as Simon bent and his hot mouth closed on Paul's left nipple. Simon sucked on him, biting, flicking with his tongue against the hard nub. Paul felt his nipples tighten sharply, and a shock arced through him from chest to groin. Simon moved to the other side, while his hands busied themselves with Paul's belt and button.

Suddenly shy, Paul reached down to cup Simon's face and pull that wandering mouth up for a kiss. He grabbed Simon's hands, pinning them momentarily. Simon returned the kiss lightly, not fighting the restraint. After a slow brush of lips and tongues, he stepped back and raised his hands, kissing each of Paul's fingers where they ringed his wrists.

"Are we still okay?" he asked gently.

Paul let go of him and nodded. "Just… go slow?"

"Slow is good." Simon smiled and leaned in for another soft kiss, lips barely parted. "Why don't you get in the shower?" He stepped back and turned away, moving a big towel on the rail, tossing down a terrycloth mat.

Without those hot eyes on him, Paul found it easier to unzip and push his jeans down. He toed out of snow-wet sneakers as his pant legs slid off. Socks. There was something unattractive about a man's bare legs in socks, and he peeled them off. Which left his boxers. Damp, sticky boxers; proof positive that whatever he was doing with Simon, his response wasn't just alcohol and opportunity. He turned toward the shower, his back to Simon, and pushed the fabric down his legs. Freeing his feet with a clumsy lurch, he kicked his underwear into a corner and shivered.

"Get in the warm water," Simon told him. "Relax."

The shower had a glass door and Paul had to step back to swing it open. As he did so, his bare hip brushed against warm skin, and he shied forward as if stung, refusing to look back. The stall was big and clean with seamless walls and floor, spray spreading wide from a large flat showerhead. He faced into the water, letting the streams run down his chest into the sticky trail of hair on his stomach, clean warmth washing over him.

Behind him, the door squeaked in opening, then shut with a soft thump. The sounds in the little cubicle became muffled, closer, darker. Paul had always liked small dark spaces. He closed his eyes and moved his face under the spray.

"Paul." Simon spoke in a bass whisper. "I've got the soap. I'm going to touch you, okay?"

Paul couldn't answer but he let his body sway back a fraction in assent. Apparently, his movement was clear enough, because warm slick hands began rubbing his shoulders. He could smell a faint herbal scent and feel the trail of lather as suds slid downward. Simon's strong fingers worked Paul's shoulders, digging into the knotted muscles there. Paul couldn't help groaning in appreciation.

"God, that's better than sex," he said, then winced as Simon gave a deep chuckle.

Simon's hands moved lower, massaging his whole back. "It shouldn't be. You *have* had sex before, haven't you?"

"Yes, of course. What sort of loser do you think I am?"

"Not a loser." Simon dropped a light kiss on Paul's shoulder. "I'm getting a hell of a kick out of being the first man to make love to you. I wouldn't mind being the first *person.* I was just curious."

"Well, I have," Paul said huffily. Then because Simon's hands were working magic down his spine, and he trusted the man, but he was nervous, he admitted, "Twice."

Simon's hands hesitated for an instant, then resumed their slow circles. "Was it good sex?"

Paul said nothing. Simon's hands slid around Paul's ribs to glide up his chest. Strong fingers molded Paul's pecs and curved downward toward his waist, slow and restrained, not touching anywhere vital. "Want to tell me?" Simon's hot mouth kissed the back of his neck, once, twice, softly. Paul was conscious of the heat of that other male body, carefully not touching, a centimeter behind his own.

"The first time was kind of a disaster," he said, his voice a little high, just to say something, to slow this down. *...a slender girl on the bed, eyes cool beneath tousled brown hair. "Wow, twenty-six seconds. That was hardly worth getting undressed for."* "The second time was nice, though."

Simon set firm hands on Paul's shoulders, turning him around. Paul resisted for a second, then rotated obligingly. Simon's eyes glowed with that odd green light as he kissed Paul firmly. "Sugar, when you've had sex with me, I'll be damned if you'll call it 'nice.'"

Simon's smooth skin was beaded with water, a mist of droplets sitting on his hair like dew on black grass. His eyes were warm, his body gave off heat like a woodstove. Paul had seen that chest before, those shoulders; his own body remembered. Simon's nipples were dark in the dense mat of hair across his chest. Unbidden, Paul's eyes dropped lower, to the deep groove that led from one muscled hip to furry groin. And yeah, Simon wasn't kidding about enjoying this.

Paul looked away, but not fast enough to avoid imprinting that image on his brain. Simon's dick was short but wide, curving a little to one side, the head swelling gently from uncut foreskin. Paul knew what other men looked like from years of PE showers, but he had never consciously paid attention. At least he didn't think he had. And the boys at school had never looked like this. He swallowed convulsively.

Simon kissed him again, wet and open-mouthed. He licked downward over Paul's chin, neck, shoulder, chest. Paul stared at the wall over Simon's shoulder, but he knew what was coming next and his body jerked in anticipation. He slid a hand into Simon's hair instinctively, trying to guide him toward a crinkling nipple. Simon resisted for a moment, biting at the muscle of Paul's chest. Then that hot mouth closed around Paul's tight bud, sucking and pulling. Paul moaned as the sensation sizzled through him.

Simon licked and bit, then began to work lower. He crouched and slid his tongue over the flat plane of Paul's belly, then lowered himself to his knees on the shower floor. Paul's hand tightened in Simon's black hair.

Simon kissed Paul's left hip. His teeth bit over the angle of bone hard enough to leave a little mark, and then he ran his tongue tip over the spot. Paul shuddered.

"Was that good or bad?" Simon murmured.

"Oh, good," Paul whispered. "Definitely." How could Simon not know? Paul was hard again, jutting out next to Simon's exploring face. Paul stared down at him, at that firm mouth moving over his skin, the big hands sliding up the sides of his thighs. Simon cupped Paul's ass and moved in to nuzzle the tawny curls in his groin. Paul ached to be touched *there*, but Simon kept teasing, licking around the area, avoiding any touch of Paul's slim shaft and flared, cut head. Paul shifted his weight, trying to make contact, but firm fingers on his ass cheeks held him still.

"Please," he whispered.

Simon growled, a low sound that went right to Paul's body and ran along his nerves. "You like this? You want more?"

"Yes." The ache in Paul's belly made it hard to think, but God, did he want more! "Yes, please."

Simon licked his cock, a stroke of heat up the side of his shaft. Paul gasped. That hot tongue found him again, swirling around the head, probing. Then Paul's dick slipped into firm, tight wetness. He was sucked deep, licked up and back. He felt Simon shift one hand to cup his butt cheek, and saw the other hand move to Simon's own jutting erection. Simon lifted his mouth off Paul's cock and traveled lower, nudging his thighs apart. He kissed Paul's balls, one side then the other, mouthing at the furry orbs with a gentle plucking of lips that made Paul shudder. All the heat in his body was rushing downward to his groin. Dimly, Paul knew he was whimpering, making small needy noises, but his voice was beyond his control now. He tugged at Simon's hair, desperate, wanting.

Simon's lips closed over his shaft again and took him in. Paul shoved forward without thinking and sank deep in that welcoming heat. He took up a rhythm by instinct, and when he realized he was thrusting and tried to stop, Simon's grip on his ass urged him deeper. Simon's mouth was expert, firm vibrating pressure and the glide of soft tongue in just the right places.

Paul's vision tunneled darkly as prickles of heat spread through his thighs and groin. *Almost. God, please.* Then he came in Simon's willing mouth. As his balls emptied themselves, he went dizzy, blinded with the rush, jolted by electric pulses of climax. He flailed with his free hand and encountered a rail on the wall, where he hung on desperately, shaking. *Holy shit.*

Simon sucked him more softly, drawing out the sensations, teasing little aftershocks from Paul's pleasure-blind body. As his climax eased down, Simon released him, then pushed his heavy dark head into Paul's thigh, nose buried in the crease of his groin. Breathing harshly, Simon worked his fist on himself hard, fast, faster, and groaned softly. Then there was only the water flowing quietly over them, muffling the sound of their shuddering breaths, washing the sweet-chlorine smell of cum from their skin.

Gently, Simon kissed Paul's thigh, his hip, his belly. He stood and folded Paul into his arms without words. Paul felt so good, standing there and being held. He let his head fall against Simon's shoulder and didn't think. *Don't think. Just feel, just be.* The relaxed, satisfied hum of his body was like nothing he remembered before. He felt like he could sleep for a year, or maybe run far and fast.

Finally, he said, "That was…"

Simon nipped at his neck. "You say nice, and I'll have to punish you."

Paul laughed, almost a sob. "No, 'nice' wasn't the word I was thinking."

Simon tightened his arms around him comfortingly, then let him go with a warm smile. He handed Paul the soap. "Here, you might need this. Again."

Paul lathered and washed, wincing at his almost painful sensitivity. He had never come three times in one evening before, although that first solo effort dimmed in memory now. He'd never come this hard ever, never had a warm solid body close to him afterward in silent companionship. Everything with Simon was entirely different. Maybe too much so.

The water turned cold, and Simon reached past him to shut it off. "Come on, get out and get dry. I don't want you getting cold after I did my best to get you hot."

The bathroom outside the shower stall was steamy. Simon passed him an outsized towel, and Paul wrapped himself in the terrycloth, covered from neck to shins. Despite the luxury, he shivered, and then felt Simon's hands on him, rubbing his back, drying him. He shrugged irritably. "Don't."

Simon stepped away to give him room and concentrated on drying his own hair, face averted. Eventually, without looking at Paul, he asked, "Are you all right?"

"Of course! No. I don't know."

Simon chuckled softly. "That covers the spectrum."

"Don't laugh at me!"

"Hey." Simon raised his hands calmingly, letting his towel slide to the floor. "Not laughing."

They stared at each other, Paul muffled in terrycloth, Simon unabashedly nude. Paul looked away. In the steam-fogged mirror, Simon's rear view was a brown blur. The tiny, dark bathroom window lurked behind a solid blind. The light bar over the sink shone too bright; their breathing echoed against too-white tiles. Paul reached for the door.

Simon, closer to the handle, swung the door to let him out into the dark hallway. The air seemed cleaner, free of steam and the scent of heated skin. *That outdoorsy woods and musk scent's not an aftershave, it's the way his skin smells.* Paul took a few steps away from the bathroom.

"The door on the right is the bedroom." From the timbre of Simon's voice, he was still standing in the bathroom, unmoving. "I have extra clothes if you want some."

Slowly, Paul turned right and went in. He was surprised to find Simon's private space scrupulously clean and neat, dominated by a king-sized bed in dark wood. *Don't look at the bed.* A polished dresser stood against one wall, a nightstand flanked the bed, and thin blue drapes curtained a large window. The polished oak floor, bare except for a braided rug, was cool under Paul's bare feet.

Simon passed Paul, still naked, and opened the top drawer of the dresser. He rummaged around, pulled out a pair of boxers and tossed them at Paul, who was too slow to stop them dropping at his feet. "Those are new. You're welcome to them, although they may fall off your skinny ass." Simon pulled on a pair of shorts of his own, eyes still guardedly not meeting Paul's. He walked over to the bed and sat on the edge. After a moment he looked up carefully and patted the comforter beside him. "Come and sit."

"It's late." Paul picked up the underwear and pulled them on, keeping the towel around him. "I should go."

"You should talk to me." Simon's tone was more uncertain than Paul had ever heard him. "Because I'm getting scared that I hurt you or frightened you or grossed you out, or something."

"No!" Paul didn't want to suggest that. He met Simon's eyes quickly. "No, that was… it's never felt like that. You were amazing."

"But…"

"I don't know. It's just too much, too fast. I don't have friends and I don't have sex and I don't think I'm gay, bi, whatever, and suddenly it's all three of those together."

"Is that so bad?"

"Not bad, but really different. Like I'm someone I don't recognize."

"Someone who's going to eat more food?" Simon teased gently.

Paul almost laughed. "Yeah, maybe. Who knows?"

"Come on then." Simon stood and pulled on a black sweatshirt from a chair by the bed. "If you need space, you've got it. Go get your clothes on. But I'm going to make you breakfast before you go."

Paul blinked and looked at his naked wrist. No watch. There was a clock by the bed, though. "It's two AM. Who the hell eats breakfast at two AM?"

"Someone who didn't eat any fucking dinner?" Simon suggested, cocking his head to one side and eyeing Paul challengingly.

"I ate…" Had he? He couldn't remember. Housework, laundry, sitting down at the computer. He'd bought lots of food. Surely he'd eaten some of it?

"I rest my case. You know where the kitchen is when you're dressed."

When Paul did finally reach the bottom of the stairs, he hesitated. He wore slightly sticky jeans over borrowed underwear, damp sneakers over bare feet, dirty shorts and wet socks wadded up in his hand. He could go out to his truck and leave. But an enticing smell of bacon wafted from the kitchen, and anyway, Paul's pride wouldn't let him sneak out the back door. Or even out the front.

Simon glanced up as Paul appeared in the kitchen. "There you are. Coffee's hot." He gestured at a bar stool pulled up to the counter. "Park it there."

Paul walked over slowly, hooked the chair out with one foot, and sat. Simon slid a mug down the counter to him, then tossed a big Ziploc after it.

"Stow your laundry in there," he said casually, as if men sat down at his table with cum-smeared shorts every day of the week. *Maybe they did.* Paul frowned, while doing as he was told. Simon lifted a last strip of bacon out of the pan onto a plate and set the food in front of Paul.

Leaning against the counter, he lifted his own mug, sipped, then gazed ruefully at Paul over the edge. "This is a little weird for me too."

"How? You *are* gay."

"Yes. But you're the first guy I've ever had in my own house. Usually I keep my sex life separate from my regular life. I do hit-and-run sex, and occasional fuck-buddies, but nothing that might get caught up in my real world."

"So what am I?"

"I don't know. Trouble, probably." Simon sighed and hauled another stool close enough to sit. "I like you. I like you a whole lot, and I want you even more than that. If I was smart, I would never have touched you. Because my real life's a mess, and the last thing I need is to have someone I care about mixed up in it. But somehow, I'm not smart around you."

Paul worked through this, feeling warm and scared at the same time. He dodged the personal and settled for asking, "How is your real life a mess?"

Simon shook his head. "I can't tell you."

"Is it your family?"

"Yeah. I probably should warn you. Some of them like to make trouble for me."

"Like that kid in the bowling alley?"

Simon laughed shortly. "Well, he'd like to. But I can handle Tommy, or any of the younger crowd. It's some of the others, my uncles." He was quiet for a minute. "Really, if *you* were going to be smart, you'd walk out my door and never look back. Although you would eat those eggs first, while they're hot, because I make awesome eggs."

Paul took a bite obediently. The eggs were good, hot and fluffy and salted. The bacon was crisp but not burned, just the way he liked it. Suddenly ravenous, he dug into the food, considering.

"If I do walk out the door," he said eventually, "it won't be because your family drove me off." He chewed his toast, and added, "After all, how much trouble can they make? I gather you work for the family business, and they could probably mess up your career, but what could they do to me? Boycott my clinic?"

Simon frowned, and his gray-green eyes looked darker. "They won't mess with your work. They're not like that. But if they decide you really are getting in the way, they might… hurt you."

"What?" Paul laughed. "Like the Mafia? Break my kneecaps?"

"No." Simon looked uneasy. "Forget I said anything but just… if this middle-aged big guy, six-four, muscles, blond hair, big nose, comes up to you somewhere, be as polite as you can and then get the hell out of there. And call me."

Paul stopped smiling, worried by Simon's tone. "One of your uncles?'

"Karl. Likely you'll never meet him but he likes to hurt things." Simon stood restlessly. "Damn, I should never have gotten you involved with me. You should eat up and go."

Paul mopped the last of his eggs with the bread, and took his plate to the sink. But when he came back, he walked behind Simon and touched his arm. "Listen, I may be freaked to hell and gone, but I'm not giving up on you unless you really want me to."

Simon's body went tense under Paul's hand. "No. Fuck, no. Or should that be fuck, yes? There's no reason they should be interested in you. And God knows I want to see you again." He slid off the stool and stepped back. "Just, if we're ever out somewhere and I suddenly tell you to go home, flat out like that, will you do it with no questions asked?"

Paul blinked. He'd been inches from leaving and never coming back, but now he was damned if someone else was going to drive him off. But Simon sounded worried. "Yeah, I could do that."

"Good." Simon's eyes lightened. "Good man. I like a guy who can take directions." He led Paul to the door, grabbing his coat off the closet knob for him. "Here. Keep warm and get some sleep. Can I see you tomorrow, or should I call first?"

Suddenly, Paul's uncertainty made a comeback. "I don't know."

"Okay." Simon opened the door. His eyes drifted to Paul's mouth, like he was thinking about a kiss, but he didn't make the move. "We'll see how it goes."

Paul stumbled, heading down the drive to his truck in the biting chill of Minnesota winter. The seat was cold, the engine protested at being asked to turn over. *How long was I inside?* As he sat waiting for the engine to warm up, looking at the house, he saw the kitchen light go out, and minutes later the bedroom went dark. Up there, Simon was sliding his warm, muscular body under the blue comforter on the bed. Paul knew that however complicated Simon's life was, he couldn't be as confused as Paul was right now. But as much as Paul's mind scrambled for traction, his body hummed in contented warmth. *How the hell did I get myself into this?* Just a week ago, his life had been simple. *But bleak and cold as a Minnesota winter.*

Chapter 8

The woodworking room of the cabinetry shop had a unique smell of fresh lumber and sawdust, of stain and oil. From the next room, the hum and buzz of power-tools and shouted conversation outside the doorway faded slowly into a background blur. Simon let the normalcy of that soak into him as he worked. There were no windows in here and the air was warm, like a den. The ventilator fan hummed smoothly. Simon liked doing fancy handwork. He could keep busy and not think.

He startled out of a daze when a hand touched his wrist. Jerking away, he spun around, then controlled himself at the sight of Alfred stepping back with his hands out and empty. The sound of tools and voices from the front workroom suddenly recrystallized in his hearing, like a radio switching back on.

"Jumpy, aren't you, boy?" Alfred said.

Simon shrugged. Alfred had been at the meet. He could figure it out.

"Take a break," Alfred told him, waving toward the door of the workshop. "Go for a run or something. Get your head back into your work."

"I'm fine." Simon turned back to his sanding, but his boss reached out and stopped him.

"If that panel was meant to be sanded flat, we wouldn't have put the carved relief-work on it."

Simon looked down. The area of the cabinet door that he was finish-sanding was definitely flatter than the last three he had done, and his hand was cramping around the sandpaper. "Shit," he muttered, opening his fingers stiffly.

"Exactly. That's going to have to be redone from scratch. If you need to be elsewhere, go, but don't screw up the job."

"Sorry, boss." Simon liked Alfred. The older werewolf had headed the carpentry unit for more than forty years, and he was one of the few who'd supported Simon in the early days. In fact, he'd volunteered to take Simon on, when Gordon had been looking for a safe, supervised job while Simon's fate hung in the balance. Alfred would do the right thing when he could, though he didn't make waves. He certainly didn't deserve to have Simon ruining his careful work. Simon laid his tools aside and stretched, eyes down in submission.

"Listen." Alfred put a hand on his arm. "Almost no one at that meet believed Cory. I mean, that boy's so angry these days his truth and lies are hard to read, but between the two of you, I don't think anyone could miss whose word was better. Not even Karl. If he'd really thought you broke oath, he wouldn't have arranged a fight. He would have dragged your carcass in and laid you at Gordon's feet."

Maybe that's what he planned. "Someone should get Cory away from Karl. He's ruining that boy. Telling lies in front of Gordon and the whole pack is damn near suicidal."

"Gordon questioned the boy, afterward. He decided that Cory was more likely deluded than lying. The kid actually believes you did something, although he can't or won't say what."

Simon shook his head. Lying to a werewolf was hard. Acute senses picked up small changes in heart rate, increased sweating, dilated pupils, scent. Lying to your Alpha, who had a presence in your head, was even harder. A kid like Cory shouldn't be capable of it.

"That's not possible," Simon protested. "I've been under oath for ten years now, and Cory's what, sixteen? I haven't been within ten feet of him or alone in a room with him in all that time. If I'd ever so much as touched him casually, it would've been before he was six." When Alfred sighed, Simon's eyes widened. "Damn it, he doesn't… what kind of sick fuck does he think I am?"

"Cory has problems. And Karl certainly isn't making them better. You need to steer clear of both of them. Gordon knows your word is good."

"I'm not sure that's enough anymore. Do we have anyone who can talk to Cory, help him out? The kid's losing it." Wolves didn't tend toward the healing professions. Quick tempers, and a tendency to regard weakness as an opportunity for advancement, were common. And wolves didn't do well around fresh blood, so medical training was out.

"I don't know anyone," Alfred said heavily. "Cory's dad thinks he's fine. Just hot-headed, you know. Stewart would like to see Cory grow up to be like Karl. He approves of the mentoring."

"Karl is using the boy. He'll mentor him right into the incinerator." Simon could've killed Cory as easily as he'd broken his leg in that fight, if he had chosen to. He looked Alfred in the eye. "How did we end up like this? Waiting for Karl to take over and top us all, with no alternatives and no control?"

"I've begun to wonder," Alfred admitted. He glanced toward the other workroom and apparently decided the whine of power tools was enough cover. He lowered his voice. "The last twenty years have been bad for the pack. We lost half of our upper ranks, the ones who might've reined in or Challenged Karl. Your parents' car was hit by the train, Lucien fell off a cliff, Oscar drowned, Derek was caught in that fire, and finally Arthur in the plane crash. For a tough species, we've been dropping like flies. We're left with old men and youngsters, and the low ranks between them. And Karl moved up four times in the aftermath."

Simon blinked. "You think..."

Alfred looked away. "I think we're no more noble than most of the human race, and some of us are just as ruthless and ambitious. Karl has always been our fixer and enforcer. If anyone could arrange accidents, while keeping his hands clean, it would be Karl. The wolves we have left are those he can dominate."

"Karl has to hold the pack, though," Simon protested. "If he scares everyone off, he'll be left Alpha of nothing. There are other packs and other tough wolves out there that the pack could appeal to."

"He has more support than you'd think. Some of the old wolves think he'll bring back the good old days of dominance and submission, and proper respect for your elders and betters. Some of the young wolves like the way he takes them out at night, not just to run but to hunt and howl, close enough to humans to feel a thrill. He encourages them to fight too. They get to give in to their wolf instincts rather than learn to master them. Makes me glad my son Geoff is far away, much as I hated seeing him go."

Geoff was unusual among the werewolves, a quiet boy with a passion for music. His horn could sing better than any wolf at moonrise, and he wrote weird eerie pieces for woodwinds and strings. He'd wanted Julliard, and managed to get accepted. Letting him go out of the pack had been cause for a long, acrimonious meeting. Simon, still in the closet back then, had supported any relaxing of pack custom and rules. He'd been on the team which found a pack near the school that would take the boy in and encouraged him to go. He probably owed some of Alfred's support to that.

"What do we do?" Simon asked. "Go after Karl with a shotgun?" He bit his tongue hard, almost unable to believe he'd said that. Threatening to kill the pack Second with human weapons was treason, almost sacrilege. But Alfred didn't look shocked.

"Almost worth it. Except there's no proof he's done anything to justify it yet. And then there's the problem of Karl being so dominant, body and will, over all of us except Gordon. I don't think any of us could look him in the eye and pull a trigger on him. Our wolves wouldn't let us."

"I could."

"Truly?" Alfred's light gray eyes bored into his own.

"Yes." Simon met that gaze, although he had to fight not to look down, not to turn aside. He raised his chin and realized he was holding back a growl.

Alfred was the one who finally blinked. "I've always had a feeling you're not as submissive as you pretend to be. But I'm not convinced you're up to Karl's weight yet."

Simon looked away and nodded. Tackling Karl sounded good when he said it, but his wolf wasn't convinced either.

Alfred punched him lightly in the arm. "Get out of here, boy. Go run or something. Come back when you're ready to fix that door panel you were wrecking."

§ § § §

Hours later, Simon ducked in the door of the North End Veterinary Clinic as the receptionist let the last client out.

"Oh, sir, excuse me but we're closing," she said, continuing to hold the door.

"That's okay." Simon held up his brown paper bag. "I brought Thai food for the doc. Hey, they gave me an extra fortune cookie too." He dug in the sack, pulled one out, and held it out to her.

The gray-haired woman eyed him doubtfully, but she let the door close as she took the cellophane wrapper.

Simon cocked his head at her. "Well, come on, let's see your fortune."

"You were here before," she said, holding the cookie package loosely in her fingers. "But I don't remember your pet."

Simon wasn't about to remind her. "I'm a friend of Dr. Hunter's. I was here the other day. My name's Simon."

"Oh, yes." She gave him the uncertain smile of someone trying to place an acquaintance, then the smile became more real as she obviously let it go. She ripped open the cellophane and pulled out the folded cookie. "The doctor's in the back, but it'll be a while before he's done."

"I'm in no rush." Simon nodded toward the cookie. "What does it say? Are you going to meet a short, dark, handsome stranger?" He waggled his eyebrows at her.

She laughed, and read. "*The world is stranger and more beautiful than you know.*"

Simon coughed.

"*What* did you say?" Paul asked as he came around the corner.

The receptionist waved her hand. "Fortune cookie."

"Ah."

"I think that one was meant for you," Simon said lightly. He knew he was staring. *I'd forgotten how beautiful he is.* Attraction hit him again, seeing this man suddenly appear. Wolf and human, he wanted to be at Paul's side. He settled for a grin, and waved the bag. "Thai food. Get it while it's hot."

Paul stared at him. "What are you doing here?"

Simon shrugged. "Delivering dinner?"

"Is everything okay, doc?" the receptionist asked, glancing back and forth between them.

"Huh?" Paul came back to himself with a start. "Yes, Elise, we're fine. I just wasn't expecting him." He smiled, although the amusement looked forced. "You can head out as soon as you've done the money and closed up. Simon, why don't you take the food back to my office and I'll join you in a few minutes."

The receptionist waited until Paul disappeared back into the clinic and then turned to Simon. "Are you really just bringing him dinner?"

"Don't you think he needs to be fed?"

"Well, yes. The doctor doesn't take real good care of himself, but…"

"So it's up to his friends to fix that." Simon waved the sack. "Cream cheese rolls, egg rolls, ginger fried rice, Pad Thai, Broccoli Delight, Sweet Basil Noodles. I got everything mild. I don't think our doctor is a spicy-food fan."

"Um, I guess not. The office is back there." She pointed.

"I know. I can find it," Simon said cheerfully. "Have a good night."

In the office, he let the cheerful smile go as he pulled out the food and arranged the containers on the desk. Savory odors rose, making his mouth water, but his stomach churned. Maybe he should've called first, before just walking in. This had seemed clever, an hour ago. Now it seemed… pushy. And he'd promised not to push.

He caught the sound of Paul's footsteps in the hallway in time to arrange himself in a chair before the vet appeared. Paul leaned in the doorway, his pose casual, but every line of his body reading tense and unhappy to Simon.

"Were you under the impression someone called for takeout?" Paul asked thinly.

Simon shrugged. "You have to eat; I have to eat. I was in the mood for Thai, and I didn't want to eat alone."

"And that's all this is? Just the two of us sharing a meal, and then you'll pick up and go?"

"If that's what you want. You know what I want, but you're driving this bus. If nothing else, I wanted to know that you ate a good dinner, and I wanted to see you. Stuff your face here and I'll go away happy. But don't waste the food. It's too good."

Paul moved slowly to his chair and sat. "Where did you go?"

"Sweet Basil," Simon told him, opening a container and holding out a cream cheese roll. "They're down in Brooklyn Park, but the food's really good and cheap."

Paul took the crisp golden roll, fingers carefully not touching Simon's, and bit into the end absently. The taste widened his eyes and he took a second big bite. "Mm. Not bad." He opened another waxed container curiously. "You drove an hour round trip to bring me Thai food?"

"Well, I figure I'll eat two thirds of this."

Paul stayed silent as they opened and divided the food. Simon handed Paul chopsticks with a challenging look. Paul responded by expertly winding basil noodles around the tips and popping them in his mouth. Simon relaxed a fraction and directed his attention to the egg rolls.

"So," Paul said after they'd both made inroads into their food, "I don't suppose you happen to know why a girl showed up here from Tam's Bakery at ten this morning, and delivered muffins?"

"Maybe you have a secret admirer. Was she a cute girl?"

"I didn't see her. I was in surgery. But my receptionist informed me that she said the doctor was to eat at least two of them."

"Someone thinks you don't eat enough."

"What is this? Do you have a thing for sumo wrestlers?"

"*Moi*?" Simon smiled. "Maybe I just want to be sure you keep your strength up." His eyes met Paul's, and for a moment the heat between them was a palpable thing. Simon broke the gaze, and busily chased the last shrimp around the container with his chopsticks.

"Is this what you call giving me space?"

"I don't know," Simon admitted to his box full of broccoli. "I don't know how to do this. I'm used to going after what I want. I've never courted someone before. When you do bar pickups there's no time to be subtle."

"How many…" Paul's voice broke off, and when Simon looked up Paul's face was red and his eyes darted away from Simon's.

"How many men have I been with?"

"You don't have to answer that. It's none of my business."

"Sure it is. But the simple answer is, I haven't kept count. I've hit the bars when I felt the urge, sometimes once a week, more often not for months at a time. Most guys were one-night stands, or more likely one hour, but I've been with three guys over the years who were fuck-buddies. Never a real lover, though. No one that was more than just fun."

"Oh." Paul sounded subdued.

"Hey," Simon said softly, trying to hit the right note. "No one recently. No one else now."

Paul picked up a piece of chicken and chewed slowly. "Okay. About one guy a month for how many years? That makes…"

"You don't want the number," Simon said quickly. "Seriously, it has nothing to do with you and me."

"Come on. Can't be that many. I mean how precocious were you?"

"I didn't have to be precocious. I'm older than you."

Paul stared at him. "No way."

"Yeah." One downside to being wolf was being carded for decades.

"I'm older than I look," Paul said.

"So am I. Look, your age is no secret, right? Four years of college, four years of vet school, two years in practice, makes you twenty-eight or so."

"Twenty-seven."

"Well, I'm thirty-three." When Paul just stared at him, Simon smiled wryly, took out his wallet, extracted his driver's license, and flipped it across the desk.

Paul eyed the front suspiciously. "Okay. Date of birth?"

"July first 1977," Simon said complacently. "Graduated high school in '95. Shall I tell you the top forty songs from that year?"

Paul slid his license back to him, an unreadable expression on his face.

"What?" Simon asked cautiously.

Paul smiled. "That's good."

"It is?"

"Yeah. The other way felt weird. There you were, so much younger than me with so much more experience and knowledge; it felt like I was stupid or pathetic. I like you much better as the older guy. But God, you look barely twenty-one. You're going to be carded until you turn gray."

"Good genetics," Simon said smugly. *If you only knew. But thank God you don't.* He pushed the thought away from him. "Tell me, do you kiss older guys?"

"You said this was just dinner."

"Do you go to hockey games with older guys?"

"What?" Paul blinked at him.

"You told me you like hockey, right?" Simon pulled the tickets out of his pocket. "Gophers against University of Wisconsin tomorrow night. Should be a good game. Starts at seven-thirty."

Paul stared at him. "I don't close the clinic until seven."

"So we'll be a little late."

"Is this like a date?"

"Not much like one. Not at a hockey game. That's a bad place to try to be out and proud. I just figured we'd have fun."

Paul's laugh was a little strangled. "Do you ever quit?"

"Winners never quit, and quitters never get fucked. So, yes or no to hockey?"

"What if I say no?"

"I can find someone who wants the tickets," Simon said easily. "They're on the blue line. Good view. I work with seven other guys, a couple of whom have kids."

"Why wouldn't you take someone else to the game?"

Simon sighed. "What part of 'I want to spend time with you' didn't you understand?"

Paul rubbed his forehead wearily. "I don't understand any of this. God, I'm tired."

"Do you want me to go now?"

Paul looked up at him, and his eyes were hot. "I want you to kiss me. I just don't freaking want to want that."

Simon sat frozen, said nothing, did nothing. After a long moment, Paul got up and came around the desk. He reached out a hand that wasn't quite steady and traced Simon's lips with one finger. Simon held on to his control and sat still, didn't kiss that wandering fingertip. Paul traced Simon's jaw, and moved up into his hair. Slowly, he bent down and fit his mouth to Simon's.

The touch was like electricity, arcing from Simon's mouth through his body. He suppressed his reaction, keeping the kiss light, opening his lips a little. Then Paul's hand tightened in his hair, and Paul's tongue headed for Simon's tonsils. Simon twisted up out of his seat, still open to the demanding kiss. He grabbed for Paul's hips, pulling their bodies together. The heat of Paul's wiry body against his quickly had him achingly hard, and he tried not to make that obvious even as he closed his arms tighter.

After a moment Paul broke the kiss, panting. "Shit."

"What?"

"Kissing you still feels like nothing else on earth. I thought maybe it wouldn't feel so good this time."

"Good is bad," Simon murmured, still holding their hips together, feeling the press of Paul's hard flesh against his belly. *Good to know it's not just me.* "I think I'm getting the hang of this. Can we be bad some more?"

Paul pulled free, although he was laughing. "You're nuts."

"Crazy Simon, they call me." Simon sobered. That was almost too true.

"Is it always like that?"

"Is which what?"

"Sex with… other men. Is it always that, um, intense?"

"Depends on who you're with," Simon said, keeping his voice light. "Good sex can be really hot, yeah, and intense. Bad sex is more uncomfortable and less satisfying than Internet porn and a bottle of baby oil. I've done both kinds, and a lot in between."

"What kind is this?" Paul's voice was almost inaudible.

"Don't you know?" He took hold of Paul's jaw and forced those gold eyes to meet his own. "This is different. This is the first time that just kissing someone makes me ache until I can't breathe. I want you, but not only in bed and not just for a night. This isn't like anything I've done before."

Too damned true. He wasn't sure why. Maybe because his wolf was somehow there on the edges, approving each time he touched Paul, breathing the scent of that clean male skin with an odd echo of satisfaction. For the first time, every part of him, man and wolf, seemed to be involved. *Meeting Paul first in wolf form probably skewed my reactions. Maybe that's why I can't seem to stay away from him.*

He let go of Paul. For him, it probably *was* just the hot sex. After all, the next best experience he'd had to compare them to was "*nice.*"

Simon put his light smile back on. "Now I'm going to kiss you for a while, and then I'm going to let you get back to all the work I'm interrupting. Tomorrow I'll pick you up after closing and we'll go see hockey."

Paul raised an eyebrow. "Really?"

"Oh, yeah." Simon pulled him hard into another kiss. No soft and restrained shit now. He used every move he knew while keeping his hands above the belt and their clothes on. When he paused for breath, Paul was glassy-eyed and his mouth was reddened and full.

"I'm not having sex with you in my office," Paul said breathlessly. "I'm just not."

"Of course not." Simon let him go abruptly and stepped back. He glanced at the mess on the desk. "I cooked, you can do the dishes. See you tomorrow, sugar." He got some satisfaction from the vision, out of the corner of his eye, of Paul holding the edge of the desk tightly and breathing hard.

I can do this. He walked out, keeping his stride loose and jaunty. He knew all about tactical retreats, though his body was not happy with him. He would run the tension off as a wolf tonight, and plan for tomorrow.

Chapter 9

Paul eyed the arena crowd with amusement. Minnesota college hockey fans were out in every shade of maroon and gold. Not that there was anything wrong with supporting your local team. After all, he'd graduated from the U of M vet school— he'd been known to cheer for many varieties of athletic Gophers. But too often the team colors, when rendered in fabric, became yellow and purple, and that was just…

"Do you think she realizes," he whispered to Simon, "she looks like a giant Easter egg?" The middle-aged lady in question wore faded striped sweats that banded her torso in something closer to lavender than maroon.

Simon snorted. "Yeah. Check out that guy." A man old enough to have grandchildren in university had his face painted with M's and a very large, stuffed Goldie Gopher on his hat. "That's dedication."

The hockey game had broken open by now, late in the third period. Up by four goals, the Minnesota team was coasting, and Paul had moved on to people-watching. He hadn't realized how much more fun it was when there was someone to share his thoughts with. "How did we ever end up as the Gophers, anyway? I mean, what kind of mascot is that? Small harmless rodents. Even a badger would eat us for a snack as we ran away squeaking."

"Could be worse," Simon whispered back. "After all, Goldie's really a chipmunk, if you want to get technical. Our team could be the Chipper Chipmunks."

The horn blew, signaling the end of the game. Fans rose to applaud as the teams circled to center ice to shake hands. Simon turned to Paul. "Fight the crowds to get out faster, or sit here and wait for the aisles to thin out?"

"I'm in no rush." Paul didn't want to move yet. Being out with Simon was fun, given the presence of an arena full of chaperones to keep it from becoming something more. Throughout the game, he'd been uncomfortably aware of Simon's warm body beside him, and he wasn't sure where he wanted the evening to go from here. A backlog of work waiting at the clinic could be used as an excuse to cut the night short, but the aching heat in his groin urged otherwise. He couldn't decide if he was being cautious or freaking cowardly.

The river of fans slowly crept up the stairs past their seats, heading for the exit. Paul didn't notice when the stream ground to a halt, but Simon surged to his feet. Paul stood up too and was startled when Simon clenched a fist on his sleeve, dragging him halfway behind Simon's body. Paul looked at the group of men who'd bucked traffic in the aisles and now filled the row in front of them.

"Karl," Simon said in an emotionless voice to the tallest of them.

Paul looked at the man. Big, blond, middle-aged, nose… check. The man's eyes were locked on Simon's, and to Paul's surprise after a moment Simon looked down, almost a bow of the head.

"Simon. What a surprise to see you here. I wouldn't have thought you were the type for sports."

"What, all those big muscled guys in uniform?" Simon said lightly. "How could I not be?"

Karl's mouth twisted. A young blond boy behind him, maybe a son or cousin, grabbed at Karl's arm. "Why are we even talking to him?" the boy asked fiercely. Karl turned swiftly. Paul couldn't see the older man's expression, but the boy let go instantly and backed up two steps, mumbling apologies.

Karl turned back to Paul and Simon. "Are you going to introduce us to your friend?"

"Wasn't planning on it." Paul could feel Simon tense and vibrating, like an engine revved up but not unleashed.

"Introduce us, Simon," the other older man said coldly.

Paul expected another refusal, but Simon said, "Paul, these are my uncles Karl and Frank, and my cousins Zach, George, and Cory."

Paul looked at the men. There wasn't much family resemblance. Karl and Frank were both big and blond, but Karl looked Scandinavian while Frank was built wider, craggier, and less fair-skinned. Zach was small and tanned but his tones were more Mediterranean olive than Simon's bronze. George was All-American, light-brown hair, fair and blue-eyed, while Cory looked like a younger version of Frank but with narrower features. Only the way they stood and moved suggested kinship. Paul had noticed the fluid grace and power that Simon brought to everything he did. *Noticed and appreciated.* To a greater or lesser degree, all these men moved like that, totally comfortable in their skins, with muscle to back it up. Even Cory, who looked about fourteen, was more jacked than most high school kids.

Normally Paul would've acknowledged an introduction by shaking hands, but neither Simon's bulk in front of him nor the men's expressions encouraged that. He settled for inclining his head a little. "Gentlemen."

The man Simon had called Frank caught Paul with a cold gaze, his pale blue eyes boring into Paul's. Paul fought the inclination to look away and eventually raised an eyebrow. *Can I help you?*

Frank's eyes narrowed. "Might not want to hang around our Simon too much. Doesn't look good, with him being a fag and all."

Paul blinked, startled. *What the hell was that?* He wondered if he was supposed to get mad or run away screaming. He wondered what kind of uncle said something like that about his nephew in public to a stranger.

He tried a dismissive shrug.

"You do know, *Paul*," Frank said harshly, "that the guy you're with would rather fuck those hockey players than watch them skate."

Paul recoiled, anger heating in his gut. Was this what Simon had to put up with at those family meetings? Treated like being gay was some kind of plague he might pass around? Like it meant Simon couldn't be around athletic guys without wanting to have sex with them? He glanced back at the rink, where the last players were clearing off the ice.

He saw Frank follow his gaze and felt the big man's sour satisfaction. Suddenly he really wanted to shake the bastard out of his complacency.

"You're kidding!" Paul said with assumed horror. For a moment most of the men looked pleased, although Karl narrowed his eyes speculatively. Paul turned to Simon. "Honey, if you're not getting enough at home you don't have to run after hockey players. I'm sure the boss would give me more time off." He batted his eyelashes at Simon and smiled narrowly in satisfaction as Frank choked and backed up a step.

"Jesus," the kid George said with disgust. "You're one of them!"

Karl didn't visibly react, except to look more intently at Paul. "Are you living in Simon's house?"

Simon shouldered Paul back farther, out from under his uncle's eye. "No, he's not. Was there anything else you wanted?"

Karl stared back at Simon, until once again Simon made that odd gesture of looking down. "Not yet," Karl said coldly. He made his way out of the seats toward the aisle, with the others following. Zach, the last of the youngsters to pass them, looked at Simon as if he would add a comment. At Simon's fierce glare, he in turn dropped his eyes and moved on by.

Simon stayed in front of Paul, watching, until the men had vanished into the thinning crowd. Then he let out a breath and turned to Paul with a wry smile. "I apologize on behalf of most of my family for the bad manners of some of my family."

"They're a charming bunch. So friendly, too." He choked a laugh. "I can't believe I said that to your Uncle Frank."

Simon began laughing too. "Neither could I. It was perfect, though. Did you see his face? God, I love you!" He stopped on an intake of breath and stared intently, frozen, their shoulders touching. After a moment he dropped his eyes from Paul's in the same odd submissive gesture he'd used to his uncles. "I'm sorry. I shouldn't have said that. Wrong place, wrong time."

Paul's mind raced like a hamster in a wheel, looking for a way out that didn't involve admitting he'd heard any of that. In the end all he could do was pretend. "Can you drop me back at the clinic?" he asked brightly. "I dumped all my charts and records on my desk so we could get here sooner. I have a couple of hours work to do yet tonight."

Simon nodded silently.

They slowly worked their way out to the street. The air outside was almost pleasant, with new snow falling in big fat flakes. The stone buildings of the university looked like a Currier-and-Ives painting, capped with lines of pristine white on every ledge and outcropping. They'd arrived late and had to park in the farthest lot. Paul walked beside Simon, trying not to notice his warm bulk, his easy stride.

Other hockey fans shared the sidewalk, voices raised in cheerful recap of the game. Once, Paul hit a patch of ice hidden by the fresh snow cover. Simon grabbed his elbow with a strong hand to keep him from a spill. The instant he was steady, Simon let go even before Paul could break free. Paul muttered a thank you, feeling that touch as if it still lingered.

The ride home in Simon's truck was dark and quiet. Which felt odd, because Simon was so seldom quiet. Paul had gotten used to the easy flow of talk, the warm, inconsequential and uncensored chatter that Simon shared with him, which made him free to comment in return. He wanted to say something, to jumpstart the conversation, get them back on familiar footing. But when he opened his mouth, what came out was, "You can't fall in love with someone in five days!"

"Okay." Simon's tone was flat.

"No, really," Paul insisted. "I mean, how much can you know about me at this point? I could be a serial killer. Neighbors always say they were nice, quiet young men. Or I might be a total slob, or a Republican, or pick my nose at the table, or, or something you'll really hate."

"Like a disco fan?" Simon asked, sounding more like himself.

"Yeah. Well, not that, that's really gross."

Simon sighed instead of laughing. "Paul, I've seen you at work and at play. I've spent hours with you. I think I know the basics. Sure, you could have bad habits that will drive me nuts, but that's not the point. I'm sorry if my saying… that… upset you, and you have a right to tell me to back off. But you can't tell me how to feel."

"But I might not even be into men, not really." *Even if sex with you was amazing. Maybe those were just the wrong girls. I put on a show for Uncle Frank, because I hate bullies, not because—*

"Doesn't matter. I've told you this isn't just about sex, the way I feel when I'm with you."

"I don't want to talk about it," Paul said perversely. "Can we drop the subject, please?"

To his annoyance, Simon didn't protest or even remind him that he'd brought it up. He just said, "Sure," in that same flat voice. Which left Paul feeling like the bad guy. But what did Simon expect? If you hit on a straight guy, probably straight guy, make him all mixed up, how can you expect him to be thrilled by a declaration of love five days later? And not even something sweet and romantic on purpose. More like a stealth declaration. Not that Paul wanted sweet and romantic, of course. Not that he knew what the fuck he did want.

The rest of the drive was long and strained. Simon stopped at the door of the clinic. He didn't get out of the truck, or even look at Paul directly. Paul slid out and hesitated, still holding the inside handle of the passenger door. He should say something. He'd enjoyed the hockey game, and he didn't want Simon to go away mad, but he didn't want to be too encouraging either. Eventually Simon said, "You're letting the snow in on the seat."

Paul shut the door with a bang. *All right then.* He turned to the clinic door, pulling out his keys. Behind him the truck engine idled. As he got the door open, he heard the truck window power down and Simon said quietly, "Will you call me?"

"Sure," Paul answered without turning around. The big tires crunched on the snow behind him, and then were gone. Paul felt lighter, and colder. The wind dropped wet flakes down his neck as he headed inside to his work.

§ § § §

Opening up the clinic next morning, in the frigid dark before midwinter's laggard dawn, was not Paul's favorite thing. A good night's sleep would've helped, but he'd had nightmares every time he drifted off— locked in a bare cupboard with a bright white light burning, and he called and screamed but no one came. Or drowning in cold water that slowly closed over his sinking head and no one would help him. Waking gasping from one of those was all too familiar. He sometimes wondered why a nightmare didn't lose its power to hurt you after the fiftieth repetition. He didn't wonder why the bad dreams were back; it always happened when he was stressed, just to make the bad times more special.

When a man jumped out of a beat-up Volvo and hurried toward him out of the dark parking lot, Paul whirled in panic, his heart pounding. The man stopped and held out a box. Paul breathed easier. Maybe getting mugged wasn't going to be the added fucktastic start to his day.

"A guy paid me to give this to you," the scruffy man said. "For the thin guy in the blue coat who gets here early. That's you."

Paul reached out and took the box. The delivery guy hurried off without waiting for a tip. Paul looked at the container. The white shape was familiar, the Tam's Bakery sticker obvious. A scrawled black Sharpie note in an unfamiliar curved feminine hand said, "The round filled ones are lemon." The sweet golden aroma of fresh donuts rose from the box.

Paul had to laugh, as he juggled box, bag, and keys, to let himself in. The gift bordered on stalking, but somehow didn't feel that way. If Simon had been waiting to make his own delivery, or if he'd put his own message on the box, that would've been too much. But this was barely on the warm side of uncomfortable. And damn it, he *had* skipped breakfast again, trying to eke out two more minutes of sleep.

He set the box on the table behind the reception desk, hesitated for a second, then took one. Not lemon-filled though. He didn't need the sensory reminder of lemon cream, of firm lips, and careful teeth, and soft probing tongue and… *shit!* He bit firmly into a cinnamon twist to erase the memory of lemon from his tongue.

The donuts turned out to be the last warm thing about his day. Every serious case he saw seemed to be trying to crash and burn on him. A diabetic cat they'd been struggling to regulate came in thin, dehydrated, and acidotic, with kidneys failing. The elderly owners made the hard choice to stop trying. Paul slipped the needle into a tiny collapsing vein on the cat's leg, and it passed almost instantly as the owners sobbed and held each other. Sarah, the technician, stowed the tiny body in the freezer for cremation. She had tears in her eyes, but she was covering the front desk and phone for Elise, who'd called in sick. There was no time to grieve.

A young Labrador came in with a broken leg. It seemed simple, until X-rays of the site showed a femur eaten away by bone cancer. The leg had broken while the dog was simply running in the yard because there was no normal bone left. At least that owner accepted a referral to the University Vet Hospital. Clinicians there would help the owner make the decision between amputation and euthanasia. Either way, the dog's chance of living out the year was not good.

Paul worked through lunch, ordering therapeutic pet foods, checking the drug log, updating the clinic website. Keeping busy was good. Especially doing things that engaged his brain enough to prevent thought. He called his weekend receptionist again and left another message asking her to come in, even just for an hour or two, to help Sarah. Then the afternoon clients began arriving.

He checked, vaccinated, swabbed, and medicated a series of routine cases. Then another young Lab appeared, with unsteady gait and vomiting. He figured she'd eaten something inappropriate. Take ten young vomiting Labs, and nine of them had eaten rotten food, dead mice, balls, shoes, rocks, sticks. Hell, he'd once had a Lab in for surgical removal of a pair of women's underwear. The real kicker had come when the wife picked the dog up at the end of the day, took one look at the retrieved fabric, and screamed that they weren't hers. Given that they were black and lacy, Paul figured the husband was in for a rough night.

And sure enough, this dog *had* eaten something. Unfortunately that something was antifreeze. The crystals were in the urine, the test kit popped a strong positive. There was an antidote, but it wasn't perfect and only worked early in the process. This owner said that the dog had been sleeping in the garage, where his old car was leaking. For the last four days she'd been getting sick and peeing in the house. Exposure had to have started days ago. Her kidney values were through the roof. Paul tried hard to push for intensive care and IV fluids elsewhere, anywhere else. There were several good referral centers in the area. She still had a small chance. But the heavyset, middle-aged man at the other end of the leash shook his head.

"I just got laid off, Doc," he said. "I don't even really got the money for today, but I had to try. I can't spend hundreds, maybe thousands, on a slim hope. Can you put her down easy for me?"

Paul could, and did. He couldn't argue with the choice. He just wished he could. He managed to do the job with a tourniquet on the leg, without calling Sarah in to hold the dog. She was having a hard enough day as it was.

By four o'clock, Sarah looked beat. Trying to do both the receptionist's job and her own, she was constantly running back and forth from the front desk to the treatment area. When a client failed to show up on time, Paul took the phone off the hook, put all the lines on hold, and sent her to take a few minutes down-time in the break room. He suggested she eat some of the damned lemon donuts. She gave him a slightly confused smile and took the offer.

While he was tending the desk, Mrs. Wickham came in the door with Pooky for her annual visit. He checked her in and led Pooky to the scale to be weighed. Two minutes later, Mrs. Wickham was bundling Pooky out the door, swearing never to set foot in his clinic again. Paul put his face in his hands. Maybe he had been less than diplomatic to suggest she was killing her beloved Pooky with food. Perhaps he shouldn't have compared the increasingly obese pug to a beachball. *No kidding.*

Not that Mrs. Wickham would be much missed, but she'd been a paying client. And she was the type to spread her displeasure far and wide. He rubbed his eyes, and hoped that very few of his other clients were her friends. Silently, he wrote "Going Elsewhere" in Pooky's file. When Sarah came up in time to greet the next client, he let her take over and went back to practice medicine where he belonged. Obviously he was a failure at interpersonal relationships.

The endless day was close to over when he heard a yell from the front. "Doctor! Quickly!" Heart revving, he ran to the door. A man staggered in with a limp Great Dane in his arms. Sarah was helping support the dog's hindquarters.

"He was hit by a car," the man panted. "Right outside our house. Damn deep snow let Duke get over the fence. Bastard in the car didn't even stop."

They hurried the dog back onto the X-ray table. Paul dove into the routine: oxygen, fluids, pain medicine. The dog's hind legs were limp, and he added steroids. When the dog's breathing seemed stable, he snapped the first X-ray. Ten minutes later he led the owner to a seat in one of the exam rooms.

The X-rays were not subtle. That clarity was the only blessing. He didn't have to wonder if he was reading things right, or missing something vital.

"That's a broken leg, isn't it?" the owner said.

Paul looked at the film, clipped up on the light box. "Yeah," he said. The smashed front leg bone was obvious. "But we have bigger problems." He pointed. "Duke has a spinal fracture." He showed the owner where the ninth thoracic vertebra was split and displaced. There was an inch of space between the two ends of the bone. The shearing force across the spinal cord had to have been severe. "He's paralyzed and has no feeling in his back legs, not even deep pain."

"But you can fix him, right?" the man said anxiously. "I mean, he needs surgery and you'll fix him."

Paul sighed. “I don’t know about the front leg. That much damage might force even a specialist to amputate. But the spine is bad. They could stabilize him, make it solid enough to heal. But he’s not likely to ever use his back legs again. And with the bad front leg…” He shook his head. “He’s a big dog, huge. You can’t carry him out to the bathroom every day while he’s healing, and he’s never going to get around on one good leg. I’ll refer you to a specialty surgeon if you want to try. But you’re looking at thousands of dollars and a lot of pain, for a very slim possibility of a good quality of life afterward.”

The owner called in his wife, and his daughter, and his brother, but in the end the decision was made. At least this dog was pre-sedated with morphine, a catheter already in his leg. The actual killing was easy. Paul shepherded the grieving crowd of Petersons out the door when it was all over.

“One left,” Sarah told him. Paul thought it might be one more than he could take. But by some gift of God, it was a small, adult, healthy cat in need of a rabies shot. No sign of even tooth problems. He sent her owner to the desk to check out and headed for his office. He wanted quiet. He needed space. And sleep, and time off, and maybe whiskey. There was a first time for everything.

At the door of his office, he remembered one more chore. He was hefting the body of the Great Dane, slippery in its black plastic shroud, trying to get it over the lip of the freezer when a voice beside him said, “Here, let me help.” With a second pair of hands, the big dog slid up and in. Paul struggled to rearrange the body in a way that would let him close the damned lid.

“That thing’s full,” Simon commented.

Paul rounded on him angrily. “I don’t need you to tell me that. What the hell are you doing here anyway?”

“Just saying hello,” Simon said cautiously.

“Well, I don’t want to hear it. And if you brought food again, I’m not hungry.”

Simon held his hands out empty. “No food. I like to vary my approach.”

“I’ve had the day from hell. The last thing I need is someone else putting demands on me.”

“Is that what I’m doing?”

Paul tried to answer and felt the edge of tears catch at his throat. He turned away, blinking. Simon stepped closer and put a hand on his arm.

Paul wheeled around. "Don't touch me," he snarled. "Don't fucking put your hands on me."

"Hey!" Simon's own voice rose. "I was offering you a hug, not a fast fuck on top of the freezer."

A choked sound from the hallway made them both look over. Sarah stood there, a hand to her mouth. "I'm so sorry. I didn't mean to interrupt."

Simon yanked his hand back as if Paul's arm had burned it. For a moment Paul just stood there. But when life keeps dumping shit on your head, at some point you have to grit your teeth and keep going. He turned toward his technician. "Hey, Sarah," he said as warmly as he could. "I'm glad you're still here. I really wanted to thank you for all your help today. This was as bad as a day gets around here, and you did way more than your share. You were amazing. If I can't get more staff in tomorrow, we'll call the routine cases and reschedule. Tonight, you should do something nice for yourself, because you deserve it. I couldn't have made it through without you."

"Thanks," Sarah said. "I mean, that's okay. It's my job, you know."

"You did more than just your job. And I appreciate it. Now get out of here, and I'll finish up. You can let Simon out while you're at it, and lock the front door behind you."

"We should talk," Simon said quietly.

"Not tonight." Paul was weary to the bone and sick of killing animals he wanted to save. He couldn't do this now. "You should go."

Simon stared at him, gray-green eyes intense, but Paul wasn't up to anything more. He turned abruptly and headed for his office. He could make it that far. He knew he could. And then he would sit down and do… something, and not think, and not get anything wrong, and not kill anything.

He closed the office door and sat down, shivering at the chill in the air. *I should put a space heater in here.* Snow had begun to beat on the window again. His desk was awash in incomplete files. Everything that could wait had done so, in the press of the day.

Randomly opening a file, he began expanding the case notes from the scribbled shorthand. *Pls thrd, memb pl, CRT=3:* "pulse thready, membranes pale, capillary refill time slow." *Damn!* He looked at the front of the chart, at the red post-it that said, "Send sympathy card." Then he laid the chart aside, carefully, as if it might break. That made enough room to fold his arms on the desk and lay his head down. Just for a moment. The first sob took him by surprise, ripped from his throat. He kept the second and the third almost silent.

§ § § §

Paul's technician didn't meet Simon's eyes as she got her things together and opened the door for him, but as he slid past her through the doorway, she said, "We had a really bad day today. You should cut him some slack, you know."

Simon glanced at her. "Don't worry. We're fine." Which was total bullshit, but he didn't think Paul would want his technician involved.

"Okay," she said dubiously. "Just, don't go away mad, 'cause he needs somebody. He's so alone."

"I don't think he would appreciate either of us prying into his private affairs."

"I'm not trying to pry," she said, sounding a little hurt. "I just feel bad. I like Dr. Hunter. He's the best vet I've ever worked with. And he's so dedicated to making this place work, you know? When things were slow last winter, he skipped his paychecks so he could pay me and Elise and not cut back our hours."

"He'd be glad to know how loyal you are," Simon broke in, trying to ease out of this conversation.

"We've talked about it, me and Elise. How he really needs a life that's not just this clinic, before he burns himself out. Now I'm worried I've messed things up for him."

Simon sighed. The woman was just being nice. "It's complicated. But if there were anything going on between Dr. Hunter and me, besides us being friends, then you happening to come by and see us wouldn't have changed that."

"I didn't realize he was gay. Elise has been trying to set him up with girls."

Thank God she failed. Not that Simon was having enormous success either. "I can't comment on his sexuality, and I'm sure you all mean well. But I think we both need to get out of the guy's hair for a bit."

She nodded, and turned to lock the door behind them. "If there's anything we can do?"

"Um, no, thank you." He set off toward his truck with a determined stride. This conversation was so over.

Simon lounged by his truck, messing with the key, until she'd driven off. He knew he should leave too. Paul would be even angrier if he hung around uninvited. But he was having a hard time persuading his wolf to go off and leave their mate in distress.

Mate. Holy shit. He'd caught himself by surprise just as much as Paul when those words came out last night. *I love you.* He hadn't meant to say it, wasn't even sure the words were more than a joke until he said them. He'd known he was attracted, concerned, infatuated even. But when he said love, the truth rang through him like something inevitable that he'd always known. And that scared the shit out of him.

He'd been almost glad that Paul ran hard and fast in the other direction. He hadn't wanted to talk about it either. But a long night of pacing, and cursing, and fighting not to go take care of Paul, eventually forced him to admit the truth. His wolf thought of this man as his mate. And so did he.

He didn't just want the lean body and the golden eyes and that electrical crackle of connection when they touched. He wanted to make Paul laugh and listen to his voice. He wanted to feed the man, and banish the circles of fatigue from under his eyes. He wanted to protect and help him, and tease him, and hold him. And, oh yeah, fuck him. He wanted all of it. But who knew what Paul wanted.

Simon hadn't survived and prospered this long by backing down. He could be cautious, even cunning, but he went after what he wanted. This was a little harder; he had to play it honest and fair. But that didn't mean he couldn't come up with a plan. Unfortunately, his wolf was having a hard time waiting and being subtle. Coming tonight had been bad timing. He should've waited for Paul to call him. He'd screwed things up. Again.

His wolf restlessness drove him to pace, eventually circling the building to the side where Paul's office window was located. Under other circumstances he could've gone wolf and watched that way, looking like a big stray dog. But Paul knew his wolf form. *Bad idea.* He eyed the building. Paul would probably be in there for hours, finishing up. He wouldn't eat. He'd go home and maybe sleep. But after that rejection, there was nothing Simon could safely do about it. Paul had to come to him now.

A light shone in the office window. The blind was half-closed. Simon couldn't make out anything through the tilted slats. Golden light spilled out onto the fresh dusting of snow, making the new flakes below the window shine and sparkle. He'd have to get in close and low down to see inside. And that would really be stalking. Simon forced himself to turn away and head back to his truck, closing his over-acute ears to the sound of a grown man crying.

Chapter 10

Simon asked for a more physical job at the shop the next day. He wasn't sure delicate finish-work would survive his distraction. Alfred set him on the big saw, ripping boards into panel-sized lengths. It was a good choice. There was satisfaction in steering the whirling steel blade through inches of maple and oak, with the smell of sawdust in his nose. The lethal sharpness of the saw forced him to pay attention, kept his mind from wandering in circles.

He took a long run at lunch break, but stayed away from his truck. No unauthorized cruising past Paul's clinic. The other men in the shop were giving him wider berth than usual. He wasn't sure if he was giving off some lethal vibe, or if they were distancing themselves for when the pack shit might hit the fan. Usually he got on fairly well with his co-workers, at least the older ones he let himself socialize with. They weren't close friends, but there was a shared camaraderie. Today, he barely got a nod and a greeting. He was preoccupied enough not to care much.

By evening, he was ready for a shower and a meal. Hot water soothed the aches in his arm, and rinsed the sawdust from his hair. He wished he could rinse the thoughts going round and round in his head as easily. He'd done nothing wrong. How could it be wrong, to admit that you… cared about someone? But Paul wasn't ready for his declaration, obviously. Simon wanted to do something cute, something romantic, and yeah, probably something stupid, to get Paul back. He had just enough sense to know that the only hope he had was to stay away and wait.

The second day was harder, but he figured he was getting more practice at not thinking about Paul. Not thinking about anything but the job under his hands. He finish-sanded flat panels like a fiend and kept away from the fine work. In the evening, he drove out to the farmhouse and put himself to work again, until around two AM he finally wore himself out enough to sleep.

By the third night, he thought he was resigned. He'd clearly screwed up his standing with Paul beyond redemption. The clincher was probably when he outed Paul to his technician, before the man was even sure in his own mind how he felt about men. He wondered how much of a clusterfuck that had become at the clinic. The technician had seemed okay with the gay, but who knew what the rest of the staff would think. Had Sarah kept her suspicions to herself, or was everyone treating Paul like a leper? If Simon had made the guy's life more miserable than ever, he should just shoot himself. He wondered how he could find out.

Werewolves didn't run to pets much. Animals tended to be wary, even when a wolf was in human form. There was no one he could persuade to take their cat to the vet for a little reconnaissance. Maybe he could pick up a one-night trick with a pet. He snorted at himself. Yeah, that would be romantic. Fuck some guy and ask him to spy on your ex-boyfriend. *Jesus, Conley, you're pathetic.*

He didn't have much appetite, but he knew he should eat. He didn't turn into some ravening wolf-monster when he was hungry, like in one movie he'd seen, but low blood sugar did shorten his already precarious temper. The last thing he needed now was to get himself into new shit with the pack by snapping at the wrong person. He was in his kitchen deciding between pasta and frozen chicken when he heard Paul's SUV. He yanked the door open as Paul raised his hand to knock.

For a moment they stared at each other. Then Paul said, "Is that hug still available?"

"Hell, yes!" Simon grabbed the man, hauled him in, and slammed the door. Then he wrapped his arms tightly around Paul's thin shoulders and buried his face in tawny hair. It took a minute before he realized that Paul was saying softly, "Simon, I need to breathe."

He eased up. "Sorry, sorry." He made himself let go. "I jumped you. I'm sorry. I just, I thought I'd totally screwed us up. I was sure you were done with me."

Paul laughed at him, slipping out of his jacket and draping it on the closet handle. "Not yet."

"Good. That's good." Simon opened the closet and hung the parka up inside, and closed the door firmly. "Can you stay? Do you want to? I was making dinner; I can fix you something. I have chicken or pasta, or there's steaks in the freezer, or I could do a stew."

Paul smiled. "Take a breath. I didn't come here just to run back out the door. But you don't have to feed me."

"I want to." Simon got a grip. "It's the Jewish grandmother in me. I take one look at you, and I want to say, 'Eat something, bubbeleh.'"

Paul tilted his head. "That's what you think of when you look at me?"

The heat in those gray-flecked gold eyes burned into Simon. "No. Not really."

"Good." Paul stepped up to him, slowly and deliberately, and raised his face for a kiss.

For a moment, Simon fought to keep his touch light and sweet and respectful. Then the heat closed in, and he plundered that offered mouth. Paul was ready and opened for his tongue, and he took more, swaying their bodies together, pulling Paul closer.

The bed was upstairs, but the couch was nearer. Simon steered them that way, not breaking the kiss. If Paul said stop, he would. But if Paul's mouth was kept busy kissing him, then he wasn't saying anything.

Simon found the couch with the back of his leg and fell into the cushions, pulling Paul down with him. He felt no resistance. Paul fisted his hands in Simon's hair as he landed on top. They ground together, shoving and frantic. Simon let his legs fall open and Paul pushed into the space, hard against him. Then it was all breath and motion, teeth and tongues, and Simon's hands on that tight sweet ass, Paul's fingers along his jaw. He ached for more than friction and pressure, but was close, close, too close to stop and back off. Simon groaned and clamped their hips together. Paul came first, moaning his climax into Simon's mouth. Simon kissed, licked, and then set his teeth in Paul's shoulder, his hips bucking out of control, thrusting hard up against Paul. Release crashed over him like a wave, leaving him blind and shaking. He locked his arms around Paul's back and just held on.

"Wow," Paul said eventually. "That was some welcome."

"We aim to please."

"Good aim." He shifted his weight, and Simon hugged him tighter, involuntarily.

"Hey." Paul's voice was soft. "I'm not going anywhere. I just want to get my sensitive bits away from your hip bone."

"Sure." Simon eased his grip and turned a little, settling Paul more comfortably between his legs. "Wouldn't want to damage those sensitive bits."

For a while they lay there, breathing together. Eventually Paul said, "This wasn't quite the way I planned it. I was going to show up at your door, we were going to talk, maybe have a drink, then…"

"Then?"

"Then. But now is good too."

"I'm sorry if I'm making this harder for you. Pushing too far too fast."

"I like it hard," Paul quipped, shifting his hips. "But yeah, this is all happening awfully fast." He turned his cheek against Simon's neck, his mouth muffled on Simon's skin. "I was going to tell you we needed to slow it down, take some time apart. But I realized I didn't want that. Then I spent too long worrying about being with another man. How could I deal with people knowing that? What if my staff found out, what would they think? How could I ever tell them? Except it turned out I didn't need to. Sarah saw us and, um, drew her own conclusion."

"Oops. I'm so sorry. I'm a fucking idiot."

"I won't argue with that. But what's done is done." Paul made a strangled sound that was almost a laugh. "The next morning my receptionist apologized for trying to set me up with her niece several times. I should've just told her I was gay. But if I'm ever looking, she has a cousin who has his own landscaping business, a really nice guy."

Simon growled. "You're not looking."

"Nope." Paul rested his head more comfortably against Simon's shoulder. "Anyhow, they think I'm gay now, and life goes on. I have good people."

Simon remembered his own coming out vividly. No reason Paul's should be quite as traumatic; it was unlikely anyone would want to kill him for it. But this exposure couldn't be easy, especially when Paul was still deciding about his own sexuality. Although the warm weight along his body suggested some decisions had been made. "Are you okay?"

"I don't know," Paul admitted. "I'm not ready to come out to my clients and march in parades. But being with you is… important at a whole different level than anything I've had before. I would go home and try not to think about you, and then in the middle of the night I couldn't think about anything else. You… make me feel good about myself, and turn me on, in a way no one else has. And walking away from that would be punishing myself for no good reason."

"I agree completely. In fact, I think we should explore the topic further." He nibbled along Paul's ear. At least with the sex, he knew what he was doing.

"Stop it," Paul said, although he was laughing. "I also realized what almost scares me more is the having-a-relationship part. I know absolutely nothing about relationships."

"I'm making it up as I go along too. I haven't told anyone I loved them since my mother died."

"No one has said that to me, and meant it, in even longer. I don't think I know what real love means. I don't know if I can be what you need. Of course, I'm not sure I understand the sex part perfectly either."

"Well, you see," Simon began, "when the daddy bird and the mommy bird love each other very, very much… *ouch*!"

Paul licked the spot he had bitten on Simon's chin. "Are you ever serious?"

"As seldom as possible. Having you here is like champagne bubbles up my nose. It makes me silly."

"Don't blame that on me. You came to me silly."

Simon moved his head back to look in Paul's eyes without squinting. Gold eyes under those long amber lashes stared back unflinchingly. Simon freed a hand to trace Paul's chin and eyebrow.

"I want this," he said, as seriously as he could. "I want you here, with me. I want to spend time getting to know you, in every way there is, and see what this thing between us can become."

"Okay."

Simon kissed him softly, just a brush of lips, and Paul nestled his head down in the curve of Simon's neck with a sigh. Simon traced his fingers over the nape of Paul's neck and the soft fine strands that lay across it. He trailed a finger down Paul's spine, feeling his back arch under the caress, like a cat. Flat shoulders, long curve of lumbar muscles, hard, lean swell of ass. He laid his hand flat and pressed, and heard Paul's breath quicken again.

"How about food? And then I'll give you a tutorial on that sex thing."

"We could skip the food," Paul suggested, nipping at him.

"Nope." Simon stood abruptly, spilling Paul off onto the floor. "For what I'm planning, you'll need to have all your strength." He stood and stretched, aware of sticky coolness at his groin. "Maybe with a detour to clean up first. If I had known you were coming back, I'd have bought more new underwear."

"I have a bag in the truck," Paul admitted shyly.

Simon stared at him, then laughed. "Can I say 'God, I love you!' now and not have you run away screaming?"

"I think so."

"Give me the keys." Simon held out his hand. "I'll get the bag for you."

"I can go."

"Nope." Simon took the keys from Paul's fingers. "For one thing, I'm better padded against the cold."

"And for another?"

Simon dropped his eyes. *For another, I don't want you out there in the truck, with the keys, in case you change your mind.*

"I'm not leaving," Paul seemed to know what he was thinking. "I didn't drive around for two hours getting up the nerve just to let myself chicken out now."

"Is it that scary, being with me?"

"Yeah, it kind of is." Paul gave him a sweet smile. "In my experience, most of the really worthwhile things are scary, going in."

Simon fetched Paul's bag for him anyway, and they took turns in the small downstairs washroom, getting clean and dry. Simon washed himself roughly, frowning at his half-hard dick. His brain understood "slowly" but his body wanted to pull Paul into bed and not get back out until morning. He needed to figure out how to keep his advances sexy but not scary, not off-putting to someone who hadn't spent years whacking off to pictures of men. He'd never been someone's first time. Paul's lack of experience worried him almost as much as it turned him on.

Paul lounged against the kitchen counter, watching him as he prepared food. The salad was ready in the refrigerator and would stretch for two people. He decided on pasta, quick and easy. He could show off his cooking to Paul another time. *Please, let there be another time.* Right now, he wanted fast. He set Paul to opening pasta sauce and dumping in sliced mushrooms.

"What is it with you and feeding me?" Paul asked as he followed directions, stirring with the wooden spoon.

"Partly I want to put about fifteen pounds on those beautiful bones of yours," Simon told him, turning down the heat under the boiling pasta. "Partly my mother's influence, I guess. She was from the South, a small town outside of Atlanta. Southern hospitality means no one comes to your house without being offered cake, or cookies, or sweet tea, or something. She taught me to cook, and I kind of equate feeding someone with caring about them." *And my wolf wants to feed you up and keep you safe.*

"She's dead, your mom?"

"Yeah. Died when I was twelve, both she and my dad, in a car accident."

"I'm sorry." Paul put a hand on his arm. His eyes were dark with compassion. "That must've been rough."

"For a while, yeah. But my Uncle Martin took me in. He wasn't a real people person, but he did care about me, and he supported me when he found out I was gay." That had perhaps been the biggest good surprise of Simon's life, until Paul showed up on his doorstep tonight. *Lighten things up.* "But he wasn't much of a cook, so I made meals for both of us. Tonight, you're getting canned pasta sauce, but sometime I'll show you what I can really do in the kitchen."

Maybe some of his mother's Southern home cooking. Paul could use a little bacon grease and stick-to-his-ribs cornbread. Or some of the Anishinaabe cooking his grandmother might've made, if he'd ever known her. He'd had to go find recipes. His dad had distanced himself as far as possible from that part of his heritage, but after he'd died, Simon had looked up stuff.

Manoomin for sure. Paul would love the wild-harvested rice and he was worth the splurge. Walleye, if he could get fresh from someone with an ice house—

Paul broke into his menu planning to ask, "No brothers or sisters?"

"Nope. Only child." Wolves never had sisters, of course. "How about you?"

"I'm an only too." Paul's face closed down, like it always did when they got close to talking about his childhood. There was something bad there, but tonight was not the time for Simon to push him to talk.

"I think this pasta's done." On impulse, Simon picked up a strand of spaghetti and tossed it at the wall. It hit and slid down wetly. He grabbed the strand and ate it before it reached the floor. "Yep," he mumbled around the pasta. "That's done."

"You are a goof." Paul's face was bright and amused again. "That's how you test pasta?"

"Never tried it before," Simon said airily. "They say if the pasta sticks, it's done." He gave an exaggerated shudder. "Actually, I don't know anyone who likes their spaghetti sticky enough to glue to a wall. This is *al dente*. Okay with you?"

"Fine." Paul was laughing.

"Then let's eat." Simon served them at the counter, keeping the presentation simple. Paper napkins, the regular plates, glasses of water. He didn't offer Paul beer. Whatever was coming, he wanted Paul completely sober for it. No excuses. He babbled about the workshop, kept Paul amused by the wacky customers and screw-ups that he'd encountered over the years. Nothing deep, nothing personal. *God, Paul's beautiful when he laughs.*

When they were done, he stuck the plates in the dishwasher, ditched the pans in the sink, and turned to look at Paul. "I know what I want for dessert. Will you come upstairs with me?"

§ § § §

Simon's voice hit Paul right in the center of his body. He was suddenly tight, and hot, and terrified. *You can do this. You decided to do this.* He couldn't answer.

Simon held out his hand, and after a long moment Paul took it. Hard, warm fingers closed around his own. Simon's scent was so familiar now, green forest and musk seeming to stroke over his skin. Every nerve ending came alert. He let Simon lead him out of the kitchen, up the narrow stairs, and into the bedroom.

Simon turned on the light and Paul looked around. Nothing looked familiar. Had the bed been that big and high before? He couldn't remember. The blue of the curtains was bright.

"Can we turn off the light?"

Simon let go of his hand and went over to the dresser. He switched on a small lamp in a dark blue shade, then flicked off the overhead. "Is this okay?"

The lamp laid a pool of light on the polished wood. Simon's shadow crawled up the wall behind him. "I guess."

Simon came back to him, smiling a little. "Sugar, you don't want the room totally dark the first time, or someone might put out an eye with their elbow. Not their own eye, obviously."

Paul couldn't help snorting. Simon stepped in closer, hands loosely clasping Paul's upper arms.

"And I want to see you," he added softly. Those hands began running up and down Paul's arms in a soothing way, gentle friction. "Relax, baby." Simon's voice was deep and slow. "I won't hurt you. I swear. Nothing that you don't want. If you like, we can do nothing more than we did downstairs. I'm in no hurry."

Paul searched for words. "I don't have another pair of dry shorts," he said hoarsely.

Simon's chuckle was electric, stroking Paul's skin. "Then we'll have to lose the underwear first." Simon's hands moved to Paul's shirt buttons, popping them open calmly. Not slowly, not portentously, just matter-of-factly. Button, button, button. Paul looked down, watching, as Simon's broad hands pushed his shirt open and slid it off his shoulders. He looked up to catch Simon's eyes, and Simon kissed him. That was better. This much Paul understood. He opened his mouth greedily, trying to lose himself in the rush of lips on lips, tongue on tongue.

Simon pulled back slightly. "Easy. Slowly. It's okay."

Simon's hands slid up under Paul's T-shirt, pushing the hem up Paul's chest with his wrists as his fingers moved higher. Paul shuddered as those rough fingertips found his nipples and pinched. Simon's thumbs stroked him with short flicking motions. Simon kissed his neck, licking, nipping, as his hands moved. Then he pulled back and hauled the cotton fabric up and off.

Paul stood half-naked in front of this man, *his lover*. So odd, so wrong, *so right*. Suddenly he wanted to be the one making the moves. He grabbed the bottom of Simon's sweatshirt and yanked it up. Simon helped him, raising his arms for the fleece to slide up and over his head, baring his hard chest, his pits dark with hair. His smell came stronger and warmer, filling Paul's head. Paul leaned forward to kiss Simon's mouth, his chin, his jaw rough with the beginnings of evening stubble. He slid his lips lower, to Simon's strong neck and curved shoulder. He opened his mouth, licking, sucking, and Simon moaned softly.

That was sweet, that he could draw that sound from Simon. Paul licked, then bit his shoulder lightly, and felt Simon jolt against him. Paul slid his hands around the man's warm back, fingers digging into smooth hard shoulders. He breathed against Simon's neck, letting his touch wander lower, tracing spine down to the elastic edge of sweatpants. *Enough.*

He stepped back. Simon eyed him, a small smile on his face, his stance easy and confident. He obviously liked to be touched; those sweatpants didn't hide much. Paul jerked his gaze back up to Simon's eyes, aware that his face was hot.

"Hey," Simon said. "I want you to look at me. I love that you were looking." Simon put his fingers in the waistband of his own sweats and slowly lowered them. Paul watched despite himself. Six-pack abs, outlined in lamplight, hipbones clean-cut above the V of groin that led downward, downward. Simon's curls were dark and thick. He kept himself trapped in the soft fabric as he pulled down, giving Paul a view of everything else, and then suddenly his cock sprang free, thick and hard, copper dark, rising out of its foreskin sheath. Simon dropped the pants and stepped out of them, naked.

Paul's jeans trapped him, uncomfortably tight. He stepped back and lowered his own hands. Simon made no move toward him as he unbuttoned, unzipped, undressed himself. He tossed his jeans, socks, and shorts over onto his shirt, before looking up again. *So. Here we are.* His cock obviously had no reservations. He was painfully hard, aching, trembling a little in time to his thudding pulse.

"Why are you over there when I'm over here?" Simon asked gently.

Paul went to him. Simon kissed him tenderly, hands on his face, making no moves toward his naked body. Paul shifted so his cock brushed Simon's hip, gliding against hot smooth skin. Simon just kissed him some more. Paul reached out, tentatively, and touched Simon's bare abdomen. Simon tensed, then laughed. "Cold hands, babe."

He took Paul's hands, breathing on them, and licked Paul's fingers into his hot mouth, sucking gently. "Now try." Simon guided Paul's hands to his hard shaft. Paul touched tentatively, running his fingers along that soft skin. He felt the hardness beneath, the ridge of bulging veins, the faint jerk and rise at his touch. He slid his hands up and over the velvet head. Slick pre-cum glided under his palm and Simon hissed. "Oh, yeah, sugar. Touch me."

Then Simon touched Paul, hands warm and firm. *Like jacking myself, except it isn't.* Paul stroked, pulled harder, felt the motions mirrored by Simon's hands on him. *Different touch and sounds and smell, hot kisses and the press of a warm thigh against my own.*

"Come to bed," Simon whispered, guiding him across the room, still kissing. They slid onto the bed. Paul sank into the pillows, Simon's weight against him, Simon's hands on him. He closed his eyes and let himself touch and be touched. Simon seemed expert, stroking, pulling, cupping Paul's scrotum with just the right pressure, stroking behind his balls with a fingertip. Fire ran through Paul's groin. He couldn't think, could barely keep his hands moving on Simon's cock. Simon closed his fingers tightly on Paul and pumped, twisting around and over.

Paul pushed up into that touch, his hands dropping to the sheets. He fumbled for something, anything, to hold on to, as his body hovered on the brink of whiteout overload. Pressure and need built in his groin, demanding release. If there was fabric between his fingers, he couldn't feel it, couldn't feel anything but Simon's hands. He opened his eyes. His vision tunneled, the periphery sparking. But in the center of his world, Simon's eyes glowed green. Paul erupted. His cock pumped into Simon's grasp, all that heat and fire arcing through him and out in spatters and wells of spunk.

When he was spent, panting, Simon moved further over him and began to thrust against Paul's hip. Paul reached down, fumbling, and trapped Simon's erection in his hands. Simon groaned, "Yeah. Touch me." Paul tightened his fists against that hot silken shaft.

Simon's pleasure needed nothing from him but steady pressure, as Simon set his own pace, harder, faster, fucking into the channel of Paul's fingers. Simon whispered his name, softly, then louder. Simon's mouth found his and he moaned against Paul's tongue as his body shuddered. Then the hot, sticky wetness of another man's cum filled Paul's hands.

"Oh, God," Simon gasped. "Oh, God, Paul, babe, sugar." He dropped his mouth against Paul's skin and mumbled inarticulately. Paul caught his name and "yes" and "sweet." After a moment, Simon eased his weight over and brushed against Paul's softening dick. Paul jolted, his body achingly sensitive. Simon laughed against his mouth. "Oh, yeah. Don't you move for a bit either." Slowly, carefully, they let go of each other. Paul worried about his messy hands, but Simon sat up, reached for tissues, and wiped them both. Paul lay still and let himself be tended. When Simon was done, he took Paul's almost-clean hands and laid them on his own six-pack abdomen, as he curled back up on his side facing Paul.

"Just keep those hands there for a bit," he murmured. "I want to feel you on me, but even I need a little recovery time."

"Even you?"

Simon laughed contentedly. "You'll see. Later. When you're ready for it."

"Are you bragging?"

Simon huffed. "It's not bragging when it's true." He stroked his hands over Paul's shoulders. "Well? Good, bad, what'd you think?"

"You know that felt good. But it wasn't…"

"Wasn't what?"

"Wasn't real sex."

Simon smiled lazily. "I figure if someone has cum on their skin, it was sex. Sugar, I could be happy doing nothing more than that with you for a month."

"But how will I know?"

"Know what, babe?"

"If I'm really gay," Paul whispered. "If this is really me."

"Feels like you, smells like you." Simon kissed his jaw. "Don't get hung up on labels, Paul. If you're happy here with me, that's what counts. If what we do in bed turns you on, we're okay. And I'd say evidence points that way. Did you see the movie *Kinsey*? Does it matter if you're a three, four, five, six, as long as you're where you want to be right now?"

"I guess." Put that way, it sounded stupid, all the agonizing he'd been doing. But still he wanted to know. How could he be so far from straight and never have realized? Was he bi, or did the fact that sex with Simon eclipsed everything he'd ever done with a woman make him gay? If a man's hands had felt better than a woman's whole body…

Simon rolled over and pushed back against him, spooning with his firm rump pressed warm and round against Paul's groin. Paul snuggled closer, suddenly wanting to hold him exactly this way. Simon's dick against his would've been… uncomfortable. Simon's dick at his ass, even more so. But this was just sweet and safe. He breathed the scent of Simon's coarse dark hair against his face and wrapped an arm around him. *Him. The man I'm in bed with.* But he couldn't make this feel anything but good.

Simon's hand pressed over his, flattening his palm against Simon's chest. "Sleep a little, babe," Simon murmured. "Time enough for other things later."

Paul had thought they would talk, or something. Make plans. But interrupted nights of bad dreams and unfulfilled want had taken their toll. His eyes drifted closed, and the world went away.

§ § § §

Simon lay in the dim pre-dawn light of his bedroom, listening to the man beside him breathe. He'd dozed and woken over and over throughout the night. Paul's body pressed warm against his own, and Simon had been hard with wanting him for hours. But he recognized Paul's boneless sleep as deep exhaustion. If he could give Paul a safe unbroken night, then sex could wait, whatever his body might think.

He wanted to stay curled up there until the sun rose, until Paul woke of his own accord and turned to him. But it was Saturday, and while he was off work, he knew the clinic was open Saturday mornings. He leaned over and kissed Paul's mouth. Paul was so deep under it took a moment of licking and nibbling before he reacted. He murmured softly, then his eyes snapped open and his body went rigid.

Simon could feel the smile curving his own mouth. “Mornin’, sugar.”

He saw Paul’s eyes go through *what the hell*, and then *oh, yeah*, before he got a small smile in return. “Good morning.”

“I don’t know when you want to go to work, but it’s six o’clock. If you need to get out early, I have time to feed you first. And if you don’t, I have time for other things first.”

“Um.” He could almost see the wheels turning in Paul’s head, and held his breath waiting for the result. He was disappointed, but not surprised, when Paul said tentatively, “I really should get up and get to work.”

“Okay. One hot breakfast coming up. You get first dibs on the shower, since I’m not going anywhere.” He rolled out of bed and moved around the room, intentionally naked, picking up Paul’s clothes, pulling fresh sweatpants and shirt out of a drawer and eventually putting them on. He dressed slowly, and paused in poses that he knew showed off his body to the man in his bed, but he wasn’t trying to change Paul’s mind. Not that he would have objected, but just having Paul’s eyes on him was good. It was like investing for the future.

Downstairs, he cooked, aware of the sound of the shower on the floor above. Aware of the man naked in his shower upstairs. He felt unnaturally buoyant, like a kite caught in thermal updrafts. No doubt something would come along to swat him out of the sky eventually, but for now life was good. Life was fucking great.

“How about later?” he said when Paul had settled himself in front of a plate of food. “What do you want to do after work?”

“Um.” Paul blushed but met his eyes. “I thought if you weren’t busy maybe I could come back here for, um…”

Simon laughed in delight. “Oh yes. Simon’s cooking school and Kama Sutra classes are always open to the discriminating student.”

“More than one student?”

“No. Not anymore.”

Paul suddenly dropped his eyes, uncomfortable. “But you used to go out with a lot of different men, right? Have you ever…”

Simon waited.

"I just want to be sure we're safe."

Ah. Not a problem, because werewolves turned out to be immune to most human diseases, including all the STD's. But maybe a different kind of problem, because he couldn't prove that. Wolves avoided medical tests at all costs, in case their *differences* were noted. Simon leaned forward.

"Paul," he said clearly. "I have always played safe, and I know I'm negative now. And I swear to you, as long as you are with me there will be no one else. I will never risk your health like that."

"Okay. That's… okay."

"Hey, you have a right to ask. In fact, you'd be pretty stupid not to. And one thing you are not, my love, is stupid."

Paul looked down and got very involved in cutting up his ham.

§ § § §

Simon washed dishes happily after Paul left for the clinic. Last night's pots were crusty but he'd have been crazy to stop on the way to bed to do dishes first. He smiled to himself. Paul was so hot, and sweet, and uncertain. And in just a few hours he would be back, and they could climb into that big bed and continue expanding his horizons. He was drying the last lid and plotting his approach when the phone rang.

"Hello?"

"Simon? It's Joshua."

"Yes?" He seldom got an unexpected call from the Third, so this was unlikely to be good news. Unless Karl had gotten hit by a bus… *Sadly, I'd have felt that.*

"Gordon needs you. Up at the lodge, as soon as possible."

"Now?" *Damn. Bad timing.*

"Yes. Bring a bag and pack for a few days in the North Country."

"What? I can't…" But Simon was talking to dead air. Joshua had hung up, certain that Simon had heard and would obey.

Shit! Fuck! Simon slammed his fist down on the counter. He couldn't go off somewhere. Not now, when Paul had finally agreed to be with him. Especially not when he couldn't even explain where he was going or for how long. But he couldn't say no to Gordon. Joshua was right; the fifteenth ranked wolf in the pack did not tell his Alpha to shove off because he was interfering with his love life. *Fuck!*

Simon packed as directed, briefs and shirts, jeans and socks. Just being in his bedroom with the smell of sex still redolent in the air made him horny. And angry, and frustrated. He threw a pair of worn socks across the room. *Damn!* He scrubbed Paul's scent from his shower stall and showered with the strong-smelling soap and then plain, resenting the way his routine erased sex with Paul from his skin. *Necessary. Safest. But damn it.*

The clinic had to come first. Gordon could wait a few more minutes. Leaving Paul unexpectedly was going to be hard enough. He wasn't going without a face-to-face explanation.

There was an unfamiliar young woman at the reception desk when he went in. In the waiting room, a beautiful pair of German Shepherds watched him, following him warily with their dark eyes. Their hackles raised as he passed them. Simon went up to the desk.

"Can you give Dr. Hunter a message? Could you tell him Simon is here, and I need a quick word with him?"

The woman's face brightened into a wide smile. "*You're* Simon," she said, holding out her hand. "I'm Mika. Mika Huong. I work Saturdays. It's so nice to meet you."

Simon shook her small hand, reflecting that the word certainly had gotten around among the staff.

"Why don't you go back to the doctor's office and I'll let him know you're here."

"It's not an emergency," Simon told her. "Just when he has a moment."

He spent about ten minutes wandering around the office, being nosy, before Paul looked in.

"Simon?" He sounded concerned. "What's wrong?"

"Nothing's wrong. At least not very wrong. I just… I got a call from my Uncle Gordon."

"The one who owns the firm?"

"Yeah. They're having some kind of problem at one of the sites, out of town, and he wants me to go take care of it."

"Now?" Simon got some satisfaction out of the fact that Paul looked as dismayed as he felt.

"Apparently." Simon shrugged. "I don't even know which site yet. He just sent down orders to pack a bag and come meet him."

"Pack a bag? You'll be away for a while?"

"Not long." *If it turns out to be long, I'm going to get back here somehow to see you.*

"If it's just the weekend, and it can wait a couple of hours, I could go with you. Like a road trip. Might be fun."

"No," Simon said sharply. Seeing Paul's face tighten he hurried to add, "Not that I wouldn't love to have you with me, but I have no clue what this is about. And if Karl or Frank is involved, I want to keep you far away from them."

"Are you sure this is all legal stuff? You almost act like you're afraid of them."

"Not afraid." *Scared shitless they might pay attention to you.* How to spin this right? Keeping pack secrets was one of the reasons he'd never had a real lover before. "I'm wary of them. It's like, um, remember in high school how there were bullies who would figure out the thing that bugged you the most, and they'd keep harping on it, trying to make you crazy? Well my uncles are like that. They would love to make me flip out, maybe go after one of them in public so they'd have an excuse to slap me down. I can keep my temper well enough. But if they go after you, I don't know what I might do. I have good control but I lose my head when you're involved."

Paul snorted.

"Which of those things don't you buy?" Simon tried to sound teasing.

"You have no control that I've seen."

"Oh, you have no idea," Simon breathed, taking one step closer. "I've been a very good boy so far."

"Really? You could do more?"

Okay, that sounded like teasing back. Simon reached over Paul's shoulder and pushed the office door shut. He looked Paul in the eye. "Want to see whose control is better?"

Paul laughed and shoved him away with one hand on his chest. "Not in my office in the middle of the work day. But you might hold that thought." They looked at each other for a moment. "You really have to go? You couldn't tell him to get someone else?"

"I wish. I would if I could. But Gordon saved my life once, at some risk to his own, and I owe him big time. When he says hop, I jump."

"Saved your life?"

"Um, yeah. Long story." And not one he should have even mentioned to a human. Being around Paul made it hard to think. "The point is, I can't say no unless my refusal involves life and death. Wanting you only feels that way." Simon tried to let his frustration show. He didn't *want* to dump Paul for the weekend. He needed Paul to believe that.

Paul nodded. "I guess I owe him then too. But… Will you call me?"

Simon winced at the uncertainty in his lover's voice. "Absolutely. Maybe too often. And if worst comes to worst, I'll give you a tutorial in phone sex."

"Get out of here." Paul reached for the door, then looked back. "Just… be careful?"

Too intense, he knows something's off. Simon found a light smile, leaned over and kissed him quickly. "Don't worry. I'll be back before you know it." Watching Paul's easy stride as he headed back to his clients, Simon hoped he was telling the truth. With pack business, nothing was certain.

§ § § §

The parking lot of the lodge only held a few vehicles when Simon arrived, which was a good sign. Impending disaster should involve the whole pack, so this was something less ominous. Which didn't mean it wasn't still trouble.

Simon entered the main room to find Gordon waiting, with Joshua, Aaron, Mark, and Mitchell lounging in the chairs in postures of fake nonchalance. Gordon looked up when Simon arrived.

"Ah, there you are," he said. "Now we just need Otto."

Simon found a seat, thinking hard. Otto was the pack's representative with the DNR, the department responsible for wildlife control. He'd been placed in that position and developed his skill with wild wolves so that he became the authority people turned to for wolf-sightings. His intervention gave the pack more security in case of an accidental sighting. Which suggested that this meeting was unrelated to Simon's own problems. He breathed a little easier.

Otto hurried in a few minutes later. "Sorry, Gordon. Had to drop the wife off first. Her car wouldn't start."

Gordon nodded. "Here's the problem." They leaned forward, attention focused. "We've had a couple of sightings up at Pine River. Whether someone in our pack has been careless, or it's a wolf from outside our pack, I don't know. There's even a chance they could be real wild wolves."

"No one told you they were going up there hunting?" Aaron asked.

"No."

The pack had a big property north of Pine River. That part of northern Minnesota was dotted with national forest lands, and close to the open spaces of the Boundary Waters and reservations. It wasn't unheard of for Minnesota's resurgent wild wolf population to be seen there. That fact, along with the size and remoteness of the pack property, made it one of the few places they could really let loose, run and hunt and howl.

The lodge here was nice, the space enough for a good run, but it was too close to the cities to be really safe. As urban sprawl made its way outward, there were more and more people about. The werewolves could run in small groups, and observers might think they were dogs if seen. But they didn't dare howl, didn't dare hunt big game, and couldn't risk a full run of the pack, more than forty strong now. The Pine River land gave them that freedom. Although even there, people might appear unexpectedly. Snowmobilers had become the bane of the wolf pack lately.

"If it was one of our pack, or rather two of them," Gordon said, "I'm going to strip their hides off slowly. Bad enough that they were seen taking down a deer outside of pack property last month. But I found out that they attacked a bull two weeks ago."

"A bull?" Mark asked. "Livestock?"

"Yes." Gordon's voice was cold.

He nodded at Otto, who said, "A month ago a farmer was checking his northern fence line, and he spotted two really big wolves, one dark and one light, hunting a whitetail buck. They made the kill while he watched, but then turned and left the carcass. He figured they got wind of him, and reported the incident to the local DNR rep up there. Then two weeks ago, on another Saturday night, one of his bulls got loose. The guy breeds bulls for the rodeo trade, and this one was a half-Brahma, two thousand pounds with big horns. It was starting to snow, and he was worried about the bull as well as about anyone the bull might come across. He followed its tracks north.

"The man said when he found his bull, it was being attacked by the same two wolves. But he said it seemed like they were playing with it, dodging in and out like bullfighters, slashing at it but not doing much damage, almost like they didn't want to kill it. He said all the wounds ended up superficial. The bull was more mad than hurt. He ran up yelling and the wolves took off. I gather he had a hell of a time getting the bull back home. He called the DNR again, this time to request relocation of the two wolves, which he described as huge and weird and overly bold around a human. The local DNR has been looking for traces without success, and the report just trickled down to me."

Gordon told the group, "What I want is for you to go find out who or what is involved, and take care of the problem so we don't get more attention focused on the area. If it's wild wolves, Otto will try to trap and relocate. If he can't, you can kill them. Take care of the bodies though, so they can't be found. We don't need legal trouble or protesters. If it's some of our pack, I want them back here in front of me. If it's strange werewolves, same thing, but if they won't come and won't tell you who their Alpha is, take them out. I don't want publicity. Is that clear?"

They all nodded, under the force of Gordon's glare.

"What are the chances they'll show up while we're there looking for them?" Aaron asked. "If they're pack, they're probably making occasional trips."

"I had a guy up there check the woods," Otto said. "There's evidence of several other recent wolf kills. Either they're living in the area or they're going up there often. If they are from our pack, they probably aren't making a three hour drive each way on weeknights, which makes the weekend our best bet."

"If necessary, you'll stay there until you do figure it out," Gordon told them. "That's why I chose all of you. First, I know where you were that first Saturday night; Aaron was with me, and the rest of you other than Otto were coping with the roof emergency at the shop." Simon nodded, remembering an evening spent cleaning up water and shoring up a roof that suddenly threatened to collapse. "With the exception of Otto, none of you have unbonded family to question your absence. You can stick with this until it's resolved. Most of you work for me, so you can get time off to do this job. Mark, you come back for your next shift, of course. But your status as a cop will give us extra insurance, if we need local cooperation."

Joshua said, "Aaron is in charge. Mark, Mitchell, Simon, you take orders from him. Otto will meet with the DNR, smooth the waters, deal with wild wolves if that's what they are. I made reservations for you at the Motel 6, two nights to start with."

"That farmer's going round telling people what big brutes those wolves were, how weird they were," Gordon added. "I want this over, now." He got up, glared at each of them in turn until they bent head or lowered eyes in acknowledgement, and then stalked out.

Joshua went through further details for them, and ten minutes later they headed north in a loose convoy. Mark's fast driving, with Mitchell riding shotgun, had them pulling away rapidly. Simon drove automatically, catching the small slips of poor traction with a practiced ease. The roads weren't that bad, really, for all the snow they'd been getting. He considered pulling over and calling Paul with an update, while he still had service, but a glance at the dashboard clock told him the vet clinic was still open. *Do not disturb Paul at work unnecessarily.* Simon put that in his new rulebook. He would make this relationship work. He'd always been good at strategy.

The Motel 6 outside Pine River wasn't a luxurious place, but the parking lot was warmed by the midafternoon sun. Simon pulled in behind Aaron. They left the cars, each with a bag over one shoulder, and went into the lobby to find Mark and Mitchell waiting.

"Otto headed for the DNR rep's house," Mark said. "Joshua got us three rooms. Otto took one key." He held out the other two to Aaron. "You tell us who rooms with who."

For a moment, Simon didn't see why that was an issue they had to wait for Aaron to decide. Then he realized the question was, *who rooms with the queer guy?* Ah. He glanced at Aaron with what he hoped was an expression of enquiry. Strict pack order would put him with Mitchell, which was probably the snag.

Mitchell was always uneasy around Simon. He ranked just above Simon in the pack, and they both knew that situation held only as long as Simon chose to let it. He was fine with his rank, for now. He had no desire to move upward. But Mitchell didn't like Simon or the awareness that Simon could probably take him if he ever chose to Challenge.

Mark he didn't know well. Megan was the friendliest of the pack wives, but Mark's shift work meant he missed a lot of the get-togethers. When he was there, his usual group included some of Simon's detractors. Simon hadn't ever had a real conversation with the pack Seventh. Aaron was even more of a mystery.

Simon was trying to be good, but his mouth opened and he said, "You know, Mitch, you've got nothing I haven't seen before." They had, after all, shifted nude side by side often enough. Mitchell's mouth twisted, his glare icy at the reminder of his exposures to Simon's gay gaze.

Aaron gave Simon a hard look and extended one key card envelope. "Mark, you're with Mitchell. Simon's with me. Meet in my room, at dusk. Both sightings were after dark, so we'll patrol tonight."

Mark and Mitchell headed out the door quickly. Aaron tossed Simon one of the plastic cards from his envelope. "I hope you don't snore."

"I hope I don't, too," Simon agreed, with a slightly exaggerated submissive look.

Aaron snorted. When they were in the room, Aaron chose his bed by tossing his bag on it. Simon gave the other bed a smack of agreement and stuck his own bag in the closet. He had so little stuff, it wasn't worth unpacking. He pulled out cold weather pants for later.

"Why do you always push people?" Aaron asked from behind him.

"I beg your pardon, sir?" Simon said, not looking up.

"You heard me. You do it consistently, about everything. One extra remark, one bit of snark past where it's safe. Why?"

"Maybe that's just my personality. Lack of control and all."

"Bullshit."

Surprised, Simon looked around at him. Aaron was sitting on the side of the bed, his eyes fixed on Simon. "That's what I thought, when I first joined this pack. That you were unable to control the impulse to quip back at people. But I've been watching you, and I don't think you lack control. You're exactly where you choose to be in the pack. You bow head to wolves you could take down in a minute, to stay in the middle. You speak up at the right moment to get your ideas heard. And sometimes your snark derails an argument, or distracts people from a line of thought they were following. But often enough, it just gets your ass whipped. So why?"

Simon shrugged, but Aaron's stare was hard and demanding. He felt the force of that gaze, almost like looking at Gordon. "We need to lighten up. As a pack. As a people. We have this tradition of rigid control of every aspect of pack members' lives. And some of it's necessary, for safety. I can't argue with that. But our young kids are less and less willing to submit to that kind of control. They aren't being brought up in authoritarian households in isolation, like we did a hundred years ago, or even fifty. If we don't give them more freedom in the areas where we can, they're going to rebel. So I'm… opening the window a little for the next guy." He grinned. "I'm good with openings."

To his surprise, Aaron laughed. "You're a brat. But I've come to believe the same. I left a pack even more rigid than this one before ending up here." He eyed Simon. "Have you ever thought you could make more of a difference from higher up?"

"Yeah. Except Karl would kill me."

"Karl." Aaron's eyes went cold. "We'll cross that bridge when we must, which may be soon. Okay. For now, you're under my authority. Which means you can snark all you like in private, but in public or in action, you take orders. Is that absolutely clear?"

"Yes, boss."

"Good boy." Aaron's grin was fierce. "Then catch a nap while you can. We'll be out all night."

Chapter 11

Nightfall found Simon stripping off his clothes in the back of Aaron's truck, parked at the end of a dirt lane. The air was frigid on his skin, but he swung the door open before shifting. He could open door handles in wolf form, but they were hard on his teeth, and vice versa. And even in a fiberglass-bodied truck, there was enough steel to make shifting easier with the door open.

In the front, Aaron got naked with the nonchalant ease of long practice. Simon watched him in the rearview, just because he could, and because looking shouldn't be a crime. Aaron was beautifully built, long hard muscles under that olive skin, not bulky like Simon, but sleek like a distance runner. He looked both taller and more powerful out of his clothes. The fine scattering of dark hair at his groin hid nothing. He was well-hung, and beautiful.

Aaron must have felt Simon's gaze, because he turned. Simon quickly looked up to his face but Aaron just raised one eyebrow, with no effort to turn away. Then he shifted, the change rushing over him with astonishing speed. He was completely silent as black wolf took the place of olive-skinned man.

Simon hurried his own shift, reaching for the energy, so bountiful out here that even the truck around him didn't block much. Large windows and open doors were sufficient, when the sky arced overhead. He held back a groan as his body twisted, pulling, reforming. It was an odd pain, shifting. Almost like that moment before orgasm, when the worst thing in the world would be to not go over, and yet it didn't exactly hurt. He felt his cells lock into wolf form, and suddenly he was back. The smell of leather and gasoline, man and fabric, was strong in his nostrils. He raised his head from the seat and shouldered out of the door.

Aaron stood on his hind legs in the snow to lean on his door and shut it, so Simon did the same. Then he paced over to the dominant wolf. Aaron's wolf was jet black without a hint of gray, brown eyes faintly glowing in the light from the cab windows. Then the cab timer turned the truck dark. Aaron became a subtle shadow against the deep gray of the snow.

Clouds masked the stars and moon overhead. Even to werewolf eyes, the world was dim. Living in cities, where there was always reflection of artificial light from something, made it easy to forget what night was really like. Out here, a velvet darkness wrapped around him, waiting to trip unwary feet if he moved wrong. Simon's wolf eyes adapted quickly, though. He saw Aaron looking at him and nodded his readiness. Aaron set out, moving swiftly through the trees. Simon set himself to follow just as fast and silently. Or almost. Jesus, Aaron was good.

They found the location where the attack on the bull had been reported. Quartering the ground, noses active, they each found several traces of the bull's blood. At least three snowfalls had covered the ground since then, and a thick layer of ice had formed with the melting and freezing. The odor of blood was faint. Although they dug into the overlying snow as far as possible around those spots, scenting carefully, neither of them could pick up the identity of the attackers. Werewolf almost certainly, not wolf, but barely a lingering trace.

After a while Aaron set out toward the farm. They moved more slowly and carefully as they approached the buildings, circling to get downwind. Once, they heard the short bark of a dog from inside the house, and they paused, but the sound was not repeated. The cattle sheltered under long roofs, huddling together against the bite of the cold air. Aaron nodded to a shed off in its own enclosure, under the arch of two old oak trees. Otto had inspected the place in human form earlier, talking to the farmer in his DNR persona, and he'd described the layout.

They approached the shed silently, low to the ground, keeping to the open spaces where the wind had cleared the loose snow down to a fine drift across the ice. They could tell the moment when the bull inside noticed their scent. His angry huffs and pawing feet were louder than Simon would have guessed. He hoped they'd be done before the farmer woke and felt the need to come investigate. They made two fast passes close to the furious animal, noses working hard, but even in wolf form, there was no trace of pack scent left on the bull's skin to guide them.

They crouched behind a snowdrift, waiting. When the bull had quieted without arousing the humans in the house, Aaron looked at Simon and motioned with his head back toward the woods. Simon ran back over the ice-crusted snow to the shelter of the trees, and stood watching as Aaron shifted. The man got up, naked in the cold, and used a branch to wipe out the faint traces of their tracks in the snow. He did it carefully and thoroughly. By the time Aaron arrived at the trees, he was shaking with cold. He dropped to shift again.

As soon as Aaron was wolf, before he could stand, Simon went over and curled around him. Werewolf metabolism could only do so much. Shared body warmth was good. With some wolves, he would've kept back, knowing they would rather freeze than let him touch them, even in wolf form. Aaron just stuck his cold nose into Simon's furry armpit and pressed close for a moment, sharing the heat. After a few minutes, he pulled back, shook, and stood.

They spent the rest of the night patrolling the area. Around three, a light snow began to fall again. It would cover their tracks near the farm more thoroughly, which was good. But snow-cover would also further hide the traces of any other wolf.

Several times, they spotted deer moving through the trees or holed up under the spreading bows of an evergreen. Each time, they circled the tempting prey, but there was no evidence of a hunter in wait. Simon's respect for Aaron as wolf kept growing. He was a silent shadow, moving like water flowing through the trees. Somehow, he caught every shift of the breeze, staying upwind despite fickle changes, so browsing deer missed detecting him until he was almost upon them. Once, when a motion in the trees suggested a possible predator, Aaron's response was lightning fast. Simon followed, submerging himself as far as he dared in wolf. Despite their serious purpose, he felt the wild joy of running at Aaron's shoulder.

When the sun cleared the horizon and trees cast long morning shadows on the ground, Aaron finally led them back to his truck. They shifted in silence and hurried to pull on clothes. Simon shuddered as his shirt slid over his head, cold as ice from a night on the truck seat. The underwear was worse. But this was a familiar end to a nighttime run, and his body quickly warmed the fabric.

At the motel, sounds told them that Mark's room was occupied. Aaron knocked, and Mark opened the door immediately. Mitchell had been sprawled out on the bed, but he sat up quickly as they entered. Aaron leaned on the dresser, at ease but still dominating the room. Simon sat on the floor, because he was tired and because it put him lower than everyone else without extra effort on his part.

Aaron said. "Looks like no one is bursting to tell me they've solved this?"

"No one's using the cabins on our property," Mark said. "There were some tire tracks, but nothing clear. At least three snows over every trace, which puts the freshest ones two weeks back. We inspected the kill sites we were assigned. Scent was useless, but at one site there were a couple of old paw prints under a pine that could still be made out under the ice. They were awfully big to be a wild wolf, only a little smaller than mine."

"I saw one specimen from an old deer carcass that my colleague brought in," Otto said. "Lots of scavengers had been at it, but the bite radius on the killing blow was big too. I'm pretty sure we're talking werewolf."

"Okay," Aaron told them. "Otto, you had some sleep. You patrol today, look for vehicles on the property, any pack member showing up unexpectedly. The rest of us will pair up again and go out tonight. Same division of the area. Meanwhile, get some rest."

Back in their room, Simon left Aaron getting ready for bed and headed out in his truck. Not that he had anywhere to go, but he wasn't making this phone call within range of sharp pack ears. To his disappointment, his call went to voice mail. He left Paul a brief message of "Not back until tomorrow at the earliest. I'll call you again." He didn't add anything Paul might not want an audience to hear, and then wondered if that had sounded cold. He wasn't used to second-guessing himself so much.

Aaron woke when Simon came back in. Actually, he probably woke before Simon touched the door, alerting to steps in the hall. Aaron's whole attitude spoke of wary alertness. Simon stripped in the dimness of the room, and Aaron neither paid attention to him, nor made a show of ignoring him. Before Simon slept, he heard the dominant wolf snoring lightly.

On the second night, the sky was clearer. Moonlight was as good as daylight to the wolves. Simon ran behind Aaron. They could stretch out at full tilt, with the pale light to show them every ice patch and hollow. Simon realized how long it had been since he had let himself run all out. When they paused on a ridge, surveying the countryside, he had to resist the urge to howl, just for the fun of it. So it took him a second, when he heard a wolf call from off to the west, to pull up out of his instincts enough to recognize a signal from a song. Aaron was already plunging down off the rocks toward the sound.

A second cry came a little further north. Aaron was really moving now, and Simon slowly dropped back despite his best efforts. They topped a hill, and below them Simon could see Mark's dark gray shape running all out. It took a moment to spot his quarry. Under the trees two hundred yards ahead, a smaller black werewolf wove through the undergrowth. Aaron had already started downhill, cutting an angle to intercept the black wolf. Simon thought about the layout of the land, and then chose his own route. There were a few rocky crags and hollows down below that would detour a running wolf. He might make them work for him.

They all ran silently now. Sharp werewolf ears could pick up the crunch of paws on crusted snow, and the puff of laboring breaths. Simon threw himself forward in a rush, came to the rise he recalled, and launched off it. The snow below cushioned him just enough, although his left foreleg twinged. Then a body crashed into his, and he felt a slash of teeth on his shoulder as the dark wolf tried to muscle past. He ducked, spun aside, and grabbed a mouthful of fur. Wolf instinct was to slash and let go, but Simon overrode it, closing his jaws on hair and skin and holding on.

Momentum tumbled both Simon and his quarry into the snow. A sudden plunge of cold snow up his nostrils made Simon open his jaws, and the black wolf yanked free. But by then Aaron was on them.

Aaron was bigger, faster, and far more deadly. The fight would've been over in ten seconds if he'd wanted to make a kill. As it was, the smaller wolf was bleeding lightly from half a dozen places before he tumbled in the snow for the last time and didn't get up again. Mark, Mitchell and Simon rose from where they had been guarding escape routes and approached.

Aaron stood over the smaller wolf, snarling. The loser didn't move. Simon had recognized Zach by taste and smell the moment they collided. He wasn't surprised that Aaron had beaten him. He wondered where Zach had gotten the nerve to fight back at all. Sheer panic, perhaps.

After a few minutes, Aaron pulled away and Zach slowly hauled himself up on four feet. When Mark led the way, Zach followed, head and tail down. Aaron brought up the rear.

At Mark's SUV, Zach climbed in unresisting. Mark shifted first, and then told Zach in a cold voice to do the same. It took several long minutes until the boy was done. He clung to the seat, shivering and naked, but raised his head to look defiantly at Mark. "No law against running the woods," he said. Cuts on his skin still trickled slowly with blood, as he glared at them all.

Mark stared back until the boy's eyes dropped. "You can wait and tell Gordon exactly what you were doing here. And with whom. Where's your vehicle?"

Zach shook his head without speaking.

"Did your buddy escape and leave you here? What kind of gutless coward were you running with?"

Zach shivered at Mark's tone, but didn't look up.

"Look at me when I'm talking to you." The boy's chin jerked up as he tried to meet Mark's eyes, but he couldn't hold it. Dominance was clear-cut in the pack. Slowly, Zach's gaze dropped until his head bowed deeply. Mark sighed. He dug a blanket out of the back and passed it over. "Wrap up in that. Do you have clothes somewhere, or did your buddy take off with them?"

Zach shrugged without lifting his head.

"Right," Mark said. "We'll find you some pants at the motel." Mitchell joined them in the car, crowding Zach against the door as he too shifted. Zach pulled as far into the corner as he could, huddled into the blanket. Mitchell dressed quickly.

"We'll bring him down to the city," Mark told Aaron, with a slight note of question to grant Aaron the right to alter the plan. Aaron nodded his still-furry head and stepped back. Mark was right below Aaron in rank, and he and Mitchell should handle Zach with ease. Still, Aaron waited at the side of the road with Simon silent at his shoulder, until Mark pulled away.

Four hours later the pack had gathered in the meeting room, under Gordon's eye. Zach sat on the floor in the center, dressed in loose sweats, with Aaron silent behind him. The rest of the ranks sat still, without the usual chatter or restlessness.

When Gordon said, "We are met," the response rolled back sharp and cold. Simon had a moment of sympathy for the boy, remembering how that felt.

"Zach," Gordon said, and the young man looked up slowly. "You were seen, twice, by humans near Pine River. Once you were taking down a deer outside our boundaries. Once you actually had the stupidity to attack a cow."

"It wasn't a cow, it was a bull," Zach protested. The growl from the pack made it clear they were not impressed.

"Do you want to tell me how that disaster happened?"

"No, sir," Zach mumbled.

"Tell me anyway." The force of Gordon's demand jolted Zach visibly.

"We were just running, not even hunting that time. Then there it was. There wasn't even a fence. The bull was loose, and it swung these big horns at us, and… it was just instinct. You know. We're wolves, hunters, when prey like that suddenly appears you go after it." Zach's voice trailed off.

"And you couldn't control your instincts?" Gordon said coldly.

Simon winced. That was the first law of the pack. Control yourself. Do nothing that would endanger the security of the pack.

"Well I could have, sure. I just… there was no one out there, and that bastard was close and big and challenging. It was only fun, you know. We didn't really hurt it."

"But you were seen."

Zach looked up, his fear starting to show as he realized there was more at stake here than being reprimanded for unsanctioned hunting. "The human didn't see anything. I mean, we were wolf and we didn't change. We broke up the trail good so he could never have tracked us. We just looked like big wolves. We didn't risk security."

"I got a report of two giant wolves playing with a cow without seeming to want to kill it," Gordon said. "Odd, uncanny wolves. What does that sound like to you?"

Zach was silent. The whole pack waited for Gordon, as he stared down at the boy. "Who was with you?"

Zach shook his head, even though he was trembling with the effort. Gordon raised his eyes to look over the assembled wolves. "Who was with him? Better to come forward now instead of waiting until I make him give me your name."

For a moment there was no sound but breathing, and then Jason stood shakily from the outermost ring. "I was."

"Come up here," Gordon said. His words didn't sound like much, but Jason jerked as if shoved, and made his stumbling way up to Zach's side. Simon winced. Jason was barely sixteen, a baby by werewolf standards. Zach wasn't that much older, but adult enough that he should've known better.

Gordon stared hard at Jason in turn. "Did he make you go with him or was it your free choice?" he asked. Zach had rank on Jason as well as age. The kid could wiggle out of the worst of this if he said he had been forced. But Jason shook his head and managed to say, "Choice."

Gordon sighed. "Now we decide what the penalty should be for this mess."

Joseph rose from the outer walls, where the pack elders kept watch. "They are young," he said icily, "but they know the law as well as any of us. Since his father died, my grandson Zach hasn't listened to me, or indeed to anyone. He has no control of his own, and he rejects mine. All our young wolves must learn the cost."

Pete scrambled to his feet. "They're boys. My Jason is sixteen! They were careless, reckless perhaps, but they meant no harm. It was an accident that they were seen, and no real damage has come of it. They didn't break security on purpose."

"Law is law," Marcus said heavily from his seat. "Being seen with the deer off our land was just reckless. Going after the bull was criminally stupid. Exposure level stupid."

"But not enough to deserve death," Pete protested. Simon saw Jason's face blanch as he realized what penalty was hanging over him. Zach only looked more defiant. Simon thought hard, without inspiration. Werewolf law was severe and tended to all-or-nothing solutions. They had no jails, no other ways to control lawbreakers. Basically, you could take an oath, beat the shit out of someone, or kill him. When there was danger to the pack, leaving someone alive was usually considered an unacceptable risk. The pack's northern property had several deep mine shafts, and an incinerator that had once been a kiln. If an accident couldn't be staged, then people just disappeared. Bodies were disposed of, totally.

They'd all been raised to accept that. No one individual was worth more than the pack. But the younger wolves had never seen an execution. Gordon had kept things well in hand and luck had been good for years.

However much safer it might make the pack, including him, Simon didn't want these boys to pay heavily for a few bad choices. He'd been newly wolf, not even fourteen, at the last lawbreaker's execution. He and Andy were assigned to clean out the kiln after it cooled. He didn't want to see Cory and George and the other boys forced to deal with the ashes of their friends. But it would be a mistake for Simon to speak up now. He himself was Gordon's least-popular act of leniency.

Several wolves rose together, a few speaking for force of law and others for just a good beating in a mix of voices. Then Karl stood slowly and eyed the other wolves until everyone was seated again. "I think we need to make a clear example here," he said. "Our young wolves are getting rebellious, thinking pack law is no more than custom." His cold gaze flicked over Simon, and then moved on. "However, I don't want to sacrifice these youngsters. I have found a solution which we have not used in generations, but which fits this situation well. It's called lock mentoring." He looked back at Gordon. "You may not have thought of it."

"Actually, I have," Gordon said. "I'm glad you agree with my choice." His hard gaze swept out over the pack. "Joshua, bring the bag."

Karl looked irritated at being anticipated, but sat down without comment. Joshua carried over a small duffle, which he set down by Gordon's feet. "In the older days of our pack," Gordon said, "lock mentoring was common. As is the case now, any young wolf who didn't have a living father was assigned a mentor, who was responsible for his training and behavior. And every mentor had full control of his young wolf, up to life or death. In those days, any pup whose control or obedience was less than perfect was locked." Gordon reached into the back and pulled out a length of fine chain, and a small padlock. "When a boy is locked, the chain is placed around his neck and locked tight. A wolf's neck is bigger than a man's at the same weight. Try to shift while locked, and the chain will tighten around your wolf's neck. Maybe it will only embed in your flesh, maybe it will choke off your air, maybe even cut through your jugular vein."

He looked down at the two boys. "I don't recommend testing it. Most who tried it, died." He scanned the assembled wolves. "The mentor holds the key. Under his discretion, the chain may be removed temporarily for supervised shifting. The mentor and Alpha together decided when the lock was no longer needed. A minimum of one year was usual. A maximum of five was set. A boy still rebellious, or uncontrolled, after five years of supervision, was never going to learn. If he was not ready then, he died."

Gordon frowned. "A hundred and twenty years ago, when Byron was Alpha, he made all the boys wear locks. For the smallest infraction, he would force them to try to shift while chained. Their pain was part of the cruelty and severity with which he ruled the pack, and when Sylvester took him down fifteen years later, the practice of locks was completely abandoned.

"But that left beatings and clean killing in its place as the only way to discipline lawbreakers. I've thought for a long time that gives me too few options. Perhaps it's time to try locks again." Gordon allowed himself a small smile. "A sixteen-year-old who never does anything reckless and stupid is unnatural. The problem is when they choose a version of reckless and stupid that endangers the pack. Perhaps our boys do need a reminder of why human rules can be messed with, and why ours are lethal. I would prefer that they don't have to die to make that lesson stick."

He looked at the two boys again. "It's not just your own lives you may be saving," he told them. "Make this work, show that you can learn from your mentors, and we will keep this option open." His stare became harder. "There is nothing magic about these chains. They can be cut, the lock can be forced, if you have strong enough tools. But if you do that, if you try to run or defy me, not only will we track you down and kill you, it will also mean that the next one of your friends who screws up won't be offered this option. They will die, fast and hard. So think well, and tell me if you accept the locks."

Jason stammered, "Yes, Alpha."

Zach looked up, his face tight. "What other choice do we have?" he asked bitterly.

"You can always be killed."

"Like my father."

Karl spoke up. "Your father's death was an accident. Yours would not be."

Zach hesitated and then looked only at Gordon. "Yes Alpha, I accept this penalty for my mistakes."

"Good," Gordon said. There was a rustle of breath around the circle, Simon's sigh part of it. The Alpha had spoken. No one would die tonight.

"I volunteer to serve as mentor for Zach," Karl said clearly. "I believe he can learn, given the right guidance."

Simon winced, thinking of being under Karl's full control at the age of twenty. He wondered if this was part of Karl's plans; it hadn't escaped his notice that both boys were among the crowd that seemed to follow Karl around. Had he encouraged the boys to run wild? Clearly he'd had the lock solution ready, if Gordon hadn't come up with it independently. Control over a teenage werewolf would seem like more trouble than it was worth, but Zach was smart, really smart, and good with technology. Maybe Karl had a use for him.

Gordon smiled at Karl, but there was something sharp behind the smile. "Thank you for the offer, Second. But you have too many duties to spare the time for mentoring a teenager. I have other mentors in mind."

Simon had been watching Zach, and he saw what looked like relief pass over the boy's face. It was a good sign, he thought. Zach might have followed Karl, but not so blindly that he wanted his life in Karl's hands. Maybe the boy could learn.

He watched as Gordon completed the arrangements. Zach was given to Alfred, to provide both mentoring and a new job and new home away from his friends, and perhaps not incidentally away from his grandfather. Looking at Joseph's dour scowl, Simon thought Zach would be far better off. The boy's grandfather was known for his strict traditional views. Simon had never seen an affectionate gesture toward the boy from that bitter old man.

Jason was sent to Brian to live and attend a new school. The boy looked shell-shocked, but made no protest. Karl's expression was sour. The choice of mentors was no doubt totally unlike where he would have put the boys.

Gordon turned to Pete, after Brian accepted the charge. "You will tell your wife that Jason was caught vandalizing property up north. Tell her you made arrangements that no charges would be filed, as long as he breaks off his old contacts and friends and goes to stay with his uncle. She can visit him there. But he may not go home. Can you make that stick?"

"I can," Pete agreed. "I'll persuade her it was this or jail. She'll miss him, but she'll agree." Pete's wife was spouse and mother to werewolves, but she was not pack. Some of the wives were true mates, bound to their husbands in the deeper way that involved the wolf as well as the man. Those women could be trusted with the pack secrets, but unbonded wives like Pete's couldn't.

The wives who were not so deeply trusted were kept outside of pack life. They knew nothing of werewolves, of dominance, of the code and laws their husbands lived and sometimes died by. It was hard on their husbands, but the burden of secrecy was the same regarding those women as for any other human contact. Break the secret, and both wolf and human would disappear. There was too much risk to let an unhappy spouse have access to that kind of knowledge. If they weren't trusted enough to be bondmates, then they weren't safe with pack secrets. Jason's mother couldn't be told what her son was truly being punished for.

Gordon then had each of the boys step up in turn and receive the chain locked tight about their necks. Though there was no magic involved, Jason flinched violently when the padlock snapped home. Zach took it stoically and then flipped the lock with a fingertip.

"It's kind of punk," he said, although he looked off to one side and not into Gordon's eyes. "Maybe I'll start a new trend."

Gordon sighed and waved a hand to Alfred and Brian. "Gentlemen, you have your charges. Good luck." He looked around the circle, catching them all with a clear, cold gaze. "This meet is concluded. Good night all." Gordon's stride as he left the room suggested he did not want to be detained, and even Karl watched him go without comment.

"Glad they didn't do that to you ten years ago," Andy murmured at Simon's elbow.

"Yeah, well," Simon pointed out, "it wasn't what I was doing while I was a wolf that worried them. No point in keeping me from shifting."

"Right." Andy sighed. "I'm glad Gordon chose the locks, instead of turning Karl loose on them." He lowered his voice to a breath. "No kid should die for something that dumb, and I don't know if he'd have stopped with a beating.

I don't know Jason well, but Zach's kind of cool. He's just been wild since his dad died."

"I can understand that," Simon agreed, as they left the room in their turn. "I feel sorry for Pete, though. How do you tell your wife her kid's being sent away, without giving her any say in the decision?"

"Better than telling her he had an accident and died," Andy pointed out. "But yeah, it'd be easier if they were real mates. Maybe he'll try the bond again."

"What do you mean, try?" Simon asked. "I thought it just happened, or didn't."

"That's not what I heard."

"What have you heard?" Simon asked curiously. "Because you know, strangely enough, no one has discussed the process of mate-bonding with me."

Andy snorted. "The way I understand it, you and your wife obviously have to really trust each other and all. But then, if you think you might bond, you still have to do it on purpose. You kind of reach for the energy, like you were going to shift, while you're touching your mate. I heard it works best during sex. Anyway, if you do it right, you, um, pull the energy sort of through them and there you are, bonded. If it doesn't work, you just don't link up. But you have to try for a bond."

"What if you don't do it right and you pull so much energy that you shift there in the bed? You'd be in deep trouble, or at least your wife would," Simon said.

"You don't pull it all the way. Just feel for it, like you're testing if you're too shielded or not. God, bonding would be a mess otherwise. No one would dare try."

"I suppose." Simon considered the process. "It's hard to picture how that works."

"Well, it's not something you'll ever worry about," Andy pointed out.

Simon managed to keep from demanding why his friend was so certain. *They barely tolerate gay sex. What would they think about gay love?* He mumbled his agreement and glanced at his watch. The sun wasn't yet up, but he'd have to hustle if he wanted to catch Paul before the clinic opened. Suddenly he wanted that more than food or sleep. Almost more than breath.

Chapter 12

Paul arrived at the clinic on Monday morning with a vague headache and a serious bad mood. He didn't want to be clingy or unreasonable, but surely you don't tell someone you love them and then disappear for two days with one lousy voice mail. One cold and non-committal voice mail. Or maybe you did, if you were Simon. After all, he didn't really know much about Simon. Not to mention, the family mafia thing was spooky. Maybe he needed to back off a little, before he got too involved.

That resolve lasted until the moment a man in dark sweats and a parka pushed away from the wall of the clinic near the door and approached him, box in hand, as he got out of his truck. He knew that walk at the first stride.

"Donuts?" Simon's tone was whimsical but his eyes were hot and needy.

"And where the fuck have you been?" Paul said, more roughly than he intended, because it was yell or kiss the man.

"Away. And now I'm back. Can we go inside? I have a serious need to hold you, and I don't think you want me to do that here in the parking lot."

Paul led the way in, aware of Simon's heated presence close behind him as he relocked the door and headed back to his office. He took off his jacket and hung it up, not looking behind him. He kicked off his boots and slipped into work shoes. He was reaching for the lab coat on its hook when the bakery box hit the desk. Then his arms were grabbed, he was whirled around, and Simon's mouth took possession of his.

And okay, so much for the backing-off part. Paul's mouth opened of its own accord to take Simon's tongue. They slammed together, pressed up against each other and to hell with it, he grabbed Simon just as hard, wrapping his arms around those muscular shoulders. He gasped into Simon's mouth as their thighs collided, groins brushed.

Simon broke the kiss to pull Paul's head against his shoulder and kiss his neck. "God, I needed that," he said, one arm still clamped around Paul. "Needed you."

Paul eased back. "Are you okay?"

"I am now." Simon grinned almost believably. "It was just a long drive, and some nasty vandalism, and not the way I wanted to spend the weekend, you know?"

Paul pulled free and leaned on the desk. "And what happened to phone sex?"

Simon's expression went rueful. "Rooming with Uncle Aaron cramped my style."

"Ah." Paul smiled. That explained the plain vanilla voice mail. "Have I met Uncle Aaron?" He couldn't remember the name of the guy with Karl at the hockey game, just cold pale blue eyes and bad attitude.

"No. Aaron's okay, actually. But believe me when I tell you he doesn't want to hear me describing my dick to my boyfriend."

"Is that what you were planning?" *Is that who I am?*

"Maybe," Simon said. "But now we can do show *and* tell, much more fun." Suddenly his head went up. "Someone's coming in. They have a key."

"I don't hear anything." Paul looked at his watch. "That'll be Elise, though." He stepped back out of Simon's reach. It took more resolve than he expected. "I need to get to work."

"Tonight," Simon told him. "My place. I'll supply steaks. I'm ready to eat some meat."

Paul blinked at the double entendre. "Can I bring anything?"

"Yourself. Your toothbrush." Simon tilted his head challengingly.

Paul couldn't answer, but he nodded.

Simon crowded against him and kissed him quickly. "You're so cute when you turn bright red. I can see myself out. Call me when you're done here, okay?"

Paul watched him go, then suddenly decided to follow him up to the front. He was twenty-seven years old, and Elise wasn't his mother. He wasn't sneaking around with a secret date. In fact, he kind of wanted her to envy his good fortune. Not many people had a guy who looked like Simon bringing them donuts and cooking for them. He took the pastries with him and made it to the front desk in time to see Elise relocking the door behind Simon.

"Good morning, Doctor," she said. "Did you have a nice weekend?"

Paul hurried to say, "It was kind of boring. Simon was out of town." Because he wanted her to envy him but at the same time he didn't want to think she was picturing him having sex. And maybe he was a little schizophrenic about the whole thing. With a firm headshake, he forced his private life from his thoughts and concentrated on work. "So," he said firmly, "have a donut and remind me what's on the surgery schedule this morning."

The day went smoothly. He cruised through his routine. The sick animals had minor problems; nothing was trying to die on him. He only thought about Simon every, well, five or six minutes. But passing thoughts, mostly. His work was absorbing. He thought he would get out on time, and his imagination kept veering in directions that made him glad he was wearing a loose lab coat. Then he pulled Mrs. Cromwell's cat Daphne out of the carrier and realized his day wasn't quite done yet.

Mrs. Cromwell's cats were almost as old in cat years as she was in human years. The other cat, Chloe, had been slowly failing as her kidneys shut down. Paul had spent a lot of time discussing quality-of-life with Mrs. Cromwell. Daphne was supposed to be the healthy one. But it didn't take much handling to see that she was thin and dehydrated. Half an hour later Paul had diagnosed diabetes and an infection. Treatable, at least, which was a huge relief.

But it meant fluids and insulin and antibiotics for Daphne. It also meant spending almost an hour with her elderly owner. First, she had to be convinced that her beloved cat wouldn't hate her if she started administering insulin shots. Then she had to be shown how, and told about diet and rechecks. Paul tried to dump some of the client education on his technician, but Mrs. Cromwell said Sarah's voice was too fast and high-pitched to hear properly. Paul controlled his impatience and spent another half hour with her. By the time the gray-haired lady was helped out to her car with the carrier, and sent on her way, it was late. By the time Paul was finally done with charts and ready to lock up, it was later. He hesitated before calling Simon.

"Hey!" Simon didn't sound too upset. "You ready to blow that Popsicle stand at last? Or blow something even more fun?"

Paul choked. "Um, yeah, I'm done. But I thought… it's after eight, and by the time I go home and change, and get to your place, it'll be nine. Maybe you want to reschedule?"

"Paul," Simon growled. "I've been holding my breath waiting for you. And *not* holding other parts of my anatomy because I'm expecting you to do that for me. Are you really too tired?"

"No. But…"

"Okay," Simon said firmly. "Then get your hot ass over here. Forget the changing and the toothbrush. I'll lend you one of mine. The salad is made, the steaks will be done ten minutes after you walk in the door. Don't keep a hungry man waiting."

Paul drove on autopilot, till he was almost shocked to find himself in Simon's driveway. Parking the truck, walking up to the door, had an odd dreamlike quality to it. Then Simon opened the door and pulled him into a hug, and the strangeness vanished.

Food was ready quickly. Simon kept the conversation light and teasing, and Paul found that he was hungry. It'd been a long time since he'd indulged in a steak. He would've felt guilty about the expense, except that Simon devoured a slab of meat twice the size of Paul's.

At the end of the meal, Simon opened a beer and handed Paul one.

"I don't know," Paul said doubtfully.

"Just one," Simon told him. "I want you relaxed, but not drunk enough to disconnect your brain. 'Cause I'm planning to blow your… mind."

"Promises, promises," Paul teased back. He'd never been good with small talk. But somehow with Simon it was easy. He didn't worry about sounding stupid.

Simon smiled, slow and sexy. He tipped his bottle up, chugging the beer so that Paul could see the muscles in his throat working. A drop of amber liquid escaped and trickled down his neck. The room felt suddenly warm.

Simon stood his empty bottle on the table, slid gracefully to his knees in front of Paul's chair, and reached for him. The first kiss, bent over and awkward, deepened slowly. Simon pulled Paul's head down farther to meet his hot, beer-flavored tongue. He kissed, licked, and nibbled his way to Paul's throat.

"Finish your damned beer," he said, his voice husky. "And come upstairs."

Paul took a couple of sips and slid the bottle away. "Okay."

In the bedroom, in the low gleam of the lamp, Simon stripped slowly. His body moved with that unique combination of power and grace, muscles flexing and gliding as he pulled up his shirt. He stretched his arms high over his head with the fabric, then toweled the T-shirt across his back, taut biceps round as coconuts. He dropped his pants, kicked them away, and approached Paul. His briefs did more to showcase than hide his arousal.

"Hey, sugar." Simon kissed Paul's neck. "You're slow." He eased Paul's clothes off deftly. Warm fingertips glided across Paul's skin, but Simon didn't grab him, didn't kiss or lick or even stroke him. He just watched his own hands, eyes glowing green in the lamp light, as each part of Paul's body was revealed. Paul trembled with anticipation by the time the last inch of his boxers was pulled carefully clear of his feet.

"Simon."

"Yeah?"

"I want…"

"What, sugar?" Simon stood in front of him, and slowly, so slowly, slid his own white briefs down over gorgeous skin, until he was naked. *And hard. And beautiful. God!* "What do you want?" Simon repeated.

"I don't know." Paul dropped his gaze under the heat of those green eyes.

"That's okay." Simon took his hand and waited until Paul looked up to smile at him. "Come to bed. We'll figure it out."

Sliding under the covers with Simon was like stepping into a furnace. Heat licked over Paul's skin. Simon touched him, kissed him leisurely. Simon's weight slid over him. Simon's mouth was everywhere, burning him down to aching need. The covers slid away unnoticed. When Simon's lips finally closed over his cock, taking him firmly into that wet heat, Paul cried out.

The surge of need was almost too much. He shoved upward, arching his back, driving against Simon's experienced tongue.

Warm fingers circled him, massaged him. He felt Simon's fingertips glide over his perineum, pressing just there. A jolt of electricity arced from Simon's fingertips to Paul's groin. Paul fisted his hands in Simon's hair, torn between pushing him down and pulling him off, that coarse hair something to cling to as he lost his balance, lost control. Climax slammed through him, taking his breath. At a distance he could hear himself crying out, but closer there was only the throbbing pulse of his body in release.

When Paul could think again, Simon's head was pillowed on his thigh. One of his big hot hands was playing idly with Paul's chest hair, winding scant auburn curls around broad fingers. Simon turned his head to press a kiss to Paul's trembling skin. Paul jerked in aftershock. His breath came short.

Simon gave a satisfied chuckle. "Is your mind blown?"

"I don't know about my mind," Paul breathed. "Other parts, though, oh, yeah."

Simon slid up the bed beside him, until their faces were level. "I loved that. You're so hot."

Paul kissed him. There was a trace of salt slick on Simon's lips. *Mine.* Paul wasn't sure if that was too weird. *If he can do it, I can kiss him afterward.* He deepened the kiss deliberately. Simon leaned into it. Paul felt the hard length of him against one thigh. He lifted himself on his elbow and pushed Simon down on the bed.

Slowly, Paul drew one fingertip down the muscled brown body, shoulder to flank to hip to groin. After a moment, Simon lay back and let him look. Paul had touched him before, and more than touched. But…

Dense dark curls couldn't begin to hide Simon's erection. Paul slid his fingertips closer. Simon's cock was bigger than his own, definitely wider. Warm-toned skin darkened to near-purple on the broad head, emerging from that helmet of foreskin. He touched lightly with a finger, sliding up the length of a swollen knotted vein, and Simon jerked in response. Paul could see Simon's pulse throbbing at the base of his shaft, fast and hard. He kept his finger moving upward. Odd how this hard part of a man could be the softest, like fine velvet to the touch.

A glistening drop of pre-cum appeared. Paul eyed it, and then slowly, deliberately, bent and touched his tongue to the liquid. Simon hissed. The flavor was odd, like salty vanilla, like nothing else. But it was a clean taste, not unpleasant. Paul licked again, with a little more tongue pressure. Simon caught his breath as Paul's mouth moved on him. "You don't have to."

"I want to," Paul said. Because he suddenly did. "But I don't know how."

"Oh, you're doing fine," Simon breathed. "Just touch me, lick me, it's all good, babe."

Paul explored, using his mouth and lips, licking and kissing his way down the hard length. The curls at the base had a musky scent, intense and wild, and he buried his face there for a moment. Then he rose up and took Simon partway into his mouth. He sucked, stroking with his tongue, feeling smooth roundness of the head and soft fold of foreskin against the roof of his mouth. He had no idea what he was doing. He had been far beyond paying attention when Simon did this to him. He tried to take Simon's whole length in deep and had to back off, gagging.

"I'm sorry," he began.

"Hey," Simon grabbed his hand and kissed it. "It's fine. You're making me crazy. But you don't have to deep-throat me to be amazing." He closed Paul's fist around the base of his erection, squeezing a little. "Like this, sugar, just like this." His eyes were glowing hot, and his smile was pure sex. He made their joint hands wave his dick in Paul's direction. "Does the little boy want a lollypop?"

Paul had to laugh. Suddenly the anxiety fell away. This was Simon, who apparently loved him. He didn't have to be perfect. He bent again, to tease with his lips and tongue, and then took in just the head. This he could manage. He sucked, licked around inside his mouth, and pumped firmly with his hand along Simon's shaft. Simon's rising gasps encouraged him to find a rhythm, sucking fast and hard. Simon groaned, arching into his hand. It was so good, so sweet, making the man respond like this.

"Paul," Simon moaned. "Oh, sugar, now. Gonna come, babe!"

The first jet of spunk hit the roof of Paul's mouth and he backed off as hot cum splashed his chin and chest. He swallowed a little, spit a little into his hand. And then he laughed, because Simon was gasping in sheer pleasure, and he'd done this right.

"God, baby." Simon snagged a towel off the bedside table with one outflung hand. "You may not be a pro, but you are one fucking talented amateur." He reached for Paul, helping to wipe him clean. Then he pulled Paul into a hard embrace. "Mine," he said fiercely. "You're mine, and you're awesome. Thank you."

Paul snuggled in happily against Simon's shoulder. "Only fair," he returned. "And everything I know I've learned from you."

Simon made a sound like a purr, or a happy growl, against Paul's hair. "Give me a few minutes." He pulled the covers over them, and wrapped a leg across Paul's. "And we'll move on to the next lesson."

It was close to three AM when Paul felt Simon shudder to yet another climax, pressed against his hip, and then sigh down into silence.

"Babe," Simon's voice was soft and deep. "I never thought I'd say this, but you've worn me out." Paul nodded sleepily against Simon's shoulder. The heavy weight of Simon's body moved around, and Paul was pulled into a spoon. Simon's dick was against his ass this time, but he was too tired and happy to worry. Simon's big warm arms around him were soothing, and Simon had made love to him twice over, without ever pushing beyond where Paul felt safe.

They'd used hands and mouths and bodies. But although Paul had been expecting, maybe willing, to let Simon go further, the other man had never asked. Paul pushed back with his hips, testing still, pressing his ass into Simon's groin. All he got was a sleepy chuckle and a tightening of Simon's hold.

"Go to sleep, sugar," Simon's voice said in his ear. "Tomorrow's coming way too soon." As Paul drifted off, he heard one last murmur. "I love you." And he almost said it back.

§ § § §

Wednesday afternoon, Simon was assigned to the back room of the shop, staining a pile of fine trim-strips for a bookcase installation. As his hands moved through the routine task, he considered a trip to the grocery store. He had some things left in his fridge, but feeding Paul up was his new hobby. The man would eat all right, if you put a meal in front of him. He just didn't seem to give food appropriate priority.

Werewolves knew better than to be careless about feeding themselves. A hungry werewolf might start looking at inappropriate things as prey. Bad idea for some stranger to catch you growling hungrily at a rabbit on the lawn. Most werewolves knew at least basic cooking. Simon considered it an art.

Maybe a roast chicken. Simon could do stuffing, or mashed potatoes and gravy. He didn't know Paul's preferences yet, but he planned to have fun finding out. All of them. He couldn't hold back a smile, here in private. Paul might be inexperienced, and a little shy, but he was amazingly sensitive and willing. And a quick learner. Three nights together had Simon's body humming like a top at the slightest thought of the guy. He knew Paul still worried about full penetration sex. Simon didn't feel the slightest need to push for that. Straight folk might not consider it sex unless someone was getting fucked, but part of the fun was exploring all the options. Paul wasn't going to be laid flat on a bed with his ass open until he himself was begging for it. Although then… Simon felt himself getting hard in anticipation. Oh yeah, that was going to be fun too.

The clock on the wall chimed the hour. Simon put a last stroke of stain on pale wood and stood the strips in the drying rack. Ten minutes to put things away and clean up and then he would head out. Maybe go to Byerlys. The Twin Cities' fanciest grocery store had a great line in dessert pastries. Watching Paul lick whipped cream off his lips was on Simon's to-do list for the night.

When he shrugged into his coat and glanced at his cell phone, there was a new text message. As he headed for the parking lot, he flipped the phone open and viewed it.

~Gordon is sending me to meet you at Bunker Hills golf course, 7 pm

From a blocked incoming number. Simon started his truck to warm up the cab while he considered. It wasn't unheard of for Gordon to pass errands around, but it was very odd for the wolf not to give his name. *Might be some trick of Karl's.* After all, it wasn't paranoia when they really were out to get you.

~Who is this? Couldn't hurt to ask, even if it was someone whose rank would earn him a slap-back for questioning them. But as minutes trickled by there was no answer.

Better ask Gordon, Simon decided, just to find out who he was meeting. Then if the meet was legit, he'd get a name of who to expect, and if Gordon said, *meeting where?* then he'd know something bad was up.

Unfortunately, Gordon's phone went straight to voice mail. Simon hung up without leaving a message, and tried his home number. Gordon's wife answered.

"Simon?" she said, and in response to his asking for Gordon, "Didn't you know? He and Karl are flying to Chicago tonight. They're probably in the air right now. They have two days of meetings about that supplier bankruptcy, to try to get as many pennies on the dollar back as we can. They'll be back on Saturday. Do you want to leave a message?"

"No," Simon said slowly. "That's okay. I can call later, if necessary."

If Karl was flying out with Gordon, then he wasn't lurking in wait at the golf course. It was unusual for both top wolves to be gone, but Simon suspected that Gordon didn't want to leave Karl alone with the pack right now. If the message wasn't from Karl, then Simon figured he could handle just about anyone else. If Gordon had needed to head out of town, then an errand for Simon was more likely to be real. He put the truck in gear and headed for the park.

The golf course parking lot was deserted when Simon arrived at six-thirty. In the daytime, there might be several people out cross-country skiing on the snowy expanse of the course, but darkness had fallen and the breeze had picked up. Even Minnesotans didn't usually court frostbite to that degree. Well, not often.

The cold expanse of pavement and ice lay silent. Small wisps of dry snow, insubstantial as mist, swirled around the ground in unseen eddies of wind. His contact might drive up any minute and hand him an assignment from Gordon, but something about the isolated quality of the place made Simon's hackles rise. No reason for two wolves in their human forms to meet so privately, unless something was wrong. And then surely Gordon would have called directly? Simon suddenly wanted to get out of plain sight.

He pulled his truck around to a semi-secluded spot. In the distance, up the hill, the parking area for the restaurant was busy enough. He might try to lose himself in the crowd there, but his view of the golf course would be limited. After a few more minutes of waiting, he gave in to temptation. The floor space in the truck was more cramped than the seat, but he'd done this before. He dropped down well out of sight, shucked his clothes, and shifted. The bulk of the truck around him absorbed some of the shift energy, but only slowed his transition. Eventually he was fur-clad and ready.

A practiced bite on the door handle let him out into the night. If he was wrong, there'd be no harm done. He would scope out his contact, go back to the truck, and shift back to human for the meet. But he wanted the sharper senses and mobility of his wolf form. If someone like Frank in wolf form was waiting to jump him, he'd be dead if he showed up as a human.

The cold wind brought a host of scents to his nose. The restaurant up the hill must've been having a special on some kind of fish, probably walleye. Closer in, he could smell the hot metal and rubber of his own truck and a faint wash of gasoline and exhaust from the hill parking. A careful scan of the local area brought no scent of humans or of wolves, but he needed to get further away from his truck.

Carefully, low to the ground, he crept away. As the smell of his pickup faded, he could detect another vehicle that'd passed through recently. *Come and gone.* He'd arrived early on purpose; he could hardly have missed his contact. Maybe just someone who mistook the turnoff for the restaurant.

He was a hundred yards from his truck when he slipped, one paw finding ice under the loose snow. He caught himself easily, but as he lurched forward something slammed against his shoulder, burning across his skin. The sharp snap of sound reached him an instant later. He rolled, dodging, before his conscious mind caught up and said, *gunshot!*

He ran a broken pattern, bitterly aware of how his dark coat stood out against the snow. A second shot caught him in the right rear leg with a sharp flash of pain and he went down, scrabbling on the ice, smelling his own blood. He scrambled up on three legs. His truck was too far. He needed to get out of sight. He launched himself up a towering snow mound left by a plow, struggling up and over. A third shot burned across his head beside his right ear, and he tumbled down the other side into deep snow. Then he picked himself up and ran on three legs.

Where? Who? Where? His mind scrambled for purchase, while his wolf body was getting them into the nearest trees. Behind him and up to the left, he heard an engine start. Half-aware, he veered away from the road. *Need safety. Run.* His wolf took over, sending him as fast as his limping gait could manage over the snowy ground. He was leaving a blood trail. If he'd been unhurt, he could've circled and tried an ambush. In this condition, that was too risky. His wolf fought for control, to get him to safety, running on. And on.

Human awareness gradually surfaced again as his body slowed. His head throbbed, and his vision pulsed in and out hazily. Sharp breaths tore at his lungs. He could smell fresh blood still dripping, but not as much now. Looking around, he cursed silently. In his half-aware state, he'd taken himself to a place his wolf thought he'd find help. The North End Veterinary Clinic.

Simon stopped short, panting hard. *Okay, think options.* This was at least a place he could break into and find medical supplies, maybe clean clothes, and a phone. He knew where the alarms were now, had seen Paul's code when they left together. He could shift back to human indoors in warmth and safety. Unless…

"Wolf!" Paul's voice came high and shocked. "What the hell?"

Simon looked around, equally shocked to see Paul walking toward him from behind his truck. *Slow, stupid, unaware...* He should run, but before he could move, Paul was there, wrapping that damned scarf around his neck.

"Come on, baby." Paul pulled Simon toward the door and unlocked it. "I can't believe it! Not again. Come on, let me help you." Dazed, Simon went with him, until his common sense surfaced and he tried to put on the brakes. Unfortunately, they were already inside the door. Simon pulled away, hard, ripping the scarf out of Paul's hands, but the sudden release rocked him off his feet. He tried to catch himself with his bad leg and went down, his vision tunneling into dizziness.

When he came back out of it, he was being led down the passage to the kennel. He didn't remember getting up, but he must have. He had come thirty feet without being aware of moving. And then Paul pushed him into the second concrete run and closed the door.

"Hang on, baby," Paul crooned as he pushed the lock pin home in the latch. "I'll be right back. I need to turn off my truck and get some things. I'll be right back." He glared at Simon. "Try to escape again, Wolf, and I'll kick your furry butt, got it? Stay." He ran out, closing the door as he went. Simon was alone, in wolf form, in his lover's clinic. Again.

Out, out, out! His head beat in time to that fervent need. There might just be time.

§ § § §

Paul skidded on the ice outside the clinic as he ran for his truck. He couldn't believe this. Didn't believe it, except that there was fresh blood on the snow at his feet. He'd been ready to leave, heading for Simon's house. Each time was easier, sweeter, to get in his truck and drive toward affection and warmth and food. *And sex, don't forget the sex.*

Then as he was scraping the ice off his mirror, a big dog staggered into his parking lot. He knew that shape of head, the massive body. But Wolf was in New Jersey. At least Simon said he was. Safe and happy. Not here bleeding in the snow again.

But as he handled the big dog, there was no mistaking him, and there was no missing the blood crusting black fur over the dog's big head, the slow drip from the right shoulder, the useless right hind leg. He hadn't done a full exam. Just enough to show that for all his new injuries Wolf wasn't pale, wasn't shocky this time. Just injured and bleeding and *here*. Then he locked the dog up temporarily.

Turn off the truck. Drop the keys in your jacket pocket with the door keys. Head back inside. He tried not to think, tried to concentrate only on the medical problem at hand. Because if he stopped, he would know that Simon had lied. There was no other answer. Not even Lassie herself could make it back from New Jersey on foot in two weeks. If Wolf was here, it was because he never left. And if that was true, then Simon lied about something important, and not just once.

It made no sense. Why would Simon have taken up with Paul, who could expose him for animal abuse as soon as he caught sight of Wolf again? How did someone whose hands were always gentle let this happen to their pet? *Wolf's not going back to him*, Paul vowed, heading back toward the clinic. *And neither am I.*

The pain of that hit him hard in the belly, and he stumbled. Because he had trusted Simon, and not just with his body. He'd really believed Simon when he said words like *love* and *different from anyone else*. Paul realized he had been falling in love himself. *Hell, be truthful. You fucking fell all the way.* And now he knew the bastard was a liar.

He meant to go back to his office first, take off his outerwear, put on a lab coat, and become Doctor Hunter again. But suddenly he had to take another look at Wolf. Before anything else. Because maybe Wolf had littermates, and this one just looked like him, or maybe Simon's friend had dumped the dog off along the road, or maybe he was hallucinating, or something, anything, that didn't make Simon a lying son of a bitch. Paul dumped his coat on the entry floor, kicked off his snowy boots, and ran in sock feet back to the kennels.

He yanked open the door and stared at that second run. And then he did decide he was hallucinating. Or drunk. Or something. Because that wasn't Wolf in the run, his black coat wet with blood. It was Simon, standing naked, his fingers jammed through the bars struggling with the difficult latch pin. The one Paul had used to keep the escape-artist dog in there.

Simon's head snapped up as Paul stared at him. For a moment Simon's eyes met his, flaring green as Paul had never seen them. Then Simon's hands dropped to fists at his sides and he turned away. "Shit." The word came very low and quiet, almost drowned out by Paul's rapid harsh breathing.

"Shit, shit, shit." With each rising iteration, Simon banged his forehead against the cement block wall of the run. And to Paul's horror, a growing patch of blood appeared on the block, beginning to drip…

"Jesus! Simon!" Paul grabbed the lock pin, extracting it with a practiced squeeze and twist. He yanked the door open, and got his hand between that dark head and the wall for the next blow. And he felt Simon pull the motion back, barely brushing his palm rather than crushing his hand against concrete.

And yet there was blood thick and wet on his hand. "Let me see." He grabbed Simon's chin, turning his head. But that wasn't a raw scrape on Simon's forehead. It was a deep, bleeding furrow, plowed from the right temple through Simon's hair above his ear. Blood was crusted around it in the coarse black hair, just like… *not going there.* But he couldn't stop his eyes from dropping down that familiar form. Hard chest, flat stomach, soft unhappy dick, and he paused there because he didn't want to look lower. *Wimp.* Tight, hairy thigh, muscles jumping and quivering in reaction to a deep, ragged two-inch hole in the muscle. Leg shaking, toes barely touching the ground. *Right hind leg.*

"Turn around," Paul said, his voice high and distant. Simon looked up at him again, his expression one Paul had never seen. Anger, pain, fear? Some of all of those? But after a moment he pivoted a half step and turned his back.

The back of Simon's right thigh was punctured by a small inflamed hole, blood running in streaks down the back of his knee and calf. Across his broad shoulders, another deep bloody groove ran from the nape of Simon's neck to the base of his right shoulder blade, marking the burn of swift metal through unresisting skin. Head, shoulder, leg. *Not going there!*

"You've been shot," Paul said.

Simon turned and gave him an expressionless stare. "No kidding."

"We should call the police."

Simon snorted. "I'd love to hear that call. What are you going to say?" His voice rose in mimicry. "Officer, I have a naked werewolf with bullet wounds in my kennel."

Paul opened his mouth to retort, swallowed twice, and finally came out with, "Werewolf?"

Simon stepped forward and cupped Paul's face in his hands, staring intently into his eyes. "Not likely, right? You're just tired, hallucinating a little. You were ready to leave when I turned up naked and bleeding on your doorstep. I told you I'd been assaulted, and you brought me inside to help. That's all."

"And I didn't call the cops because?"

"I asked you not to. Too embarrassed, too traumatized."

"So I locked you in my kennel?"

"You were hallucinating, thought I was a dog for a moment. I don't hold it against you."

Paul stared back into those intense gray-green eyes. "If you're trying to hypnotize me or brainwash me or something, it's not working."

"I know." Simon let go of him. "I can't do shit like that. But I wish to God I could. You need to forget this. You need to have never known it in the first place."

"Why? Okay, this freaks me out. But… but I can deal with the truth. I have so many questions…"

"Exactly. Questions. You know how people talk about dangerous secrets like, *if I told you that I'd have to kill you*? Well, this is that kind of secret. People die to keep it."

Paul stared at him. "You're going to kill me?"

"No!" Simon exclaimed. "God, no. Paul, you can't think that. I love you, I'd never hurt you. But I don't know if I can keep you alive if the rest of the pack suspects that you know something."

"The rest of the pack?"

Simon's smile came out twisted and bitter, so far from his usual humor. "Remember Uncle Karl and Uncle Frank?"

"Werewolves?" Paul couldn't believe he was saying that.

"Oh, yeah."

Paul scrambled to wrap his mind around this. "Is all your family…?"

"Werewolves. They're my pack."

"And the kid in the bowling alley?"

"Tommy," Simon supplied. "He's just a pup. I'm not worried about Tommy."

Paul nodded slowly. "But you are worried."

"Hell, no," Simon whispered. "I'm terrified."

That was a word he never expected to hear from Simon. Although obviously he didn't know Simon anywhere near as well as he'd thought. He was about to ask another question when Simon swayed and caught himself with one hand on the kennel wall. *Idiot!* Paul leaped forward to support him, wrapping an arm around his muscular waist.

"Come on. You've been shot, you fool. Come and sit down." He supported an unresisting Simon out into the treatment room. Chair, chair… there was a tall stool at the microscope. Not ideal for a dizzy patient, but he hooked it over and eased Simon down onto the seat. He grabbed a big towel out of the clean basket and wrapped it around Simon's shoulders. Simon had closed his eyes, but now they sprang open.

"We need to figure this out," he said, sliding forward as if to get up.

"We need to bandage you up so you stop leaking blood on my floor," Paul said tartly, pushing him back. "Then we'll figure out whatever." He parted Simon's hair with careful fingers and then paused, looking at the blood on his own skin. "Simon, this… condition. It's not contagious, is it?"

"No, babe, no. Not by blood, not by bite, it's genetic. But if you're worried…" He moved forward again.

Paul shook his head angrily. "Just shut up." He tried to close off his mind and concentrate on the medical. He could do this. He checked the scalp wound. It was shallow, skimming over the skull bones. No palpable fracture. "How many fingers?" he asked, holding up three.

"Twenty-six," Simon said. "And a half. Do you have any aspirin?"

"After I check you out." Simon's pupils were equal and responsive. He could track a finger left and right. And he was lucid. Well, assuming that any of this was lucid. The farther Paul got from the kennel, the harder it was to believe.

Simon's leg wound was bad, a shot right through the muscle mass, with a ragged exit. Simon had put weight on it, so the bone was probably intact, but it had to hurt like hell. "I could get you morphine. I'll list the DEA log for your dog."

"No!" Simon snapped. "We'll have to get rid of the Wolf record. Anyway, I don't want anything that might make me fuzzy."

"Aspirin or ibuprofen. Or Rimadyl?" *Would a werewolf use a dog pain med? Would ibuprofen give him stomach ulcers like a real dog? What's safe?*

Simon took ibuprofen, swallowing four while Paul got out bandage materials. "Should I put stitches in any of these?" Paul asked. "If you were a dog, I'd flush and debride and close the wounds."

"Just bandage. I heal fast. And when I shift, the stitches end up in the wrong place. I had a hell of a time getting the last ones out."

Paul paused in the act of selecting a Telfa pad for Simon's thigh. "Yeah. Wait a minute. You had a broken front leg… arm… leg last time you were Wolf. But out there tonight, you were running on it. And I haven't seen…" He could hardly have missed fractured ribs, gashes, a broken arm…

"I heal fast," Simon repeated. He reached out slowly and guided Paul's hand to the middle of his left forearm. "You can still feel a little of the healing callus." Paul palpated the arm underneath his fingers. The bones were solid, but careful touch found a smooth thickening, just about where Wolf's radius and ulna would've been broken.

He snatched his hand back and swallowed. “You healed in two weeks?”

“I healed in a few days,” Simon said softly. “Remember when we went bowling? It was almost healed then.”

When they went bowling. That afternoon seemed like another lifetime. Simon had been favoring his arm then. He said he fell. He said… *more lies.*

Silently, Paul washed the mess off Simon’s leg with disinfectant. The wounds still trickled a little rivulet of blood. He applied gentle pressure on each side with gauze sponges. *That has to hurt.* Simon’s muscles twitched, but he made no sound. “This should be flushed out well,” Paul told him, aiming for a professional tone. “Otherwise there’s a high risk of infection.”

“Werewolves don’t get infections. Or almost never, and if we do, a shift usually gets rid of them. Just cover it up.”

Paul nodded. *Telfa, gauze, Vet-rap bandage, tape; don’t think, don’t think.* He cleaned and covered the shoulder wound, winding the gauze around Simon’s chest and up over the shoulder. The head wound was in a tricky spot.

“Just leave that one,” Simon said when Paul reached for the clippers. “It’s too hard to bandage. It’ll heal soon enough anyway.” He picked up a wad of big gauze sponges and pressed them against his temple. “Fuck, that hurts.”

“Surprise.” Paul sat on the edge of the X-ray table. “Simon, why was someone shooting at you? Did they think you were a stray dog, or did they know who you were?”

“Oh, they knew.” Simon took the gauze off the head wound, dropped a few soaked layers, and reapplied it.

“Who?”

“Sugar, I’ll tell you everything I can,” Simon said tiredly. “Later. Right now, we need to decide what to do to keep you safe.”

“You really think I’m in danger?”

Simon sighed. “There’s one really unbreakable rule in the pack. No humans can find out about us. You wouldn’t be the first person killed to keep this secret.”

“Have you ever…?” Paul wasn’t sure he wanted to know, except he did.

Simon didn't pretend to misunderstand. "Not me personally. At least, not yet. But if it was necessary, really no other choice, I might have to. We're a rare species, trying to survive surrounded by millions of humans. We don't have super strength, or immortality, or mental powers like in the stories. We survive by not being seen."

"But surely there must be people you can trust?" Paul protested.

"Probably there are. But how do you decide, when the cost of being wrong may be extermination? Or worse yet, being swept up into some secret lab and life in captivity, to be used, bred, dissected. I trust you. But my Alpha, our pack leader, can't afford to let me make that judgment. Pack law forbids it, even if he wanted to."

"What do we do?"

"We could try to run," Simon said heavily. "I have an escape kit prepared, because, well, just because. But I'm betting you don't have false ID ready to go."

"False ID?" Paul was having a hard time taking this seriously.

"Oh, yeah. If we're judged a threat to pack security, every wolf everywhere will be looking for us. In this modern age, we use the Internet like regular humans do. We even have some wolves who are adept enough to be called hackers. We'd have to drop out of sight like going into witness protection, but without the help."

"We?"

"I got you into this mess. I'm not letting you deal with it alone. Besides, they'll have to go through me to get to you."

"Are you in trouble too then?"

"From the moment I said the word werewolf and didn't immediately break your neck, I'm as dead as you are," Simon told him.

"Surely there are other options," Paul protested. "I have my clinic, I have patients, surgeries scheduled. I can't up and leave."

"The only other choice is to bluff it out. Tell them the story that has me arriving naked and human on your doorstep. If you never saw me as wolf, and have no suspicion, then you're just my human friend. No risk, no problem."

"What's the catch?" Paul asked. "That seems like a no-brainer."

"Two possibilities. First one is that the guy who shot me followed me here and saw us together in the parking lot. I don't think I was followed, but I wasn't thinking clearly after he clipped my skull with that bullet. Second problem would be if Gordon or one of the high-ranked wolves starts asking me questions."

"Why is that a problem?" Paul asked bitterly. "Seems to me like you're an amazingly good liar. I certainly bought everything you told me."

"I'm really sorry." Simon *sounded* contrite. *Although how could you tell with a good liar?* "I told you the truth whenever I could. But sometimes I lied, and lied well, because both our lives depended on it."

"So do it again," Paul snapped.

"It's not that easy. Lying to a werewolf is much more difficult. We can almost smell a lie. There are body changes, all kinds of tells. And my Alpha is, well, in my mind in a way. Not like telepathy, but he can feel my emotions, if he tries. Lying to the Alpha is usually fatal."

Paul frowned. "I don't know enough. How can I make a decision? I'm not sure I even believe this myself anymore. Maybe I am hallucinating. Maybe this is all a dream. So, dream boy, you tell me what we should do."

Simon sat silently for several minutes. The furnace kicked on with a whirr. The lights buzzed. Simon pulled the gauze away from his head, inspected the stain, and put on a new pad. Finally, he looked up. "I think," he said slowly, "that running is in some ways riskier than staying. If we run, we're automatically guilty. They'll never stop hunting us. If we stay, change nothing, lie well, the cover story could work. There's no reason Gordon will suspect a problem, and if he doesn't suspect, he won't ask the right questions. We could be safe, as long as I wasn't followed."

"And the cover story is that I've never seen you as… Wolf?"

"Right." Simon slid off the chair, using a hand on the exam table to support himself. "We need to clean any trace of my wolf self out of the clinic. The blood in the kennel, footprints, everything. We need to get rid of the old medical record. If there's no trace of my wolf form associated with the clinic, then we should be clear. I'm your human friend. I'm allowed that."

"I can't delete you completely," Paul said. "Things like the drug log are handwritten, and I'd be in deep shit if I try to modify them. But we could change your record. I can make 'Wolf' a yellow Lab mix, change your first name and address, things like that."

"Maybe that will be enough," Simon said. "Do you have any clothes I can wear?"

Paul helped Simon back to the office and found scrubs and a sweatshirt that Simon could just fit into. He forced himself to ignore the reaction of his body to the sight of Simon squeezing into thin, skin-tight cotton. The man who had been his lover was… something else. He would have to get used to being alone again.

"I can clean the floors," Simon said, "if you get the records."

"Shut up, sit down, and drink some fluids," Paul snapped. He stomped out to the reception area for a cup of water from the cooler. He was suddenly furious at Simon, and scared for him, and confused. He needed to get a grip. *Scrubbing floors might be good therapy.*

He handed Simon the cup. "What do I need to do?"

"Any place inside the clinic that I touched as Wolf needs to be scrubbed with the stinkiest disinfectant you have. Mop all the floors. Clean the kennel walls. Seriously, I can help. I'm better already."

Paul shook his head. "You sit there and think hard about what we need to do. Give the pain med a chance to kick in. I've cleaned my own floors before." *Back when I was just starting, when this clinic was a dream almost out of reach and every penny counted.* He didn't want to lose this, even for Simon.

He poured disinfectant into the mop bucket at triple strength, choosing bleach over the less scented chlorhex. The kennel wall was rough painted concrete. The blood from Simon's head made an ink-blot pattern on the grainy surface. *What imaginary creature does this look like to you, crazy person? Do you believe in werewolves?*

Paul pulled on exam gloves and dipped a wad of paper towels in the bleach. He scrubbed the wall over and over, until the rough texture shredded the towels in his hand. *Enough. Surely that was enough.* He put the garbage in a plastic bag, and rinsed, rinsed again, flooded the sealed floor with a lake of bleach solution that slowly swirled down the drain in the gutter. *Wash all this away.*

He refilled the bucket and mopped obsessively. Kennel floor, hallway, reception, treatment room. The smell of bleach rose until his eyes watered. *Good thing there are no animals staying overnight. Elise has the cats home with her till I get the furnace controls checked. No other animals here... but the werewolf. Shit.*

He heard a sound behind him and found Simon standing there, leaning against the wall watching him.

"The stuff with your human blood on it is okay, right? I don't have to dig it out of the garbage? Or should I…" Simon caught him by the arm as he turned to the garbage can.

"Paul, baby, no." The man's deep voice was soft and hesitant. "I'm allowed to be here as a human. You've had trash pickup from last week, the old splint and stuff, right?"

"Yes, Mondays."

"Then that's okay." Simon looked around. "The X-ray table?" he said diffidently. "And that cage I was in the first night?"

"Done." Paul barked a laugh. "*The first night.* I still don't believe this. I must be crazy, hallucinating. I've… seen you, been with you, and yet you say you're not human. What does that make me? Besides insane?"

"Human," Simon whispered. "Amazing, sweet, smart, taken-unaware human. Paul, this would be hard for anyone. Just please, *please*, stick with me for now, all right? Let us try to make this safe. Afterward… afterward you can fall apart, or kill me or whatever you need."

"Afterward." Paul stared hard at him. *Do the next thing.* "The computer record still needs to be fixed. And you need to sit down before you fall down." But he didn't touch Simon, despite the way he was leaning on the walls as he trailed Paul back to his office.

At the keyboard on his desk, Paul dug into the computer records, changing all the particulars that he could about Wolf. He dropped his estimate of the dog's weight to a hundred and forty pounds, changed breed and color.

Simon watched him type from the spare chair, his eyes shadowed.

Paul remembered Wolf, the massive shaggy patience of him in that ward as Paul worked on charts at his cage-side. He remembered the feeling of connection even then, the affection that came all unbidden from the first moment he looked at the big dog. *Magic? Some kind of spell? Or just... Simon.*

His cell phone photo of Wolf was linked to the file and he pulled it up to delete it. Simon leaned forward as the image appeared on the screen.

"That's me, all right."

Paul looked at it, his hand hovering over the delete button. "You made a convincing dog. You wagged your tail at me and licked my face, you bastard."

"You fed me dog kibble," Simon countered.

"You ate it."

Paul looked at Simon and suddenly they both snorted with laughter. Paul held his ribs, whooping. "I vaccinated you for rabies, you know. You're lucky I didn't neuter you while you were under."

Simon choked and gave him a dark look. "You're lucky you didn't try."

Suddenly another thought occurred to Paul. "Simon, I put up posters with your picture. As Wolf, with my name on them." He pulled up the files with the poster artwork he had so quickly cobbled together. *Have you seen this dog?*

"I picked up twenty the next day," Simon told him. "Was that all of them?"

"Yeah." Paul breathed a sigh of relief. "Okay." He flushed the photo and the copies of the lost dog poster. He emptied the trash icon. "You know, I've heard they can retrieve data unless you scrub it somehow. But I don't know how to do that."

"It'll be okay. If they're suspicious enough to put a hacker onto your computer, we're already up shit creek. The goal is to never have them get that suspicious."

Paul nodded slowly and then thought of his technician. "Sarah saw you. The wolf you."

"If they aren't suspicious, they won't bother to talk to her. She only saw me once anyway, from the kennel door. She probably wouldn't remember more than just a big furry mutt."

Paul printed a new page for the written record, filled it back in, changed the label. All the old paper went into the shredder, and Simon emptied the resulting shreds into the trash in the kennel that contained the dog poop. A good shake of the can, and no one was going to want to go digging through there.

Finally, Paul said, “That’s everything I can think of.”

“Can you drive me to my place?” Simon asked diffidently. “I came on foot, and it’s a long way home. And we need to dump that trash bag in a dumpster somewhere. And, um, your scarf and gloves that you handled Wolf with should go in it too.”

“My favorite gloves.” That was half tease, half lament.

“I’ll buy you new ones? Extra-soft leather?” Simon might be trying for whimsical but all he managed to look was exhausted. “And please get the truck interior detailed tomorrow morning on your way in. Ask them to focus on the back. Okay?”

Paul bit down hard on a rush of protective affection. *Shot, outed— he must feel like shit.* “Of course I’ll drive you. Anything else would look weird. If you’d really showed up on my doorstep bleeding, I’m not likely to send you home in a cab. In fact, I’m coming inside with you. I wouldn’t leave someone with a head wound alone. It’ll be less suspicious, and you promised to answer some questions. Because, mister, you have a lot of ’splaining to do.”

Chapter 13

Simon let Paul help him out to the truck, shivering as his feet, clad only in Paul's socks, met the ice of the parking lot. He wished the ibuprofen would kick in so he could think properly. His head felt like a Jamaican steel band had moved in and started playing at full volume. The ringing made it hard to even hear properly.

He half expected another bullet as he stepped out the clinic door. Or Karl, looming up out of the darkness. But no, Karl was in Chicago. Which had to be good, because no one else had as much of a hard-on for him. Except obviously, whoever shot him. He wished he could think.

Paul drove silently, heater cranked and blasting lukewarm air. Simon waited for more questions, but he realized Paul wasn't going to speak to him in the car. *Is he afraid, or just disbelieving? Disgusted? Angry?* He'd never meant to tell Paul anything that would put him in danger. He wondered how many other wolves had sat with someone they loved, who'd unintentionally been exposed, and counted their lover's life expectancy in hours. He wondered if they should've run, should run even now. If he was wrong…

They stopped at a dumpster behind an Arby's to dispose of the bag of trash. The smell of grease and fried meat woke Simon for a moment. His wolf-self demanded food, right now. *Not here. Not yet.*

The next thing he noticed was the familiar jolt as they turned into his driveway. That was bad; that he'd been so out of it he'd stopped paying attention. Loss of focus was dangerous. He wouldn't hear someone coming until too late. But his disorientation also meant running away would be a really bad idea, until he had healed a bit more. He waited for Paul come around and help him down and into the house.

His house had always been sanctuary, but never as much as now. He bolted the door and made Paul take him on a circuit to be sure all his blackout drapes were in place. He put the lock bar across the dog door.

"Why have a dog door?" Paul asked. "If Wolf is really you?"

"There are times I come home in wolf form," Simon said, "and teeth aren't good with keys and doorknobs."

"Ah."

Paul supported him to the kitchen and lowered him into a chair. Then he took a seat at the other end of the table and looked at him. Simon met his gaze. He didn't want to have this conversation. Didn't want Paul to stare at him like he was some freaky stranger. Didn't want to compound his mistakes. But the horse was out of the barn, and that door couldn't be locked again. Paul was entitled to have his questions answered. His curiosity was one of the bright and shining things about his lover, that vibrant eagerness to know what and how and why. If Paul died for his lapse of care, at least it shouldn't be from ignorance.

His landline on the counter blinked steadily. Messages. No doubt the pack had felt his injury again, and the last thing he needed was someone showing up on his doorstep tonight. Not that they'd come even when he'd been near death last time, compared to which this was a minor mishap. He reached over anyway and hit the voicemail playback.

Aaron: *"I know Karl is out of town, but if this is more than some kind of accident and you need help, call me."*

A surprising offer, but the last person he wanted to see right now was Aaron. Well, second last after Gordon. He couldn't lie to his Alpha, but he had a feeling lying to Aaron would be beyond him too. He hit the next one.

Megan: *"Mark says you got dinged up again. He says you're fine, but let me know if I should call Sue to get her first aid kit out, if you need patching up. Call me."*

And the phone's new-message counter changed to zero. Two messages. That was it. Although he was somewhat surprised *anyone* had cared. Minor injuries were common and of little concern for active adult wolves. Other than the disorientation, he'd felt worse than this a time or two.

Nothing from Gordon. But perhaps he hadn't even felt Simon's pain off in Chicago or had discounted it as minor. Distance did make the bonds grow weaker. Just as well.

He hesitated but then dialed Mark's number. It rang three times and Megan answered.

"Simon here," he said. "I'm fine, just a little sore like Mark said. No worries."

"Would you tell me if there was a real problem?"

And risk you, and thereby risk Mark tearing me limb from limb? No. "Sure," he lied. "Just banged my head. I'll be fine in the morning."

"You'd better be. I'd hate to have wasted my last frozen coffeecake on someone who was going to drop dead."

"Not dropping dead." That at least was the truth. "Promise."

"Take care of yourself, Simon. This is not a good time to become accident-prone."

"Yes, ma'am."

"And don't call me ma'am." She hung up.

Simon put the phone back into the base, fiddling to get it in straight, stalling for time. But eventually he had to look up and meet Paul's eyes. The silence felt deafening.

"So," Paul said finally. "Werewolves."

"Yep." Simon forced a smile. "Teeth and claws and things that go bump in the night. Oh, wait, it's the human in me that likes to bump in the night."

Paul shook his head, but his expression lightened. "Do you, like, shift into a wolf at the full moon?"

"Moon has nothing to do with it. A clear sky makes things a little easier, but the phase of the moon is irrelevant."

"Help me here," Paul said. "I want to understand who you are, what you are. Hell, from my viewpoint you look more like a dog shapeshifter. Your wolf form isn't true to life, you know."

"Too big. That's conservation of mass. And the broader head we believe is to allow a bigger brain, since we think like humans even in wolf form."

"You don't know for sure why you look like that?"

"Do humans know where they come from? We have our myths, of course. Some say we're descended from gods who mated with wolves."

"Like Zeus and the swan," Paul said bemusedly.

"If you say so." He tried a wry smile. "Figures a geek like you would know all the kinky myths." Paul just blinked at him. *Okay, that went over big.* He let the smile fade. "All we have is oral legend, passed down from before we had anything written. So who can tell, really? You want to hear this?"

"Speak."

Simon barked once like a dog. The ripple of unwilling amusement across Paul's face was his reward. *Amused* was good. "Yes, master. Well, in one legend the gods descended to earth in a land of snow and ice, and it would not sustain them. And they did not wish to die. So they looked around for a form that would allow them to survive, one that was master of this cold place. And they saw wolves. And they merged themselves with the wolves, and became us." He waggled an eyebrow. "Didn't realize you were dating a god, did you?"

"Jesus, Simon, nothing's serious with you, is it? Maybe I am drunk. Maybe this is all a hallucination of some kind."

"Can I tuck you in on the couch and have you wake up believing that tomorrow?" Simon asked. *God, to be able to turn back time!*

Paul shook his head. "No. No, you can't. You said that's one theory."

"There are others. I knew a wolf who was with the Army in Europe during the Second World War. He said he met a Russian wolf who swore we were the creations of a powerful wizard, made by his magic as servants and protectors for his castle. Then there are the folks who blame aliens."

"Aliens. Yeah, right."

Simon kicked at him under the table and bit back a grunt of pain. *Gotta remember not to do that with a bullet wound.* "You asked."

"So I did, although you're not exactly answering. What do you believe?"

"Oh, I like the aliens theory," Simon said airily. "Some ET's playing around in the Earth's genetic sandbox. Because I don't believe in gods, and our genetics are surely screwed up. But it could be magic. Someone once said technology which is too advanced to understand is indistinguishable from magic. We've never found any other magic out there, no vampires, no wizards, no spells, no fairies. Well, other than me. And we've looked. But no one can actually explain how we shift."

Paul nodded slowly. "Yeah, turning into a wolf is just… can you shift whenever you want to? It seems so unreal. I'm not sure what to believe."

Simon rubbed his aching head. "Whenever I want, up to a point. Shifting does take some effort, some energy. It's possible to be too exhausted to shift, even when you need to." He hesitated. "Actually, I should shift now. Shifting speeds up healing. Our bodies seem to reassemble in the new form with fewer injured cells. And right now, I can't afford to be this handicapped." He began stripping off his shirt, wincing at the pull on his shoulder. "Can you help me get the bandages off?"

"You're probably still bleeding." But Paul reached slowly for the tape on his neck.

"Bandages shaped for a human will just tangle up my wolf," Simon told him. "I'll clean up the blood later." When he was fully naked, he paused. "You don't actually have to watch this."

"No!" If the situation hadn't been so serious, Simon would've smiled at Paul's quick retort. "I want to see. I admit I'm curious, and, and this is the real proof, isn't it? No tricks possible."

"I guess." Simon thought a moment. "I'm going to shift to wolf. The transition may take up to a couple of minutes, depending on how tired I am. Shifting may hurt me, especially with my injured leg, so I might make noises but don't worry. I'll be fine once I've shifted. Just don't try to touch me in the middle of it." He had a moment's worry about whether his wolf form, suddenly emerging in pain and injured, might snap at Paul without realizing the mistake. But he felt reassurance from his wolf-self. This was their mate; sight, scent, and sound. No mistakes would be made.

Paul nodded, his eyes dilated, but alert, interested.

"I may not be able to switch back again right away. Usually four shifts in a row are within my limits, but tonight, I'll probably need to wait and eat as wolf and rest first."

"So where's the dog kibble?" Paul asked.

Simon managed a laugh. "If you find kibble in this house, *you* can eat it. There's hamburger in the freezer. I might get you to thaw it in the microwave for me. Raw is fine. I'll switch back as soon as I can. Shall I go ahead?"

Paul looked uncertain, but nodded.

"Okay." Simon lay down, concentrated, *reached.* Finding the strength was harder than usual, but the energy was there. His body twisted, reforming. The muscles in his thigh screamed complaint as they shortened and flattened around that tunnel of torn flesh, but he clenched his jaw despite the shifting of his teeth and made no sound. *Mustn't frighten Paul.* Pain came in flashes, sharp from his leg, throbbing from his head and shoulder, along with the stretch and twist and lurch of nausea and disorientation that were so familiar. He couldn't judge time, but soon enough the sensations ebbed, and he looked at the world through wolf eyes.

He pushed to his feet carefully, testing his injured hind leg. The wound felt better, stronger and more able to support him, but still damned sore. He twisted his neck, rolled a shoulder, testing his healing. *Or stalling. Look up.* He raised his head.

Paul was staring at him. It was odd, how his wolf saw this man differently. To his human-self, there was always an edge of awareness of the man's body, of lean muscle and pale smooth skin. His wolf didn't care about that. For the wolf, Paul was scent and movement, breath and heart. His wolf was fiercely possessive. *Mine!* This was his man, to protect and keep, and his body mattered not at all. Only those gray-gold eyes caught them both equally, staring into his soul, wolf or man. Simon felt his tail wagging slowly.

"Wolf?" Paul said tentatively, and then, "Simon?"

Simon went to him, pleased to find that his back leg would bear his weight. He dropped his jaw open in his lupine smile. *Hi! It's me!* He butted Paul's chest gently with his head, leaving a smear of blood on his shirt. *Oops, not fully healed.* He licked at the stain with his tongue apologetically.

"No, Wolf," Paul's hand blocked him. "That doesn't matter. Can you… do you understand what I'm saying when I talk to you?"

Simon sat down and nodded his head.

"But you can't talk?"

Simon whined, then managed a gentle headshake. *Ouch.* He was better, but that graze had clearly rung his bell harder than he'd realized.

"So you think like a man even though you look… never mind. I'm not going to play twenty questions with you. You can tell me when you're, um, human again." Paul eyed him speculatively. "Can you shift back now?"

Simon considered. Could he? Maybe, but he felt awfully tired, and the distant energy seemed unreachable. Maybe better outside, but there was no need to risk that. He got up and padded over to the refrigerator. With a practiced swipe, he hooked his front nails around the edge of the door and pulled it open.

Paul came to stand behind him as he surveyed the contents. "You said there was hamburger in the freezer."

Simon eyed the big beef roast on the middle shelf. To hell with frozen hamburger. But that tasty meat was behind the condiment bottles. Pulling it out would make a mess. Of course, this time he had human hands available to get it for him. He whined at Paul and pointed with his nose.

"The roast?" Paul's eyes went a little wide. "You think your master wants you to eat that? Except, shit, you are your master, right? Seriously, you want me to give you that?"

Simon could smell the juicy raw scent of it, even through the wrapping. He nodded and whined again.

"Well, okay." Paul worked the big piece of beef out from behind the other food. "But remember this was your idea. Let me get the plastic wrap off. Do you want it cut up?"

Simon shook his head carefully, too hungry to wait. He licked at his lips as the scent wafted out. *Smooth. Let your boyfriend see you drooling over a hunk of raw beef.* Fortunately, Paul didn't seem to notice. He laid the roast down on one of Simon's dinner plates and stood back. Simon meant to eat slowly, show some restraint. But when the taste hit his tongue, he tore into the meat as fast as he could. Two minutes later he looked up, licking his jowls, and remembered he had an audience.

"I'm glad your table manners are better in human form," Paul said shakily.

Damn. The last thing Simon wanted was to scare Paul. He went over to the sink, rose up on his hind legs despite the pain, and nudged on the cold tap. After a long drink, he let the water flow over his lips and chin. He wasn't going over to Paul with beef blood on his face. When he was sure he was clean he dropped back to the floor.

Back in his seat, Paul watched him closely, maybe warily. Simon deliberately wiped his muzzle on the kitchen towel, in as human a fashion as he could manage. He took hold of the edge of the towel in his teeth and carefully pulled the hem to hang straight on the rod. Then he walked over and sat down in front of Paul.

Paul reached out automatically to pet him, then froze in mid motion. "You don't seriously want me to pet your ears, do you?"

Simon's back leg was too sore to sit up and beg, but he waved one paw in the air and then bumped his head against Paul's hand. "You're a goof," Paul told him. Simon bumped again. Automatically, those long fingers dug in at the base of his good ear, rubbing hard. *Aaah.* Simon leaned into the touch. As Paul moved to scratch Simon's furry chest and rub his chin, Simon thought he might've figured out why dogs allowed themselves to be domesticated. Nothing had ever felt as good as human fingers— *Paul's* fingers— finding all his favorite soothing spots. He grinned up at Paul.

Paul said, "Are you going to change back to human soon?"

Can I? Simon considered it, *reached* tentatively, and then shook his head. Not yet. He leaned up against Paul's leg. Paul's hand moved slowly to the bullet wound on Simon's scalp, parting the fur gently.

"This is impressive. If I hadn't seen it fresh, I'd say this was several days old already. It's barely bleeding and the ends are granulating in. Let me check your leg."

Simon got up obligingly and turned so his wounded thigh was visible. Paul laughed. "Man, I wish my regular patients understood me like that." He bent to look. "Yeah, this one's healing too, although the exit wound still looks pretty raw. You'll want to take it easy for a while yet."

Simon nodded. *Damn, it's frustrating not being able to talk back. Maybe some more food would help.* He got up and headed back to the fridge, popping the door open easily.

"What now?" Paul came over and pointed at a pan of liquid on the top shelf. "Those look like pork chops marinating. Want those?"

Simon growled. Those were dinner. Carefully prepared for tomorrow's human dinner to wow Paul. He tapped the milk carton with his nose. In his wolf form, he loved all things dairy, but slippery, crushable milk cartons were hard to handle with teeth, so he seldom bothered. He followed Paul eagerly, limping a little, as his mate found a bowl in the cupboard and filled it for him. He lapped down the creamy white stuff and begged for more, until the carton was empty. His stomach felt delightfully full. Normally he would nap now and shift afterward, but he didn't want to sleep without talking to Paul. He paced the floor carefully, trying to encourage his body to digest the food. He felt better, less wiped. Maybe that much food and rest would be enough.

He chose a spot on the floor well away from Paul's feet and laid himself down, breathed deeply for calm, for focus, then *reached* and pushed himself out. He felt the shift overtake him but the changes came hard, painful and slow.

Shift energy reached him in pulses, mimicking the throbbing of his head, moving his transition forward and then ebbing before he could get over the hump. He heard himself whine, distantly. The world had turned gray and fragmented. Then from somewhere he heard Paul say, "Simon, are you all right?" Paul sounded frightened. Simon pushed *hard,* and suddenly he was back, coming together in his human skin, his bare hip protesting the hard floor. Everything ached, but his eyes saw human colors, and his tongue licked dry human lips. He breathed jerkily, too tired to get up.

Paul knelt beside him. "Are you okay? Can you hear me?"

"Don't shout," Simon muttered. "My head hurts." He struggled to sit up, and Paul put an arm around his shoulders to help, fine tremors shaking him. Simon squinted up at him. "Is there a problem?"

"You took a long time. I got worried. But maybe it takes longer to go back to human?"

"Not usually. How long was I out?"

"Almost ten minutes."

Simon shuddered. He'd never needed even half that long. He must've really pushed it to the edge. *Damned stupid move. What if I got stuck, and Gordon sensed it and sent help and someone found Paul watching? Idiot!* Well, he was done now, although almost too tired to get up off the floor.

"Will you come to bed with me?" he asked. The uncertain expression on Paul's face had him immediately explaining, "That's not a proposition. I mean it would be, but right now I'm too tired to do anything sexy. I know you want to talk, and I'll answer any questions you like, but can we please, please do that in a nice soft bed?"

"I guess," Paul said slowly. "I do want to know more." He helped Simon to stand and make his way up the stairs. As Simon slid naked under the covers, Paul hesitated and then took off his shirt and pants. For the first time, though, he left his boxers on as he climbed in on his side of the bed.

At least he's here, Simon told himself. *Don't push.* He rolled on his side, bad leg up, and looked at Paul. His lover lay stiffly on his back, not touching him, staring up at the ceiling.

"What do you want to know?" Simon asked.

"You said your genetics were screwed up. Does that mean you're really, I mean provably, genetically, not human, even when you look a hundred percent homo sapiens?"

"Werewolves don't make good scientists. Too restless. But we've married a few. We've recently found out that our cells have extra chromosomes that seem to be dormant in human form, and carry a big hunk of DNA attached to the Y chromosome that's an odd jumble of code they haven't figured out. Who knows where it came from or what it does, exactly? But the anomalies are there to be seen if someone looks." He tried to lighten it up. "Maybe it's from all those interspecies matings, 'cause everyone knows that gods' and aliens' prime directive is to fuck humans." He grinned at Paul over the throb of his aching head. "I like to fuck humans. One particular human."

Paul flicked his shoulder sharply with a fingertip. "Stay on topic here. You're saying you have human genes plus something."

"Turns out all our cells carry a full human genome, a wolf one, and that chunk of extra whatever."

"Sounds messy," Paul said. "Usually extra chromosomes cause problems."

"I'm no scientist. Somehow we handle it, use what we need."

"When you're a wolf, how close are you to a real wolf? I mean, the drugs I used seemed to work, and the X-rays looked normal."

"We can pass for real wolf, or at least wolf-dog, and real human. As long as we don't have DNA testing. Which is why we're still walking around undetected. But, on the downside, that means no superpowers. If neither ordinary man nor wolf can do something, odds are we can't either. If we are made by magic, there are a few things I wish the wizard had added in."

"Would you be fertile with a real female human or wolf?" Paul asked, and then quickly added, "You don't have to answer that."

"No problem," Simon said. "The answer is yes. We have to be. Because there are no female werewolves."

"None?"

"We marry human women. Some of them never manage to have children, but when a woman does carry a baby to term it's always a boy, with the potential to shift. We're not sure yet what it takes to fertilize a human egg and produce a werewolf baby. Most pregnancies are lost really early. Only a few make it past three months. But we need humans to survive."

"But then…" Paul finally turned to him, eyes puzzled in the dim light. "Surely there are humans who know who and what you are. I mean, they marry you, have your babies."

"Some of the women are never told the truth. We have conflicts, bad marriages, and even divorces these days. Some men never trust their wives enough to share the secret. But yes, some of the women become bonded mates. That's when a man and his wolf-self both accept and trust the woman. If he decides to, the man links to her with the shift energy. It's hard to describe. After that she's bound to him, emotionally, and vice versa, and through him to the pack. The Alpha can sense her too. If that happens, then she's considered safe with the pack secrets."

Paul nodded slowly. "Which almost sounds more like magic than science. No way to tell, I guess. Does your pack have any wives like that?"

"Yes. Five. And eight wives who are not yet bondmates. We're a big pack, forty-four of us. But some are too young for marriage, and a dozen have outlived their wives."

"Outlived… how long do you live?" Paul whispered.

"We're not immortal or anything," Simon hurried to tell him. "Shifting slows aging down some, but time spent as a wolf may speed it up. A hundred and twenty is not unusual, a hundred and fifty is."

"So you could outlive me by fifty years."

"Or I could be hit by a bus tomorrow. Or be shot."

"Speaking of which, the wolf thing is fascinating, but I want to know who shot you."

Simon did too. "I wish I knew. I have some guesses, but… it's a dumb thing to have done, even before the guy missed. Frank's stupid enough, but I don't think he'd do it unless Karl told him to, and Karl's out of town. Although maybe, on second thought, that gives him a handy alibi while he sends someone else after me. There are a couple of the younger wolves who really don't like me right now, and a couple of the older ones who might break tradition for Karl."

"Why don't they like you?" Paul asked. "Other than the fact that you're irritating and annoying as hell?"

"Aw, how sweet." Simon bared his teeth in a grin. "They mostly don't like me because I'm gay. According to pack traditions, I should've been disposed of when they found out. Werewolf culture is *not* gay-friendly. But Gordon, my Alpha, let me live and stay in the pack. And not at the bottom of the dominance ranks either. Some of them can't handle that. And I've pushed for other progressive changes, which the older traditionalists don't want. Plus, I think Karl's using me as a scapegoat in some long-range play to take down Gordon. Of course, he probably chose me because he already hates my guts."

"One big happy family."

"Oh, yeah. We can make the Mafia look like a bunch of pussycats. Those aliens who made us must've been real big on rank and status, because we're more dominance-conscious than any real wolf pack."

"You're saying you don't know who shot you, or why, or whether they'll try again?"

"Nope." Simon was suddenly too exhausted to keep his eyes open. He yawned widely. "But I'm alive, and we're together, and no one's pounding on my door accusing me of breaking pack law, at least not yet. So far, so good."

He reached out to barely touch Paul's arm with one finger. "Sugar, I have to sleep. Will you stay here, where I'll know you're safe? Please?"

He waited only long enough to hear Paul softly say, "All right," before he was out like a light.

§ § § §

Paul looked at the sleeping man next to him. This was the strangest night of his life. He could feel the warmth of that muscular tanned body, so familiar, but also alien now. He wondered what Simon's normal body temperature was. Wolves commonly ran a hundred and one, but if werewolves were that feverish in their human form, those human mothers would be dragging their sons to the doctor for fever-of-unknown-origin testing, which clearly hadn't happened…

He sighed. He was thinking about the scientific details because he didn't want to face the personal ones. Simon wasn't human. How was he supposed to deal with that?

He snorted softly. Maybe he could write a new self-help book: *How to Cope when Your Lover is an Alien Werewolf.* Although, aside from the fact that the public notice would apparently get him killed, the market would be small. The other people who might need the book couldn't be allowed to know about it.

He could understand the men being reluctant to share the secret with their girlfriends or even wives. How odd, to realize that the man who had been in your mouth, or in your body, wasn't human. There was a squick factor, thinking that those body parts you caressed, licked, kissed, could… change. He might be into men in ways he'd never recognized, but he wasn't into bestiality.

Ah, at last, a side benefit. This made being gay the least of his worries, almost comfortingly normal. But how much harder for a woman, especially if she was pregnant, to think that the child she was carrying inside her could transform into a wolf. Simon said they never changed by chance, never without choice, but still. It would take a special woman to accept that.

So, could he accept Simon? Did he even want to try?

He wondered whether he should be afraid of being bitten, of being attacked, and decided no. He couldn't make himself scared of Simon in either body. Maybe if he hadn't met Wolf first as a dog and trusted him already. He wouldn't want to be on the wrong side of a two-hundred-pound wolf with jaws that could gnaw cleanly through an eight-inch roast. But he was certain Wolf would never hurt him. Or Simon in wolf form wouldn't. It was hard not to think of them as two separate beings.

Okay, not afraid. But could he stay with Simon, touch him, be with him, and not keep thinking *monster, alien*? He let his eyes run over that familiar face. Copper skin, dark thick hair and lashes, high cheekbones, strong nose. And that mouth.

As if aware of his gaze, Simon twisted on the sheet, muttering something. His hand swept out and found Paul's wrist. Strong fingers locked around Paul's hand and pulled his palm in against Simon's chest. Then, hugging Paul's hand to him like a teddy bear, Simon smiled softly in his sleep and quieted.

Paul fought back a yawn. He was bone tired himself, and for tonight, he'd promised to stay. Time enough tomorrow to think further ahead. He slid down in the sheets, and found himself turning automatically to fit up against Simon. Familiar skin, well-known scent, cherished warmth. His body had no doubts where it belonged. But his mind was not so sure. He dozed uneasily as the hours passed.

By early morning he was restless enough to get up. Simon had released his hand, and Paul was able to slip out of bed slowly without waking him. Simon must be beyond exhausted, he thought. He'd never before so much as stirred in the night without seeing those gray-green eyes snap open, alert and aware. He bent and pulled on his clothes, moving slowly and silently. A clink of coins in his pocket betrayed him, and he glanced up to find Simon looking at him.

"Are you leaving?" Simon asked. His tone was probably meant to sound calm, but Paul heard the anxiety.

"I still have to work today," he hedged. "If we're pretending nothing major happened. If you weren't hurt enough for the police or the hospital, then I would go to work."

"It's five AM."

"Well, if you keep dragging me out with my work unfinished to go bowling or watch you turn into a werewolf, you'll have to let me go back to work early," Paul quipped feebly.

Simon nodded. They both knew he'd already been in the parking lot, leaving, last night. There was no critical work waiting for him.

"Are you coming back?" Simon whispered.

"I don't know," Paul said slowly. "I need to think. I won't betray you. You know that. But I was starting… I don't know if I can be with you like this."

"You could still be in danger," Simon said urgently. "I want to keep you safe. I don't want you out there alone."

"I need to think. If your, um, pack is after us, it doesn't sound like being together will make much difference. And if they don't suspect a problem, then you acting like a bodyguard might make them start wondering."

"Okay." Simon dropped his eyes. "Can I make you breakfast, before you go?" His voice was hoarse.

Suddenly Paul couldn't speak, couldn't stay here one more minute. He shook his head silently and slipped out of the room, closing the door behind him. The house was silent around him as he went down the stairs. The light was still on in the kitchen, gold across the polished floor, casting a triangle of brightness into the hall. He found his boots and coat in the dimness and shoved his bare feet in, closed a couple of jacket buttons. There was no sound from upstairs. Paul wasn't sure if he wanted Simon to come after him, or was afraid he would. All he knew was that he needed to go, *now*.

The cold caught him like a hand around his throat as he stepped outside. His truck wore a layer of frost, the locks stiff. The engine started with a whirr of complaint. He pulled out of the drive, not looking back, because he didn't want to know if Simon was watching him go. He made it five blocks before the blurring of his vision forced him to pull over. Then he parked against the snow bank on the deserted street and put his head on his arms, eyes prickling.

No one will ever love you, stupid, ugly, no one will ever want you. If you love someone, they'll just ditch you and leave. Knowing where the words came from didn't keep them out of his head. He'd been so close to love with Simon, and now…

Well, what now? Now he knew loving Simon would be even more difficult than he'd thought. But did that change how he felt? Did it change how Simon felt? Could he trust anything Simon said, when there'd been a lie that enormous between them? And yet how could he blame Simon for lying? Paul remembered Karl, his pale eyes hard and speculative. And Frank, with his vicious words. *If you knew both those men could become wolves— each bigger and meaner than Simon's wolf— would you take a chance on enraging them if you didn't have to?*

He banged his head gently on his arms, folded over the steering wheel. He'd always relied on logic and science to get him through, because emotion could trap you. But logic wasn't cutting it here.

Okay. *When all else fails, simply do the next thing.* The next thing was work. He could always work and lose himself in the demands of his profession. Go home, shower, get dressed, grab a clean lab coat, go to the clinic, check the overnight reports of yesterday's blood work, prepare for surgeries. He could use the familiar routine to block thought, for now. He rubbed at his eyes and sat back up. Go home, shower, get dressed… get the damned SUV detailed inside and out… He bit his lip hard and put the truck in gear.

§ § § §

Simon waited until he heard Paul's SUV start and pull away before he got out of bed. He'd longed to run after Paul, wanted to stop him, at least guard him. His wolf pushed at him, hard, not to let their mate leave. But he couldn't keep Paul here by force. That would destroy any chance of having him here by choice. And he couldn't think of words to make the man stay. Even though he was usually so good with words.

At least he'd heard nothing except the sounds Paul made, *leaving*. No waiting wolves, no attack, no pursuit. So now he had to get up and go on.

He took a cab to Bunker Hills. His truck sat where he'd left it, windows frosted white. He paid off the cab and approached the vehicle, senses on alert. Nothing moved, nothing smelled off. He circled all the way around, but there was no sign it had been touched. His clothes and keys were still where he'd left them in the cab.

He got in, started the engine, cranked the defroster, and considered the layout. *If I wanted to shoot at me, running in the snow, from that direction… There.* The shot angle suggested someone had parked on the access road and then lain in wait with the gun on top of one of the snow banks. Or maybe fired from inside a vehicle, something high enough to see over the snow mounds.

The road was well enough used that no tire tracks stood out in the rutted snow. He found the location of his ambush. The smell of gunpowder lingered, but there was no trace he could pick up of who the gunman was. *Or woman?* But no, he'd been shot at as a wolf. Of the women who might conceivably hate him, Frank's wife, Zach's mother, and Jason's, were all wives but not true mates. They might be convinced to hold a grudge against him, but not given the knowledge to shoot at his other form. And the bonded wives didn't have cause.

A packmate then, which he'd already believed was the case. The packed snow mound the shooter could have used for elevation was too hard-compressed to show footprints or stride length. But the lack of even a trace of scent suggested the shooter had stayed in his vehicle.

He shook his head. The whole attack was so *stupid.* A dead dog might not draw a lot of interest, but a dog shot to death would be a police matter. Even the sound of gunshots within the suburban Twin Cities was likely to be investigated. To top it off, whoever set up the ambush here had no reason to expect he'd present a target as a wolf. Would they have fired on his human form?

If they'd killed him in human form, there was a real risk his body would've been seen before they could drive back to the parking lot and collect it. The golf course restaurant hadn't been far away. And these days, DNA collection at a murder scene was the rule, meaning unless they got all the blood as well, they'd be leaving behind dangerous trace evidence. They'd risked pack safety with this dumb-ass move. They should be grateful he'd survived. If his murder had revealed the great secret, every wolf on earth would've wanted a turn at killing the murdering idiot. Slowly.

Someone desperate, senile, young, or just crazy? The categories didn't eliminate as many suspects as he'd have liked, which said something about the current state of the pack. The shooter might still smell of gunpowder, if he had been careless about cleanup. He could hardly go around sniffing suspects' hands though. The young ones were out of bounds by oath, the senile were hard to get to, and he could imagine the look on Frank's face if he tried.

Simon backtracked to the spot where he'd been shot. Someone had at least driven over the blood, grinding it into the slush. You had to know it was there to pick up the traces. He climbed the snow hill that he'd desperately scaled last night. His floundering three-legged path through the snowy field on the other side was evident. No footprints followed his trail. The whole thing smelled more like one crazy wolf than a conspiracy.

He followed his own tracks, noting and carefully treading under the drips of blood in the snow, stamping fresh over the top. *I ran westward, until I reached the first road.* There was more traffic now than on a weekday evening. When a break came, he crossed the road and cast up and down the other side for obvious tracks that might lead a pursuer. To his pleasure, he found none.

Even with whatever weird fugue state he had been in, he had somehow had the sense to use the slushy, traveled road to break up his trail. If he had been followed, or if someone thought to track him later, his trail wouldn't lead them straight to Paul. Of course, if you plotted his direction and knew his habits, there weren't many other places he could've been going. Still, suspicion wasn't proof.

The big question now was whether to report his shooting to the pack. The last thing Simon wanted was to be questioned about the event. But if Gordon heard about it from other sources, his silence would look odd. He snorted. Queer, even. Maybe he could pull off claiming it looked like just more gay-bashing, not worth a mention. He'd seem dumb, for missing the security implications of a shooting in a public place, but he'd made a career of being underestimated. He decided on no report, for now.

At work, he found it hard to concentrate. Zach was there, working for his new mentor. The chain circled the boy's neck, but he seemed more relaxed than Simon had ever seen him. He showed no surprise at Simon's healthy arrival—no change of heart rate, no dilated pupils, no shift of scent to indicate strong emotions. If he was holding a grudge against Simon for the torn hamstring or for taking him down at Pine River, he hid it well. Simon snagged a hammer the boy had used and sniffed it, but there was no transferred gunpowder scent, as far as his human nose could tell.

Alfred cornered Simon at lunch break and asked him point blank why he smelled of blood. Simon fibbed about falling on the ice and slicing open his head. Alfred gave him a look that said, *you're not fooling me*, but didn't press him further. Casual conversation produced the information that Zach had been out somewhere the previous evening, so he had no alibi from Alfred.

As the day wore on, Simon found himself jumping every time he was approached. He dropped a tool on his foot, gouged a piece of wood when the door suddenly opened while he was carving. His subconscious was waiting for a shot out of the dark, a wolf leaping on him, a summons from his Alpha, some kind of reaction to last night. His stability was made worse by his wolf who wanted to ditch work and go protect Paul.

He tried to control himself, laugh at the errors, joke with people. He probably looked guilty as hell. Which would lead to people trying to figure out what he was guilty of.

Alfred chased him out at quitting time. "I don't know what's going on," he said. "But whatever your problem is, keep it out of here. Is someone Challenging you?"

"No," Simon told him. "Just, um, a fight with my boyfriend."

Alfred snorted in disbelief. "And he brained you with a frying pan? Right. Get out of here before you break something. But Simon." He waited until Simon looked up to meet his eyes. "If you need help, call me."

Simon stopped, surprised at the offer. Alfred wouldn't have said those words if he knew what was really at stake, but still, a second offer of help warmed some cold place inside him. "Thank you."

He went home. Anything else would be a mistake, but home was dark and empty. He moved room to room, too restless to settle. He found a pair of Paul's socks under the couch, a cup he'd used on the bookcase. His scent was everywhere.

He has to come back on his own.

If he comes back. Finding out your lover was a werewolf was the kind of thing that led to breakups and therapy, not happy endings. That untimely truth-bomb had been forced on them out of the blue, but maybe Simon could've explained it better, handled it better…

He made his way into the kitchen. His stomach was growling at the lateness of the hour, and a werewolf needed food. Especially after a stunt like shifting while wounded three times. He was still running on empty, and being smart meant staying fed and healthy, ready for whatever came. He opened the fridge. Four pork chops sat in his favorite marinade, the smell of soy sauce and honey filling the fridge. He closed the door again. *Not that.* His stomach rolled queasily, half hunger, half stress.

Dry cereal and an inane game show on TV seemed like a plan. He was snacking from the box when he heard Paul's SUV turn in the driveway. This time, he waited for the doorbell before going to the door. Paul would come in person, whatever he'd decided, out of courtesy. Just because he was here didn't mean he'd stay. Simon opened the door.

Shuffling on the doorstep, Paul looked up at him, a hint of color across his cheekbones. "Rumor says the right guy can get a good dinner at this address."

"Best in town," Simon agreed, fighting down the rapid beat of his heart. "For the right guy."

"And am I?" That sounded like more banter, but there was something so uncertain about Paul's voice that Simon barely kept himself from grabbing, hugging, kissing.

"Mine," Simon said, as firmly as he dared. "You're mine. And absolutely right."

Paul's face brightened. Simon wondered how Paul could possibly have doubted his welcome. *Remember that; he's less certain of me than he should be.* For now, he pulled the door open wide.

Paul held up a bakery box as he came in. The scent of chocolate wafted out. "I brought dessert."

Simon took the treat from him and set the box on the hall table. He locked his hands behind his back to keep from helping take off Paul's coat, putting away his boots, making sure that he'd stay. "Are you hungry? I still have those chops you were going to let me eat last night." *Idiot! Remind him you're a carnivorous wolf.*

But there was genuine humor in Paul's smile. "Sure. Sounds good." He followed Simon into the kitchen, perching one hip on a stool as Simon turned on the oven and began getting out food. Finally, Simon couldn't wait anymore.

"Have you thought about… what you want to do?"

"Yeah," Paul said slowly. "You had a secret you didn't tell me. But we haven't been together that long. I shouldn't expect to know all your secrets. I asked myself, what if you'd waited for a while to tell me you had cancer? Would I stay and try to work it out, or would I bail? What if you were divorced with a kid? What if you were an ex-con or an alcoholic trying to stay sober? By the time I got to, what if you were a werewolf, I'd said *stay* so many times, the answer was obvious. This is weirder than the rest. But the answer's the same. If we can work it out, I want you. If you still want me?"

"Jesus, Paul!" Simon pulled a strangled breath. "How can you not know?" He dropped the broccoli in the sink, stalked over to Paul, and cupped his lover's face in his hands. For a long moment, he stared into those gold eyes, watching the dilating pupils darken them as the scent of mutual desire rose. His first kiss was gentle. The second wasn't.

"Wait, wait," Simon murmured, even though he was the one pinning Paul up against the counter, grinding their bodies together. "I'm tired of washing shorts. I want you naked."

"Upstairs?" Paul panted.

"Couch is closer." They stumbled there together, shedding clothes. Paul's knees hit the couch, toppling him under Simon, hot and eager, where he belonged. Simon gave himself to the feel of mouth on mouth, and the slide and thrust of hard muscle and smooth skin. He let his whole weight pin his lover to the couch. Instead of objecting, Paul's arms came tight around him, pulling him down. As the need rose and rose, Simon bit down, taking Paul's hot neck between his teeth. Not to hurt, just enough, just to mark him. *Mine. Oh, God!* He felt Paul shuddering in response, and the friction became slick and wet and so good. Now! He came hard, shaking, pressing tighter against his lover. Then the heat slowly receded, leaving him limp.

"Simon, I need to breathe," Paul said. "You weigh a ton."

Simon moved over. He was still held in the circle of Paul's arms. He looked cross-eyed at Paul's pale skin, marked by the red arcs of Simon's bite. He liked the look. *Mine.* But he kissed the spot gently and licked the skin. "Did I hurt you?"

"Who? Where?" Paul smiled, his eyes closed. "God, hurt me like that anytime, Simon. Wow." Simon felt a shudder pass through the slim body under him.

After a few minutes, Simon picked up his head. “The oven’s on. And you need to eat.” He straightened his arms and pushed up, then bent his head to kiss Paul’s full, reddened mouth. Paul lay relaxed and boneless under him, eyes still closed. “I’m not looking at your naked anything,” Simon said. “I’m getting up and making dinner and not looking at you.”

Paul laughed and slid out from under him. “Yeah, go cook my dinner for me.” He yelped as Simon pinned him back down.

“I may be your dog,” Simon growled in mock displeasure, “but I’m not your bitch. Ask nicely.”

Paul looked up at him, eyes sparkling. “Pretty please? Pretty, pretty please, with a cherry on top?”

Simon held back the impulse to say what he wanted with Paul’s cherry. Too soon for that. Way too soon. Instead he kissed him. “That’s better.” He rolled off and stood up. “Now, do you want potatoes or rice with your pork chops?”

“Rice.” Paul reached for his boxers. “You know, it might’ve been easier to wash our shorts than the couch.”

“I don’t care,” Simon said. “I wanted you naked.” He paused at the entrance to the kitchen. “You will stay? Tonight?”

Paul met his eyes and nodded. “I’ll stay.”

Chapter 14

Amazing the difference a day made, Simon reflected, as he bent to his work the next afternoon. No attacks, no accusations regarding Paul, no sign of any fallout from his attempted murder. There might still be problems coming— almost certainly would be, unless he could find out who wanted him dead so badly— but he felt mellow and replete. Gordon would be back tomorrow, which might mean a summons. But today he and Paul were okay. They were a hell of a lot better than okay.

Simon worked the polyurethane finish into the grooves of the scrollwork, laying it on smooth and perfect. The strong smell of the solvents bothered his nose, but the clear even shine was beautiful. The odor was probably what kept him from realizing who'd walked into the room.

"Simon?"

He jerked up at the sound of Aaron's voice and whirled around. The brush he dropped made a wet splat, marring the perfect finish. *Easy, easy, look innocent.*

"Aaron? What's up?"

"Joshua wants to see you." Aaron's face gave nothing away, but his posture was stiff and wary. Alfred had followed him in and looked back and forth between Aaron and Simon, but his body language was submissive. There were five steps of rank between Aaron and Alfred. Which was more than enough.

"How urgent is it?" Simon asked, as if out of idle curiosity. "This finish will dry badly if I don't get the whole piece done at once."

"Alfred will find someone to finish the work. Joshua wants you now."

Shit, shit, shit. But this summons still could be unrelated to Paul. If Joshua had found out about the shooting, that didn't mean he suspected anything else. "Okay," Simon said easily. "Let me get my hands clean and I'll follow you."

"I'll wait. My instructions are to bring you right away."

Simon nodded, controlling every muscle, every reaction. "I'll be right with you then." He stepped into the bathroom and shut the door. As he applied cleanser to his hands, he thought furiously. He had his cell phone in his pocket, but he could hear Aaron standing just outside the door. No way to call Paul without being heard. He could text, but Aaron might pick up the click of the keys, and if Paul didn't erase the message it could be damning. Anyhow, he didn't think Paul could get away from the pack if they were looking for him. His man didn't have a sneaky bone in his body. If the shit was hitting the fan, bluffing it out was still their best strategy.

He stepped out and nodded to Alfred, watching from across the room. "It's late. I guess I'll see you Monday, unless Joshua's sending me to Pine River again."

Alfred nodded back. "See you." His eyes were troubled.

Simon followed Aaron out into the parking lot. He couldn't keep his wolf from calculating their chances. *Jump that way, run through there.* Even if he could escape, he couldn't run until he knew if Paul was caught up in whatever this was. His heart dropped another notch when he saw Dan waiting in the back of Aaron's Hummer. *Another body for this unknown job, or muscle to help keep me from escaping?* No way to tell. He told himself to think positive. Fear would show in his body language. He got in beside Aaron.

"Hey," he asked conversationally, "did Joshua tell you what was so urgent it couldn't wait for Gordon to get back?"

"I imagine he'll tell you what he wants you to know."

Okay, that wasn't his imagination. Aaron was definitely keeping a cool distance, which meant Simon was in trouble. The only question now was how much.

Aaron drove out to the lodge, a short, silent trip. Simon focused on trying to look unworried, even though the other two wolves were carefully not looking at him. Dan in the back occasionally whistled quietly, too soft and tunelessly to make out the song. It was freaking annoying.

At the lodge, they made their way through the great room to Gordon's office. Dan peeled off at the door and took a post outside it; Aaron ushered Simon through. The doors closed behind them with the swoosh of good soundproofing. A private office had to be designed differently when everyone around had wolf-sharp ears. Joshua sat behind the desk. He looked up as Simon and Aaron entered, and his face looked old and worn. *I'm definitely in trouble.*

"You sent for me, Third?" Simon asked, bowing his head. No faking here. Joshua could still dominate him and they both knew it.

"You've been accused of a variety of crimes. Some of which I doubt, given the source and the lack of evidence. But they include breaking secrecy, so I'm forced to pursue the matter."

Simon knew his shock showed. *Let it. Anyone would be shocked.* "Who made an accusation like that?" he asked hotly. *Anger, fear; let them come.* The more strong emotions in play, the harder it was to tell lies from truth.

Joshua turned to Aaron. "Have them bring the boy," he said heavily. Aaron went to the door, and passed the word to Dan.

Boy. There were several candidates, but Simon was not surprised when Brian came in, bringing Cory with him. Cory stared at Simon, his eyes hot and wild.

"What's he doing here?" Cory asked. "He should be dead."

"Quiet," Joshua snapped, and the weight of his rank loomed heavy on them all. "I'll ask the questions. You answer them."

Cory dropped his eyes and bowed his head. He trembled, less like fear than a runner waiting for the starter's gun, muscles bunching and twitching. Simon moved farther from the wall and eased his stance into something more ready and balanced, just in case.

"You've accused Simon of breaking secrecy with a human," Joshua said. "What's your evidence?"

"I saw it. He went into his faggot friend's clinic as wolf and came out as a man."

"When was this?" Aaron asked sharply.

"Wednesday night," Cory muttered.

"And you're only reporting it now?" Joshua said sharply.

"I wanted to take care of it myself," Cory said loudly. "I wanted to be sure. He shouldn't get away with this. He gets away with everything. He should be dead."

"Were you the one who shot me?" Simon asked.

Both Joshua and Aaron snapped around to stare at him. Cory glared, but said nothing.

"You were," Simon said. "You brainless fool. Did you even think about what would happen if you killed me? If the police had my body and did DNA testing? If you were seen or arrested? Sweet Christ, stop worrying about me and worry about yourself!"

"Explain," Joshua commanded.

Simon laid out the events of Wednesday evening, although he claimed to have shifted human before encountering Paul at the clinic. He saw the anger grow in Joshua and Aaron's eyes as they recognized the risks Cory had taken. When he was done, Joshua rounded on Cory.

"Is this true?" he snapped.

"He's lying. He went in as a wolf. I was watching. I knew he'd head for his ass-buddy's place." Cory's lip drew up in a sneer. "I've been watching our Simon closely, and Karl said…" He stopped.

"Karl said what?" Joshua asked.

"Nothing. Just that Gordon would let that slimy bastard get away with anything! It was up to me to stop him. Don't you see?"

"Enough!" Joshua snarled. "What I see is that you're so obsessed you can't even understand the risks you took. You could have wrecked us all. And beyond that, it's not your place to take pack discipline into your own hands. It's not even Karl's place. Our Alpha decides."

"But he won't. Don't you see? That, that motherfucker Simon is walking around free and Gordon does nothing about it! He never has, he never will! So I had to…"

"Stop." Joshua's voice vibrated with command, and Cory's rant was cut off in mid-word by the force of the pack Third. Joshua turned to Brian.

"Take the boy and put him in the holding cell. See that he's taken care of until Gordon gets back tomorrow. The Alpha will decide what to do with him."

"With me?" Cory began to struggle as Brian's hand clamped down on his arm. "What about him, huh?" He pointed a shaking finger at Simon, his voice rising to a shriek. "What about him? I told you what he's done. He should be locked up, not me."

Brian shook him, and Simon saw the boy's face twist at the pain in his arm.

"Enough," Brian growled. "Tell it to the Alpha."

They all watched the sputtering boy hauled out of the room, babbling incoherent rage. Joshua waved Dan to give Brian a hand, and the closing door cut off the noise. After a moment of staring at the closed door in dismay, Joshua's attention returned to Simon. "That boy hates you."

"I know." Simon frowned. "He's beyond rational. I think something must have happened to him once, something he blames me for. That might be an honest mistake, or he may have been encouraged to think his abuser was me." He didn't say who that encouragement would've come from. They all knew.

Joshua sighed. "Gordon will have little choice with that one."

Simon gritted his teeth, cursing under his breath, but Joshua was right. Unstable wolves could not be allowed to live. The stakes were too high, and cures too slow— one slip, one rampage in fur, could doom a whole race.

"It's a pity. He's so young." Joshua's gaze sharpened. "However. Just because he's not completely sane doesn't mean he doesn't sometimes tell the truth. He says you betrayed our secret to your lover. You say you didn't. Say that again, straight out."

Simon gazed into Joshua's eyes as directly as he knew how. "I have done nothing, in word or deed, with Paul that compromises pack safety." Which was plain and simple truth. Paul would never expose them.

Joshua shook his head minutely. "I would swear that was truth, but I have to be sure. The boy's story also rang true. I've sent Mark to check things out."

Simon's head snapped up in alarm. "What's Mark going to do?"

"Don't worry," Aaron said. "He's going to talk to Paul and check the clinic. If he's fully convinced all is well, the accusation may go no further than that. If he's not sure, he'll bring Paul back here for a chat."

"Paul has a practice to run," Simon protested. The last place he wanted his incurably honest mate was here, under Joshua's and Aaron's eyes. Well, maybe better than under Karl's, but still. "You can't haul him out here by force. You don't want him to think we're some kind of criminals."

"Relax," Joshua said, although it was more command than reassurance. "If he comes, it will be willingly, at the end of his work day. Now sit in that chair and be silent."

Reluctantly, unable to do anything but obey, Simon took the designated chair. Letting him sit might seem like a courtesy, but it took him off his feet and away from the door and window. With Aaron lounging against the wall at his ease, watching him, escape would be very difficult. Simon kept his lip from curling up with an effort. They could have saved themselves the trouble. If Mark was bringing Paul here, then Simon wasn't going anywhere else.

Time ticked slowly by. Joshua shuffled papers on the desk, making it look like he was working. The tension in his jaw, and the wandering of his eyes, betrayed the fact that he wasn't paying much attention to the words in front of him. Aaron stood still as stone, as if he could hold his place forever.

Finally, there was a sharp rap on the door. Aaron opened it to admit Brian, followed by Paul and Mark. Simon's eyes flew to Paul's face. His lover looked worried but not hurt. Simon stood and bowed his head to Brian, disguising a move to get his feet balanced and under him with the courtesy.

Joshua looked at Paul, his expression unreadable. "Doctor Hunter. Welcome."

"Um, I don't suppose you want to tell me why I'm here?" Paul said. "That guy," he pointed at Mark, "said Simon needed my help."

"He does." Joshua turned to Mark. "Report."

"I checked the computer. The doctor was looking up werewolves on the Internet."

"I was not!" Paul said hotly. "That's a lie!" A moment later he paled, clearly realizing that he should have been confused, not defensive. "Werewolves are too trendy, way overdone," he said in a rush. "Same for vampires, pixies, half-demon half-elf warriors with fairy godmothers. The current fantasy stuff is getting ridiculous. I have better things to do than look up vampires online."

The redirection was well done, and it fooled no one. Simon closed his eyes for an instant and prepared.

Mark shook his head. "I found traces of Simon's wolf inside the clinic, in the box of sharps and in the housing of the clipper," he said regretfully.

One leap and a grab let Simon to shove Paul into a corner and put himself between the vulnerable human and the other wolves. His speed wouldn't save them. They were cut off from the window and the door, and he couldn't take on this high-powered group of wolves on his best day. But he had to try.

He met Joshua's eyes and did not look down.

"Simon," Joshua said quietly. "Don't make this harder. If you have any defense, tell me now."

"All right," Simon said, mind racing. "Paul knows the truth. But I haven't endangered the pack. I wasn't lying about that." He took a breath and told the big lie. "He's my bonded mate. He has a right to know."

"He's what!" Joshua exclaimed. The other wolves stared at him.

"We're bonded," Simon said. "He's tied to me, man and wolf, as truly as Susan is to Gordon."

"That's impossible," Mark said loudly. "You can't bond a man."

"How do you know?" Simon challenged him. "He's my lover and my mate. The bond doesn't require anything else. We're proof of that."

"I've never heard of such a thing," Joshua said.

"So maybe we're the first. After all, how many gay werewolves have you known? And of those, how many lived to be old enough to fall in love, not just in lust? How many handled the energy as well as I do, could change as fast? I don't know why it worked, but it did."

Joshua shook his head. "That can't be right."

"Ask Gordon," Simon said. "My Alpha can tell. We'll stand in front of him and he'll tell you what he senses." That lie would get them a day, when they otherwise wouldn't have an hour. He would lie to God and the Devil himself to gain another day for Paul.

He waited. At least Paul had the sense to keep silent. Aaron took a step toward them, and Simon growled in his throat. There would be no time to shift, but he knew how to fight in his human form too. He might kill one or two before they took him down.

Aaron held out his empty hands. "Easy, Simon. You'd fight us for this man?"

"You'll have to go through me to touch a hair on his head."

"Because he's your mate?"

"Yes." Aaron's eyes were almost harder to meet than Joshua's, but Simon held them. It was truth, after all. Perhaps they hadn't bonded, but this was his mate.

After a minute, Aaron turned to Joshua. "I'm no Alpha. It could be true. I don't want to be wrong. I say we hold them for Gordon."

Joshua blew out a breath. "I agree."

"That can't be true," Mark protested. "It just can't."

"Do you have proof?" Joshua asked sharply.

Mark looked down. "No."

"Then we wait." He turned to Brian. "Cory's in the cell. You and Mark secure the east guest suite. Board up the windows, put a bolt on the door. Tell me when it's ready."

Brian inclined his head. "Yes, Third." The tension in the room eased once Mark and Brian were gone. Still, Simon held his place in front of Paul. Aaron kept station between the window and the door, and Joshua had come out from behind the desk. Simon thought he might've had a chance on his own. Go through Aaron, out the window, and run. But even if by a miracle he could take Aaron, Paul would never make it.

"Simon," Aaron said, his voice quiet. "For what it's worth, I'm sorry about this. I knew Cory was irrational about you. I should've kept a closer watch on him."

"That was my job," Joshua said. "Or rather, it should have been Karl's as enforcer."

They were all silent for a while, thinking about all the twisted ways Karl was doing his job. Simon heard Paul's rapid shallow breathing behind him. He wanted to reassure him, but didn't dare ease his hair-trigger readiness. If things suddenly got bad, he was Paul's only line of defense, and having Paul scared and ready to run might give them a chance. Probably not, but just maybe… if he kept Aaron and Joshua busy, Paul might get away. He nodded slightly toward the window and hoped that Paul had seen the motion.

"Don't try it," Aaron said quietly. "I don't want to hurt either of you, but with pack safety at stake, I won't let you run."

Simon glared at him and made no reply. If it came down to Paul's life, no one would be *letting* him do anything.

"Will Gordon really acknowledge your bond?" Joshua asked.

"Ah," Simon said. "Now that's a different question. The bond is there, and he'll sense it. But as Alpha, he'll be the only one who can tell for sure, other than me. Will he be willing to take on the reaction of the pack from Karl and Frank on down and actually confirm that I'm telling the truth, or not?"

"You think he would lie about a bond?" Aaron sounded curious, not scandalized.

"I think Gordon's hold on the pack is balanced on a knife edge," Simon said. "And this could be the weight that topples him off. When you have that much at stake, the truth becomes more fluid."

"Like you swearing you hadn't endangered the pack, rather than swearing you hadn't told Paul anything," Aaron suggested.

So Aaron had noticed. And had said nothing at the time. "Yes. Like that."

Eventually Mark and Brian came back in. "The suite's secure," Mark reported.

"You're certain?"

"Yes," Brian agreed. "They won't get out without power tools or a stash of C-4."

"Good." Joshua looked at Simon. "I want you and Doctor Hunter to stay put until Gordon arrives tomorrow. If you go quietly, you can stay in the suite. It's really quite comfortable. I stayed there with my wife once, years ago. If you fight us, we can tie you to a couple of chairs. The wait will be a lot less pleasant."

"But I have patients coming in tomorrow morning," Paul protested. "Appointments start at eight. I can't just stay here." He sounded so reasonable, Simon wondered if he hadn't grasped how close to death they really were.

"I'm afraid you have no choice, Doctor," Joshua said. "This is life and death for us, which overrides your work. I'm sorry."

"Can I at least call my technician," Paul asked. "I can tell her to get in a relief vet, or reschedule the clients?" When Joshua began to shake his head, Paul added, "Look, I'm not stupid. I won't say anything that might get an innocent girl mixed up in this mess. Some of those animals are sick. Let me make sure they'll be taken care of."

After a moment Joshua said, "All right." He gestured to the desk. "Use this phone, on speaker."

Paul brushed past Simon on his way over to the desk. Simon wanted to grab him and shove him back to safety. Except there wasn't real safety hiding in a corner. Acting calm and innocent, as Paul was doing, was probably a better strategy for survival.

Paul contacted Sarah and gave her instructions, claiming to have the flu. "Okay," the technician said. "I can do that. Will you be in Monday?"

Paul glanced around at the men in the room and said calmly, "I expect so. I'll call you otherwise. And Sarah, thank you for all you're doing. You and the rest of the staff have always gone above and beyond the call of duty for me, and I appreciate it very much." He placed the receiver quietly in the base and looked at Simon. "So, shall we check out this suite?"

Simon smiled, just for him. "Sure babe," he said. "I get first dibs on the shower."

The suite was up a flight of stairs, taken with Joshua and Mark ahead of them, Aaron and Brian behind. If they hadn't been locked in, Simon might've liked their new quarters. The upstairs rooms were as nice as a good hotel. They were used when someone came to town on business from another pack, or if a pack member wanted a night away in a safe place with a little land around to run on. A couple of pack members had spent second honeymoons here after bonding their mates.

The front room was a sitting area, with a couch and chairs, a desk and table. Doors opened into a large bedroom with a king-sized bed and an adjoining bathroom. Usually. two large windows would give a view over the property, down to the pond. But sheets of plywood had been put in place, screwed on the outside of the window frames. Simon prowled the rooms, testing the windows for movement, tapping walls, checking the size of the ventilator fan, while Paul stood in the sitting room and watched him. Finally Simon slammed his fist into the unmoving door.

"We're not going anywhere," he growled in frustration.

"I gathered," Paul said dryly.

Simon went to him slowly, eyes lowered. "I'm so sorry. So sorry. I thought I could bluff it out and you wouldn't have to be involved. Guess I wasn't that good at bluffing my pack superiors."

"But I thought…"

Simon had his hand over Paul's mouth before the rest of that sentence could come out. *If I was Joshua, I'd have someone out there listening.*

"Come on," he said clearly. "It'll be half a day before Gordon arrives to sort this out. Right now, I could use a hot shower." He put teasing into his voice, but not into his expression. "Want to scrub my back?"

"Sure." Paul's voice sounded thin. "What do I get in return?"

"That's for me to know and you to find out." Simon held out a hand, and after a moment Paul let himself be led into the bathroom. Simon shut the door, locked it, then turned on the fan and started the water running in the shower. "I think we can talk in here," he said softly.

"But not out there?" Paul asked, matching his tone.

"We werewolves may not have the fictional superpowers," Simon told him, "but some things do carry over from one body to another. In wolf form, we still think like humans, and see fairly well and in color, though not human-sharp. In human shape, our noses and ears are more acute than you'd expect.

These guest rooms are built pretty soundproof, but if there's a guard in the hallway, he might be able to hear us through the door."

Paul nodded. "Is someone out there?"

"I think so," Simon said. "I think I heard him jump when I banged the door."

Paul nodded again. "Okay." He sat on the toilet lid and looked up at Simon. "You are bluffing about the mate thing, right? Because I don't remember signing up for that."

"Yeah, still bluffing," Simon said. "Although I'd do it in a minute if it would save your life. But they were right. I don't think it's ever been done with a man, and I don't know how. Luckily, until Gordon gets here, they don't know that."

"But he'll be able to tell?"

"Yes," Simon explained. "The Alpha has a deeper connection with his wolves than the rest of the pack. He can sense a mate bond, if it's there. Which ours isn't."

"What about that idea you planted? That he might lie about it for, um, political reasons. You could say he's lying."

"Doesn't help us. No one's going to go against Gordon, if he doesn't support our story. All the good that will do is to keep a sliver of doubt alive. Maybe it'll help the next two guys in this situation."

"What else can we do?"

Simon paced, as well as he could in a bathroom with about eight feet of clear floor space. Paul was looking at him like he might pull a lifesaving rabbit out of his hat, but Simon knew he was pretty much out of rabbits. *Pity, you might distract wolves by letting loose a bunch of rabbits.* Concentrate.

"We have to get out of here. Before Gordon comes."

"How?"

"Yeah, that's the problem." Simon strode another turn, pivot, paced back. "This suite has two outside walls, but the building is log-built. No way we're going through the walls without power tools. The third wall is this one, covered with the tub enclosure. The suites are designed that way, for privacy.

Which would be great if we really were here for a night of fun and hot sex. But which sucks as an escape route. Still, maybe we can get through here if we have to. But not quietly. The only other wall is the one out into the hallway. In wolf form I can chew through drywall, but not fast enough to keep a guard from hearing me before I've made a big enough hole."

"Ceiling?" Paul asked, looking up. The bathroom had a flat plaster ceiling above them.

"Maybe," Simon said. "Floor is useless. I know they put a layer of concrete in between the floors, for noise prevention. But there's only the attic above us, so maybe they didn't bother up there."

"And then?"

"That's the other problem," Simon admitted. "We have to get out of the building, and then we have to get away from the pack. I have a car with false ID and money at a storage facility."

"Why?" Paul interrupted.

"Because of Karl. He's part of the reason we're in this mess. I've been ready to run if I needed to for over a year, since Arthur died."

"Arthur?" Paul was rubbing his forehead.

"I'll fill you in on pack politics later, when we're cuddled up somewhere with the leisure to talk."

Paul's smile was twisted. "You're an incurable optimist. It's part of your charm."

Simon strode over and kissed him, hard. "That's me, Prince Charming. Let me take you away from all this."

Paul swept a gesture at the ceiling. "Go for it."

Simon looked around the bathroom. No tools, not even a wooden-handled plunger, and the shower rod was lightweight aluminum. "Get up, babe, and let me look under your ass." Paul frowned at him, but did so. Nope, stupid flimsy flat plastic toilet seat. Simon opened the door as quietly as he could, slipped out, and came back with the desk chair from the front room. He motioned Paul to the corner of the room, climbed on the toilet, and thrust the legs of the chair up into the ceiling, hard. There was a shower of white plaster dust, and three of the legs went through. But Simon felt the jolt in his arms as the deepest leg hit something hard just eight inches in.

He put the chair down quietly, arms shaking with the need for control. Jumping lightly, he hooked his fingertips into the torn hole in the plaster and pulled. A big chunk of ceiling came down on him, and he slipped off the toilet with a graceless thud. Then looked up.

He would've cursed, but he couldn't think of anything foul enough. Above him, the torn ceiling revealed a few wires and conduits, running through an eight-inch space between the lath and plaster of the ceiling, and a solid concrete layer. *Fucking Warren and his build-it-noise-proof-for-security construction.* The place had been built all too well, long before Simon was born.

"Can we squeeze through there?" Paul said doubtfully.

"No chance," Simon told him. "Not even for a skinny dweeb like you."

"*I may be dumb, but I'm not a dweeb*," Paul quoted, with a lilting rhythm.

"*You're just a sucker with low self-esteem.*" Simon capped the line from the song, and then winced. "Sugar, I'm sorry. That just came out. It's funny in the song."

"But it's a little too close for comfort, don't you think?" Paul said painfully.

"If I wasn't covered in plaster dust, I'd hug you. Babe, you are neither dumb, nor a sucker. And we're going to live to work on the self-esteem thing, okay? Later."

"So now what?"

Simon sat on the toilet in his turn. *Now what?* He knew his limits. Worse, he knew Paul's limits. "I'm thinking."

Paul came over and squatted beside him to look up at his face. Simon reached out and brushed a strand of streaked blond hair off Paul's forehead. The smear of plaster dust from his finger was only one shade lighter than that fair skin. Humans were so breakable.

"Sugar," he said. "You need to promise me, if this mess comes down to fighting, you'll stay behind me and let me do it. If there's a chance to run, go for it, but if it comes down to a fight, that's my job."

"Oh, that helps my self-esteem," Paul retorted. "You don't think I can defend myself."

"I'm not doubting your courage, but werewolves are all about fighting." Simon's wolf was close to the surface, eager to take on someone, anyone, in Paul's defense. He tried to explain. "I'm as fit and trained as I can make myself, and I've learned from the best. I might surprise them in a fight. But, if they hurt you… Babe, you think I'm civilized because I took you bowling and let you put turquoise bandages on me."

"Bowling's not that civilized."

"Shut up." Simon leaned forward and kissed him, hard. "Just listen. Werewolves gain things from having a wolf half, but we also lose things. We're more likely to act on instinct. If I have to fight, I'll take on Karl or Frank, or whoever they set on me, and do my best to be smart about it. But if you're badly hurt, my wolf will take apart anyone between us. Anyone. I won't care if it's Aaron or my friend Andy or that dumb kid Tommy. And if I lose control, it's over."

"You wouldn't," Paul said, sounding certain.

Simon looked down. "I love that you trust me that much, but you shouldn't. When I shift, I am a wolf, not a dog. And so are the others. I'll die before they put a hand on you, but if it comes to that, once I'm dead… don't fight. They'll force Karl to do it clean and fast, if you don't fight." He closed his eyes against the picture of Paul standing over his dead body in a circle of wolves, waiting for Karl.

Paul's fingers were warm against his cheek. "Are you giving up? You?"

He forced himself to say, "No, of course not. There's always a Plan B." He stood up to pace again. "Okay. They have to open that door sometime. Maybe not until they're taking us to Gordon, but hopefully before then with food. I can take on two, maybe three of the pack, as long as they aren't in the top six. Most werewolves are in good shape. But very few of them train their human body the way I have. If I can keep them too busy to shift, I can win."

"Then what?"

"You keep a towel around your neck, a big one. If you get the chance, head for the window we passed halfway down the stairs. Use the towel for protection from the glass and go through it." He closed his eyes for a moment, imagining Paul falling toward the snow. "It's a long drop. Try to roll when you land. Then head for the nearest vehicle. With luck, I'll be right behind you and I can hotwire it."

"You know how to do that?"

"I learned a few essential skills." Simon forced a grin. "You can't outrun them on foot, but if we can get away in a car, we have a chance."

Paul looked doubtful. "That sounds more like Plan F or something."

"Everyone's a critic," Simon snarled.

Paul reached out and caught his arm as he paced by. "Simon, there's one option you haven't talked about. What if we really were, um, bonded?"

Simon stopped. *Sure he'd thought about it. God, had he thought about it, but...*

"I don't know how to do the bond. I've heard vague descriptions but, well, with shifting, the first time takes a mentor, someone to show you how. No one figures it out on their own, the first time they try. There must be a procedure for bonding, but I don't know it. And from all I've heard, for the bond, we have to both be ready before there's any hope of succeeding."

"What do we have to lose by trying?"

Simon shook his head, hard, regret and fear choking him. "We weren't supposed to be like this. I was going to take my time, go slow. I was going to charm you, seduce you. You were going to fall in love with me eventually, but..." He grabbed Paul's chin. "Look me in the eye and tell me that if I'd asked you to marry me yesterday, you would've said yes."

"No," Paul said steadily. "I probably wouldn't have."

Simon dropped his hand. "Right. And mate bonding is even closer than marriage. You're in each other's heads. Not telepathy, but a sense of where the other one is and how they feel. I've seen Gordon and Susan find each other without a second of hesitation from miles away. You have to be ready for that kind of trust. And as far as I know, it can never be undone."

"Okay. You're right. I'm not ready to sign up for that. Except, my choice is bond with you or die, well, I don't want to die. And I definitely don't want to see you dead."

"I don't want you to bond with me because you are forced to!" Simon put a fist over his mouth. *I swore never to force Paul, never to coerce him. And* damn *Cory for making me break my promise.* He didn't want them to die, but what kind of hell would it be to live bound to Paul, with Paul desperate to get free?

"But don't you see?" Paul said. "You told me bonding only works if you have that kind of trust already. So if it works, that means we were going there anyway. We just took the plunge a little sooner."

Simon stared at him. Did Paul really believe that? He hadn't thought of it that way, that success would be its own confirmation. But what if they tried and failed? *I have a chance to keep Paul alive and I'm too chicken to try it? Sure I could lose him, if he hates what I end up doing to him, but is that worse than having Karl rip out his throat?* The answer to that was pretty damned obvious. "You want me to try?"

"I want you to tell me more about bonding. I think we're coming to the end of our options."

"Okay." Simon looked around at the debris and then down at himself. "Look, let's clean up, and take this damned shower. We can talk in there, while I get the plaster off me."

"We're a day away from being dead and you're thinking about sex?"

"I was thinking about private conversation. But mate bonding is also about sex, so yeah. That too."

Paul just watched him as he soaked one of the towels and used it to wipe most of the plaster dust into a corner of the bathroom. But when Simon began stripping off his clothes and shaking them out, Paul slowly got undressed too. Simon went ahead of him into the shower and yanked the curtain across behind Paul, enclosing them in warm steam. The lodge had an excellent water heater. They weren't going to run out any time soon. He stuck his head under the spray, rinsing the plaster from his hair.

"So talk," Paul said, "because you're hogging all the water."

Simon turned and pulled Paul into the spray with him. He ran wet fingers over Paul's face, washing away the dust marks of his own hands. He slid his touch down to Paul's lean shoulders.

"Mate bonding?" Paul prompted him.

"What I have been told is that if you're ready, you have to be touching each other, preferably having sex. Then the wolf half of the pair reaches out for the energy that we use to shift, and somehow links their wife to themselves with it."

"Somehow?"

"I told you I never read the manual on this."

Paul sighed. "I was hoping you had more information than *somehow*."

"I never expected to need it."

"I guess I can understand that." Paul looked at Simon, shaking hair and water out of his eyes. "Do you think, if this hadn't happened, you would ever have tried to do the bond with me anyway?"

Simon opened his mouth to say an automatic *yes*, and then rephrased it. "Paul, my wolf half recognized you as mate before my human half ever met you. Then my human half walked into that clinic and saw you in person, and it was all over. So yes, I think someday, if you put up with me that long, I would've tried to bond you, to put an end to the lies between us."

"Would you have asked me first?"

Would I? Information was supposed to *follow* the bond, he realized. He hadn't thought about the fact that bonding must almost never happen with informed consent. Although he'd bet the occasional inquisitive wife had been quickly bound after the fact. "Pack law would have forbidden that," he said honestly. "So probably not. Because if I told you and then failed, we'd have been back in this position."

Paul ran a slick finger from Simon's shoulder to his hip. "This position's not all bad."

Simon caught his finger and kissed it. "So." He took a deep breath, without letting go of Paul's hand. "Paul Hunter, will you marry me?"

"What?"

"Sugar, I want that. I want it all. Say yes to marriage and bonding and all of it. If you can."

Paul looked down for a moment, watching the water as it swirled down the drain. Simon realized he was holding his own breath. "I'm not ready,"

Paul said without looking at Simon. "I'm not close to ready. I've always been alone and I don't know how to be with someone else. Not that I don't love you, but I'm not sure I can be half of a couple. Definitely not yet."

"I would've given you time. God, I would have waited as long as you needed. But they've taken that option away from us."

"And you're certain about me? You're already sure I'm the man you want, despite all my cracks and flaws and how screwed up I am?"

"You're mine, Paul. You're what I want, who I need. Being rushed into this doesn't have anything to do with how sure I am."

"I wish…"

Simon wished too, wished he could be doing this right, about two years down the road when Paul was comfortable with him and ready for more. "Maybe we don't have to push your commitment that far. Maybe we can do the bond for now, and then slowly work in the rest of a relationship."

Paul shook his head. "From what you've said, that's setting ourselves up to fail. You said the bond requires trust and commitment to work. I think your instinct about *marry me* was the right one. If we go into this hedging our bets, what's the chance we'll manage to bond?"

None. Simon bit his tongue and waited, staring at Paul's averted head. The water darkened his gold hair to ochre and trickled down his sculpted cheek like drops of sweat. The shower beat a soft, rhythmic pattern on his skin. Simon held his breath,

When Paul looked up, his eyes were steady and clear. "Then yes. I would've waited, I'm not really ready, but you already mean more to me than anyone I ever met. More than I imagined I could feel."

"I'll try—" Simon's throat closed on all the things he wanted to promise.

"Shhh." Paul touched Simon's lips. "You already try so damned hard. Yes. I'll marry you and stay with you, and let you in my life and my head. If tonight is all we get, then I want tonight. And if by some miracle we get out of here in one piece, then we'll figure out how a future together will work."

Simon kissed him. He wanted to be gentle and romantic, but he wasn't capable of keeping it that way when he was kissing Paul naked in the shower. When he pulled back, they both were smiling.

Paul said, “Shall we do this thing?”

“Tonight.” Simon didn’t want to discourage Paul, but they had to take every chance they might get. “I’m far from sure the bonding will work or I’d do it now. But as it is, let’s see if they bring us food. If we get a chance to make a break out the door, the odds may be better than hoping the bond will work and be recognized by the pack. If we don’t get a chance to go, then tonight I’ll do my best.”

Paul nodded hesitantly. “Okay.”

Simon eyed him. “Did you want to try now?”

Paul shook his head. “Just weird to work myself up to it and then stop. But no, tonight’s soon enough.”

They turned off the water, dried, and dressed. Simon stopped with just his boxers and T-shirt. He could change shape in those without being severely hampered, and cold didn’t bother him much. Besides, the rest of his things were lost in white dust. He led Paul into the bedroom and pulled back the covers on the bed.

“Let’s talk here,” he suggested. “More private than the front room.”

Paul hesitated then crawled under the bedspread in his clothes. Simon felt him shivering and pulled Paul in against his own warmth. He really should stand ready by the door for the chance that it might open, but he desperately needed a little time. With all that was going on, remembering to feed them was probably low on the pack’s agenda.

“Do you have any friends in the pack you could go to for help?” Paul asked.

Simon shook his head against the pillow. “No one with the rank and skills to do any good. Anyway, while there’re *some* problems my friends might help me with, risking pack safety isn’t one of them. Hell, if the risk of wolves being outed was really true, I might be hunting me down myself.”

“Bit tricky, that.”

“Mm.”

“Okay,” Paul added as Simon pulled him closer, “while we’re waiting for dinner and, um, all that, can you tell me about the pack? Who were the people in that room?”

Simon only hesitated a moment. There couldn’t be much harm now, and if they were overheard, none of his opinions could be much of a secret.

“Sure.” He ran through names and ranks, Alpha to Seventh.

“If you got rid of Karl, would Joshua automatically move up?”

“Maybe. Unless he was Challenged. Rank is a mix of the physical presence and fighting skills and mental will and dominance. Joshua’s getting older. He must be pushing ninety now. Someone might see a chance that he’s not able to hold position anymore.”

“That guy’s *ninety*?”

“Eighty-nine.” Simon shrugged. “Gordon’s a hundred and ten, which is old for an Alpha. It’s hard to stay on top that long. Brian’s almost the same age. Karl’s only sixty-two, which is about prime for an Alpha. That’s part of the problem. Other than Karl and Frank, our top five are older. They have the will, but if it comes down to fighting, they might lose. Which is no doubt why Karl is pushing things.”

“And if Karl becomes Alpha?”

“That’s why I had an escape kit.”

“Which we can’t get to.”

“Yeah. Minor flaw.” Simon kissed Paul’s shoulder. “We’ll figure it out.” *We will.* “That’s the top seven.” He went on listing names, faces, characters. It gave him something to say as he lay there and waited for the chance to *do* something. Paul stopped him around number twenty-five.

“Okay, enough.” He made a short sound. “It’s weird.”

“You think?”

“No.” Paul smacked his arm. “I mean, the fact that you have this rigid linear dominance structure. No hesitation. X is above Y and below Z. Real wolves don’t do that. I mean, there’s an alpha male and female, who do most of the breeding, and the lower wolves do have dominance relationships, but it’s more fluid than that. The wolf who ranks second when the pack feeds from a kill may not be near the top when claiming the best sleeping spots. I wonder why you're so rigid. Are all packs like that?"

"As far as I know. Any wolf I've met could tell you his position in the pack by number, or name his Third or Fifth without hesitation. Some of us think it's what you get mixing wolf dominance with human brains. Others think our forbearers were real autocratic SOBs. No wait, the sons of bitches are us."

"Do you ever mate with…?" Paul began, and then said quickly, "No, ick, I don't want to know."

"It's been done," Simon admitted. "Trying to increase the pack. Because we're so outnumbered by humans. But you don't get viable babies."

"Someone tried?"

Simon hugged Paul against him. Full disclosure here. Paul had to know what he was thinking about signing up for. "We have very few children. This pack has done far better than most, actually. I heard one Alpha in Montana tried for a while to mate local wild wolves and several of his pack, about fifty years ago. I don't know the details but word went out it was a total failure."

"Good."

"I guess. But I can understand his motives. There are two packs here in this area. The other is south of the Cities. Between us, we have seventy-four wolves, and nine boys under thirteen. In an area with a human population over three million. Is it any wonder we feel threatened by those numbers?"

"Mm," Paul agreed. "But if you ever do come out, *not* breeding with animals will definitely be the way to go."

Simon snorted. "Yeah. Talk about bad publicity. Although I worry more about the military coming in and sweeping us all up into some top-secret research program, never to be heard of again. It wouldn't take much of a sweep. And we don't do well in captivity." He closed his eyes, thinking back. "My uncle told me once about this wolf he knew, got picked up for assault after a bar fight out of town. His injuries healed fast, of course, and the other guy lost an eye, so he was convicted. The pack couldn't get to him to help him escape. My uncle said he used a zipper on his clothes and sawed through a leg artery, killed himself because he couldn't face ten years locked up. This was long enough ago, there was no awkward blood testing. Nowadays, we'd spend a mint and move heaven and earth to get a wolf out of custody."

Paul shook his head. "How do you cut an artery with a zipper?"

"Back and forth, for a long time, like chewing your foot off in a trap. We are wolf, underneath, as much as human."

"But you said you have other non-human DNA besides wolf. Has anyone ever shifted to some other form?"

"God, no." Simon shuddered. "That would be… beyond weird. We know where we stand, as wolves and as men. As something else, wizard, creature, whatever… how could we live with humans, mate with humans if we were that alien?" The idea squicked him out far more than was rational.

"Shh." Paul rubbed his arm. "I was just asking."

"Yeah. You just hit a hot button. That DNA crap is like a time bomb lurking inside of us, and no one knows what could happen if scientists get hold of us and start studying it. Could they warp us, change us by force, learn to control us like an Alpha does? Or would some ancient curse kill us all for revealing the wizard's secrets? We don't really want to know those answers. We're not afraid of villagers with pitchforks and torches now. We're terrified of guys in white coats with those electro-whatsit gels."

"Electrophoresis," Paul said automatically. "Sure, I get that."

"These days, secrecy is even more vital than in the past. Because outing one of us now could lead them to us all, no matter how good we are at hiding. Motion analysis, DNA testing, hell, sniffer dogs— they'd have a dozen ways to find us. That's why even my friends in the pack wouldn't cut us any slack on this topic." *If I still have friends in the pack.*

For a moment they lay in silence. Simon listened to Paul breathing and wondered what he was thinking about. Was he wondering how he got into this mess? Regretting his decisions? Without Simon, Paul would've gone home from work today to his quiet, safe house and an evening meal.

Of course, the old Paul might well have forgotten to eat that meal, working himself to death. *Don't wallow in guilt. Plan forward, don't look back.* "We should go get ready. In case they do come open the door."

"Are you sure this is a better bet than trying the bond?" Paul asked hesitantly.

"Everything's a long shot now." Simon rolled out of the bed and paced into the outer room. Paul followed him. "Get a towel," Simon reminded him.

"Be careful if you go through the window. No good escaping the wolves and cutting an artery on the glass."

Paul went into the bathroom without a word and came out with the bath towel around his neck.

Simon was glad Paul wasn't asking more questions. *This is a dumb plan. There's no chance in hell.* But the bond thing was worse. Because bonding not only had to happen, it had to be accepted as real and equal by a bunch of homophobic wolves. Two ridiculous longshots. *We're screwed.*

If this was his last night on earth, he should be spending it in bed with Paul. Not walking around in front of the door, trying to work the stiffness out of his bad leg. Paul sat hip-slung on the corner of the desk, watching him pace. Simon turned, bent, stretched, and paced again. Paul's sigh suggested he was being irritating, but he couldn't stop.

Two hours later, he'd practically worn a track in the carpet by the door. He consulted his internal time sense. It was after nine. "I don't think they're going to feed us at all," he murmured.

Paul checked his watch. "Probably not."

"It may not be intentional," Simon said, irrationally wanting to defend his pack. "Things are probably pretty shaken up."

"Doesn't matter. I'm not hungry anyway."

Simon was. His wolf wanted to fuel up for battle, for running, for whatever might come. But he could live without. "You're not hungry?" He made his voice low and suggestive.

"Huh?"

"Not at all?" He stalked over to the desk and ran a hand across the curve of Paul's neck. "I've got something you could eat, little boy." He scraped a nail down Paul's chest.

"Cut it out," Paul said, although he was half laughing. "That tickles."

"How about this?" Simon twisted suddenly to pin him, licking the sensitive spot in the hollow of Paul's throat. Paul gasped in response and then stilled.

"Simon, what are you thinking?"

Simon kissed him. "I'm thinking we aren't going to get a chance to run away tonight. I'm thinking if I have time left with you, I don't want to spend it talking about wolf biology. Not when human biology is so much more, um, interesting."

Paul's eyes went big, staring up at him from his pale face. His lips parted. Simon loved that mouth. He bent for a kiss, sweet and slow.

"And the bond thing?" Paul said when they broke the kiss. "Are you thinking about that?"

"Yeah." Simon waited.

"What do I have to do?"

"I don't know," Simon admitted. "All I can do is, I don't know, feel for an opportunity. Try to follow the description."

"While we have sex."

Simon hid his face in Paul's shoulder. "I don't want to ask for sex like this. Dear God, I want to spend every minute we have left having sex with you, but not like this."

Paul pushed Simon away to look him in the eye. "If this is all there is, I want everything we can have. If you try the bond thing and it doesn't work, then at least we get the sex." He nipped at Simon's jaw. "Since when have you turned down free sex?"

Admiration for Paul's gallant courage, joking in the face of the unknown, filled Simon's heart. "Never." He nodded toward the bedroom. "We could get more comfortable."

Paul slid off the desk and led the way. At the bedroom door he stopped and switched off the light. In the dim glow leaking from the bathroom, he turned and looked at Simon. "I figure we can have fun. And if the bond thing is meant to happen, then maybe…"

Simon pulled him in and kissed him again, harder. "Right. Although you know, maybe we don't have to actually…"

"Fuck?"

Hearing the word from Paul sent a jolt through Simon's body.

"I want to," Paul added. "I would've waited, but you know me. The original elephant's child, insatiable curiosity. This time with the emphasis on insatiable." His smile was only slightly uncertain. "So, big boy, are you going to show me what I've been missing?"

"God, I love you," Simon told him. "Get naked."

Paul laughed for real and wriggled out of Simon's hold. Simon yanked off his own boxers and watched as his lover undressed. He knew every line of that lean body now, would recognize it in a picture after a hundred years. He could draw the column of Paul's neck, the single line of the scar that ran down the back of one arm, the parallel arcs of his ribs, the graceful curve of hip and ass. Despite impending disaster, Simon was aroused at the sight, hard and ready. He slid under the sheet and lifted it for Paul to join him.

Paul said, "What do you want me to do?"

"Go slow." Simon nuzzled in against his shoulder. He brushed his lips over soft skin. "I've been waiting to do this with you and I'm not going to rush it." He bent to his task, shutting out everything but this man, his reactions, his need. Despite his valiant words, Paul had been no more than half hard climbing into bed. Simon was going to change that.

He used his mouth and hands, licking and biting, stroking over the smooth muscles and flat belly. He felt the moment when Paul let himself relax into that touch. Simon moved lower, licking, and took Paul's cock in his mouth.

"I thought…" Paul's voice was rough.

Simon lifted his head to smile his wickedest smile. "We'll get there. Patience, Grasshopper."

He loved doing this with Paul, loved this taste in his mouth, the hard shaft with flaring velvet head under his tongue. He moved lower, mouthing over tight round balls, spreading Paul's thighs to kiss the sensitive band of skin between testicles and ass. Paul moaned, but as Simon licked lower, toward his opening, Paul tensed again under his hands. *Shit. How to make this good for both of us?*

He moved back up, mouthing the underside of Paul's shaft, and felt Paul shudder with pleasure again. He thought hard, then wrapped his arms around Paul and rolled them over, putting Paul on top.

"What?"

“Lots of options in the toy box,” Simon told him, looking up. “Kiss me.” Paul did as he was ordered. “Now go get the lotion from the bathroom.”

Paul hesitated. “Do we need a condom?” His voice was barely audible.

Simon smiled at him. “Werewolf, remember. We don’t get infections. We’re safe. And with you I don’t have to pretend to be human. I want skin on skin.”

Paul looked away for a moment but then slid out of bed.

Simon watched him walk to the bathroom and return with the sample-sized bottle. “Hand that over, and get back in here.”

Paul slid into the bed, draped across Simon. Simon could feel his cock, hard against Simon’s hip. But not as hard as he had been. Time to fix that. He squirted a big dab of lotion in his hand and reached down, felt Paul jolt as he applied it not to Paul’s ass but over his cock in one slick glide from tip to base.

“What are you doing, Simon?”

Simon took another glob and reached down on himself, working with a fingertip. Not as slick as his favorite lubes, but greasy enough. His mouth twitched at the thought that Joshua’s habitual cheapness was having an unexpected benefit. Cheap oily lotion made a better lubricant. He slid his finger deeper. “It occurred to me that you can be in me, as easily as I can be in you. In fact, easier. I’m going to make you do all the work.” A moment’s burn and stretch, and he added a second finger.

Paul stared at him, eyes dark. “You want to do that?”

“Oh, hell, yeah.” He had never been pinned underneath another man for sex before, not even for a 69. He’d certainly never bottomed for anyone; his wolf wouldn’t have allowed the vulnerability. But he trusted Paul. He could do this.

He spread his legs and bent his knees, catching Paul’s hips between his thighs. Paul still looked uncertain. Simon reared up to kiss him. “I want you. I want you on top of me and inside me. I want to make love with you now, Paul.”

Paul bent to kiss him back, and Simon sucked his lover’s tongue into his mouth. He heard Paul moan. That cock against Simon’s belly wasn’t soft now. Simon reached down, using slick fingers to rub them both, stroking their shafts together. Paul gasped and thrust into his fingers. *Yeah, get eager, want me like I want you.*

Letting go of himself, he took Paul in his fist, squeezing, stroking, guiding him down until Paul's tip brushed Simon's opening. That silk rub of skin on skin was electric. His groan was totally sincere. *Fuck the whys of it. I need him.*

"Now, sugar," he whispered. "Fuck me."

Paul tensed, arms braced, and pushed into Simon's ass. Simon tried to relax, to allow this, as his body fought entry. His wolf wasn't protesting, but he hadn't prepped enough, wasn't open enough. He closed his eyes and took a deep breath of Paul's heated male scent. *My mate. My lover. Goddamn sex on a stick and all mine.* He breathed in the heady essence of Paul's skin, the scent that lingered in his bed when they'd pleasured each other to a boneless content. *My mate.*

Then the tight muscle gave way, letting Paul into his body. Opening up did hurt, a little. More of a stretchy, prickly burn than real pain, an odd fullness. *Paul's inside me.* He breathed out and bore down, feeling Paul slide deeper, feeling his own body, used to accommodating stretch and transformation, relax to this new sensation. Taking Paul this way felt perfectly right. *One flesh. No wonder they use those words.*

Amazing heat arced from Simon's ass to his groin and down his thighs, as Paul nudged his prostate. He whimpered, his attention narrowed down to the exquisite sensations between his legs. Without thinking, he locked his hands on Paul's ass, pulling him deeper. He slid his legs higher and angled his hips up, feeling the hot pressure squeezing over him deep inside.

"Oh, yeah," he murmured. "Oh, God, that's good. Move now."

His cock head slid against Paul's belly, while Paul's slow, building thrusts stroked him inside. Unfamiliar pleasure rose in him, sharp and electric and needy inside and out, and he moaned against Paul's mouth. Paul was making eager sounds now too. He pumped down against Simon, sliding deeper each time.

"Simon." Paul's breath sounded short. "Simon!"

"Hard," Simon told him. "Fast. Now." There was something he should remember. He tried to think against the rush and build of dark fire throughout his body. *The bond.* It was hard to think, to do anything, but arch and drive up against Paul. Simon tried to reach out, to find that shift energy outside. He was lost in his body's pleasure, on the edge of coming undone.

For a moment he thought he touched the shift energy, and his body tensed hard. *Not shifting, just touching.* Then they both crashed into climax, slick hot cum spreading on him and in him. Paul cried out, wordless and rough. Simon wrapped his arms around his lover's shoulders and pulled him down, their bodies locked together. He reached for the energy, trying to pull it around somehow, pass it to Paul. *There, there, almost there.* That golden light escaped him, sliding through his touch, skittering along the surface of Paul's skin but no deeper. He could easily touch the energy now, could've shifted to wolf, if he'd wanted to freak Paul out forever, but he couldn't reach it *through* Paul.

He felt for Paul's emotions, looked in the bright place his bonds lived for something new, knowing he'd failed. Whatever he was supposed to do, he hadn't done it.

Paul shuddered in his arms, aftershocks rocking him. Simon held him close, kissing his shoulder, his hair, whatever he could reach. Slowly, Paul's heart eased its pounding. Simon kissed him over the throbbing pulse in his neck.

"Okay," Paul said softly. "That was… amazingly awesome. Are you okay, Simon?"

"I'll let you know when I can feel my extremities again. Major redistribution of blood supply. Readjusting now." He laughed, trying to cover his disappointment, and kissed Paul again. "Wow. I've never bottomed for anyone, but I can tell you I was missing out. Thank you."

"You've never?" Paul said anxiously. "But I thought…"

"Never trusted anyone enough. You, I trust."

"Did I… was I too rough?"

"God, no," Simon said, and then in the interest of honesty, added, "It hurt some, right at first, but not half as much as it felt good. And after that, definitely feeling no pain. You can fuck me any time."

Paul blushed, but he gave Simon another kiss, before moving off to the side. Simon felt Paul slip out of him and bit back a whine, half soreness, half emptiness. His whole body was still winding down, shaking with each touch, as Paul's thigh brushed his. He already missed being filled. He felt loose and wet and empty. He pulled Paul down on him and locked him in a tight embrace.

They lay that way for a long time, before Paul said, "What about the bond?"

Simon had to shake his head. "There was almost something, for a moment. Like that tip-of-the-tongue thing, where you can taste the word you need but it's just not there."

Paul nodded. "Do you need to stop and not think about it for a while, like with tip-of-the-tongue? Or do we need more practice?"

Simon twisted to look at Paul's face. He was flushed, but his eyes were steady.

"God." Simon kissed him and pulled him in again. "What an offer. I don't know. Lie here with me for a bit and then yeah, maybe we'll try again. What have we got to lose?" Then he shook his head. "No, no, don't think about that. Talk to me. Tell me something I don't know about you. I've been spilling my guts here. It's your turn."

Paul nodded against his hair and wriggled in more comfortably. "Okay, what do you want to know?"

"Anything, everything. What was your favorite TV show as a kid? Did you ever play hooky from school?" Maybe he was asking the wrong things. He had noticed how Paul avoided any mention of his childhood. He ran his hand over Paul's lean naked back. "Or tell me about your friends, your family."

Paul shuddered. *From the touch or the question?* "You don't have to answer that," Simon said quickly. "Not if it's bad. Tell me about your pets."

§ § § §

Paul smooshed his face into the pillow against Simon's shoulder and breathed deep. *He doesn't know. Tell him about vet school, or buying the clinic.* But Simon had asked Paul to marry him. However forced the situation was, they might come out of it bound together. Simon had a right to know how screwed up Paul was. He'd bared some of his own demons, including what sounded like… Paul's thoughts shied away from the words *complicity to murder*. There'd been some kind of violence in Simon's past, anyway. Paul's childhood might be nothing by comparison.

"My family was pretty dysfunctional, at least after my dad died."

Simon took a sharp breath, and his hands closed on Paul's skin. "You don't have to tell me."

"No, I want to." To Paul's surprise he did. Here in Simon's arms, for this instant as safe as he'd ever been, it hurt less than he expected to look back.

"Okay, then I'll listen."

"It's not that big a deal. My father died when I was eleven. Up until then, we were a pretty normal family, although my dad was always the involved parent, the one who did things with me. I don't think my mother wanted kids. She didn't really care about me, but she would do anything for my dad, so she faked it well enough. Then he got cancer."

"I'm sorry."

"Pancreatic. It was fast and hard, and after the funeral my mother started drinking. Not all the time. About once a month she'd come home on a Friday night with a bottle, and then I knew a weekend from hell was coming. I never knew what it would be. Sometimes it was no worse than hours on our knees in front of this shrine she built in her room, while she cried and prayed for my father's soul and for the devil to be cast out of me."

"What devil?"

"I don't know. She wouldn't explain. Just that I was possessed of the devil and he had to be driven out. Sometimes she would lock me in the closet under the stairs for two days with a blanket and a bucket, and the light on bright." Paul shivered, remembering the first time, the musty smell and the cold hard floor, bright under the single bulb, and not knowing if she was ever coming back to let him out. *It's over. I'm past that now.*

"She never hurt me, and as I got older, she stopped locking me up, but she was… crazy. Inconsistently crazy. That's not PC. I should have sympathy and I do but… I never knew if she would be civil and almost normal, or cold and ignore me, or spend hours straight pacing around my bed, ranting at me about my failings, her problems, and how they were all my fault. Me and my demon."

"You know she was wrong, babe."

"Yeah, I do. It never made sense in my head, but it took a long time to convince my gut to stop believing her. She could use words like knives, deep into all my secret fears. Sometimes she'd go twenty-four hours at a stretch, not a moment's sleep, raving and cursing me until her voice was raw. And then she'd crash for days. She'd hole up in her room, forget to cook or pay bills or anything." Paul sighed. "Thinking back…" *God, it was easier with Simon's bulk pressed warm against him.* "I've wondered if she was psychotic, or manic-depressive and trying to treat her own pain with the alcohol. But at the time, all I knew was that home was another name for hell."

"And there was no one to rescue you?"

"No other family. And I covered up for her, all the time." Paul thought about the energy he'd put into keeping anyone from knowing when his home life fell apart. "She was all I had. Nowhere else to go. And mostly she was okay, just cold and distant. And she was my mother."

"Didn't anyone suspect? Your teachers or neighbors, or someone?"

"I'm sure some of them realized she drank. But it wasn't like I went around covered in bruises. She held down a job, went to church. One of my teachers must have guessed I was struggling, because she gave me some information from Al-Anon and Alateen. Probably saved my life. I finally faced the fact that I couldn't save her, I could only save myself. I studied my ass off, got the grades and some scholarship money and loans, and went off to college. And never went back, never looked back."

Simon was silent for a while. Paul held his breath waiting. He wasn't sure for what. Pity? Condemnation? Anger? He'd walked away from that part of his life, and locked it all up in his head, never told anyone. He'd left his mother in her own personal hell, after opening the prison gates of his own. Leaving had been pure survival, but guilt still rose up sometimes in the middle of the night.

After a minute, Simon blew out a breath and kissed his neck hard. "I am *so* glad you got out okay."

"Depends on your definition of okay. Sometimes I think I'm pretty screwed up."

"Not in my book, sugar. I do wish I could turn back time and share my mom with you. She would've been crazy about you. She was… well, everything it sounds like your mom wasn't."

Paul sighed. "Sometimes I wonder if I should go back home and check on her. I don't even know if she's still alive." *Didn't want to know if she needed me, afraid I'd say yes, afraid I'd say no.*

"When you're ready," Simon told him, "we can go together."

"I wouldn't inflict her on you."

"Hey." Simon nipped at him gently. "I'm giving you a set of mutant homicidal relatives. You think I can't handle one alcoholic mother-in-law?"

Paul laughed, choked, feeling some long-suppressed darkness drain out of him, leaving him light and free. "Of course you could. I can't wait to introduce you to her. God, what a scene." He tried to imagine Mom and Simon in the same room and failed, but the idea didn't scare him— *Simon can handle a hell of a lot and still laugh*— and for once thinking of his mother almost didn't hurt. "Let's deal with your relatives first."

That sobered them both. Paul's anger built, red-tinged and sharp. He finally had a life, had a friend and lover, a profession that was more than just a job, a place to belong, and they wanted to take it away from him. Well, to hell with them! He slid back more squarely over Simon and kissed him, licking over Simon's soft lower lip, and then biting along the strong angle of his jaw.

"Mmm," Simon said appreciatively. "What was that for?"

"Being you. Being with me. Being the sexiest thing I've ever lain on top of."

"I don't think that's saying a lot." Simon chuckled, but his gaze was soft and warm.

They kissed lazily, tasting, moving gently together, as if they had all the time in the world. Paul wanted that. He wanted everything he could have with Simon. Slowly, under the soft brush of Simon's hands, his dick began stirring. Desire seeped up through him like warm water rising. He slid sideways. The sheets were cool under his skin as he rolled to his back beside Simon.

"You on top," he said huskily.

"Are you sure?"

He couldn't say it again, but he nodded. Simon slowly fitted himself over Paul's body, chest to chest, legs intertwined. His weight pinned Paul down. Simon kissed him, leisurely and thoroughly. His cock was hard against Paul's belly, but he didn't move, beyond the slow caresses of lips and tongue. Paul tried to push up, but he was caged by hard bone and muscle.

"Slow," Simon said. "I want you completely ready for me."

He was licked and kissed, stroked, massaged, tantalized with butterfly brushes of fingers and lips. Simon knew how to make him want more. His whole body thrummed like a bowstring under Simon's touch, and when he would've sped up the pace, Simon pinned his wrists to the bed and started over at the top. By the third time Simon had kissed his way down Paul's body, only to barely brush the tip of his aching cock with one finger, Paul was ready to swear.

"Please," he said. "I need more."

"Roll over," Simon told him softly.

He obeyed, hesitation giving way to burning need. *Something, anything.* Simon's mouth slid from Paul's shoulder down his spine, biting and kissing, as his hands molded Paul's ass. Paul felt that warm tongue move lower, lower. It felt so good, although something in him still resisted. When Simon would have licked him, down there, he shifted away a little. Then he jolted as Simon bit his ass, hard.

"Mine," Simon growled. "You're mine." His teeth pinned Paul's shoulder while his hands spread Paul's ass. Then the cool of lotion slipped against Paul's hot skin, and he felt the gentle pressure of Simon's finger. Paul whimpered as he opened for that touch. Not from pain, just one last surrender. Suddenly he didn't care. He wanted this. Wanted to be spread on the bed, be topped and filled by this man. He pushed back into Simon's hand and moaned at the heat as Simon's finger slid deep, crooked and drew sparks from that touch.

"Oh, yeah," Simon grated in his ear. "Yeah, babe. Let me…" The pressure increased as Simon worked him open with more fingers, the climbing stretch eased by a steady drizzle of oily liquid. Paul arched, taking Simon's touch inside him, feeling the hard length of Simon's cock rubbing against his thigh. Simon's fingers were electric pleasure but he suddenly wanted more, wanted Simon on him and in him. "Please. Simon, please."

"On your knees," Simon ordered. Paul struggled to obey, letting those strong hard hands lift and spread him. Then Simon whispered, "Now relax, sugar. I want you now." And Simon's cock pressed against him, slick and hot. He wanted it, needed it, gasped as his body gave way and let Simon inside. A short sharp pain made him flinch, then a prickling, burning fullness blurred his vision.

"Oh, God," he whispered. "God, Simon. Wait, slow."

Simon held still, letting him relax to being filled. Simon supported Paul's hips with one hand. With the other, he reached around and stroked Paul, wet and slippery with lotion. Paul realized he'd softened as he responded to that touch, hardening again. Simon's touch felt different. Being stroked and jacked while he was full with Simon's cock made the sensation run deeper, burning over his nerves in unfamiliar places. The pain had faded, almost lost from memory.

"More," he begged. "Please, more. Ah… oh, mmm." Slowly, far too slowly, Simon pressed deeper into him, a gently steady rolling push and release, but Paul was flying now. He didn't want gentle. He shoved back, trying to deepen and quicken the rhythm. His breath came in quick gasps. *In* was good. *Out* dragged fire right through him. *Holy God!* Simon's cock rode over just the right spot inside him, and the icy hot rush almost made Paul's legs collapse from under him.

"Oh, baby," Simon moaned. "Oh, sugar, if you do that I have to move. I have to…"

Paul pushed back harder, begging with his body. Simon growled, deep in his throat, and then he arched over Paul's back, an arm locked around Paul's chest. His hips slammed forward in frantic rhythm. Paul groaned, jerking hard, feeling pain and orgasm battling to burn up through him, until he tipped over the edge. Rushing white heat inside him emptied out through Simon's fingers in one throbbing, shuddering climax. He felt Simon's teeth in his neck, and then Simon kissed the spot. He heard Simon growl "Mine," and then more softly "Oh, sugar, Paul, sweetheart. Oh, Jesus." His ass was hot and wet and sore, clenching and full and aching, and his whole body trembled in Simon's arms as aftershocks sizzled along his nerves.

Slowly, gently, Simon disentangled them. Paul couldn't have moved if his life depended on it. He let himself be eased onto his side in the circle of Simon's arms, against the cum-damp sheets. He kept breathing.

"Baby?" Simon's voice sounded small and tentative.

Paul roused himself for a soft kiss on the nearest skin, over the curve of Simon's biceps. He couldn't say anything. His whole body echoed with the thought, *this is what I was made for.* To be here, like this, with this man. If things had been different, he might never have known. He kissed Simon again, brushing the fine hairs of Simon's upper arm with gentle lips.

Simon rose up over him, to look him in the eyes. Paul stared back, sinking into that green gaze. He wanted to ask about the bond, but he didn't dare. Because there'd been one moment where he had felt the boundaries of his skin blur, where he and Simon had become one merged being with a shared need, shared goal, shared breath. If that hadn't bonded them, then he couldn't imagine anything doing it tonight. And after tonight they were out of time. Taking a slow, ragged breath, Simon gathered him back in close.

"Damn," Simon said softly. "Damn it to hell." And Paul knew they'd failed.

Chapter 15

Simon felt the wolf inside him pacing in frustration, throwing its weight against the boundaries of his mind. His wolf wanted to shift, to chew his way out into the hallway, fight whoever was out there. His wolf was a freaking idiot. Although come four AM, if he hadn't had a better idea, he might try it.

The problem was that the lodge had to be full of pack members. With the two of them locked up here, and Cory imprisoned in the cell downstairs, Joshua would've called in enough help to keep them under control. Simon could fight one guard in the hall, if it wasn't Brian or Aaron. But then they had to get out of the building, and cross open ground to the cars, and get one started. Surprise would help them; it took most wolves a moment to change, so the first pursuit would be human. But he'd seen how fast Aaron could shift. And Paul probably couldn't outrun or outfight any of the pack, even in their human forms. Running would be last-ditch desperation.

Simon held Paul close, spooned against him from shoulder to ankle. They'd gone to the bathroom and cleaned up, sharing the space with a casual intimacy Simon had never known before. Paul had been a little awkward, carefully not looking at the wrong moments, but quietly determined to stay with him, as if unwilling to lose even one moment that they might share. He hadn't once complained about Simon's failure, hadn't ever told Simon this was all his fault. But it was.

He'd known things were going to hell with Karl. He should have stayed away from Paul and his clinic, as wolf and man. Twenty years of control, and he picked now, with this bright and brilliant, vulnerable human, to lose it.

He wondered if Andy was among the wolves called in on guard duty. Andy was single and would be available for the work, although so low in the pack he barely topped Cory. Easy-going Andy slid out from under trouble and walked away at the first sign of a fight. Simon wondered if he might not try to stop them, if he turned out to be the wolf between them and freedom. It hardly mattered. The odds of reaching that point were basically nil.

Paul lay still and silent. Simon wondered if he was remembering, thinking, planning, praying? The human God presumably had no use for werewolves, but Paul was human. Would it do any good to pray? *Help him, save him and you can do what you like with me.* Had Paul prayed when his crazy mother locked him under the stairs? There was a lot of misery out there in the world, and not a lot of evidence of a deity who gave a shit.

Simon's stomach rumbled, and his mind reached out automatically, seeking shift energy. He needed to eat. Werewolf metabolism was demanding. Shift energy could maintain you for a while, bolster your reserves, but the body needed calories. Still the shift energy did provide that extra kick. Simon touched it out there and tried to pull a few threads into himself. Uncle Martin had taught him to do this, store a little for later without actually shifting. It didn't stay. That golden warmth would sieve through his mind like sand out of closed fist, gradually ebbing away. But for a while, it could give you a boost.

Simon wondered if he could give some of that to Paul. Maybe help him run faster, longer, some kind of edge that might give them a chance. He reached out and tried to wrap the energy around Paul. He pictured the man in his mind, every familiar and beloved inch. He tried dragging the energy into himself from around Paul's body, around the thighs which pressed against his and that firm ass tight to his groin, and the lean shoulders under his arm, and the tawny hair. Soak him in it somehow. Maybe a little would seep in. *Guard him, help him, shield him.* The gold light wove around Paul in his mind. *Is it helping?*

Paul suddenly jolted in his arms. "What the hell?"

"What?" Simon asked.

"I don't know," Paul said. "I was dizzy for a moment. I feel fine now. Aftershocks I guess."

Simon opened his mouth to ask if Paul felt like he had more energy and then froze. Because he didn't have to ask. Because in Simon's mind, next to the brightness that was Gordon, and the roiling energy that was the pack, was a warm tawny-gold something that was Paul. Simon closed his eyes. Opened them. Still there.

Silently, Simon disentangled himself from Paul and the sheets and slipped out of bed.

"Shower?" Paul asked without stirring.

"In a minute." Simon walked softly through the room and then out into the front entry. He could feel the pull, could find Paul's presence without any outer senses, stronger than a packmate, stronger even than his Alpha. *There, he's over there.* Paul was worried, unhappy, nervous but not terrified, more disbelieving than afraid. Simon could sense the faint overlay of confusion and anxiety. *Holy, holy, holy shit!* Only one thing that could be.

Simon padded back into the bedroom and slid in to face Paul. He framed his lover's face with his hands and kissed him ferociously. Paul returned the kiss trustingly, eyes open.

"Paul Hunter," Simon said. "Will you be mine, till death do us part?"

"Might not be long," Paul pointed out. "But yeah. What the hell. It'll be a great ride for as long as it lasts."

"Might be longer than you think. We're bonded."

"Simon, don't…" Paul began, then he stopped, staring at Simon's face. "You're serious?"

"Completely." Simon grinned, a combination of relief, dizzy exaltation, and fear hitting him all at once.

"You *are* serious." Paul frowned. "But when? I thought it didn't work."

"So did I. I was just playing with the energy, afterward, and, well, I guess you don't have to be having sex to complete the bond."

"You mean we had all that sex for nothing?"

Simon was about to retort when he saw the grin growing across Paul's face. "You fool." He punched Paul's ribs lightly.

"It worked," Paul said wonderingly. "Are you sure? I don't feel any different."

"I do. I could find you in a blizzard from a mile away."

"Hm. So I can never again lie to you about where I've been?"

"Well, I have to be paying attention…" Simon began, and then added, "Shit, we'll worry about that stuff later, if we survive." He stretched out, rubbing one foot over Paul's ankle. "Survival's still not a done deal."

"Tell me. What happens next?"

Simon dropped down on the pillows with a huff of breath, thinking about it. "I see several ways this could go. First problem could be what I suggested—Gordon sees the bond, but he denies it so he doesn't have to open up this can of gay worms, keep things simple, with the pack already riled up."

"Killing us would be easier?"

"Yeah. Precedent, you know. That would be an unfortunate but familiar tragedy. You bonded to me will freak them out royally."

"Would Gordon be likely to lie? What's he like?"

"He's strong. Fair, smart, relatively open-minded for a man as old as he is. But he's also tired, and sad. Arthur, his Second who died, was as close as Gordon ever had to a son. He has no actual children; Arthur was his nephew. He cares about the pack, and I'm sure he's worried about what Karl will do with us once he's gone. Pack well-being will trump the rights of any single wolf for Gordon."

"If he does admit we're bonded. What then?"

Simon had to grin. "Then all hell breaks loose. The traditionalists will want me dead, the moderates will be shocked, who knows how it will go down."

"But we have a chance?" Paul said tentatively.

"Yeah. Better than before, anyway. Although my other worry is that Gordon will ask *when* we bonded. The gap between disclosure and bonding could give him something to hang me on without having to lie to the pack about the bond."

"Should we still try to run?"

"No," Simon decided. "Running was always just slower suicide. I'll claim my right under pack law to tell my mate whatever I choose."

"Mate. Sounds weird, like I should get down on all fours and run around for you."

Simon let himself leer. "Kinky, babe. But we'll save that for next weekend."

"Bastard." Paul kicked his ankle. "What now?"

"Now." Simon stretched luxuriously. He felt like an elephant had slid off his back. Despite still-looming disaster, he wanted to sing, or giggle, run in circles… *Bonded. To Paul. Holy yes!* "Now, we sleep. Nothing else we can do, and we need all our energy tomorrow. Unless… do you want to talk about it more? This changes things, permanently." Sudden apprehension overlaid the euphoria. Paul would have a thousand questions and Simon wasn't sure he had any good answers.

But Paul's hair whispered against Simon's shoulder as he shook his head. "No, I… not now. Not tonight. You're sure this bond thing is a done deal?"

"Certain."

"I need to sleep. I can't think straight." Paul curled up on his side, pressed into the curve of Simon's hip. "Tomorrow, yeah, we have to talk. Tonight… would you just hold on to me so I can sleep?"

"Anytime. Always." Simon pulled Paul in tight and wrapped his arms around him.

Morning came and went without contact, or breakfast. Simon tried pounding on the suite door, demanding to talk to someone. But although he could hear a man shifting weight from one foot to the other out in the hall, there was no direct response.

Paul grew more and more subdued. Simon expected those delayed questions, but Paul hadn't said five words since they woke up. He kept a distance between them, accepting a morning kiss or touch on the arm lightly and then moving away. Simon wanted to ask what was wrong, but he was afraid of the answer. In the dark, in the heat of the bed, Paul had accepted permanent bonding. In the light of day, he might be wondering what he'd gotten himself into. Or maybe he was finally recognizing how precarious their situation was.

Simon had heard that a mate bond was strongest in the first day after it formed. He stretched out on an easy chair and closed his eyes, trying to focus on what Paul was feeling, looking for a clue, somewhere to start. He could sense Paul, all right, but the waves of emotion he picked up on were so mixed and shifting he couldn't make sense of them. Everything from love to nausea seemed to be combined in there. Maybe it was no wonder Paul didn't want to start a conversation.

They were sitting on opposite sides of the room, watching a reality show on TV, when Simon heard footsteps in the hall. He leaped up and between Paul and the door before it opened.

Aaron, Mark, Karl. Good thing running isn't the only option we have left. We wouldn't have made it ten feet with that group. Karl simmered with dark excitement. Mark looked troubled. Aaron was as cool and expressionless as ever.

"The Alpha commands your presence at meet," Karl said.

"Good," Simon returned cheerfully. "I want to get this over with. Do you realize no one brought us breakfast? Or dinner. I'm starved."

Aaron gave him one long look, slanted under indrawn brows, and then turned to Paul. "Doctor Hunter, I apologize for our poor hospitality. We need you to come with us too."

Simon was pleased to see Paul stand easily, like a man going off to work. "Sure, I have to get back to the clinic as soon as we're done."

Karl grinned at Paul sharply. "Has Simon even told you what's going on?"

Paul returned the look, although his smile was tight. "I'm his mate. Of course he's told me."

Mark grunted, like a punch in the gut, to hear Paul say it that way. He turned his reaction into a hand gesture down the hall, and then turned and led the way. Simon put Paul behind Mark and ahead of himself. He wanted his own body between Karl and his mate. His wolf was agitated, angry, and he practiced deep breathing as they walked. *Calm, stay calm.* He had a feeling that the one who lost his cool today would be the one who died.

Downstairs, the door to the meet room was open. Mark stood aside and let Paul and Simon pass him. The pack was already assembled, row on row. They sat silent and intense. No chatting today about last night's game or the cost overrun on the new project. Every eye was on Simon as he entered. He slipped a hand under Paul's arm to guide him. This would be as fraught with risks as walking on thin ice.

Simon bowed his head to Gordon, at the front of the room. "You sent for me, Alpha?"

"Yes." Gordon's voice was cold. He nodded to an open space to his right. "You and Doctor Hunter stand there for the moment, Simon, and keep your mouth shut unless I speak to you."

Simon inclined his head again, and led Paul to their designated spot. His wolf was thinking automatically about who was closest, and where behind them was a corner to put Paul into, if fighting came.

Gordon turned to Aaron. "Ask Brian to bring the boy." There was a long silence, as Aaron ran his errand. Then the pack stirred, rustling, as Aaron, Brian, and Cory came in. Gordon turned to Cory, sadness in his eyes. "Come up here, son." Simon could feel the command in Gordon's voice. "Stand in front of me."

Cory looked bad, pale and disheveled, but he walked with a wolf's innate grace to stand facing his Alpha, and lowered his eyes.

"Tell me," Gordon commanded. "Did you shoot Simon?"

The movement and intake of breath from the wolves almost covered Cory's breathed, "Yes." Simon guessed that most of his packmates hadn't been told exactly why the meet was happening.

"In public," Gordon continued. "Without regard for secrecy or concealment?" *Which is a far bigger crime than trying to murder me*, Simon thought. Well, from Gordon's point of view.

"Yes." Cory looked up, his eyes bright and frantic. "I had to. Don't you see? No one was doing anything! He was walking around, like he was one of us. I had to do it."

"Simon is one of us."

"Not really." Cory's words tumbled over themselves in his eagerness to explain. "He's not like us. He does things, foul dirty things, and then he smiles, like it's nothing, like it's okay to be a slimy faggot bastard. Like what he does is okay!"

"What things does he do?" Gordon's voice was lower, hypnotic.

"He touches," Cory whispered, harsh and wet. "They wait and pretend to be your friend and then… He does things to kids. Someone did. A man… I remember a man did, and Karl said Simon, he was… and no one saw, no one cared. I remember… I have to stop him."

"Cory," Gordon snapped. "Look at me." The boy's eyes snapped to his Alpha's. "Have you ever seen Simon do anything to a child with your own eyes?"

"Yes!" Cory shouted, and then softer, "No. There was a man, and Karl said, I don't know…" His eyes dropped, and then when he looked up it was in desperate appeal. "It had to be Simon, don't you see? I don't know who, but it had to be Simon. He's one of them, he's the only one. Karl said it must have been. He was so big, so big, and dark and… if it wasn't Simon, he's still a faggot." Cory's voice became louder, frantic. "He's still not one of us. He needs to die. I'll kill him, I will, I'll kill, first chance, I will…" The boy's body began to slump, and Simon felt the prickle as shift energy ran over him. Cory was going wolf.

Gordon snapped, "Stop!"

Cory's human lip lifted in a near-wolf snarl, and Simon saw the change beginning to take him.

He barely caught the nod from Gordon to Karl, but there was no way to miss Karl's response. One fast blow with the edge of his hand and a sickening crunch. Cory's body dropped like a stone, boneless and still, firming back into human. Paul gasped and there was a moan from some of the watching wolves. They all felt the shock. That was not just an incapacitating strike, but a killing blow. Even a werewolf did not survive a broken neck.

Gordon stared at Karl, who looked back blandly. "As you commanded, Alpha."

Gordon eyed him a moment longer. If anything, Karl's expression grew more confident. If Gordon had meant him to contain Cory, not kill him, saying so now would force their Alpha to discipline his Second, and Simon doubted Gordon could make that stick.

Eventually, Gordon looked out over the crowd of wolves. "Stewart?"

Cory's father stood silently. His face was shocked and uncomprehending, but not protesting.

"Your son was broken beyond safe healing," Gordon said to him. "When this meet is done, we will help you take his body home."

"Yes, Alpha," Stewart whispered.

Simon could sense the depth of Paul's distress over their bond and moved to put his shoulder in front of Paul's. Now was not the time for Paul to make any protest. What was done to Cory was done, wrong or right. Now it would be their turn, and death could come just as suddenly.

The pack held silent as Brian went to Cory's huddled form, lifted him, and laid him against the wall by the door. They watched as the big man straightened the boy's body, folded his hands on his chest, and closed the staring eyes.

Gordon was the first to look away. "Now Simon," he said. "Come forward."

Simon took two steps forward and turned to face his Alpha squarely. At his shoulder, Paul moved with him unbidden. Simon let their bodies touch, feeling Paul's presence through the bond, his fear and fury and shock reverberating in Simon's mind. Surely Gordon must feel it too.

"Simon Conley, you are accused of allowing this human to find out about us, at a risk to the pack and all wolves."

"We're allowed to tell our bond mates our secrets," Simon said, sticking to absolute truth. "Paul is my mate. I have broken no law."

That brought a roar of protest from the wolves. Gordon snarled for silence, and above the chopped off comments, Karl said, "There's more to a bond mate than fucking, Simon. Just because he's in your bed doesn't give him any rights."

"It wouldn't," Simon agreed cheerfully. "Except that we have a true mate bond, solid and linked. Ask Gordon, if you don't believe me."

There was dead silence. Karl bit back a retort, and instead after a moment turned to Gordon with a twisted smile. "Well, Alpha? Will you tell Simon that he's never going to have a mate bond, or shall I?"

Gordon stared at Simon intently. "Come closer." Simon took three steps, painfully aware of the distance between himself and Paul. Karl was closer to Paul than Gordon was. Simon made himself stand relaxed and look up at his Alpha. Gordon's eyes bored into him.

Simon remembered the other times he had done this: his first day as pack, when he had taken oath to join them; the desperate day of his outing when he had taken oath again to live. Gordon reached out a hand, still strong and sure despite the thinning of the skin over prominent joints. Gordon's fingers brushed his hair.

"My Simon," he said softly. "Never quite what I expect." He raised his voice, speaking clearly. "They are bound. Solid and true as any mate bond I have witnessed. I swear as Alpha that this is true."

The protest was like a wave breaking over them. Wolves shouted oaths, questions, some even laughed in disbelief. To Simon's left, Karl strode forward toward Gordon shouting, "No! You fool! You can't accept this. I Challenge you!"

Gordon turned abruptly toward Karl, just as the younger man swung a hand at him. Simon was never sure if Karl planned the strike, or if he meant a ritual blow of Challenge. Perhaps meeting Gordon's eyes at the last moment scared him. Whichever, he caught Gordon not with his open hand but with the edge, and with the full, violent strength of his arm. Old necks break as easily as young ones. Gordon fell, dead.

For an instant there was silence. Then an anguished moan rolled over the assembled men. Simon felt the grief and shock, in his head, in his heart, in his bones. That bright place where Gordon had been was empty, and the pack-sense roiled with darkness. But there was still a bright amber light in Simon's head, and that was his sole focus now. Before the rest of the pack had recovered, he moved fast, shoving Paul back into the corner of the room and tugging off his own clothes. He forced his shift as fast and hard as he ever had.

When he was in fur, he staggered to his feet in front of Paul. Not much time had passed, since Karl still stood silent and human in front of the pack, above Gordon's body. He was staring hard at the wolves, running his eyes over the ranks. *Looking for Challenges.* Simon looked at them too, seeing shock, anger, grief. No one moved for a long time. Then slowly Joshua rose to his feet, looking straight at Karl.

"That was no true Challenge," he said coldly.

"It was intended to be," Karl replied. "And anyway, it's done." He narrowed his eyes. "Or are you Challenging me now?"

Simon watched Joshua want to say yes, but realize that was suicide. With the pack grieving, angry and divided, Joshua didn't have wholehearted support. And without it, Karl's relative youth, size, and strength were too big an advantage. Joshua was still whippy and fast for a ninety-year-old wolf, but that wouldn't be enough. Eventually he dropped his eyes. "No Challenge," he said, although he didn't name Karl as Alpha.

"Now we move on," Karl said, when no one else moved or spoke. He turned his attention to Simon, guarding Paul in the corner. "First, this freak show."

Simon growled, letting his teeth show. Karl wasn't his Alpha, not yet, not ever. Karl would have to go through him to get Paul, and after he did, perhaps he'd be weakened enough for Joshua to make a successful Challenge. That might be Simon's last gift to the pack, whether they recognized it or not.

"Not yet." Aaron's voice came clear and strong. "I Challenge you, Karl."

Karl swung around. "You? You're sixth in this pack. Wait for your betters ahead of you."

"What they won't take on, I will," Aaron said. "You aren't fit to be Alpha. You're a scheming, vicious manipulator who used a confused, traumatized boy to make your play, and you will take this pack straight to hell. Which I cannot allow. I'm sure my superiors in rank will let me be the one to make this Challenge."

"I doubt it," Karl said contemptuously, but Simon heard a false note. *He's worried*, he realized. *Of all of us, Aaron makes him afraid.* "You're not even of this pack, really. You haven't been here long enough to have the right to Challenge for Alpha."

"Scared, are you?" Aaron moved toward Karl with that flowing grace that was particularly his. "Looking for someone else to stop me?"

"I'm not afraid of you," Karl snarled. "If none of them will stop you, then I will."

"Here and now. This pack needs to know who leads them right now."

"Done. In fur, then. I accept your Challenge." Karl began pulling off his shirt as he spoke.

The other men moved quickly, taking places around the walls, leaving the center of the room open. Simon snarled, and snapped when necessary, to keep everyone away from Paul. There was no way to know how this would end, or who might prove to be an enemy. If Aaron could at least injure Karl, they might yet survive, but the way the pack reacted to his bond with Paul showed Karl wasn't the only threat.

Brian moved Gordon's body in turn to a place by the door. Tears ran down the big man's face, although his expression was fixed and hard. A hundred years of friendship had ended with one blow of Karl's hand. Simon had no doubt where Brian's support was going.

When the space was clear, Karl and Aaron stood facing each other, naked and ready.

"I am Alpha of this pack, by seniority and right of combat. You're a rank outsider," Karl said.

"You will die for what you have done to this pack, and not least to that boy," Aaron returned.

Joshua snarled from his spot by the wall. "Enough. Fight."

They shifted. Aaron was faster by a good margin, fur rippling over skin, muscle and bone transforming in seconds. He was on four feet, watching with glowing dark eyes, as Karl completed his shift. And still Aaron waited, as custom required, until the bigger wolf was up and ready. Simon wanted to shout at him not to waste an advantage, but it was clear that Aaron was not making Karl's mistake. This contest would be seen to be completely fair.

At first glance, the odds seemed heavily in Karl's favor. The gray wolf was larger, stronger, and lightning fast, as he lunged in for the first strike. Again and again, Simon expected Aaron to be borne down by Karl's weight and speed. But gradually he realized that as fast as Karl was, Aaron was faster.

The smaller black wolf was never quite where Karl thought he would be. With each pass, Aaron leapt free, and after the first few minutes, it was Karl who was bleeding from slashed wounds along his flanks and ribs. Wolves fought, when they must, in swift arcing lunges. Usually there was a snap, or a slash, and then the attacker leapt away. They seldom grabbed and held. As long as Aaron didn't have to close in with Karl, speed was worth more than size.

Simon glanced around the room. All eyes were locked on the two wolves in the center. The pack rocked with the rhythm of attack and retreat. Whoever they were supporting, each wolf's will was set behind his candidate. A true Alpha could draw strength and energy from his pack. If all else was equal, the wolf with more support would have an edge. Impossible to tell in this room who that would be.

Suddenly Aaron seemed to slip, dropping one shoulder to the floor. Karl closed in on him. But in a flurry of fighting, it was Aaron who ended up with his jaws in Karl's neck. For once he held tight, as Karl flung himself backward, trying to dislodge his attacker. Aaron clung, in unwolflike tenacity, working his way deeper as Karl slammed him against the floor. Slowly, slowly, Karl's fighting ebbed as Aaron's hold on his neck tightened.

A growl echoed off to Simon's right, and then a huge tawny wolf lunged at Aaron, knocking him off Karl. All three wolves went rolling, scrabbling for purchase. Simon leaped out of his corner before anyone else moved. He alone was shifted and available in that moment. He slammed into Frank, driving the other wolf away from the main fight. Then all his attention was taken by his own desperate struggle to survive.

Frank rounded on him with a snarl so high-pitched it was almost a scream. His bulk slammed Simon backward, as his teeth fastened in Simon's shoulder. With a wrench, Simon pulled loose, leaving a hunk of fur and skin in the tawny wolf's jaws. *Speed, go for speed.* As with Aaron, his only hope in this contest was to keep out of the bigger wolf's reach. *Fast in and slash. Dive and roll away as a real wolf never would.* Simon blessed his mentor's training, as he caught Frank again and again, marking the big wolf's skin briefly as he sped back out of range. Once his flank brushed against Aaron's, as they each leaped clear of their opponents. Otherwise, his attention was focused on Frank alone. He danced on the edge of death. One miscalculation and those big jaws would crush him. But there was a manic glee in finally, *finally*, being allowed to fight full out and kill.

It was Frank who miscalculated, distracted perhaps by the clashing wolves behind them. For an instant he took his eyes off Simon. In that moment Simon went in low and nailed a hamstring on one tawny back leg. Frank went down.

Simon darted in again, slashing. Frank tried to rise to meet him, but Simon came again, and again, forcing the bigger wolf to turn and then turn back, his useless hind leg hampering him. A whirl the other direction and Frank went down again. This time, instead of backing off, Simon lunged in and caught Frank's muzzle in his own jaws. He clamped down hard.

Frank struggled with every ounce of muscle he possessed, straining his neck and shoulders to throw Simon off. But Simon bit down harder.

Blood flowed freely, and Frank's breathing took on a wet harsh quality. Simon felt the big wolf slumping, his chest rattling. He held his death grip, following Frank's head to the floor.

Then from behind him, he heard Paul's dismayed voice. "Simon! You'll kill him!"

That was the point, wasn't it? But Simon's wolf felt their mate's distress. And Frank was down, if not dead. Perhaps that was enough. Simon let go slowly, watching Frank lie gasping wetly for breath. Gradually, Simon backed up toward Paul's corner a step or two. Frank made no move to get up.

A snarl of pain rose from the other fight, as Aaron caught Karl's foreleg in his jaws. Karl's muscle tore as he pulled free. Both wolves were breathing harder now, but it was Karl whose sides heaved, wet with blood, while Aaron still moved easily. Simon turned to watch the struggle for Alpha.

He barely heard the rush, as Frank came up off the floor behind him. Frank's lunge was not at Simon, but a crippled leap toward Paul in his corner. Only the lamed rear leg hampered Frank enough to let Simon's desperate jump succeed. His own long canine teeth slashed through Frank's neck, even as his shoulder threw Frank's leap off balance. They went down in a heap, right at Paul's feet. This time, Simon followed with a second neck bite that opened the artery. Hot red blood pumped over them both for a few moments and then stopped.

No regrets.

Simon rose quickly, shouldering Paul deeper into the corner with his body against the human's thighs. Then he set himself to guard. When Paul reached for Simon's wounded shoulder, he growled the man back. No time for that now.

Out on the floor, Karl was tiring. His lunges became shorter, and when he retreated, he took time for breath, before resuming the fight. Aaron still played a waiting game, melting away from each rush with a snap and a bite. Again and again, Karl moved in, but now they could all see the end coming. In a lesser fight, Karl would have the choice of lying down and baring his neck in surrender. But there was only one way this fight for Alpha would end.

That moment came suddenly. Karl lunged in, and Aaron rose up inside his path rather than away. Karl's bite found Aaron's cheek, but Aaron's jaws closed around Karl's throat. Werewolf jaws were strong. They all heard the crunch of cartilage giving under white teeth, and then the scent of blood rose strongly. Aaron rode Karl's body to the ground, ready to bite again, but it was over. The big gray wolf managed a few more gurgling breaths and then lay still.

The assembled pack made no sound, not in sorrow, not in approval. *Everyone's in shock.* Slowly, but still with his usual grace, Aaron rose from Karl's body. His shift back to human was again swift. Blood ran down his neck and into his mouth from his torn cheek, and open wounds gaped over his ribs and hip. Aaron looked around at them and said calmly, "If you gentlemen will excuse me for a moment, this blood is annoying." He shifted again, black wolf rising and stretching for a moment in blood-matted fur. Then yet another shift, and when he stood in skin, the wounds on his face and body were scabbing over, and the flow had ceased.

"Better," Aaron said easily, as if multiple shifts after an all-out fight were routine. He walked over to where his blue sweatpants lay in a heap, bent over with care, and pulled them on. With steady hands, he rolled the waistband down, to keep it off a laceration over his hip, but made no move to pick up his shirt.

"Now," he said. "Where were we?"

The assembled pack stared at him in silence for a several long breaths. Then Joshua stepped forward slowly toward him. "You beat Karl, fairly and with honor. I don't deny that. But I question whether you can hold this pack."

Aaron didn't seem angry. "Say your piece," he told the older man calmly.

"Karl was right about one thing," Joshua told him. "You're a newcomer here. You've kept to yourself. We respect you, but we don't know you, and you don't know us. This pack has a long history, and we've never been led by an outsider."

Aaron raised an eyebrow. "Are you Challenging me now?"

"No," Joshua said steadily. "Not yet."

"You would lose," Aaron told him confidently.

"Perhaps." That was just pride on Joshua's part. Even wounded, Simon had no doubt that Aaron would be able to outfight Joshua. "But unless you convince the pack to accept you, this will go badly."

"I have a different answer," Aaron said. "I propose we split the pack."

"We what?" Joshua was not the only one startled. All around Simon, men broke the silence with low-voiced exclamations.

"Split the pack. It's the logical answer. And it needs doing. We have forty-one wolves here." He glanced over at Frank's still body. "No, forty. Still, too many. This pack is more fertile than most, and we've grown too big. A full pack run is now something that no Minnesotan is going to mistake for a regular pack of wild wolves. And trying to get all these people to pull together is like herding cats. Split the pack in two. We'll be healthier and safer for it."

Joshua eyed him carefully. "Split it how?"

"Let them choose," Aaron said. "I'm Alpha now, but you're right, some of your wolves will never accept me. So keep them as your own. You're next in rank. You could've led the pack, if Gordon had failed when you were younger, or if Karl had been less strong. Let each wolf come up and swear to you or to me. Let the split fall as it may."

"You think any of them will go with you?"

"Oh, some will," Aaron said. "Some are mine already." He looked over at Simon, standing guard over Paul. "Simon," he said clearly. "Your mate is safe with us. Shift back now."

Simon felt the push in his head, as strong as he had ever felt from Gordon. The shift began running over his body, even before he could think about obeying or not. A minute later, he was climbing back up on two feet, his shoulder throbbing, his eyes fixed on Aaron. And that once-empty Alpha's place in his head held a cool blue presence.

"Simon," Aaron said almost gaily, "will you swear to me as your Alpha, to take your place in my pack under my authority?"

"I will." Simon felt the *click* as his link to his new Alpha took hold. *Yes, there, done.* His wolf was content. Aaron was strongest and would keep them safe.

Aaron held his eyes for another long moment. "And you really are bonded to Paul," he added eventually. "I had wondered if Gordon was fooling himself, but obviously not. Welcome to my pack, Paul Hunter."

Paul nodded, but didn't speak. Aaron turned to look at the other wolves. "My pack will probably be smaller," he told them. "And therefore poorer, even if we are given a fair share of the joint funds. I will adjust traditions where it makes sense to do so." He gave Paul a pointed nod. "But I will not tolerate lawbreaking if it endangers us. I can and will be quite, um, lethal if it is required." He glanced over at Karl's body, then continued, "Simon will be part of my pack, and his mate is under my protection. If you join me, Paul will also be under your protection. If you cannot stomach that kind of change, stay here. But think about this." His eyes glowed as he looked around.

"As werewolves, we're all fighting a rearguard action to stay secret. I believe we will fail in my lifetime. There are too many people, too many cameras and satellites and blood tests and regulations. One day we will be discovered. And how our people are treated then may depend on what we have become. If we are a violent people who kill our young, and tolerate no dissent, we will have a hard time finding human champions. And without humans to speak for us, we may not survive. I intend my pack to survive."

He paused, and Joshua nodded to him. "If you will accept their choices," Joshua said clearly, "I'll call the roll. Each wolf will come up and choose his Alpha."

"Do it."

In the pregnant pause, the assembled men eyed their two leaders, minds surely racing through the future possibilities. Simon whispered to Paul, "Look well, O wolves." When Paul made a small choked sound, Simon muttered. "Loved *The Jungle Book* as a kid. I've always wanted to say that."

Then Joshua called, "Brian?"

Brian rose and came forward. To Aaron he said, "I wish you well with your pack, and I would almost join you, except… except that I've been dominant to you, and old habits die hard. And I think my old pack shouldn't lose all its troublemakers." He turned to Joshua. "I will swear to you, old friend." And so it began.

To Simon's surprise, Mark chose Aaron. Aaron greeted his choice with a return inclination of his head and a simple, "Second." For a moment, Simon was angry. It wasn't Mark who took on Frank, the number five wolf, for Aaron's sake. Surely Simon had proved his own worth. Luckily common sense reasserted itself before he could open his big mouth to protest.

After all, do you really want to be stuck with all the duties of Second for a new pack right now? Do you want to worry about Mark pushing at your heels? The answer was a resounding *No*. So by the time Aaron swung his acute gaze to Simon, no doubt sensing that moment of anger, Simon was able to return a bland smile. *Fine with me.* Aaron gave him a microscopic nod and moved on.

Most wolves chose Joshua and the security of the old pack. But several, including Lucas, Richard and Damian, gave oath to Aaron. When Simon's name was called, Aaron simply looked at him and said, "Mine." It was odd how that slid warmth through Simon, in a way that Gordon's grudging acceptance never had. He felt a little tension drain away, settling into his new place. Andy picked Aaron with a cheerful grin Simon's way. Then it was Zach's turn.

The young man walked up to the front, his head high. He looked at Joshua. "I want to choose Aaron," he said.

From his place among the seniors by the wall, Zach's grandfather snapped, "No, boy."

Zach gave the old man one steady look and then continued to Joshua, "But Alfred holds my key and he chose you."

"That arrangement was set by Gordon," Joshua said. "I'm reluctant to change it."

Aaron nodded. "I agree that Zach should wear the lock as our Alpha decreed. But he's twenty, and free to make his own decisions. Perhaps we could choose a new mentor for his lock. If Alfred is willing to pass the responsibility on."

Alfred said from his place, "Zach will do fine either way. If he wants to go, I wouldn't hold him."

"Lucas, then," Aaron said. "Will you take the boy's key?"

Lucas startled. "You want me to mentor a young one? What kind of role model do you think I am?"

Aaron looked at him with a surprising glint of humor. "Perhaps it will be good for you. Will you do it?"

Lucas's smile twisted. "I will. And on your head be it." He turned to Zach. "Come here boy." Zach walked over and looked him in the eye. "Well enough," Lucas said after a moment. "Take your oath."

When they were done, Aaron and Joshua looked at each other. "Eleven in my pack," Aaron said. "Twenty-nine in yours. You're still too big, but it's a start." He looked around the room, at the wolves drawn into two groups, the bodies, the blood on the floor. "I suggest, Joshua, that we discuss territory, and money, and protocol tomorrow. I have one wounded, we have four dead, and we have more than enough cleanup to do."

"I agree." Joshua seemed to have grown taller and sharper as his wolves pledged to him, although Aaron remained just… Aaron. *No need for change*, Simon thought.

"What about him?" Stewart demanded, stepping forward and pointing toward Simon with his chin. "My boy made accusations here that were never even discussed. Does he just walk away?"

Joshua sighed. "Stewart, we all grieve for your loss. But your boy was confused and manipulated into accusing Simon. Gordon knew this, I'm certain of it, and Aaron can see the truth. If someone hurt your boy, now or when he was small, it was not Simon. It was probably not even one of us. For all our flaws, werewolves do not harm the women and children. But you may have to live with never knowing who it was. Karl saw to that."

Stewart frowned and then looked down. "I want to take the boy home to his mother," he said roughly. "This will be hard enough for her. I don't want him to disappear, so she has to wonder forever what became of him."

Joshua turned to Brian. "What do you say, Second? Can you arrange it so the accident looks good enough to let his mother have the body?"

Brian's eyes unfocused for a moment as he thought. "Forty minutes gone by, and a single blow," he said. "It won't be easy to fit a scenario to that. I can try."

"What do you need?" Joshua asked.

"The old barn," Brian said. "Mitchell, Connor, Otto."

"They're yours," Joshua agreed. "Do it now. Stewart, you may take the boy but—" Joshua stared at him sharply. "If Brian can't make it good enough to pass inspection without causing the humans to take samples and start investigations, then he will burn the body, and you will settle for that."

"Yes, Alpha," Stewart agreed.

Simon watched in silence as the men passed out of the room. Stewart bent to lift his son in his arms. Cory's blond head fell back limply as his father shifted his body. The boy's slack mouth and eyes dropped open. Connor jumped to help. Simon felt intense grief and anger from behind him as Paul watched the father carry out his son. He kept his back turned though. *This isn't all settled between Paul and me*, he realized. They might be bonded, but the violence in that sealed concrete room wouldn't make things easier. The acid of Paul's emotions burned in Simon's mind.

Aaron turned to Mark. "Karl and Frank are yours. I imagine they went snowmobiling for the weekend. There are a few places where the ice is surprisingly thin, even with all the cold. People fall through into the water every year."

"Yes, Alpha."

Joshua was nodding. "I think Gordon went with them. They've all been friends for a long time. It would be no surprise that they spent the weekend together. But let Susan have the time she needs with his body first. There's no rush if we use that scenario, and she deserves her rights."

Aaron turned to Lucas. "You're a good hand with the medical supplies. See to Simon."

"What about seeing to you?" Lucas asked, opening a cupboard on the wall.

"I'll take some bandaging and skin glue when you're done with him," Aaron agreed. "Patrick, Andy, deal with the floor. Richard, Dan, help with the bodies."

The other wolves began filing toward the door. Simon could hear the voices, lowered still in grief and shock, as they passed down the hallway into the human warmth of the common room. Lucas wiped the blood off Simon with a damp towel and began wrapping gauze around his shoulder, drawing the torn flesh together. Simon hissed through his teeth as the pain suddenly hit him. And at last he turned to look at his mate, standing mute and pale in his corner.

Chapter 16

Paul had passed beyond shock to some odd ethereal existence where this all made sense. *Boy seems crazy? Kill him. Bad guy takes over the pack? Turn into a wolf and kill him too. Sure, why not? Someone else objects— hey, you know how to fix that.* Maybe the way to survive around crazies was to be crazy too. Because when Simon had gone Wolf and ripped into that big tawny beast, Paul had felt a rush of exhilaration. Terrified, sure, sick, yeah, but also pure hot anger and satisfaction that was almost a sexual pleasure at the fight. He'd never felt that way about violence before.

Perhaps coming so close to dying had changed him. First in front of the whole pack as a security threat, and then in that moment when the wounded tan wolf leapt at him from the floor, his fear had been so thick and bright it almost choked him. Those white fangs had snapped together less than a foot from the arm he had flung up to cover his throat. Even now, his heart pounded in his chest in memory. He'd been around some dangerous dogs in his time, and even an angry bull, but never like that. Never something so focused, so vicious, that had flat out wanted him dead.

Two men began uncoiling a hose. Disbelievingly, Paul noticed that there was a fucking drain in the center of the floor. *They were prepared for blood.* Others slid the bodies of the two dead wolves into huge plastic bags. The bodies hadn't changed back to human. He'd thought when werewolves died, they would go back to human. But then, what the hell did he know? *When werewolves died— when has that ever been in my wheelhouse?*

The dead stayed wolf. How did someone cope with that? You could hardly tell some un-clued-in woman that this furry wolf-carcass was really her husband's body. Although if he'd heard right, the dead were slated to disappear into a frozen lake. No body to be found. Wait seven years before you declare them legally deceased. How fair was that?

But then fairness didn't enter the room with this alien pack, did it? He wondered how he would describe what he'd seen. Was that four murders? Two murders and two justifiable homicides? And what if the person died in wolf form; did that make it euthanasia, or felony dog fighting? The teenaged kid was hardest to get past. Gordon gave a signal; Karl struck the blow. Had Gordon intended to be fatal, or was that Karl's overreaction? If both men were now dead, did it matter? Except it did. Because one way, the boy's death was another unjustified murder by a dangerous man, and the other way, the slaughter was pack policy. And if he was pack now, was he supporting the murder of children?

He had to get out of that room.

He was aware of Simon's eyes on him, over the shoulder of the man bandaging him, but Paul couldn't meet his gaze. He made his way toward the door, walking wide around the living and the dead. At the door, he had to step back to allow two elderly women to enter. They were holding each other up, both weeping. The smaller of the two slid to her knees beside Gordon's body and stroked his hair out of his staring eyes with a trembling hand, closing the lids. Her friend knelt beside her and wrapped an arm around her shoulders.

Paul averted his eyes and went out. The blank corridor through which they'd entered extended in both directions. Paul looked left at the staircase they'd come down, with an exit beyond, and right toward a bright area filled with voices. He wanted to leave, but the door to the outside was clearly alarmed. As little as he wanted to enter that bright room, he was even less eager to trigger an alarm in this building full of werewolves. There had to be another door somewhere.

The bright room was far larger than he had expected. Soft furniture, small tables, rugs and a fireplace made up a warm great room. Longer tables near one wall held a variety of food. The smell of pastries was obscene over the smell of blood and death in his nose. Paul took three steps along the wall, before he turned away and was sick right there on the floor.

Painful spasms ripped through his gut. *Guess it's lucky I haven't eaten recently.* Strings of yellow bile dripped from his mouth. He held himself braced against the wall with one hand and dug frantically in his pockets for a tissue with the other. Then a wad of napkins was shoved into his hand, and a strong arm braced his shoulders.

He wiped his mouth, and looked up angrily. *How dare Simon touch me now!* But the eyes that met his were hazel and worried, in the face of a tall, plain woman.

"Are you all right?" she said. "Would you like to sit down?"

Paul glanced around. Simon wasn't in sight. The men who'd come out of that slaughter-ground were standing in groups, talking urgently. Some of them cast glances his way, but none seemed to be staring. Many of them were eating. His stomach heaved again.

When the nausea eased, he let the woman guide him to a chair in a secluded corner. He dropped down into the seat, blotting at his mouth. The woman sat on the low table in front of him. She kept a hand on his arm and looked anxiously into his face.

Paul summoned up a small smile and eased his arm free. "I'm fine, thank you. I'll clean that up in a minute."

"Don't worry about it," she said. "Can I get you something? A glass of water?"

Paul shook his head. *How about ten milligrams of Valium and a fast car?* On second thought, don't drug and drive. He'd settle for the car.

The woman was looking at him intently. "You're new. And… you don't seem like a wolf." When he didn't respond, she said, "I'm Megan, Mark's wife and bondmate."

"Paul," he said automatically. "I'm Simon's…" *What was he?* Still Simon's something, though. If he concentrated, he could feel where Simon was in the room behind him. There was no denying the link.

"Simon Conley?" she said, and then incredulously, "You're Simon's *bondmate*? He really did it?"

Paul closed his eyes and spat acid saliva and bile into the napkins. With his eyes still shut he said, "I guess he did."

The woman's hand landed cool on his forehead. "You poor thing. What an introduction to the pack! And you can't have been bonded very long."

Paul was about to say, *twelve hours*, when he remembered the security issues. He settled for, "Less than a week."

"Who's been advising you?" the woman asked.

Paul opened his eyes to glance at her. "Advising?"

"Well, yes. The bond is confusing at first, even once you find out what's going on. And then the pack, the whole life. You should have one of the mated wives helping you figure things out."

Paul shook his head mutely.

Megan made a tsking sound. "That Simon, he should've asked me, if Susan wouldn't do it. She's too old to like changes, but that's no excuse. No matter how long you've known your mate, the bond is a shock and you should have help." She paused, and when Paul didn't comment she asked, "How long have you been with Simon, anyway? He kept you very secret."

How long? A lifetime, by some measures. It was hard to come up with a number. "Two weeks," he said finally.

"What!" Megan seemed outraged. "That's not just stupid, that's practically criminal. He bonded you after two weeks? I didn't even think that could be done. How can you possibly know you want this forever? What in God's name was the man thinking?"

Paul shrugged lethargically. Thinking didn't seem to have been a big feature of this whole mess. *Feeling. Reacting.* "Maybe he thought that if we didn't do this now, we wouldn't live long enough to get the chance."

A sound from the hallway made him look over. The room fell silent as four men appeared, carrying the pair of big black plastic bags through to the front entrance and out into the cold. Paul stared after them. "If Karl had won that fight," he said, "I think that would've been our bodies going out in bags."

Megan nodded slowly. "Can you tell me what happened?" she asked in a near-whisper. "I heard bits and pieces as the men came out, but Mark is still back there."

He didn't want to remember anything, didn't want to go there. But she was offering him help and support. He tried to explain. The story made less sense than it should have. He forgot some of the names, didn't know who pledged to whom. He didn't even know who had died in tawny wolf form, *under Simon's teeth.* Paul wrapped his arms around his stomach and hugged himself in. *Don't think, don't remember how you felt glad when he died.*

Megan nodded, looking as if she understood his garbled story. "That would've been Frank, probably. He was stupid enough, and devoted to Karl enough. God, what a mess." She sighed heavily. "We knew out here when Gordon died, of course. Susan felt his death through her bond. I thought she was going to faint."

"She could tell he was dead?" Paul repeated. *Of course she could. I can feel Simon alive over there now. I would know.* Was that curse or comfort?

"Well, sure," Megan said. "She knew he was furious about something, but she said he wasn't afraid, just sad and blazingly angry. And then suddenly he was dead."

Paul processed that. "She could tell what he was feeling in there?"

"Of course she could tell, that close and that strong. You won't always feel Simon as strongly as you did the first day, but you'll always get a hint of what he's feeling if you try." She flushed. "We knew this was a bad meet, not just business. I guess we were all tuned in to our mates more than normal."

"So the bond lets you feel what your, um, mate is feeling, not just where he is?" Paul asked. Simon had said something about being in each other's heads, but he'd somehow failed to realize it would go both ways.

"You haven't noticed that?" Megan said curiously. "Simon didn't tell you? The first twenty-four hours were the strongest, of course, but you'll always have some connection. Simon should have explained."

"I don't think Simon knows a hell of a lot more than I do," Paul said bitterly. "He wasn't expecting this either."

Megan patted his arm. "That's why you need an advisor. So you don't think you're going crazy."

Paul's laugh came short and sharp. *A little late for that.* Although maybe that explained the feelings he had when Simon fought the tan wolf. Maybe that fierce pleasure was Simon's and not his own. Was it better to have felt that way himself or to be bonded to the man who had? And what would happen if he couldn't tell what he felt from what Simon did? He closed his eyes again and held his head tight in his hands, to keep his skull from exploding.

And there the sensation was, his *mate*, coming toward him from behind. He could feel worry and sorrow and concern and okay, love, wrapped up in a package that was Simon. He didn't look up, just felt for that presence. He knew when Simon crouched down beside his chair.

"Paul?" Simon's voice was very tentative. "Are you okay?"

"Can I leave now? Because I need to get the hell out of here."

"Sure," Simon said, although he sounded less than certain. "Sure. Let me just… um, is your car here?"

"No," Paul said, eyes still shut. "I came with… whoever it was. They said you needed me urgently, and a ride would be faster than driving myself."

"Right." There was a rustle as Simon stood. "Let me… I'll find our coats and get some kind of transportation, and I'll be back, okay. Don't go anywhere, babe. Okay? Just wait here for me."

Paul sat silent, *feeling* Simon hurry off.

"He's worried about you," Megan said after a minute. "Are you two going to be all right?"

How the hell should I know? He nodded anyway. Something pressed on his hand, a sharp sensation odd enough to make him open his eyes.

"Mark's coming; I have to go." Megan recapped her pen and tapped the numbers she'd written on his hand. "That's my cell phone. Call me anytime. Even if it turns out Mark pledged differently from Simon, I'll help you all I can. Some of the wolves are going to be bastards about you and Simon, but I like him. Call me."

Paul followed her with his eyes as she hurried across the room. Just as she reached the corridor, a familiar-looking lean man of middle height appeared. He reached out as Megan stepped forward, and they almost flowed into one another. The man held her in a tight embrace, his head against hers, bodies melded. They were nearly the same height, and Paul had the momentary impression they were one person. Then they broke apart, and both headed off down the hallway. Paul noticed that the man held Megan's hand in his own. Bondmates. Huh. Right now, he had no particular desire to hug Simon.

§ § § §

Simon rose from his position crouched in the snow outside Paul's apartment building and shook himself. His wolf form didn't mind the cold, but holding still was making him stiff and his wounded shoulder ached. And he was going to have to get some food soon. Except he didn't want to leave Paul unprotected.

He'd dropped Paul off in the borrowed car after a silent drive. He could feel the walls Paul had put up between them. It would've taken a braver man than him to storm that silence. But after Paul disappeared into the building, Simon had been swamped by worries.

There were still pack members who hated him. There might be some who had been influenced by Karl, like Cory was. They might hate him even more for killing Frank. And while wives and children were usually protected from the pack by the very nature of wolves, Paul was neither woman nor child. Simon couldn't shake the idea that someone might try to get at him by hurting Paul.

So here he was hours later, making yet another circuit of the building. His senses were on alert for any pack member, but he didn't expect the one who showed up. Aaron swung his legs out of the Hummer and stood with a weariness less fluid than his usual grace. The wound on his face had partially healed. He looked over directly at where Simon lay concealed beneath the stairs.

"Come here, Simon," he said.

Simon sighed and paced out to look up at his Alpha.

Aaron pinched the bridge of his nose tiredly, looking down at him. Then he fisted one hand in Simon's ruff at the neck. "Come on," he said. "We need to talk to that mate of yours, and then I need to talk to you." When Simon dug in his toes and refused to budge, Aaron gave his fur a firm tug. "Now, Simon. I promise you, Paul's not sleeping."

Aaron was Simon's Alpha without doubt. At the command of "Come," his body followed cooperatively at Aaron's heels, even as his mind tried to protest.

Paul wasn't going to be happy to see them. He could feel his mate's turmoil in his bond. Paul wouldn't welcome any intrusion right now, particularly his.

Aaron led him up the stairs and unerringly to Paul's door. He pushed the doorbell. When there was no answer, he pushed again. Eventually, Simon felt Paul approach the door, and then it swung open.

"What do you want?" Paul didn't sound inviting.

Aaron pushed past him, dragging Simon along. "I found this mutt lurking outside your door," he said, giving Simon a shake. "I need to talk to you both. Go change, Simon."

I hear and obey, master. There was nothing to be gained by defying Aaron, and Simon wanted to be able to put in his two cents. He padded to the bathroom and shifted, trying to do the freaky, non-human thing out of Paul's sight. Shifting was hard, as his hungry, abused body protested doing this again. A sharp mental push sent him flying over the threshold, though. When he looked up, both Aaron and Paul were in the doorway staring down at him.

"You have taken yourself to the limit, haven't you?" Aaron said, his tone more cool than sympathetic. "Paul, find him something warm to wrap up in."

Paul turned without comment and fetched a comforter from the bed. Aaron gave Simon a hand up, wrapped the quilt around him, bundled him to the living room, and shoved him down in one of the armchairs. He pointed to the other and said to Paul, "You. There."

"What the hell?" Paul began. Simon winced, but Aaron didn't seem to take offense.

"You're both exhausted, hungry, and angry," he said. "Which in Simon's case is as dangerous as it is foolish. So I'm going to make food for you and talk to you, and you're damned well going to listen to me."

"Why should I?" Paul demanded.

Aaron snorted. "Because, present evidence to the contrary, you're not stupid." He stalked over to the refrigerator and poured out two glasses of milk. "Here, start with this."

Simon gulped his, aware of his starving cells waking up and begging for more. Aaron opened a couple of cans of thick soup and poured them into a pan on the stove.

"Okay," he said. "While that heats, we talk." He walked over and sat on the couch facing them. His brown eyes surveyed them for a moment, then his expression softened. "Did you know, the Alpha bond is apparently like the mate bond. The first twenty-four hours are intense. I took oath from ten wolves today, and I can feel every fucking one of them in my head. And I use the adjective on purpose. You know what the most common response to facing death is?"

Simon let out a little snort.

Aaron's grin was wry. "Yeah, that. When you consider that one of my wolves is Lucas, I haven't been this horny in about thirty years." He sobered, turning to Paul. "At the same time, the worst pain in my head is that guy." He nodded at Simon. "He's been sitting out there in the snow, freezing his bad shoulder, worried stiff about you until I can hardly think."

To Simon's surprise, Paul looked down, his face flushing.

"I didn't ask him to come in," Simon defended him quickly. "I didn't tell him…"

"Sit there and shut up," Aaron said, without force. Simon did as he was told anyway. "Paul. I'm not asking you to go to bed with him," Aaron said. "In fact, I'll probably appreciate it if you don't, until the first intensity of this bonding wears off. But I need you to let him inside, and talk to him, and just be together tonight. Don't fight the bond till you both hurt. Not now. All right?"

"I guess."

"Good." Aaron turned to Simon. "Now I have pack business with you. First question; you beat Frank fair and square, but I named Mark as Second. Frank topped Mark. Are we going to have a problem?"

"Nope," Simon said cheerfully. His position in the pack was the least of his worries right now. "In fact, I'm happy to stay fifth, behind Mark, Lucas, and Richard, like I was before, if that keeps the peace. It's no skin off my nose, which is more than I can say if I fight them."

Aaron's chuckle sounded relieved. "Then let's leave the ranks that way for now. Although, down the road, one of them may feel compelled to prove it's not just your choice that keeps you down there."

"Sufficient unto the day," Simon said.

"Second question," Aaron went on. "Are you going to have a problem with Zach?"

"Zach?" Simon asked, confused. "Why?"

"He came to me to confess that he'd been part of the murderous attempt on your life," Aaron pointed out. "Some people might hold a grudge."

Simon snorted. "I took his leg out on the first pass. And he was sent into that fight by some high-ranking wolves he'd have a hard time defying. I'll let it go, this time." He let his grin go wolfish. "Tell him if he tries again, I'll take out all four of his legs."

Aaron nodded. "I'll pass that message along." He rose and went to the stove, where the soup was beginning to bubble, the smell of beef and carrots making Simon's mouth water. Aaron dished a quarter or so into one bowl, and poured the rest into another. Paul got the small serving, Simon the large.

"Now eat," Aaron said. "Paul, a werewolf needs to eat, even more than a human does. Not only do we use a lot of energy, especially if we're healing or shifting, but a hungry werewolf is also likely to do less thinking and more acting on instinct. And wolf instincts are seldom helpful in the modern world. So yell at him if you're mad, but make sure he's fed first, all right?"

"Is that my job?" Paul asked. He hadn't yet taken a bite. Simon shoveled food into his own mouth to drown the temptation to answer.

Aaron looked serious. "Paul Hunter," he said formally. "I wish I could offer you a choice, but you are pack now and forever. You are Simon's mate. I don't know any way to change that. It's up to you to figure out how you'll live with it."

"Or die with it?" Paul asked acidly. "Like that boy?"

Aaron eyed him steadily. "What would you have wanted us to do? The boy was not just a little troubled but out of control. He attempted murder twice, with teeth and with a gun. He began an uncontrolled shift out of pure anger, with his Alpha right there forbidding it. Should we have turned him over to human authorities, to be tried and locked up in a human jail? Or attempted to treat him with a human therapist, who could never know the real nature of his problems? Do you think it would have been safe for that boy to get really angry around a human?"

Paul shook his head. "There had to be some other answer."

Aaron sighed. "If you figure one out, please God tell me for next time. But for now… have you never put a dog to sleep just because it was aggressive? Maybe a young, healthy dog with years of life ahead of it, but you looked at that animal and you knew that there was no safe way to keep it around? You wanted to work with the dog, desensitize and train it, but the chance that someone would get badly hurt in the process was just too high?"

Paul looked down.

"You could lock the dog in a cage forever, for safety, but that would be even more cruel," Aaron went on. "And we have no werewolf mental wards and no jails."

"You're not dogs," Paul said, but his voice was less sharp.

"We're not human either. And most of us would far rather be dead than in a cage. Wolves chew off a leg to run free." He frowned silently for a moment, then visibly pushed the problem away. "Eat your soup. You both need the calories, and Simon has more healing to do."

"What about you?" Simon said. "You were hurt worse than I was, and you're running around doing work."

"Being Alpha comes with some perks," Aaron told him. "I can pull energy from my pack bonds for shifting and healing, and I've done both." He added, "Actually that got me thinking. I wonder if the prejudice we feel against homosexuality in werewolves is because it opens the possibility of a mate bond between two wolves. If they could share energy and strength, a wolf bonded to another wolf might have a real advantage against ordinary packmates. They might be hard to stop. It certainly opens up new concerns. Fortunately, you bonded to a human, so we can put that possibility off until we come to it."

Simon looked over at Paul. If he could take energy from Paul, he hoped he'd never let that happen. He was asking enough of the man without doing some kind of vampire number on him. He was going to have to talk to Mark about this bond thing sooner, not later.

Aaron stood and looked down at them. "Paul, you need to talk to your mate. We are what we are, but the violence you saw today is a rare thing even for us. Gordon was Alpha for fifty years without a death fight for rank. And there are humans out there who are as bad as Karl was, and worse. Don't throw away the good with the bad." He headed to the door and turned back with a hand on the knob. "Simon?"

"Yes, Alpha?"

"Tomorrow. Ten AM at the lodge. We're going to negotiate terms between the packs. I want your cockeyed view of things, if only to keep Joshua off balance. And tonight." Aaron's grin was rakish. "If you actually have the chance to get laid, take it. Don't mind me. No one else has. If I had a lover waiting for me, I'd be there now." He nodded to Paul. "Take care of my wolf, Doctor Hunter."

Paul sighed heavily as the door closed behind Aaron. He took a spoonful of thick soup, chewed, and swallowed slowly. "So that's our Alpha," he said eventually.

Simon couldn't hold back a grin at the word "our." "Yeah. He's got a different style than Gordon had, but I think I like it." He scraped the bottom of his bowl with the spoon and looked over, putting on his best wistful expression. He knew Paul had a heavy caretaker vibe, and he *was* still hungry. "Is there more soup?"

"Probably not." Paul carried his own plate to the sink. "I can find you something else." He opened the refrigerator. "I don't suppose you want carrots? I have bread and peanut butter."

"Any jam?"

Paul shook his head and checked the cupboard. "Marshmallow fluff."

"Ack. Just glue my jaws together now. Didn't they make you take courses in nutrition at that college of yours?"

"I once studied a pig farm. The farmer fed the pigs surplus candy bars, wrappers and all. He ground them up with soy and vitamins for a complete and balanced diet."

"Yummy," Simon returned. "Okay, lay the marshmallow fluff on me."

Paul looked at him, and the heat in both their faces reflected the inadvertent image that presented.

"I didn't mean it that way," Simon said in a small voice, although he couldn't help adding hopefully, "Unless you want to? I could live with that. Really."

"Goof." Paul began assembling the sticky sandwich. Simon sat huddled in his comforter, waiting and thinking. He was with his mate now, and that simmering pain and anger he'd been getting from Paul was muted. He felt warm and tired, but he still had miles to go. Metaphorically speaking.

"Um, do you have to go in to the clinic tomorrow?" he asked tentatively.

"I should." Paul slapped on the upper slice of bread and brought the food over. "Who knows how the relief vet left things this morning."

"But not early, right?" Simon gulped the gluey sandwich down, working the roof of his mouth clean with his tongue, and put on a hopeful tone. "I mean, tomorrow's Sunday so we can sleep in first, can't we?"

"We?" Paul looked at him hard.

Simon tilted his head. He missed having a tail; he would be wagging for all he was worth. Eventually Paul snorted and dropped his eyes.

Okay, enough. Simon slipped out of the comforter and slid to his knees beside his mate's chair. He could fight this battle naked; in fact better that way. He could feel the effort Paul was making not to look.

"Babe," he said quietly. "I'm sorry. I'm so sorry you were in danger, and I'm sorry you saw the worst of what we can be. Although maybe it's good that you realize I can't be a tame lapdog, even for you. I'm sorry you were pressured into bonding with me, but I'm not sorry you said yes. Are you?" His pulse pounded in his ears as he waited for the answer.

After a long silent minute Paul shook his head. "No, I'm not."

Simon let out his breath and rested his cheek on Paul's jeans-clad knee. "Thank God." He breathed slowly. Paul's leg was warm under his cheek. Eventually, Paul touched his hair, stroking, twirling a curl through his fingers with a gentle tug.

"Maybe we need to start over," Simon said eventually into the worn denim. "Just dating, getting to know each other better. If that's what you want." He got no answer beyond the slow drift of fingertips over his head and down across the back of his neck. His whole body tightened at the touch of skin, although he made an effort not to show it. He wondered if any of the heat rising in him was coming from Paul. It was hard to separate his feelings from his mate's.

"I could sleep on the floor, if you prefer," he went on, holding himself rigidly still. *Do not rub your cheek on his thigh. Do not press in closer.* "In wolf form, if you really can't stand to have me close tonight. If you are uncomfortable having a killer in your bed." Until he heard the bitter tone of his own voice, he hadn't realized how much that bothered him. A sudden wave of pain and regret drowned the heat. *I killed Frank.* For the first time, he'd closed jaws on a living thinking person and deliberately taken his life. He would do it again in an instant to keep Paul unhurt but… but…

Paul cupped his chin and raised him, eye to eye. "Don't," he said simply. "You did everything to save me. I've handed out death with a syringe, when it was necessary. What you did was one step further and harder but… it'll be okay."

"Will it?" Simon asked. No play-acting here, when Paul could feel his heart. Just painful uncertainty. "If there'd been another choice…"

"You gave him a second chance," Paul reminded him. "And he used that mercy to come after me, intent on murder. So thank you for my life."

Paul could've died. Changing his fight would mean changing that moment when Paul lived and Frank died. Simon raised a hand in turn to reach behind Paul's head and pull Paul's mouth down to his. *Mine. Safe.*

Paul leaned back and smiled at him. "You know what I think?"

"What?"

"Aaron was right. There's one good way to respond to death. And looking at you naked, I'm wondering what sex will be like when I can feel exactly what you're feeling."

The rush of desire arced between them, echoed and redoubled down the bond. Paul's eyes went hot, the dark gold shining in response to Simon's stare. Simon rose slowly, watching Paul watch him. His body drew taut, shivering with anticipation. The ache of his healing shoulder, the fatigue of his muscles, vanished in that wave of heat. From Paul's mind, the heat rebounded back to him, melding his want with Paul's. He could *feel* the rising need in his lover's body, and the glow of affection, heart to heart, as their eyes met.

He held out his hand to his mate. "Come on, sugar. Let's go help the rest of the pack blow Aaron's mind."

#######

Unsettled Interlude

(Hidden Wolves 1.15)

Paul woke slowly, to the awareness that he was very warm, weighted down, and a bit sore. Behind his slitted eyelids, he could see a tiny crescent of hazy morning light. He took only a second to remember that the *warm and weighted down* part was Simon, draped across him like a living hot water bottle. The sore part was… also Simon.

Paul moved his legs slightly on the sheets, feeling the pull of sensitized skin. He thought the motion was subtle, but Simon immediately tensed and pushed away from him. "Are you okay?"

"I'm fine." Paul opened his eyes and sure enough, Simon was braced above him, staring down at him with a little frown creasing his brow. "You're hovering."

"More like landing on you." Simon wriggled his hips against Paul's thighs.

Despite the joke, his eyes seemed wary. Paul tried to recapture some of his righteous anger from the evening before, his frustrated fury at Simon and Aaron and all the werewolf bullshit, but those emotions felt distant. In this familiar room, with Simon smiling and the brightness of a winter morning filtering through the curtains, the last two days could've all been a dream. Except for the way he could *feel*, somewhere inside his head, that Simon was actually more hungry and worried than horny.

Paul gave him a push. "Get off and we'll get some breakfast."

Simon rolled gracefully away and bounced to his feet. "I'll cook if you want a shower."

Paul leaned up on his elbow and looked over at his, um, mate. Looking at Simon was never a hardship. He wasn't classically handsome, but he was sculpted and solid, with smooth, brown skin wrapped over curved, hard muscle. His green eyes shone under hair that was nearly black. Across his flat pecs, a dusting of equally dark curls led the eye downward to a clear six-pack. And on down, to that… Paul jerked his gaze upward, to meet Simon's grin.

"It's all yours," Simon said.

"I was actually thinking pancakes," Paul suggested.

"I'll do my best. Although I remember you were down to marshmallow fluff and stale bread, so it may not be easy. Some kind of French toast, perhaps."

Paul swung his legs out and stood up, hiding a wince as he moved. Last night had been, well, intense. He walked over to Simon and didn't hesitate as he closed the last foot of space. Simon wrapped strong arms around him in a hug, and he returned it, laying his head on Simon's good shoulder. This was what he'd always craved and never had. Someone he could go to and be welcome, held, loved, without question. He still couldn't believe the permanence was true, but he couldn't deny the sweet echo of relief and pleasure and affection that filled them both, over that wacky bond in his head. *How can I disbelieve his love when I can feel it?*

"You don't really have to cook for me."

"I offered. I want to. Cooking's a way to show the love."

That word again— the thing Paul had never thought he'd be worthy of. The thing he still couldn't quite understand he'd found, and didn't feel he deserved. Simon loved him. Of all the incredible events of the last two days, of werewolves and captivity, murder and mind-bonds, that was the one that felt most like fiction. Amazing, I-wish-it-was-true fiction. He closed his eyes and opened his mouth against Simon's bare neck, tasting the salt tang of sweat on his lips. So good. Surely this had to be real? "I love you too."

"I know." Simon leaned back, tilting his head so their mouths came together. He kissed Paul with a careful hunger Paul could feel. "Love you more."

That was probably another of Simon's jokes, but it might well be true. "I'm sorry."

"No. God, I was kidding."

Paul burrowed his face against the uninjured side of Simon's neck. "I'm not good for you. I'm married to my work and not going to be social," he mumbled. "You have all these people, these friends, and I'm going to be the weird guy in the corner who doesn't talk to them. And I don't handle being told what to do well. That's part of why I leaped at the chance to buy my own clinic. I question everything, and I'll probably get you into trouble again."

"Hush. Paul, look at me?" When he refused to lift his head, Simon pressed a kiss against his hair and chuckled. "If you don't think I can find trouble on my own, you haven't been watching. If you're around to hold me like this when it's over, I'll have no complaints."

That Paul could do. They stood pressed together, naked in the cool room. Paul focused on the heat of Simon everywhere they touched and the chill of the air whispering over his spine, until Simon said, "As much as I love this, Aaron told me to show up at ten, and it's after nine. I don't think our new Alpha has much patience with lateness."

"And I should check the clinic." Paul had to force his arms to let go. "Shower. I was going to shower."

"Yeah. Get clean and come have some marshmallow fluff pancakes."

He'd thought that was a joke, but apparently fluff could substitute adequately for pancake syrup. They were finishing up when Simon's phone rang. They both jumped in alarm, and Paul had to grab for his tipping coffee mug. He sucked the spilled coffee off his finger and listened. After that first surge of mutual alarm, Simon's presence in Paul's head felt calm and alert. Paul told his jangling nerves to stand down.

"Yes sir… Okay… I was wondering… That would work… I'll tell him."

Simon tapped out of the phone and stared down at it.

"Tell me what?"

"That was Aaron. He's sending Lucas to watch out for you today, while I'm busy backing him up in the pack negotiations." Simon wrinkled his nose, sounding as irritated as he ever got. "You'd think he could manage without me. Joshua sure doesn't love me enough to give our pack a bigger share, just because I'm standing behind Aaron. More likely the reverse."

Paul would've liked to keep Simon close for a while. Simon was his anchor in this newly-overturned life he seemed to be leading. But Paul was an adult, not a kid who needed his teddy bear, and maybe Aaron was deliberately detaching them for a few hours. "Maybe Aaron hopes seeing you will unsettle Joshua. Or guilt-trip him." Joshua now led the pack that had been ready to rip Simon to shreds for loving another man. Paul hoped the old werewolf would feel some kind of remorse, though he wasn't holding his breath.

"Maybe. And then we'll meet as a pack tonight at five. Aaron's house."

"Which is where?"

"Just let me know whether you're here or the clinic around four thirty and I'll come by and pick you up. Then next time you'll know."

Paul nodded slowly. "Okay. And I'll be fine with, um, Lucas? I don't even know who he is. Is he playing bodyguard? Or making sure I don't go to the cops or something?" The whole overwhelming avalanche of new shit loomed again, and he took a shallow breath. "I'm not a threat." *Although maybe I should be.* He was the one who read mysteries and scoffed at the heroes for not going to the cops when things happened. Like deaths. *"I saw this guy turn into a wolf and then he was killed and dropped into a lake..."* Maybe not.

"Bodyguard, absolutely," Simon said. "The worst should be over, but you and I are certain to be unpopular for a while. Lucas is an older guy, medium height and build, brown hair, easy smile. I'll, uh, text him and ask him to come to the door before I leave, so I can introduce you."

"He's in our pack?" *Pack. Our pack.* He repeated the words a few more times silently, but the idea only got more ridiculous with repetition.

Simon eyed him cautiously but said, "Yes. He swore to Aaron."

Paul nodded. For some reason, Aaron's name was like a bell, ringing through the confusion and clearing his head. Whether because he was Alpha, or just because he was someone Paul had actually met, Aaron felt real. "Okay."

"I wish I could stay. I know we should talk and I probably should've woken you earlier. But you looked so cute sleeping."

Paul wrapped his fist in the front of the sweatshirt Simon was wearing and pulled him against the table to give him a hard, sticky-sweet kiss. "I am not cute. Now. This meeting. I'll get to see everybody? Learn some of the rules?"

"Yeah."

"So that'll be good. We can talk after. And talk some more tomorrow. And probably the next day. But in between..." He could feel Simon's intense worry, and hated being a big part of that. He repeated the kiss, longer this time. "With everything that I'm confused about and doubting, I don't doubt you. Okay? I know you, um, love me. I trust you. My life feels turned upside down, but at the center of the good part is you, and that makes everything worthwhile." He would believe that. He had to.

Simon kissed him back. "Okay. And a lot better than okay."

§ § § §

Work at the vet clinic was a good distraction. Paul checked on the few kenneled animals who were staying the weekend and paused to give the clinic cats some loving. The younger two were willing to chase their catnip mice across the floor when he jiggled and tossed them. Old Sally gave him a disdainful glare from her slightly-crossed eyes, until he took the hint to rub her cheeks, scratch her arched back, and refill her bowl. It was all so *normal.*

Lucas seemed nice enough. Could you call a werewolf *nice*? He looked like a man in his forties, which presumably meant he was a lot older. He'd given Paul a nod and a firm handshake, and then insisted on driving his own car to the clinic and patrolling in his own way. He was out there somewhere. Paul wondered if a look out the clinic window would give him a glimpse of a middle-aged man in a dark parka, or an improbably big wolf. He didn't check.

After half an hour of mouse-tossing and a bribe of extra loose catnip, the younger cats were finally done playing and settled in a heap, grooming each other and purring in a slightly drunken slur. Paul picked up Sally and retreated to his office. She deigned to curl up on his lap and sleep, while he did paperwork and read journals. His coffee got cold, but getting more would have meant displacing her. He stroked her rounded back gently and she twitched an ear in response. Her fur was warm velvet under his fingers.

A dog barked, back in the kennel. *Trouble?* But the sounds seemed more like boredom than alarm. Paul's heart rate settled back to normal. He set his journal aside and closed his eyes. *Had Simon sensed that, my instant of surprise and alarm? Can my freaking* mate *somehow feel the texture of Sally's coat, taste the stale coffee?*

Paul tried to reach out with his mind toward Simon. He really had no clue what the hell he was doing. *Simon. THAT WAY.* Like a ribbon of light behind his eyelids, the *something* that was Simon led off into infinite darkness. Eyes still shut, Paul raised his hand to point toward it. He opened his eyes. His finger pointed to the left side of the poster of dog dental hygiene on the west wall. Hm.

He pushed his rolling chair away from the desk and spun it around. Sally yowled in surprise, dug her claws into his leg, and jumped down in high offense. From sanctuary under his desk, she paused to wash her paw and glare at him.

"Sorry I made you sound like a frightened chicken, your Majesty," he said.

She gave her paw another lick, to show her unconcern, before stalking out of the room. Paul closed his eyes and spun the chair until he felt dizzy. Eyes screwed shut, he felt for that shining ribbon of Simon again. *THAT WAY.* He opened his eyes. Sure enough, he was pointing right at the signs of early gum disease.

He tried to blank his mind and sense what Simon was feeling. It was hard to tell. A little apprehension? A hint of hunger? But Paul had missed his own lunch. Maybe that was just him. Simon's shoulder had still been scabbed and sore that morning. Could he feel that pain? After a long moment of mental navel-gazing Paul decided he felt nothing that couldn't simply be imagination. But… *THAT WAY.* Whatever else was or wasn't true, he knew as surely as the beat of his own heart that Simon was there, west and slightly north, at the end of that ribbon of light.

He made himself go back to the computer and pull up work. The vaccine reminders needed to be adjusted for the new protocol. He rested his chin on one hand and began browsing the files, pecking at the keyboard to change a word here and there.

The sound of knocking made him jump. He jerked his head up, and smacked the keyboard with his elbow. His dormant screen came back to life, and he realized he'd been drowsing with his head down on his hand. His fingers tingled with returning circulation.

The knocking came again, from out front at the main door. As he stood quickly, he realized he knew perfectly well who was summoning him so loudly. *THAT WAY.* Sure enough, Simon stood on the doorstep, hands cupped around his face to see in through the glass. Paul pulled out his key and unlocked the door. "Impatient much?"

"You didn't answer my text or the first two times I knocked. I was getting worried."

Paul was going to say something about working hard but Simon's warm kiss drove the thought from his brain. He swayed forward, relishing the mix of cold clothes and warm skin, of a cool dry hand on the nape of his neck and a hot, wet tongue exploring his mouth. *Mmm. Nice.*

When he shivered, though, Simon pushed him back inside and pulled the door shut behind them. "Come on, babe. Pack meeting in thirty. Shut things down and get your coat."

"It's that late?"

Simon chuckled. "You really get caught up in your work, don't you? Yeah, it is. Can I help?"

"No." Paul tried to gather his sleep-scattered wits. Or maybe his Simon-scattered wits, because what he really wanted right now was to pull Simon back into a dark corner and try that kiss again. "No, the kennel worker will be in later and she'll take care of things. I just need to shut down the office."

Instead of waiting up front, Simon followed him back down the hall. Halfway there, Sally came around the corner, spotted Simon, and managed one loud hiss for form's sake before scuttling away as fast as her legs could go. Paul had to laugh. "You'll be one veterinary spouse who never gets asked to help out at the clinic."

Simon grinned, teeth bared. "I don't know. No mean dog will ever bite you with me around."

"They'll run away in a panic. Not a lot better."

"It is to me." Simon caught him by the wrist and pulled him around, pinning Paul between his body and the wall. Simon kissed him again, short hard kisses that made his lips tingle and his whole body strain to get closer. "Nothing gets to hurt you with me around."

Over the bond, Paul felt a flash of anxiety despite the strong words. He gentled his kisses, raising his hands to run his thumbs over Simon's cheekbones. "You've made sure of that. We're safe, right?"

"Yeah." Simon closed his eyes for one last long kiss. "Unless we make the Alpha mad by showing up late, in which case all bets are off, so get your gorgeous ass in gear." He moved back and let Paul past.

Paul drove them while Simon gave him directions. Aaron's house turned out to be quite ordinary, a bit bigger than Simon's, on a fair-sized lot framed in cedar hedges. Several cars stood parked along the street, but Simon had Paul pull past them and turn into the driveway. "Alpha's orders. We park close."

Paul turned off the key and sat for a moment. There was no reason this pack meeting should devolve into bloodshed and murder. There were, in fact, good reasons why it wouldn't. But he didn't get out of the car. Eventually Simon came around and opened his door. "Ready?"

"As I'll ever be." It still took a heart-pounding effort to slide out and lock the car.

When he followed Simon in the unlocked front door, his first reaction was surprise at how normal everything seemed. Beyond the entryway, space opened up into a large front living room. Several men and the woman who'd introduced herself as Megan sat or stood around, drinking what smelled like coffee and eating, of all things, donuts. The scene was ordinary, and boring, and banal, until every head in the room turned toward them. Paul stopped so fast that Simon ran into his shoulder, rocking him.

"Oh, there you are." Megan jumped to her feet and came over to them. "Here, this is fresh." She put her mug into Paul's hand. "Come sit down and eat something." She led them to the armchair she'd vacated and pushed Paul gently into it, perching herself on the arm beside him. Paul was aware of Simon standing behind them. Simon might look at ease, as he accepted a donut from someone, but Paul could feel his tension.

"I'll introduce you to everyone afterward," Megan stage-whispered to him. "I know all the best stories."

At that moment, Aaron appeared through a doorway, and everyone's attention locked on him. Aaron seemed unconcerned, giving Simon and Paul a nod and leaning up against the fireplace. Paul noticed that two of the men who'd been standing quickly found places to sit, without taking their eyes off their Alpha. Aaron bit into a pastry, licked a bit of sugar off his lips, and gave them a small smile.

"Might as well get started, as soon as Lucas comes in from scouting around. We'll meet in here for tonight. Tomorrow I'll draft someone to clean out my basement for a more private space when we need it." The front door opened and Lucas came in, glanced around, and gave Aaron a little salute. A young guy slid off the couch to sit on the floor, and Lucas took his place.

Aaron said simply, "We are met."

"We are met," all the men responded as one, catching Paul by surprise. He noticed Megan said nothing either, so presumably that was all right.

"Welcome." A single word, in Aaron's calm voice, but somehow it resonated through Paul, warmed him and settled in his bones. He found himself leaning forward. Aaron gazed around the room, touching upon each man there in turn, and Paul felt the weight of his attention for a moment when that intense look came to him.

"You all know each other," Aaron continued. "All but one. That's Paul, Simon's mate. All of you need to introduce yourselves to him after the meet ends. He needs to know who to trust. This is our pack now— the thirteen of us in this room, plus Richard's unbonded wife, Alicia, and Mark and Megan's little Nick."

He paused. "Some of you have friends who swore to Joshua. Some even have relatives who did. And now they're on the other side of the line between packs. They are North pack, we are West. We may have secrets, decisions, choices that they not only can't help with, but can't find out about. I need to hear that you are all clear on that."

"Yes, Alpha."

Once again, Paul had missed some signal for that chorus of response. He nodded, trying not to feel like a new initiate at a cult prayer meeting. Simon put a hand on his shoulder. Paul noticed that Simon and Mark were the only two men besides Aaron still standing. He twisted to look up and catch Simon's eye, wondering if there was a reason for him not to get comfortable. Simon gave him a quick smile, but nudged his chin with one finger as if to point his attention back to Aaron.

"I'm going to keep tonight short," Aaron told them. "I'll ask a few things from you that aren't traditional, to make our transition to a pack easier. First, you all know where you stood in rank, relative to those around you. Maybe this looks like a chance to test that, to shake things up. But don't. For the next month, I don't want any Challenges at all. After that, we'll see. But for now, the last thing we need is instability." He turned a hard stare on each man in turn, until they'd all looked down in acquiescence.

"This will be pack headquarters. Again, that's for now. It's my home and I'll want it back, but for now the downstairs will be for pack. The upstairs is private. We're also losing any claim to the old pack lodge and its grounds. That's not unexpected, but it will limit us to this one little space. Keep your eyes open for another property where we might be able to meet and run. Once I know how the money stands, we'll discuss our options further."

Aaron glanced at Paul again, his gaze intent. "This pack has two mates, Megan and Paul. They are now equals in pack eyes. However you would treat Megan, whatever would be allowed or not, you'll treat Paul exactly the same. Except for one thing. Don't mention him outside our pack. Not to anyone. Joshua is enforcing the same rule for his wolves. I don't know if there will eventually be wider trouble about having Simon and Paul in our pack, but it's possible. You all know where I stand on that— I did enough speech-making yesterday. The longer we can keep our men a secret and let the world move forward, the less of a concern it will be when someone does find out. With luck, by then, someone else's pack will be knee-deep in a crisis when our story becomes widely known. Is that clear?"

"Yes, Alpha." This time Paul had managed to join in. Go him.

"Vincent has volunteered to be my secretary." Aaron nodded to an elderly man seated on the floor near the windows. The man dropped his gaze in response. "Give him all your contact information. It'll be memorized and the written record kept safely locked away, I assure you. But I need to know how to find you all. You can tithe to him too, until we get a pack account set up. The rest is details." Aaron sighed and a little of the tension left his posture. Paul could feel Simon relax a fraction too, and only then realized how tightly his lover had been wound.

"I'll be in contact with all of you. No doubt very frequently for the next few weeks, as we get set up. This is a big change, and I intend our pack to come through it as well as possible. That means all of us need to keep each other informed of anything that might be relevant to the pack. My door is open to you for any comments, problems, suggestions, concerns. If you don't feel like bringing something up directly to me, talk to Vincent.

"For tonight, welcome Paul. Meet each other again in this new pack. Remember, you may have liked Brian, or trusted Alfred, but they answer to a different Alpha now. Their priorities aren't yours. Here, in this room, is your family.

"And eat the damned donuts because David bought out half the store and if you leave them with me, even my metabolism will be overwhelmed by the sugar." A young teenager flushed and looked down, until the dark-haired boy beside him coaxed him into a high-five.

Aaron smiled at them. "This meet is concluded."

Paul thought that low-key ending caught the other men by surprise too. More than one twitched and stared at Aaron intently.

"There will be plenty more," Aaron said mildly. "We're all tired. And donuts are no substitute for dinner. We'll start with introductions, contact information, and then spend a few minutes reminding yourselves who's still allowed to sneak up behind you in the dark. Then go relax. I'll be meeting with Joshua again tomorrow. And probably the next day. And we'll probably have long and contentious discussions about more than one problem, as they arise. For tonight, we need time to bond and become pack in truth. We'll run together in fur soon and really settle in."

He pushed away from the brick of the fireplace, smiled around the room, and then came and dropped to sit on the floor by Paul's knee, looking up at him. "Tell me, Doctor Hunter, did your clinic do all right while you were, um, detained?"

"Yeah. No disasters."

Simon came to sit by Paul's other knee, a hand on his calf, head leaning against him. Megan looked down at them and then laughed. "Aaron, you'd better stand up if you want this bunch to mingle."

Aaron and Paul both looked around. Every wolf in the room was now sitting on the floor, except the two youngest who sprawled on their stomachs, legs waving in totally unconvincing casualness. Aaron sighed. "I'm not a reigning monarch. You're allowed to have your heads higher than mine."

"Force of personality, boss," Simon drawled. "This is more comfortable."

Aaron laughed and stood. "Well, I'll go make more coffee then. Let the effect wear off."

As soon as Aaron had left the room, the men around Paul turned to him with a name and a handshake. The crowd felt like more than ten or nine or whatever the number was. He'd never been good in groups. He met each grip, some firmer, others fast and light, murmured some kind of response, and gave up on remembering names. Simon at his knee didn't rise, but turned a steady look on each of them. Megan leaned over closer to Paul to whisper, "Relax. You're safe as houses with this bunch now, and you're making Simon nervous."

Paul thought the nerves were pretty mutual, but he tried to follow her directions. Family. It had been a long time since he'd had real family. He looked around at this room full of strangers and wondered if they'd ever feel that way to him. He tried to relax and pretend he was comfortable in the crowd.

"I'll come see you and help you get pack stuff figured out," Megan offered. "I assume you're moving into Simon's place?"

And holy cow, there went the whole relaxing thing right out the window. Paul's stomach lurched with uncertainty. "I don't know. We haven't talked about it." Paul glanced down at Simon whose eyes were fixed somewhere about the level of Paul's ankle.

"And I've put my foot in it, haven't I?" She laughed. "What I don't know about gay guys could fill an encyclopedia. I'm so sorry. I assumed bonded mates would live together, but there's no real reason you'd have to."

"Megan, darlin'," Simon said, "I adore you and I'm really glad you're going to be friends with Paul, and you can just kill that topic deader than a doornail right the fuck now, okay?"

"Got it." She bent and kissed his cheek. Paul could feel Simon's surprise and pleasure at the gesture. "I need to get home and relieve the babysitter anyway. She has a hot date. Paul, you still have my number?"

"Yes." He'd written it down off his hand onto paper, before his shower yesterday. Before his first shower.

"So call me."

The meeting or party or whatever the gathering became wound down quickly after that. Paul took a deep breath of cold evening air as they walked to his SUV. He started the engine, waited for Simon to close his door, and then hesitated, turning to look at him. "Do you want me to move in with you?"

"Um. Yeah, I do. But I know living together's a big step. I know you weren't planning on any of this and…"

Paul stopped him with a hand on his arm. "In simple words, why?"

"Because I love you. Because I need you near me and if you don't move into my house, I'll have to hang around yours, and yours is harder to defend."

"And smaller."

"And on top of a bunch of strangers. And not nearly as well stocked with food."

"That could be fixed."

"And has a little, cramped kitchen where I'll have a harder time cooking for you."

"A fatal flaw."

"Well, I think so."

Paul sighed. "I know it must feel to you like I keep blowing hot and cold. Close to you one minute and then shoving you away and sniping at you the next."

"Not really," Simon said unconvincingly. "Okay, yes, sometimes."

"I feel like we short-circuited a whole chunk of what we should've done together. It's not you. Never think that. I do believe you're the guy I was meant to end up with. The *person* I was meant to, even if I wasn't expecting that to be a man. But it feels like I was time warped from the first date straight to the wedding, and missed all the bits in between."

Simon nodded slowly. "I can see that. For me, you just feel, I don't know, so *right*, that I'm not missing that part. I'm ready to dive in and be mates. But I can absolutely understand that you might not be."

Paul hesitated. His apartment wasn't anything more than a place to lay his head. He already felt more at home in Simon's welcoming house than he ever had in his own place. It was just a big step. But then so was marriage, and they'd effectively done that. And anyway… "If I keep the apartment, the nights I don't have you staying over, where would you be?"

Simon dropped his eyes and didn't answer.

"Outside in the freaking snow keeping watch, am I right?"

"I'm not sure the danger's over. I can't relax. Not yet."

Paul nodded slowly. A rush of affection nearly overwhelmed him. His? Simon's? Did it matter? He leaned toward Simon, knowing he would be met, caught, kissed. Why would he want to live without that?

"I like your house," he said reflectively. "It has a bigger bed, and two bathrooms, and that kitchen. With the good food. And the chef." He leaned further into Simon's arms, feeling his strength holding him up. He'd never, before he'd met Simon, taken a plunge into the unknown without planning and list-making and pros and cons. Since meeting Simon, he'd done nothing but plunge. Yet never in his life had he felt this safe. *So strange. And yet so good.* He straightened in his seat and put the truck in gear. "If we go by my place first and pick up some of my clothes," he said, "we can be home in less than an hour."

§ § § §

Simon's breath came hard and fast, and he closed his eyes tightly. Bright flashing lights seemed to be going off in his head as his body jolted in aftershocks, and he wondered vaguely Paul could see them too. His body and brain buzzed and settled, wrung out and pretty much offline. The disorientation wasn't helped by a rap of hard knuckles on his temple.

His eyes popped open and he stared down at the gorgeous man under him. "What the hell was that for?' He tried to sound upset, to hide the deep delight humming through him.

Clearly he didn't manage, because Paul glared up at him. "You were looking smug."

Simon couldn't stop the grin that spread across his face. "I made you scream. In a good way."

"Yeah." Paul's beautiful mouth curved in an answering smile, until he rubbed the grin away with the tips of his fingers. Simon noted with satisfaction that his lover's hand was shaking slightly. And he didn't have to wonder about why. The warm intimacy of their mate bond made it obvious that the tremors were from sensory overload of the best kind. Paul reached up to pull Simon down for a kiss and then shoved him back. "Now get off me; you weigh a ton."

Obediently, Simon braced himself on his arms and moved sideways. Paul gave a tiny moan as they separated. His eyelashes fluttered half closed over his gorgeous eyes. Simon thought that was about the sexiest sight ever. He kissed Paul's throat before reaching for tissues and attending to the less romantic parts of cleaning up.

By the time they were wiped and clean and wrapped up together under the blankets, Paul seemed restless. Simon sighed internally. The whole of this Tuesday had felt long, and coaxing Paul to bed before dinner was as far as his evening planning had gone. He'd have loved just a few minutes of blissed-out sleep, before the next thing that would come along and jolt him back to hair-trigger alertness. But he didn't say so. Really, staying awake to talk to Paul wasn't a hardship. "What's bugging you?"

"Not bugging." Paul rolled on his side to look at Simon. "I was just wondering, what would you say to a pair of kittens?"

"Um. 'Hi, snack food?' Ouch!" He made the effort to sound injured by the kick to his shin.

"Be serious."

"Maybe that was me being serious. Okay, not really. Although if it was bunnies…" Maybe better not to go there. "You mean like pets? For us?"

"Yeah."

"I'd say that was a bad idea. Remember how the clinic cats feel about me?"

"But you were wolfed up the first time they saw you. It makes sense that they'd still be nervous."

"Paul, animals in general don't like us, even in human form. Might be something about our scent. The way wolf packs managed to have horses to ride in the past was by taking the foals away from their dams at birth and hand-raising them. Then they would accept the wolves as normal. Same thing for farm dogs and cows; we had to breed lines that became used to wolves. We used to have a bigger problem back when horses were common. Some wolves really provoked a reaction from them even in human form, especially if the wolf got angry. I heard there were even a few accusations of witchcraft back when. I guess it looks odd if you yell at a guy and his horse immediately freaks out and throws him on his head."

Paul was listening closely, with that air of rapt attention he got whenever Simon explained wolf life. Like he was going to write a scientific paper or something. Simon couldn't help leaning in to kiss the little crease between Paul's tawny eyebrows. Paul laughed, but pulled back slightly. "But if we got the kittens at birth, they might adjust okay?"

"Wouldn't that be cruel, taking them away from their mother?"

"Not in this case." Paul cuddled in against Simon's side, an unselfconscious motion that Simon treasured. Who'd have thought Paul would be this at ease in his bed so fast? At least, when he wasn't overthinking it. Simon figured the mate bond must be helping things, his own joy at Paul's touch spreading through the bond and relaxing Paul in turn.

"At the clinic yesterday," Paul said, "a girl brought in her cat. She was worried it had a tumor or something, because its belly had become big really fast. But the cat was just pregnant. One night's adventure after sneaking outside six weeks ago. I took an x-ray, to show the owner because she was still worried, and there were eleven kittens in there. I've never seen a litter that big and I doubt the mom can nurse eleven. Some will probably have to be fostered anyway. I was thinking we might take a couple. I could keep them at the clinic in the daytime. The staff would love to bottle-feed babies, and with you having this house and both of us around, we'd have time for pets. We *are* both going to be here together from now on, right?"

Simon wasn't sure if that was a real question or a distraction from the kitten thing. But he *always* took Paul seriously on this topic. "Absolutely. Now and forever. Cross my heart." He swept his finger over his chest dramatically. Okay, he took it as seriously as he was able to.

Paul snorted. "So. Kittens, yes?"

Simon sighed. "I want you to have whatever makes you happy but…" He'd been trying not to admit that more trouble was probably coming, and he didn't want to hand any more hostages to fortune, small creatures that Paul might love. If they owned kittens, what were the odds that at some point a hostile wolf might not grab one and use it to lure Paul into danger? Although… Simon sighed again. You could lure Paul into danger by threatening to harm a stray alley cat. It was probably a moot point. "When do we have to decide?"

"They're not due for about three weeks yet. Barely visible on the x-ray. The mom's going to look like a basketball before they're born."

"Give me a little time. Let me think about it." Simon tried to lighten things up. "After all, litter boxes in the bathroom, cat hair on my pillow… I don't know."

"I'll clean the litter boxes every day, Mom. I swear."

"Damned straight you will." Shit. That sounded like giving in and he was still convinced this was a bad idea. He needed to practice saying no to Paul. *I need to try even once saying no to Paul.*

Although kissing Paul was a hell of a lot easier. He decided to practice that for a while. Paul slid a hand into Simon's hair and kissed back enthusiastically. When they broke for breath, they stayed face to face, looking at each other. Slowly, Simon watched the light in Paul's golden eyes fade and darken and wondered what he was thinking.

Paul ran a finger over Simon's temple into his hair, over new unblemished skin. The graze from Cory's bullet had healed and even the scar had faded during Simon's last shift. "I love the way you heal. I love knowing you'll be okay if you get hurt." He continued to stroke slowly over Simon's face.

Simon sighed, kissed those wandering fingers, and pulled his human mate in tightly against him. If only Paul could heal like that, Simon would worry a hell of a lot less. But it was Paul whose thoughts were trailing down into darkness now, in a way that Simon had felt before. "What, babe?"

"Huh?"

"You're thinking too much again, and it's making you sad. Want to share?"

"Nothing new. And I'm still trying to decide if it's nice or creepy that you can tell what I'm thinking."

"Feeling, not thinking." Simon brushed his lips over Paul's soft hair. A few stray blond strands tickled his cheek. "I'd prefer that you decide it's nice. We'll both be happier."

"Mm." In Simon's encircling arms, Paul's muscles slowly moved from post-sex laxness to stiff and tense.

"What are you thinking about, that makes you feel so unhappy?"

"Three guesses."

Simon didn't need the extra two. In the days since the werewolves' disastrous explosion and the splitting of the packs, they'd talked a lot. He knew Paul's hot buttons, and the flavors of his emotions. This much sadness was easy to figure out. "Cory."

"Yeah. I still struggle with that. Maybe he could've healed eventually too, gotten well again mentally, if he'd had the time and help. But the pack didn't give him that time. They killed him— boom— for the sin of being mentally ill. If you could tell me that was all Karl's doing, I'd be okay. But you won't."

"I can't."

"If that's still pack policy, I don't think I can live with it. I've tried, but… I think I need to get out as soon as we can. Not away from you but out of the pack."

Simon took a careful breath. Paul had hinted at this before but not come out and said the words. "Are you asking me to choose between you and the pack?"

"No!" Then Paul hesitated. "Maybe. I hadn't thought about it like that. I guess I figured, after the way they treated you, as soon as we were safe to leave, you would."

"Wolves don't just walk out on their packs."

"But this situation's different, isn't it? If you don't have to worry about Karl coming after you, then why would you want to stay? They rejected you first. They locked you up, put you on trial. Sure, the worst of them are with the other pack now—" Simon heard a stutter in Paul's voice that was probably him biting back the words, "*or dead.*" "But even the guys in our pack were part of all that. You didn't have even one friend good enough to take your side when you really needed them."

Simon winced but said, "Aaron took my side."

"Aaron. I guess so, but he had ulterior motives. He wanted to be Alpha, and now he is. Would he force you to stay in the pack, if you wanted to go?"

"Maybe not. But I *don't* want to leave." How could he say this so a human could understand? "It's more than just the pack being my family. You're my closest family now. But the pack is my people, my kind. They're the only ones who really know what I am from the inside out. They're blood and bond. Leaving a pack is desperately hard for any werewolf."

"I thought Aaron said he'd done it, wandered alone for years without a pack."

Aaron had been incredibly busy in the last three days, but he'd spared a couple of hours to spend with Paul and talked more about his past than Simon would've expected. "Yeah, he did. But Aaron's unusual. Don't judge the rest of us by Aaron. Going lone wolf… It's not natural. If we decide to travel, or work abroad, or join the military— well that's not an option any more with DNA sampling. But if wolves move away from our pack for any reason, we almost always do it in groups, or at least a pair. One of your own to watch your back and remind you of home. And we come back when we can."

"And having your mate wouldn't be enough?"

Damn. He could feel the hurt in Paul. But it wasn't that simple. "Right now, there's this place in my head where the whole pack exists. I can feel them, especially my Alpha, and it grounds me. I'd be lost and empty in my head without them."

"So if it came down to them or me, you'd choose the pack?"

"God, no." Simon tightened his arms around his mate and wrapped one leg up over Paul's hip. "I choose you, first, always, and forever. But I'd prefer not to have to choose."

"They kill kids," Paul whispered hoarsely. "If we stay with the pack, I'm part of that. How can I be part of that? How can human mates ever accept the rules of the pack?"

"Because all of the choices are shitty. We're not harsh to be cruel, and not just because we can, but because we're not safe any other way. Safety trumps everything else."

"It shouldn't. What was that quote? '*Those who give up liberty for security will eventually find they have neither.*'"

Simon gritted his teeth and searched for an explanation that would make sense to Paul. He'd thought that bonding his mate, linking him to the pack, would be the hard part. Creating the bond was turning out to be the least of his challenges.

"A hundred and fifty years ago our ways seemed normal. Back then, if you were crazy and human, you were locked away somewhere awful for life. If you were really lucky, you could hope to not be abused and treated like an animal in those hells. We wolves could consider ourselves merciful by comparison. Some places hung thieves, and sodomy was still punishable by death, even in countries as civilized as England."

"Okay, a hundred years ago, we humans were just as brutal as you wolves. But we've made some progress and you haven't?"

Simon really, *really* hated the "you" and "we" parts of this conversation. "Not exactly. Well, sort of, although humans still manage some pretty stunning brutality. I guess the packs are now out there on the fringe with the less civilized humans. But the thing that puts us out there isn't that we're really more bloodthirsty than humans. It's the threat of discovery."

"You justify everything that way."

"Not justify. Explain."

"Would it really be so bad, for werewolves to be outed to the human world?"

"Exposure might be survivable. I hope so, because like Aaron says, it's probably going to happen. But humans don't have a reputation for treating outsiders well. Especially if we have something humans want. We all have nightmares of our whole species disappearing into some government black box, never to be seen again. To be dissected for our differences, or brainwashed and blackmailed into spying for them. Or bred forcibly to make an army of wolves they would control."

"Hate to say it, Simon, but in the modern warfare era, you guys are probably not that big of an asset."

"Maybe not." Simon sighed. "But I'm sure the military would find a use for us. In the mountains of Afghanistan or acting like feral dogs spying around the cities of China. Something. And they sure as hell would be interested in the healing and some of the communications."

"Maybe you all need to come out at once. More people than they could ever hide or suppress. On TV maybe." Paul's eyes lit with amusement. "Imagine on all the talk shows, a bunch of wolves shifting in front of the viewers' eyes. Or on the news networks. Something that could never be taken back or hidden from the public."

Simon shook his head. "Then two days later, you can imagine the radio talk-shows ranting about the threat of werewolves as God-knows what. Disease carriers, because everyone knows it's contagious by a bite. Saboteurs, terrorists, aliens, a threat to Mom, apple pie and the American way. And crying for quarantines and visible ID tags, branding, and who knows, maybe concentration camps, muzzles. It would be a circus."

"Worth getting through it, surely, to join the human race in the open?"

"Maybe. Depending on how much support we get, and whether we could avoid being used as a handy excuse for everything from nuclear armament to racial profiling. Or if we have something they want, like our healing. Ask my grandmother's people how easy it is to survive when white folk with guns want something you have."

Paul bit his lip. "I'm sorry. You're right but… you're sacrificing your own kids to stay hidden."

Simon turned so he could see Paul's face better in the dim of the room. "It's not my call anyway and thank God for that. Coming out depends on the Alphas. If Aaron forbade it, not one of the pack would back me up and they'd stop me by force if I tried. If Aaron commanded it, every man would be on camera stripping naked."

Simon felt Paul's uneasiness. "That's wrong too, for one man to have that kind of power."

"You humans give the President of the United States a nuclear holocaust button. No society is perfect or safe from abuse, and each one has its own balances. We've survived this long by being rigid and ruthless in our obedience and concealment. It's hard to break free from that."

Paul's hand moved on Simon's thigh, almost unconsciously tracing the site of other now-healed scars. The gesture was absently fond, but Simon felt a tingling warmth of arousal build in the wake of that touch. Simon pressed up closer. Maybe Paul could be distracted. But his serious lover's mind was locked in problem-solving mode.

"Still, that doesn't make all the violence right. We can't just do nothing. *I* can't do nothing. I'm part of this wolf shit now, and something has to change." His rubbing fingers tightened into a fist, pressing hard on Simon's leg. "I wish… Damn, I wish I had the guts to stand up in front of the pack and say so. If you won't leave the pack then… Humans improved because people within the society protested and agitated and fought to make us better. Maybe eventually, when I get up the fucking nerve, that's going to be my role in the pack."

Simon winced and closed his eyes, imagining his Paul standing up at a pack meeting and speaking out for civil rights for mentally impaired werewolves. Aaron would do him the courtesy of listening, but the odds were it would *not* go over well.

He was distracted by the ping of a text message on his phone. If he'd been alone, he'd have checked it but in front of Paul he hesitated.

"Don't you need to get that?" Paul asked.

Simon shrugged, but a slight flavor of suspicion and hurt lurked behind Paul's words, and maybe it was time to stop dodging this topic too.

"Shift change," he said.

Paul's eyes narrowed. "Shifts of what?"

"Aaron has someone out there watching for us at night. He lets me know who."

"Every night? And you didn't tell me? Are they, like, *watching* us, right now?"

"No, Paul, no. They're watching out *for* us. Guarding us. Looking for strangers, guys from the other packs, threats. They can't see in here or feel anything that happens between us. Pack sense isn't that clear between random members, I promise." And thank God for that, because although every member of Aaron's pack had knowingly chosen Paul, in choosing Aaron, Simon bet none of them wanted to know the details. He tried a small smile. "I can't even tell who's out there right now, unless they get hurt enough for me to notice their pain. Aaron messages me the shifts. Or you could run out and whack them with a frying pan, and then I'd know."

The humor was an epic fail. Paul said, "Was this your idea?"

"Aaron's."

"So the threat isn't over. He thinks you're still in danger."

"Maybe. He's being careful. It's early days yet, and some of Joshua's pack really don't like us."

Paul sighed tiredly. "And that's why you haven't been sleeping. Because you think trouble's still coming."

"I think it might. But I trust Aaron to keep us safe." Mostly. If it could be done. The not-sleeping thing wasn't lack of confidence, exactly, just realism, and awareness that the rest of the pack couldn't take on every top wolf of Joshua's.

"I like Aaron but I don't really know him well enough to trust him with your life, if there's a real threat." Paul's eyes were wide.

"You will." Simon mentally touched the solid presence in his mind that was Aaron. "We're his now, his pack. He'll defend you against the world, if need be." Simon knew there was a chance the best Aaron could do wouldn't be enough, but they'd deal with the crisis if it came. No need for both of them to be constantly wound up. He took a deep breath and tried to project calm and faith through the mate bond.

Paul nodded, but his gaze was still shadowed. "What do you think is coming? Or who?"

Enough serious stuff. Simon grinned and slid down Paul's body. "Oh, babe," he breathed, "right now I know exactly who's *coming*." And he let Paul feel the heat rising in him as he bent his head to prove his point.

Paul's hand fisted in his hair. Simon arched his neck at the pull and looked reluctantly away from the delectable sight in front of him to meet Paul's irritated look. He wanted to get Paul all hot and bothered and then suck him into unconsciousness, not debate this further. He grabbed for a topic that would distract Paul from pack politics and to his horror heard himself say, "Given any more thought to calling your mother?"

"Shit." Paul shoved him back roughly and slid over across the bed.

Simon pounded his forehead silently on the mattress. *Dumb, dumb, dumb! With a capital D. Like thinking about Paul's cold and alcoholic mother would put him in the mood for sex.*

Simon rolled on his back and watched as Paul stood up and began hunting around for his clothes. "I'm sorry."

Paul gave him a glare and yanked on a pair of boxers.

Simon sighed and got out of bed, easing closer to his irritated mate. The waves of annoyance coming from Paul made touching him seem like a bad idea. "I'm an idiot." One thing pack politics taught you was that there was a time to roll over, bare your throat, and get the beating over with. "A moron. Totally without sense or consideration. I was trying to change the subject. I shouldn't have brought her up. It's totally none of my business."

Paul glanced at him. "That's the only thing you've said that I disagree with. If I have to deal with the pack, then you get a share of my mother."

Except you won't share. Simon still knew little more than what Paul had told him on their mating night. "I was still stupid. Like distracting someone from a bad tooth by hitting their broken toe with a hammer."

Paul snorted, and the look he gave Simon was closer to exasperated humor. "Nice analogy. My mother is not a broken toe."

"Something painful anyway." Privately, Simon figured she'd been a hell of a lot worse than any broken bone. He tentatively reached out to touch Paul's arm. The mate bond gave that little surge that they got from touching. And yeah, under Paul's annoyance was the flavor of old pain. Simon moved slowly closer. "We should do something fun right now. Go out to eat maybe. That's Damian out there. I have no problem with running him around town a bit."

Paul's fingers paused on his shirt buttons, then resumed their task, closing them over his bare chest. "I think you owe me some home cooking."

"How do you figure that? I just got done doing all the work."

"Foot in mouth penalty."

"Okay. You really don't want to go out?"

"I really don't. I want to eat here and not have to feel you worry, even if now I get why. I can listen to you gripe about how much weight I need to put on instead. It's irritating in a completely different way."

"I can do that." Simon thought Paul was still too thin. Between work and stress and refusing to slow down, those fifteen pounds Simon had vowed to put on him were slow in coming.

They finished dressing and made their way down to the kitchen. Simon pulled open the refrigerator and inspected the contents. He needed to shop for food. He needed to do a bunch of errands, actually. Aaron had decided Simon was better off not going to his job at the workshop until Joshua's wolves calmed down a bit. Simon figured that meant he'd be back at work in five or six years. If he was lucky. But he hadn't been using his free time productively.

Paul knew Simon wasn't working at the shop, but he hadn't told Paul that he spent most of his unemployed hours hanging around outside the clinic, keeping watch. Okay, all of them. Really, he should relax enough to go buy a few groceries. Maybe he could find a pack-brother who would take a daytime hour to watch Paul. Or who liked to buy food.

"We need to shop," Paul said, peering over his shoulder.

"True. We should do it together." *Great idea, that would be even safer.* "We can hold up cucumbers in the produce section and make suggestive gestures at each other with them."

"Oh, now that sounds appealing." But Paul snickered.

Before Simon had a chance to elaborate on the topic, there was a knock on the kitchen door. His response was pure reflex. *Shove Paul into a safe corner away from the door. Put your bulk in front of him. Probe toward the door with every sense to decide if this is a strange werewolf out there...* And then relax sheepishly when you realize it's just Andy, and an assassin wouldn't be likely to knock on the door first.

Simon pictured himself pounding his paranoid head on something harder than a mattress this time. A moment later, he realized that Paul behind him was still taut with fear. Simon stepped away and turned to give him a reassuring smile. "No, it's okay. False alarm. It's Andy."

"Your friend Andy?"

"Yes, of course." Except there was no "of course" for Paul. A human couldn't hear Andy's breathing, recognize his scent, or know by pack sense that the man outside was a friend.

Paul's stance eased. "Jesus, you're jumpy. And you're getting worse. Are you going to let him in?"

Simon took two long strides and pulled open the door. "Damn it, Andy, is there something wrong with ringing the front doorbell like a normal person?"

"I could hear that you two were back here. Anyway, Damian's hanging around out front."

"If he didn't notice you coming around back, he is so damned fired."

"Nah, of course he noticed. But this way he didn't get in my face. Damien's letting his promotion from pack Seventeenth to Sixth go to his head."

"He's not a bigger fish, it's a smaller pond."

"You rank him. You can tell him that. I can't." Andy tilted his head quizzically. "You gonna let me in?"

"Sure." Simon realized he had his body wedged into the opening of the door. It took a surprising effort to step back and pull the door wide for Andy to enter. This was *Andy*, dammit. Anyone less of a threat was hard to picture.

Andy stepped past him, pulling off his wool gloves. He gave Paul a lopsided smile. "Hi. We met formally at that pack thing, but I figured it was time to get to know the guy who is going to have to put up with this lunatic for a lifetime."

"Oh, that's nice," Simon growled, only half joking. "Trying to put my mate off me."

"That's the point of bondmates, isn't it? That it can't be done?" Then Andy apparently saw a hint of truth behind Simon's mock anger and sobered. "You guys *are* really bonded, aren't you?"

Simon rubbed his forehead tiredly. Even Andy was doubting the wrong part of this. "Yes, Andy, we are, but like with getting married, the wedding isn't the end of the process. And we don't need you questioning our bond."

"Should I go?"

"No," Paul said clearly. "Just because Simon is a dick and jumping at shadows, doesn't mean you should put up with that. I for one would like to meet someone from the pack who doesn't have the urge to make me disappear and get their old lives back."

To his credit, Andy looked appalled. "Someone said that?"

"Not exactly, but it seems logical. The pack has no reason to like me and you would all breathe easier with me gone."

Simon reached out a hand toward him. "Paul…"

Andy shook his head firmly. "No. Aaron would smack down anyone who said that. Maybe even anyone who thought it too loud; our Alpha is scary good." He unzipped his parka and pulled it off. "Paul, you're pack. Unless you break a law beyond repair, you're ours now. Just like Megan. Well, she's a lot cuter."

Simon could feel Paul relax a bit, and he silently blessed Andy. "Sorry, Andy. I'm touchy these days. You want a coffee?"

"I wouldn't say no."

Making coffee was good. Measuring grounds with the intense aroma filling his nose, the sound of water coming to a boil, the sweetness of the cocoa powder in his own mug, and behind it the murmur of voices as Andy and Paul made tentative small talk. It was all basic stuff— where'd you grow up, and do you have any brothers, and do you like hockey? How about those Gophers? Simon heard Paul chuckle, and he reached for his homemade cookies. If Andy was entertaining Paul, he would bribe his friend to stay longer. It was never hard to convince Andy to eat. And then Paul might eat some too. To hell with no sweets before dinner. Any calories were good calories.

By the time the coffee was gone, Paul was acting almost normal and he'd eaten two cookies. Andy'd had six, but Simon didn't begrudge them. Andy reached for a seventh and then pulled his hand back.

"Go for it," Simon said. "I can bake more."

"Is that what you're doing these days? Being the happy househusband?"

"No," Paul said. "He's hanging around me all day, patrolling the clinic, being all intense and broody."

Simon stared at him. "You knew that?"

"Simon, I can tell where you are if I pay attention." Paul sighed. "In an odd way, I'm glad to find out you think you have a real reason to stay so close. I was beginning to wonder if being bonded was another word for being joined at the hip."

"You could have asked me."

"Would you have told me the truth?"

Andy looked back and forth between them. "What am I not getting?"

"Simon thinks we're going to have trouble. Like real teeth-in-your-throat kind of trouble."

"What does Aaron say?" Andy asked immediately.

Paul smiled slightly. "Your all-knowing Alpha? I'm not sure. He hasn't mentioned any specific threats to me, just made vague suggestions to be careful. But he apparently set up this patrol thing Damian is doing. For damned sure I'm going to ask him next time I see him. Insist that he levels with me."

"You're going to insist. To the Alpha. Our Alpha."

"Maybe not," Paul admitted. "When he's not here, I think of him like any other calm, smart, decisive kind of guy. Like we're equals. But when he's sitting there across from me somehow it's different."

"Oh, yeah." Andy stood and reached for his jacket. "Well, I'll let Aaron worry about it, and you two can get back to… uh, what you were doing." He grinned slyly at them. "'Night Simon, Paul."

When Simon turned back to Paul after closing and locking the door, his mate's face was flushed.

"He knew what we were doing? Or was that just a guess, because we're, like, newly bonded."

"Um. He could probably smell it." Truth. He was aiming to be truthful with Paul, always. Annoying how often he was tempted to shade things a bit, to downplay the weirdness of being pack. But ignorance wouldn't be a service to Paul in the end. "You remember how careful I was about cleanup, back before. It's hard not to notice that scent."

"Ah."

"Does it bother you, that he can tell? I mean, even a human could've guessed, like you said. Because this is like being newly-wed."

Paul's face was still pink, but the shine in his eyes changed slightly. "Is it?"

"Oh, yes." Simon moved closer. "The beginning of everything. When you can't get enough of your husband's smell and his taste and the touch of his hands."

Paul didn't take a step forward, but he did hold still as Simon slid his arms around Paul's waist.

"Husband. But we're not married."

"We can be." Simon kissed his neck, where the muscles were still a little tight. "As soon or as late as you like. Tell me what you want." He kissed the sharp angle of Paul's jaw, the bridge of his straight nose, the smooth skin of his temple. Paul's eyes burned gold, darkening as his breath sped up. "Tell me what you'd like. I kind of like saying 'husband' but I'm not, um, wedded to it. Shall I call you mate? Lover? What would please you?"

Paul put a hand on Simon's cheek and turned him for a real kiss. Simon opened his mate bond as wide as it would go, feeling the brush of lips on lips, the smooth slide of tongues, echoed, doubled and redoubled. Paul leaned back and looked at him. "Call me Paul. And you know damned well what I like."

Yeah. Simon tightened his arms, pulling them together. He figured he was becoming pretty expert at figuring that out, and even more willing to give Paul's pleasures further study. Tomorrow was another day. *Carpe noctem.* Seize the night.

#######

If you enjoyed meeting the Hidden Wolves, take a look at how Aaron copes with his new pack, and one young wolf in particular, who challenges him as a man, not just as an Alpha…

Excerpt from *Unexpected Demands* *(Hidden Wolves Book 2)*

Chapter 1

I'm running through the woods, full out on four legs, over leaves so dry they crumble beneath me. The air's heavy and hot, summer's last breath.

I'm not running for my life. If he catches me, our fight will mean death for one of us, but the death will probably be his. He's old now, his hair streaked with gray as a man, his wolf's muzzle frosted white. A senior, a veteran who never quite made Alpha, and bitter with it. He taught me well; in my desperate fury, I could beat him.

But if I kill him, I'm not sure I'll be sane afterward. I can feel the black abyss hovering, an emotionless darkness where I could go and let my wolf take over. My wolf wouldn't hesitate. Hatred runs hot and acid in my throat and only iron control keeps me from turning to finish this. I'm running for my soul, and there are heavy footfalls coming fast through the dry leaves behind me...

Shit. I'd dozed off.

I smacked the side of my head. A stupid gesture, but there was no one else in the room to see it, and the impact jolted me back to the present. *I'm not that seventeen-year-old youngster, haven't been for thirty years.* Bad enough that the nightmares had invaded my sleep again, disrupting my scant hours of rest. I'd be damned if I'd let them sneak up on me when I was awake. Well, nominally awake.

I allowed myself a moment, put my head in my hands and closed my eyes. *Breathe, for one minute, don't think and just breathe.* I'd taught myself meditation long ago, for control when control was the difference between life and death. I used those skills now to gather energy. I was tired.

Make that fucking exhausted.

Of course, I was also angry, and frustrated, and worried. *And admit it, Aaron David Tremaine, scared.* Actually, you could take one of those charts from school, the name-your-emotions ones with the silly faces, and put a check next to all the negatives, and that would pretty much sum up my current state.

And don't forget the one that's not on any kids' chart: horny. After thirteen years of locking my needs away where sexual desire couldn't endanger me, one tumultuous night a week ago had brought my body roaring back to life, worse than ever. And it wasn't even a night when *I* got any sex.

Maybe being tired was good. Exhaustion took the edge off all the rest.

I rubbed my face briskly, sat up in my chair, and laid my hands flat on the desk. This was no time to be indulging myself. When you're the Alpha of a werewolf pack, even a pack as small and non-traditional as mine, you have to *be* Alpha. No doubts, no worries, at least where the lower-ranked wolves can see you. I'd been faking that all week, ever since pack leadership had fallen into my hands.

Since I ripped pack dominance from Karl's bleeding, dying body.

A rap on the door startled me, then the door flung open before I could respond. Vincent rushed in. His normal air of detached amusement was replaced with a frown. "Aaron, there's trouble at Simon's."

"Damn." I leaped up immediately. "Local wolves?"

"Yeah."

"Do you know who or how many?"

"Nope."

"Who's on guard duty?"

"Andy."

"Son-of-a-bitch." That was only a figure of speech. There are no female werewolves. If there were, maybe we'd have a more relaxed attitude about sex and reproduction, and this whole mess wouldn't be happening.

I didn't mean the phrase as an insult to Andy either. He was just the wrong person to be on deck for any kind of trouble. Young, submissive, and easygoing,

Andy had the softest personality of any of my wolves. *And if anyone hurts him and I catch up to them, they're going to be eating through a straw for a month, werewolf healing or not.*

"Do you want me with you?" Vincent asked eagerly. The old wolf had been a surprise addition to my pack. I hadn't expected any of the seniors to come my way. He'd appointed himself my secretary, and was so useful I had no desire to depose him, even though secretly I thought he decided to be mine mainly out of boredom. Joining my pack gave him a ringside seat at the circus. Some people weren't made for retirement.

Unfortunately, Vincent wasn't above stirring up a little extra excitement, just to see what happened. That was the last thing I needed. "No. Stay here. Call Joshua and tell him I'm about to come down on some wolf of his. Again."

Vincent made a face. He'd have preferred the chance of a fight over having to call the no doubt pissed off Alpha of a now-separate pack. Especially since Joshua was too dour for Vincent to have much fun riling him up. But as my secretary, he'd make the call, and— I gave him a hard glare until he dropped his eyes and bent his head— he would control his impulse to be snide. I left him subdued, pulling out his phone.

Simon rented a small house with a white-fenced yard. Fences and lawn set the building back far enough from the neighbors for privacy, which was turning out to be a good thing. This wasn't our first go-round with trouble.

When I pulled in the driveway, four men stood at the front steps. On the bottom stair, a stocky, brown-haired man with a reddened face glared upward. He looked in his late thirties, but I knew he was sixty-six. I also knew he was short-tempered, right-handed, of barely average intelligence, and as violently homophobic as they come. Dan. Shit.

The man on the walkway behind him might've been his clone, but for the lighter hair and eyes: Geoffrey. He'd been eighth ranked in our old pack, and was now Joshua's Third, and not a stupid man. But he was cold, and calculating, and had no love for any wolf of mine.

At the top of the steps stood my two men. Andy was dressed for the weather, his gloved hands clenched into fists, the hood of his jacket pushed back to give him a full range of vision. His breath streamed out in puffs of white, and I could practically taste his fear, but he held his ground. Behind him, oblivious to having a T-shirt and bare feet on the frozen porch, Simon loomed still as stone. Not tall, but powerful, built like a fighter with muscles rippling under his copper skin, Simon was not a wolf to take on lightly. A fact Dan apparently realized, since he was still at the bottom of those stairs.

They all swung their heads to look at me as I got out of the Hummer. Andy's posture relaxed immediately, and his anxiety across our pack bond vanished. I appreciated his faith in me, even though his confidence might be a bit premature.

Simon held his ground, unmoving, his impassive face hiding the force of the anger and fear still burning across his bond. But then he had his lover, Paul, in that house behind him. No one would get through Simon's protection to reach Paul. And he trusted no one, not even me, to take that responsibility from him.

My business was with the interlopers. "Geoffrey," I said coolly. "Dan."

"This is none of your affair, Tremaine," Dan snapped. I noted that Geoff was holding back and letting the lower-ranked wolf speak up. Interesting.

"Of course it is. My wolves, my problem. Tell me what's going on."

"I'm here to challenge that… that… thing that you're letting walk around like he's as good as the rest of us." Dan pointed a finger at Simon. I guessed the slight tremble was due to rage, not fear. Stupid of him to underestimate Simon, but that was Dan.

"In the first place," I told him, "you can't. He's not in your pack now. You want to take on one of my wolves, you have to face me first. And I don't think you want to do that." I glared at him, and needed less than two seconds for him to drop his eyes. I might've been only a few ranks ahead of him in the old pack, but I was an Alpha now, and his body knew that even better than his brain. "In the second place, Simon would wipe the floor with you, if I let him."

"Bullshit," Dan blustered. "He's nothing. Stinking faggot. He's bowed his head to me a hundred times."

"Because he chose to. Think, you fool. Simon beat Frank in a fair fight. Frank!" The big tawny wolf had been our Fifth, and a vicious fighter. In the scrambling events of that night, when I killed Karl and everything changed, perhaps the biggest surprise had been Simon rising victorious from Frank's body. I'd known he was holding back, hiding in the middle of the pack. I hadn't realized how much.

The memory of that night flitted across Dan's face too, and he paled a shade, but he wasn't the kind to ever back down. "Bullshit," he repeated. "I can take him."

I turned a calm eye to Geoffrey, who was watching us both. "Is this challenge sanctioned by your Alpha?"

Geoff shook his head. "I don't believe Dan ran it by Joshua first. But he does have a complaint."

More than the standard "gay werewolves are the spawn of Satan and should be destroyed?" "What complaint?"

"My house!" Dan sputtered. "Someone took orange spray paint and wrote things on my house!"

I turned an inadvertent snort into a cough. *Not funny, not funny.* "What things?"

Dan's face regained its red hue. "Words. Insults. He did it!" He turned to glare at Simon again. "You know he did. Cowardly, sneaking, afraid to face me. He wrecked my house!" He made a lunge up the stairs.

I grabbed his arm, and swung him around to face me. "Shut up and stand down," I snarled, with all the menace I could muster. Apparently enough, because he sagged like the air had leaked out of him. "I will look into this, and if your property was damaged, I'll see that you get compensation from the guilty party. But it damned well wasn't Simon. I've had men watching him for his protection all week." I gestured at Andy, hovering on the stoop. "Simon didn't do anything. Now go home, and let your Alpha deal with this. Unless you'd rather Challenge me?"

He didn't even try to meet my eyes. "No, Alpha."

"Go." I gave him a shove toward his parked car.

From where he stood watching, Geoff said, "Maybe the vandalism wasn't Simon this time. But your pack's out of control. You're only asking for trouble, letting this bullshit go on. Follow the law, get rid of the human who knows about us, deal with your fag, and then we can live in peace again."

"Over my dead body," I said coldly.

"Perhaps." Geoff looked me up and down, then shifted his gaze to Simon, and to Andy still trying to look tough and protective. When Geoff turned back to me, his lip curled in a sneer, although he couldn't quite meet my eyes. "Perhaps someone will take you down, and then deal with this… perversion… the way it should be handled."

"But not you." I stepped forward, pushing into his personal space, and he backed off a step, then two. "And not today. Get out of here."

I held my ground until they climbed into their car and drove away. Then I sighed. Damn. I *so* did not need this.

Behind me, Andy murmured, "I'm sorry, Aaron."

"For what?" I turned to look at him. "You did what you were supposed to. When trouble came, you called me and backed up Simon until I got here. What else could you have done?"

"I wasn't much backup," he said miserably. "Dan would've walked right over me."

"It's not your job to stand up to wolves like Dan. It's mine. You did fine." I climbed the steps and slapped his shoulder gently. "Take off, Andy. I'll be here for a while, and Damian will be on patrol soon. Go get something to eat and warm up." Not that we wolves felt the cold much.

Andy ducked his head. "Okay." He turned to Simon. "You all right, bro?"

Simon dredged up a smile. The two had been friends a long time. "I'm fine. I'm glad you didn't get dragged into a real fight, but it was good to have you here."

"Right, sure." Andy waved a hand toward the house, and called, "Bye, Paul." He pulled his hood up over his ears and headed off down the road to wherever he'd parked his car.

I turned to Simon, who was still glaring over my shoulder down the road, immovable in his doorway. "Let's take this inside," I said gently. "You're letting in the cold, and you may not feel it, but Paul does."

Simon came back to himself with a start. "Oh. Right."

He led the way into his house. Just inside the entry, in the shadows of the hall, I spotted his human mate, Paul. Simon went to him quickly, perhaps unconsciously keeping himself between me and Paul. They were about the same height, but Simon was wide, hard with muscle, while Paul was slender. Simon was decent-looking, ochre-skinned and black-haired, with regular features and that powerful build, but not remarkable unless you caught the spark of humor in his eyes.

Paul was high-cheekboned and pale, dark gold of hair and eyes, and beautiful. All the more so because he seemed unaware of it. Simon, anything but unaware, practically pissed circles around him when other men came too close. His possessive posturing would've been funny, under other circumstances.

I eyed them for a moment, then shut down the pack bond that linked me to Simon's emotions. I couldn't concentrate with the force of Simon's fear and love and worry pressing in on me. The odd bond-echo that was Paul went with him. My head felt clearer without the intense stress I'd been getting from the two men. "Can we sit down?"

Simon led the way into the living room, bringing Paul with him. He kept his hand on Paul's arm like he needed the contact. I dropped onto the couch and Paul sat in the chair across from me. Simon chose to stand behind him. Paul craned his neck back to look up at his mate and sighed, but forbore to comment.

"So," I told them, "I'll check into the spray paint thing. That's not your concern. But this pattern of threats against you is not going away."

"I didn't think it would." Simon's voice sounded as tired as I felt. "Once the word got out, I knew we'd have a problem."

"Your relationship's all over the pack websites. So far, a dozen Alphas have demanded I purge my own pack or they'll do it for me. Most are calling me a liar to my face, for taking you in as a bonded pair. They're suggesting I should be eliminated immediately myself. The mate bond thing is making the homophobes have kittens."

Paul snorted, as I'd hoped he would. Simon just looked grim.

"On the plus side…" I continued.

"There's a plus side to this?" Simon asked.

"I have eight anonymous queries from other wolves either putting out tentative feelers about joining our pack or asking me to explain how the mate bond between two men worked."

"Which helps us how? You're not going to invite strangers into the pack right now."

"No. But it's proof that eliminating you and Paul won't get rid of the issue of gay wolves. We need to address how to change, not try and stuff the gay back in the box. Which is the point I'm trying to make on the Net."

"How's that working for you?" Simon asked acidly.

"It's an uphill battle," I agreed. "But I think I'm getting a shift from '*kill them now*' to '*check the situation out and then kill them.*'"

"Which is so much better."

"Damned right it is," I snapped. Even without the bond open, I could see the darkness pulling Simon down. For a wolf who'd faced his own imminent death more than once with a can-do attitude, he was awfully negative now.

Of course, he had a good reason. We both knew there was a serious chance that Paul would not survive this coming out, even though an attacker would have to go through Simon to get to Paul, and through me to get to Simon. Problem was, if enough wolves really wanted to, they could do just that.

"You think if the others find out there are lots of queers among us, they'll magically become okay with that?" Simon asked sarcastically.

"Of course not. Even humans aren't all okay with it, and we wolves are more homophobic than they are. But the pack does change when it has to."

"What about you?" Paul interrupted. "Do we make your skin crawl, Aaron?"

That had to be a quote from someone. Simon looked stricken, and made a move to touch Paul's face, but cut the gesture short.

"No," I said, calmly and forcefully. "After I left my home pack, I met lots of humans and lived in lots of places. Gay people are just… people. But I also know how long it took me to be convinced of that, to the marrow of my bones. I know how instinctive my revulsion was, when I was young."

The truth, if not the whole truth. I remembered my father's heavy blows, his voice, "not tough enough, not wolf enough, hell, not man enough." And my fear— did he know, did he guess? I remembered not just accepting the pain but welcoming it, needing it, hoping desperately that if I took his fists well enough, the punishment might somehow work, might purge this shameful, disgusting part of me, and make me true pack. I remembered vividly how I felt each time the pain failed, each time I lived through one of his beatings and came out the other side unchanged.

And all the years afterward, stumbling to some kind of weary resignation that I wasn't ever going to change. And only later, finally, to a complete acceptance that I could be both *wolf* and *gay*. I'd been looking at gay werewolfhood from the inside, and even then, acceptance had been a long journey. And for the safety of all of us, one that had to remain secret right now.

"I still can't believe they hate gay werewolves enough to come hunt us down," Paul said.

"It's not just that," I pointed out. "There've been rumors about gay wolves who survived purging, in this pack and in others, forever. No one cared enough to make a crusade out of it. I think deep down, most of us realize that extermination isn't possible. There are lots of queer wolves already out there under cover now, as proved by those emails. Killing you won't solve that problem."

Simon snorted. "It'll just make them feel better."

Paul elbowed him in the hip. "So why are they so rabid now?"

"It's the mate bond. The idea of a gay love real enough to bond, and the fact that a human man knows our secrets and is being allowed to live because of a male-male mate bond. They don't believe that can be true, don't want it to be true. And if your bond's not true, then Simon and I are both liars and traitors to our kind, and all three of us need to die."

"To the point where they'll show up from miles away and kill us?" Paul said disbelievingly.

"Oh, yeah, babe," Simon said. "Secrecy is our holy grail. Nothing's too much when it comes to keeping the secret."

"But I haven't betrayed your secrecy. Can't there be some kind of probation for human allies? Surely they'd eventually see that I'm not a threat."

"We don't take that chance," I said quietly. "Bonded mates are safe, because they are linked to their wolves. As a bondmate, you feel what Simon feels and to a lesser degree what happens to the rest of the pack. If we're captured, imprisoned, killed, you'd experience the pain with us. That's our insurance. But if you're just his human friend, who knows? Who can say that you won't get mad at him and betray him, or get bored and leave and let the secret slip one day? The decision was made eons ago— only bondmates learn our secret and live."

"That's pretty fanatical."

I shrugged. "Yes, but it's worked so far. An absolute rule has allowed us to set a clear policy, and not depend on the judgment of any single wolf or even a single Alpha about who can be trusted. I can't even say I disagree with it. I've seen some pretty vindictive ex-wives who were once beloved spouses.

Even if our days in hiding are as numbered as I think they are, I'm no more eager to be outed to human society than most other wolves."

Paul stared at me. "So you think it's okay to go around killing people? Maybe you should kill me yourself, and just be done with it."

I shook my head, giving Simon my best Alpha glare to hold him in place. "I don't like killing. I'll go a long way to avoid it, if any other alternative is possible. We also discredit, confuse, undermine those who *think* they saw werewolves. Death is a last resort. But then, you *are* Simon's mate. You're part of my pack, you're in my head, and mine to protect, to my last breath and beyond."

"But you'd kill me, if I wasn't," Paul persisted.

He was entitled to the truth. "Maybe. If I couldn't persuade you this was all a fantasy, drug-induced hallucinations, a mental break, something. To keep Mark's little boy out of a cage for the rest of his life? To stop scientists sampling him and poking him to make him shift, an animal tortured in the name of research? Yes, I might kill you." Paul's gold eyes bored disdainfully into mine, but he wasn't going to win this one. "Tell me you humans would never do things like that to a child."

His eyes finally dropped. "We might. But that risk doesn't justify…"

"It does to me. One day, we'll have to come out to the humans, and take our chances. But the more time human society has to change, to accept the weird and wonderful and diverse, and the more time our numbers have to increase, the better our chance of survival. I won't do anything to deliberately endanger that."

"So what choices do Paul and I have?" Simon asked. "We don't have that kind of time. We can wait here until some wolf kills us, or we can try to run and hide, and pray no one finds us."

"My hope lies in the fact that it's our claim about your bond that's making them rabid. And your bond is a matter of fact, not opinion. They don't need to like you. They just need to acknowledge that you are bound together. If Paul is accepted as a packmate, he'll be a hell of a lot safer." Killing a bonded mate was only slightly less bad than killing a young pup. Under normal circumstances, it would bring the wrath of all the packs down on you. Wolves protected mates and young. But up until now, mates had always been women.

"How do we prove anything?" Simon asked. "I can sense my bond with Paul. As my Alpha, you can too. But other wolves can't tell for sure. If they won't take your word as Alpha now, what would make them change their minds?"

"They can't sense the bond directly," I pointed out. "But your connection gives you abilities that would be hard to explain any other way. With a true mate bond, you know when something happens to Paul, even from miles away. You can find each other over a big distance. You can sense each other's emotions. Those are things that can be demonstrated."

"Demonstrated? Like passing a test? You think anyone will buy that?"

"I'm trying to persuade the other packs to send a delegation to test you. We shift the emphasis from whether gay wolves should be allowed to exist in the first place, to whether they can form a true bond. The first question is a matter of opinion, and we have no hope of winning right now. The other is a fact that we can prove. Protecting and trusting our mates is instinctive. Get enough wolves convinced, make them see that you and Paul are both linked to the whole pack, and we might live through this."

Simon was shaking his head. "It's too risky."

"What other choice is there?" I asked. The silence stretched out for a while. Simon looked down at the floor. Finally I added, "We need to change opinions fast, or you have to run and go off the map. If that's your choice, I'll help you all I can. But if you run now, exile will be forever. You'll have to keep hiding, always worried about being found, isolated, unprotected."

My wolf instincts protested— *guard, protect, pack.* I didn't want to let them go, but overcoming instinct was something I worked hard for. This was their choice. "They'll hunt you. They won't let a human walk away with pack secrets. They won't stop looking. And Paul loses everything he's built here, his practice, his home, friends, everything."

"Except his life." Simon's fingers whitened on Paul's shoulder, and the young man winced silently. Just as quickly, Simon let go and rubbed gently where he had gripped too hard. "Sorry, babe," he whispered. "I'm so sorry. About all of this."

"Shut up," Paul told him. "You didn't cause the problem. We got into this together, and I don't want to run. Anyway, you were the one who told me how important the pack was to you, how hard it would be to live without packmates."

"That was before half the wolves in the known universe found out about us and decided we should be wiped off the face of the earth. Don't worry about me. That's not relevant now."

"Your needs are part of the equation. I don't want you feeling empty and alone because you decided that protecting me was more important than your ties to your pack."

Simon knelt by his chair, looking him in the eyes. I could tell this wasn't the first time they had gone around with this question. "We can't stay. It's too risky. You haven't seen how rabid some of the comments are. They all want you dead."

"And whose fault is it that I haven't seen what they're saying?" Paul's voice heated in its turn. He looked over at me. "Will you tell this idiot that I'm a big boy, and I can handle a few insults and threats? He's being all protective to the point where he won't let me read the forum postings anymore."

I could understand the protective instinct, but I raised my eyebrow at Simon. "Don't you think Paul's strong enough to be a full partner here?"

From Simon's wince, I knew I'd hit a sore spot. "It's not that. Of course he is. I just…I don't want him to see… to read what other wolves…" He trailed off.

"I think Paul's already seen us at our worst," I said gently. Simon looked as ragged as I felt. "He hasn't walked away yet."

"What will happen to you," Paul asked me, "if you let us get away?"

"Probably nothing." Nothing for Paul to worry about, anyway. I was his Alpha, not the reverse. "Some will consider my failure to hold you a breach of security, but I can handle my end. You need to think about yourselves."

"I want to stay," Paul repeated. He looked back at Simon. "I don't want to spend the rest of my life running. And more." His voice took on a deeper resonance. "Simon, in this looking-glass world I've fallen into they kill thirteen-year-olds for being gay. If you and I have a chance to change that, how can we walk away from it?"

"I can," Simon muttered. "I can walk away from anything to keep your blood inside your body where it belongs."

Paul just looked at him, his hazel-gold eyes dark and quiet. After a long time, Simon said, "Damn." He looked up at me. "All right, okay, he's right. We have to do this. Into your hands, my Alpha. Tell me what you want me to do."

That was the decision I'd wanted, but I still felt a roil of nausea. Simon was giving me control over the most precious thing in his life, and we could all end up dead. But I also had the memory of slaughtered kids walking at my shoulder. I had to do this too.

"I'll get online," I said, "and try to set up a meeting open to all the packs. If I can persuade the other Alphas to send delegates, they may not send assassins." I looked at the two hollow-eyed men in front of me. "You two get some sleep. It's Sunday, the day of rest, you know. You look like a pair of raccoons."

Paul sighed. "Simon won't sleep. A leaf hitting the ground a block away has him leaping out of bed."

"Then sleep at my house." My wolf loved the idea of having the threatened members of our pack protected under my roof. "Trust me to keep you safe. Joshua's wolves aren't going to pound on my door without *consequences*." I let my tone go hard on the word. "There's a spare room. Feel free to use the shower and the bed."

"We don't need to…" Simon began.

"You do. You can't protect Paul if you're falling over. Follow me home and get in a few solid hours of shut-eye. We'll talk again after." I put a little Alpha push into it. I apparently didn't yet have a good handle on the command part of an Alpha's power because Simon winced like I was giving him a headache, and nodded jerkily.

"All right," he said. "You're right. My brain is mush right now. Thank you."

"I'll pack a bag," Paul said. He glanced at Simon. "I can't wait till you're less exhausted." The heat that flashed between them as Simon returned his gaze almost scorched me.

Even without my Alpha bond open, my body reacted to their desire. Two hot guys, exchanging that look? *Shit. I need to get laid.* Except that complication was the last thing I could afford right now. Celibacy sucked, but it kept us all safer.

I managed a controlled tone. "I'll call Damian and let him know he should watch my house instead of yours." I'd keep the patrol on them, but trouble was much less likely at an Alpha's home— probably just as well with Damien next up. He was the hothead among my wolves. If he'd been on those steps facing Dan, I'd no doubt have arrived in the middle of a fight. I rubbed my forehead. I could use some sleep too, but this wasn't the time.

At least these two were coming back to my place. That was right; I could feel my wolf settling, satisfied. I could put them where I wanted them, behind me in any fight. Maybe my wolf was an overprotective control freak, but *my house, my protection, my rules* drained some of the exhaustion from my bones. For a few hours, I'd know exactly where Paul and Simon were and keep them safe myself.

§ § § §

Mark, my Second, was a human-trained police officer. He was also highly skilled at surreptitiously using his wolf senses at crime scenes to track down the guilty party. He grumbled about idiots keeping him from going home to his family, but agreed to go look at the graffiti for me.

Although Dan hadn't picked up any individual scent over the strong reek of spray paint, Mark wasn't as limited. His call came only ten minutes after I dispatched him to the scene of the crime. And the culprit shouldn't have come as a surprise. A disappointment, maybe, but not a surprise. I made a couple of phone calls.

I was busy on my desktop computer, trying to counter all the kill-the-fag postings on pack websites and advocate for sanity, when I heard Vincent open my front door. Then footsteps approached, followed by a hesitant tap on the study door. I let the petitioner wait a few minutes. Time to put my Alpha game face on.

I'd spent decades teaching myself to be silent and unobtrusive, to fade into a pack for safety, but the unobtrusive wolf I'd created couldn't guide this mismatched new pack of mine. *I'm the freaking Alpha.* The seismic shift in what my pack needed from me was still a work in progress. I had to speak up now, to use every ounce of strength and persuasiveness I could muster, on behalf of my wolves. To not just fight and persuade by subtlety, but decide and sometimes rule.

I'd talked more, bargained and threatened more, in the last week than in the previous seven years. *Remaking myself one more time.* Sometimes taking the lead was hard, but sometimes being Alpha felt like throwing off chains after far too long in prison. My wolf liked being dominant.

I sat up straighter and let my wolf come to the fore. The man on the other side of the door was near the bottom of my pack's rankings and urgently in need of a good father figure. Or maybe a good spanking; at this point I could go either way.

"Come in, Zach," I said in a conversational tone, not bothering to raise my voice. We may have lacked weird powers and super strength, but acute hearing? That we wolves had in spades.

The door opened slowly and the young man behind it came into my study. He was small and lightly built, with dark hair and eyes, and the smooth, easy gait of a born athlete. Of course, all my wolves had that, a gift to their human forms from the wolf. The kid had his chin up and his eyes were defiant. *Brat knows he's wrong, but he's not going to make this easy.*

"Shut the door and come here," I told him, as his mouth opened for whatever cocky greeting or justification he'd come up with while waiting. He did as I asked. By the time he reached the front of my desk, he'd taken measure of my expression, and thought better of speaking first. I let him stand there silently and just glared at him while I opened our pack bond.

I was still getting the hang of my Alpha bonds— the emotional links that bound my wolves to me, and me to them. I could hardly get worse at it than I'd been the first day. For those first interminable hours, as my pack bonded to me, the fears, doubts, excitements, and damned lusts of all my wolves had come roaring down the open bonds toward me, until I could hardly separate myself from them. Their emotions buffeted at me. A steep learning curve had been necessary for survival.

I had learned. Mostly. Now I could cut contact down to the barest thread, or open it at will. Although once open, the intensity was still excessive. From Zach, I was getting a heart-pounding mix of anxiety, embarrassment, and fear. And one hell of a headache. His for a change, not mine.

Looking more closely, I sniffed and wrinkled my nose. "Just how much did you drink last night?"

His olive skin couldn't hide his flush. "Not that much."

"I can still smell the booze on you," I said coldly. "Unless you had more again this morning?"

"Hair of the dog," he tossed off, aiming for nonchalance.

"You'll note that refers to dogs, not wolves," I snapped. "Wasn't last night's binge enough?" I didn't wait for an answer. "I'm told you decided to get drunk with some of your human friends, began cruising for trouble, and ended up spray-painting the word BIGOT in giant orange letters on the side of Dan's house. Is that right?"

I could feel his jolt of surprise when I mentioned the spray paint, the moment's hesitation when he considered denying it, and the fear that went with giving up that denial. My bonds might still be too deep for comfort when I opened them up, but at least my wolves were never going to be able to lie to me.

"I didn't plan it. Things just sort of happened."

I eyed him coldly. "How old are you?"

"Twenty-one," he said, with a touch of defiance. When my cold look didn't waver, he added, "Almost."

"Almost" was true. There was only a week left to his full majority, but almost wasn't completely, and the legal drinking age was twenty-one. Which gave me leverage, had I needed any more than being his Alpha.

"You decided that our pack wasn't in enough trouble? You had to add underage drinking, drunk driving, and vandalism to the mix? Not to mention antagonizing the fourth-ranked wolf of the only pack that's even marginally behind us right now?"

"I didn't get caught. No one will know…" He trailed off because obviously someone did know.

I sighed. "Zach, tell me. What the hell am I supposed to do with you? You're already locked down." He wore a strong narrow chain padlocked tight around his neck, an effective deterrent against shifting to a wolf form with a much thicker neck size, as a punishment for past sins. "I put you in Lucas's care with the hope you could straighten up and get it right. I figured after your grandfather's heavy hand, Lucas might seem like a good second chance. Was I wrong?"

"No. I wasn't… I didn't mean… none of this is Lucas's fault."

I leaned back in my chair and locked my hands behind my head. "Explain."

He stood still for a moment, searching for an opening, and then blurted, "Simon and our whole pack are in trouble and no one's doing anything about it!"

I raised an eyebrow. "Your answer was to spray paint a house? In front of humans?"

"I was going to put TRAITOR," he said defiantly, "But I figured that might raise questions, so I didn't. I went with BIGOT. The guys were drunk, they didn't ask why. And Dan was the one who outed Simon on the Net first."

I blinked. That was new information, if true. I knew someone had put complaints about my gay wolf out there anonymously, against both pack Alphas' explicit orders. I hadn't guessed it was Dan. Not that his breach excused Zach's actions, but still. "You know this how?"

"I'm good with computers." A little pride filtered into his anger. "When that statement went up form a new user, I knew there weren't too many people it could've come from. I checked around, pulled up some chat room logs, and traced the leak back to Dan. I have the record; I can prove it."

"I thought our board was secure," I said, startled. We'd spent enough money on keeping up the computer security. The chat room was supposed to be hack-proof. Our rules kept names, addresses, and blatant references to pack activities off the board, but we still might attract unwanted attention. No one was supposed to be able to track down pack members from comments.

Zach tossed his head, flicking the fall of black bangs out of his eyes. "Nothing's completely secure. I've… um… hacked into the chat room host's server before. And Dan's not particularly careful, uses really crap passwords. It wasn't hard to find him."

Joshua, Alpha of the North pack, would have Dan's hide, for both the security breach and the gossip. But Zach still needed a reprimand. "And then," I drawled, "instead of taking this information to Dan's Alpha or to yours, you decided to go out, get drunk, and buy some orange paint?"

His pride disappeared in a wave of embarrassment. "It wasn't like that. You were out, and Joshua had his whole pack at a meet. And while I was waiting for you, my friends called, and they had Jim's brother's pickup and some booze and the paint and… things just happened."

I sighed. I could drag the boy through his story further, but the picture was clear enough. What I should do was less so.

I hadn't planned to be Alpha. When I was forced to kill Karl to keep him from heading our pack and taking us all to hell, I got the job handed to me. I could figure it out, I knew that, but pure selfishness made me wish someone else had stepped up to the current mess. *Although be honest, Aaron, would you trust someone else with your wolves?*

An Alpha was part boss, part father, part absolute commanding officer to his wolves. The thought of someone else leading my pack astray made my wolf snarl, even though I'd never aspired to any of those roles. I'd always used persuasion far more than force of will, and the switch was jarring. I wondered how many others of the confident Alpha werewolves I'd met were paddling frantically underneath the water, trying to learn on the job. My headache throbbed behind my temples.

I'm too tired to do right by this brat tonight. Mark, my Second, was always telling me to delegate. So I would delegate. "Go home," I said, waving Zach away. "Tell your mentor the whole story and see what he thinks should be done with you. Tell Lucas I said it's his call, as long as you can walk afterward. And Zach." I sat up suddenly and fixed him with a cold stare. "No booze. None. Between now and your birthday, at least, not one drop of alcohol passes your lips. Swear it."

Zach dropped his eyes. He looked calm and controlled, but I could feel his confusion and fear, nausea, panic. The roiling mix of emotions grew surprisingly strong, as if he was terrified this was just a delay in some severe punishment. Zach's grandfather had messed that boy up more than I'd realized.

He steadied himself and raised his eyes. "I swear." His voice shook slightly.

I nodded. "Now tell me." I deliberately went conversational with my tone. Anything to dial back the fear in that boy. I restrained a sudden desire to rip his grandfather Joseph's throat out, and searched for a distraction. "Do you think you could do a little more hacking without getting caught…"

***Unexpected Demands* (Hidden Wolves Book 2)**
will rerelease in February 2021.
Find Aaron and Zach's story wherever ebooks are sold.

About the Author

I get asked about my name a lot. It's not something exotic, though. "Kaje" is pronounced just like "cage" – it's an old nickname, and my pronouns are she/her/hers. I was born in Montreal but I've lived for 30 years in Minnesota, where the two seasons are Snow-removal and Road-repair, where the mosquito is the state bird, and where winter can be breathtakingly beautiful. Minnesota's a kind, quiet (if sometimes chilly) place and it's home.

I've been writing far longer than I care to admit (*whispers – forty-five years*), mostly for my own entertainment, usually M/M romance (with added mystery, fantasy, historical, sci-fi…) I also have a few Young Adult stories (under the pen name Kira Harp).

My first professionally published book, Life Lessons, came out from MLR Press in May 2011. I have a weakness for closeted cops with honest hearts and teachers who speak their minds, and I was delighted and encouraged by the reception Mac and Tony received.

I now have a good-sized backlist in ebooks and print, including Amazon bestseller *The Rebuilding Year* and Rainbow Award winner for "Best Mystery-Thriller" *Tracefinder: Contact*. Readers can find a complete list of my books with links on my website at https://kajeharper.com/books/

I'm always pleased to have readers find me online:

Website: https://kajeharper.com/

Facebook: https://www.facebook.com/KajeHarper

Facebook group: Kaje's Conversation Corner: https://www.facebook.com/groups/208207893795147/

Goodreads Author page: https://www.goodreads.com/author/show/4769304.Kaje_Harper

Other Books by Kaje Harper

Self-Published/Indie:

Changes Coming Down (Changes #1)
Changes Going On (Changes #2)

Tracefinder: Contact (Tracefinder #1)
Tracefinder: Changes (Tracefinder #2)
Tracefinder: Choices (Tracefinder #3)

The Family We're Born With (Finding Family #1) – free novella
The Family We Make (Finding Family #2)

Rejoice, Dammit

Unfair in Love and War
(in the charity anthology Another Place in Time)

Not Your Grandfather's Magic
(in the charity anthology Wish Come True)

Don't Plan to Stay

Love and Lint Rollers

Second Act

Marked by Death (Necromancer #1)
Powered by Ghosts (Necromancer #2)
Bound by Memories (Necromancer #3)

A Midnight Clear

Audiobooks:

Into Deep Waters – Narrated by Kaleo Griffith

The Rebuilding Year – Narrated by Gomez Pugh

Life, Some Assembly Required – Narrated by Gomez Pugh

Building Forever – Narrated by Gomez Pugh

Re-releases:

The Rebuilding Year (Rebuilding Year #1)
Life, Some Assembly Required (Rebuilding Year #2)
Building Forever (Rebuilding Year #2.5)

Sole Support

Gift of the Goddess

Fair Isn't Life

Re-releasing in 2021:

Life Lessons (Life Lessons #1)
Breaking Cover (Life Lessons #2)
Home Work (Life Lessons #3)
Learning Curve (Life Lessons #4)

Unexpected Demands (Hidden Wolves #2)
Unjustified Claims (Hidden Wolves #3)
Unsafe Exposure (Hidden Wolves #4)

Storming Love: Nelson & Caleb

Full Circle

Where the Heart Is

Ghosts and Flames

Possibilities

Tumbling Dreams (currently out of print)

Stand-alone free novels:

Into Deep Waters

Nor Iron Bars a Cage

Chasing Death Metal Dreams

Lies and Consequences

Laser Visions

Stand-alone free short stories:

Like the Taste of Summer

Show Me Yours

Within Reach

Shooting Star

A full list with blurbs, and download and buy links can be found at:

http://www.kajeharper.com/books/

Made in United States
Troutdale, OR
10/05/2024